FRASIER ISLAND

SUSAN PAGE DAVIS

HARVEST HOUSE PUBLISHERS
EUGENE, OREGON

Published in association with the literary agent of Hartline Literary Agency, Pittsburgh, PA.

This is a work of fiction. Names, characters, places, and incidents are products of the author's imagination or are used fictitiously. Any resemblance to actual persons, living or dead, or to events or locales, is entirely coincidental.

Cover by Left Coast Design, Portland, Oregon

Cover photos © Photodisc/Photodisc Green/Getty Images; Diane Collins/Photonica/Getty Images

FRASIER ISLAND
Copyright © 2007 by Susan Page Davis
Published by Harvest House Publishers
Eugene, Oregon 97402
www.harvesthousepublishers.com

Library of Congress Cataloging-in-Publication Data
  Davis, Susan Page.
  Frasier Island / Susan Page Davis.
       p. cm.
  ISBN-13: 978-0-7369-2066-7 (pbk.)
  ISBN-10: 0-7369-2066-8
  1. United States. Navy—Fiction. I. Title.
  PS3604.A976F73 2007
  813.'6—dc22

                                                                         2006030635

Printed in the United States of America

         07 08 09 10 11 12 13 14 15 / LB-CF / 10 9 8 7 6 5 4 3 2

To my oldest son,
James Samuel Davis,
who challenged me to write this book
and create believable new worlds.
I'm so proud of you!
I hope to be reading one of your books soon.
Love,
Mom

Acknowledgments

Many people helped me during the writing of *Frasier Island*. My thanks go especially to my son Jim, who sparked the first germ of the story, and whose brainstorming was invaluable; to my dear husband, Jim, who edited the manuscript several times; and to my agent for this work, Tamela Hancock Murray, who pointed out a major flaw in the story line.

Former Marine Sergeant Brian Swift contributed by describing for me day-to-day life on a battle group and the routine on board ship during "West Pac" (Western Pacific deployment). Former Petty Officer Casey Vinson was consulted about ranks, chain of command, military ethics, logistics of special training and assignments, and personal relationships between Navy personnel. Retired Machinist's Mate Second Class Ken Lee gave me last-minute advice on a few crucial matters.

Retired Coast Guard Chief Warrant Officer Gilman C. Page was very helpful in his assessment of the basic premise, where a handful of military personnel mans a remote and isolated station for an extended period of time. Page was also consulted on sonar and other surveillance equipment and military routine and procedure. Besides that, he's pretty good as a big brother to buck you up when you're sure you'll never get it right!

Perhaps most of all, I'd like to thank my editor at Harvest House, Kim Moore, who believed in this story.

PROLOGUE

"Isn't she beautiful, Uncle George?"

George Hudson leaned on the box stall's Dutch door, holding his six-year-old niece up so that she could see over it, but also trying to keep her sneakers from making contact with his clean uniform. In the California spring sunlight he could see the chestnut filly wobbling as she sniffed a dim corner of the stall, investigating her new world. The foal's mother snuffled nearby, munching hay and eyeing her fuzzy offspring with maternal pride.

"Yes, she is, Cassie." He glanced at his sister, Judy, who was crowding him on the other side, watching the gangly foal and her mother. "I'm glad I was here long enough to see this."

Judy slipped her hand through his arm. "Me too. It's been great having you here this week. Do you really have to leave today?"

"Absolutely. The Navy frowns on tardiness."

"The Navy is mean," said Cassie, and George laughed.

"She's right." Judy favored him with an exaggerated scowl. "The Navy is an inflexible tyrant."

George looked from Cassie to her mother and shook his head. "I'd better get my gear before you two talk me into doing something I could be court-martialed for." He set Cassie on the ground.

"Go get your sister," Judy told her.

The little girl looked up at George with wide, solemn eyes and then darted toward the corral. Abbey was practicing precision movements with her bay gelding there, while her father watched critically from the fence.

"I don't want you to go to that place," Judy said.

George forced his attention back to his sister, but his mind was already far away. His destination pulled him, and he didn't want any further delays.

"You know nothing about my orders." He flicked a piece of timothy hay from the sleeve of her denim jacket.

"That doesn't matter. I know it's someplace where you can isolate yourself. You've implied that much. George, everyone grieves in their own way, but this isn't the time to leave your family."

He pressed his lips tightly together, holding back an impulsive reply.

"This is the time when you need your family most." Judy's brown eyes were turbulent with passion. "You asked for this assignment. You want to get away from everyone and brood. Admit it. You could have stayed in Commander Norton's office. I know you're still raw, and maybe angry, but honestly, George, being around people you love is the best thing—"

"You know what, Judy?" Even as he spoke, George knew he should keep quiet. He didn't want to hurt her. He ought to just walk away and let her remember him as the man who suffered in silence. But everyone assumed they knew what was going on inside his head these days. That's why he'd requested the transfer. He had to think for himself.

"For the last six months everyone has been telling me how I ought to feel and how I ought to act. Well, I'm tired of it. This is what I need to do now. I need to get away from everyone and be able to deal with this at my own speed."

Judy caught her breath and blinked twice. He could see her assurance wilting.

"I'm sorry," she said. "I didn't mean to smother you."

He looked off toward the mountains, wishing he'd kept quiet.

"George, I can't help worrying about you. You'll be so far away.

And you said it will be hard to contact you. What if something happens and we can't get ahold of you?"

He slid his arm around her and drew her close for an instant. "Don't worry, kiddo. I'll write when I can, and maybe even call once in a while. And you can always reach me through Earl Norton's office if there's a family crisis. But I need this." She looked doubtful, so he said again, "I won't be able to send mail out often, but when I can, I will."

"Where are you going? Antarctica?"

He chuckled. "No. I don't think we're taking much cold weather gear." Jason and the girls were walking toward them from the corral. He leaned toward Judy and whispered, "I'll be in the Pacific, but that's as much as I can tell you, and you can't even tell the kids that. Don't worry about me. I'll be safe."

Jason approached and extended his hand. "So this is it, George?"

"Yes. Thanks for putting up with me, Jason."

"No problem. You're welcome here anytime, but I know you're eager to get on with your assignment."

"I am. It's an important project, and it's something totally different from what I've done in the past. I want to be a part of it." George realized his voice had taken on an unaccustomed animation. Just talking about the new mission energized him.

"Well, I hope it will be absorbing enough to take your mind off the past." Judy's eyes glittered with unshed tears.

"It's a distraction, it's true, but I know that what I'll be doing is crucial to national security. This is what I need right now. Something that has to be done."

A tear spilled over, and Judy wiped it away with her sleeve. "I guess we'll have to live with that. Say goodbye, girls."

Cassie catapulted into his arms. "Uncle George, you're going to be gone for a long time, aren't you?"

"Yes, baby." He kissed her and pulled Abbey in close.

"We'll miss you, Uncle George," Abbey said.

"Send me a letter." His voice shook a little, and he knew he was in trouble. If he didn't get away soon, they'd have him in tears. "Abbey, you send me a picture of you and Stormy when you start winning ribbons."

"I will."

He kissed Abbey's smooth cheek and released the girls.

"Will you be here for Christmas?" Cassie asked.

It was all he could do to look into her big, liquid eyes. "No, I won't be here for Christmas." It came out a bit too gruff. He ruffled her hair and picked up his sea bag.

"I thought you liked it here," she wailed.

George froze, and then he lowered his bag slowly to the ground. He stooped close to Cassie and returned her gloomy gaze. "I love it here."

"Then why are you leaving?"

"Because I'm in the Navy, and that's what sailors do."

Judy sighed in disgust. "Please don't give my daughter a stupid explanation like that. You asked for this assignment. It was your choice."

George stared at her. What did she want him to say? Did she want him to tell the girls the bald truth, that he couldn't stand to be around people anymore? He couldn't bear to stay at the ranch and see them all mourning for him, as if they could ease his grief by taking it on themselves. He couldn't go back into Norton's office again and work with him every day, growing more and more claustrophobic as he saw the unrelenting sorrow in Earl's eyes.

He looked from Cassie's woeful face to Abbey's. It was hard leaving these kids behind when he loved them, but it wasn't as though he were abandoning his own children.

Abbey took a step closer and touched his arm. "Are you leaving because you're sad, Uncle George?"

He winced. "Sort of, I guess. But I think hard work is good for people who've…who've been through bad times." He glanced at Judy, half afraid she would rebuke him again, but she seemed somewhat mollified.

"Uncle George's work is extremely important," Jason said.

"Are you going to be a spy?" Cassie whispered.

George laughed. "No, nothing like that. I'll be more like a watchman."

"What will you be watching?" Abbey asked.

"I can't tell you."

"Will you send me a postcard?" Cassie asked.

He smiled, imagining a glossy postcard promoting the place where he would serve. Not likely. "I'll send you one from Pearl Harbor, on my way out."

He put his sea bag on the backseat and got into the car he had rented for the week. Judy rushed in for one last kiss.

"We'll be praying for you."

He bit his lip and stifled a bitter reply. They all waved as he drove out the long gravel driveway. He would miss them, but it was right for him to leave.

Before pulling onto the highway that would take him back toward the base, George stopped the car. He was starting a new epoch, leaving his former life behind. It might be years before he saw Judy, Jason, and the girls again, he knew, but they had each other. They wouldn't really miss him that much once they got back into their routines.

But he had to deal with another part of his life. He looked down at his hands on the steering wheel and slowly spread his fingers, watching his burnished gold ring reflect the sunlight. He pulled the chain that held his dog tags from beneath the neckband of his T-shirt and eased the ring off over his knuckle.

"I won't forget you," he whispered. The pain that had settled in his chest wasn't physical. He would go into this new life with her memory close to his heart, but without the outward signs of either his recent grief or the happiness he'd had only a few months ago.

Whatever Judy's methods of dealing with grief, he had his own ideas. He wouldn't look to family and God for support. He would look within himself.

He would have his own command soon, although a small one. He didn't want his subordinates speculating about his past. He wanted only to lose himself in his job for as long as it took. He'd been wounded before, and he knew that the pain would lessen slowly, over time. Someday he would realize it was gone.

Seattle, Washington
Three years later

Ensign Rachel Whitney poked a chicken nugget with her fork and pushed it around the largest section of her tray. Her stomach churned so badly she couldn't eat. In less than an hour she would receive her new assignment.

She tossed the fork down, and it ricocheted off the tray and bounced across the table. Ensign Peter Bell slapped his hand down on it, clamping it to the table.

"Take it easy, will ya, Whitney?"

Rachel pushed her tray away and leaned her elbows on the table, her head in her hands. "Sorry. This waiting is killing me."

"Get used to it. If you're assigned monitoring duty, that's all you'll do for the next six months to a year—wait." Bell placed the fork on her abandoned tray.

Monica Rawley, the only other woman in Rachel's class at the U.S. Navy's Special Warfare Training Center, threw her a withering look. "If they send me to that creepy island you want so badly, I'll absolutely die."

"Yeah, I want to be where there are some chicks at least," said Michael Gustafson, on the other side of Rawley. "Imagine being stuck in the middle of nowhere for six months with two or three other guys."

Bell grimaced. "I'd rather not."

"Personally, I'd like a larger selection to choose from," Monica said, and the half dozen men sharing their table hooted.

"I hope they send me to Alaska," said Bill White.

"Not me. I want the Persian Gulf." Gustafson turned his attention back to his food.

Bell shoved back his chair. "I'm getting more coffee. Anyone want anything?"

"I think I'll just go over to 7B and wait." Rachel stood and picked up her tray.

Rawley shook her head. "They're not going to post the new assignments until 1300. You might as well finish your lunch."

"Not hungry."

As Rachel cleared her tray, she heard White say under his breath, "If she wasn't so standoffish, she could be a lot of fun."

"Fun?" Gustafson made no attempt to lower his voice. "She's not what I'd consider a party girl. Never goes out. Always studying."

"Trust me, Rachel's not the fun-loving type," Rawley said, and Rachel turned and strode for the door.

She and Monica were uneasy roommates. Monica had a hardened prettiness, and she gravitated toward flirtations. Rachel was sure they would someday land her in trouble with the Navy. On the other hand, Rachel had determined that nothing, not even love, would stand between her and her career. As a result, she'd sidestepped all attempts at romance, and Monica had branded her heartless.

Right now, all she wanted was to be somewhere else. Home, maybe. She felt a strong pull toward her family and regretted the walls she had built around herself.

Her route to the classroom took her past the mailboxes, and she decided to stop long enough to check hers. They'd all be leaving within twenty-four hours, but there was still a chance she'd get some last-minute mail from home.

She slid her key into the slot and cranked it. The head came off in her hand, and she stared down at it in disbelief.

"Oh, man!" She kicked the concrete wall beneath the bank of mailboxes.

"Ouch!" Bill White came up behind her. "You've got to watch that temper, Whitney."

"Oh, yeah?"

He held up both hands, his keys dangling from one. "Take it easy. No one's trying to deep six you. Just settle down."

She said between clenched teeth, "I broke my key."

He laughed, and she threw her shoulders back.

"You think that's funny?"

"Well, yeah."

Rachel sighed and watched helplessly as he opened his own box, knowing the officer in charge of mail was away for the lunch hour, and she wouldn't be able to see if she had any letters until later. Of course, she wouldn't blame her family if they didn't write. Her anger had spilled over at home too, and during the last few years tension had run high.

She'd received a letter from her father two weeks ago, though, saying that they loved her and wished her success. He even said they hoped she'd have time enough to come home for a visit before she left for her new assignment. She'd written back, just a brief note, unsure of what to say, but the exchange had softened her heart.

She loved her parents and her brothers, though her constant chafing kept her at odds with them. Although she'd never shared the cause of her anger with them, they felt it. She wanted to have a better relationship with all of them. A lump formed in her throat as she considered whether or not she would go home tomorrow. Was there a return letter in her box, waiting for her? Maybe one from her mother? She stared malevolently at her mailbox, and the broken stub of the key glinted back at her.

White smiled to himself as he shuffled several envelopes, and she felt a stab of regret. Of all the trainees in her group, he'd been friendliest to her, ignoring her remoteness. He wasn't bad-looking, and he could be good company when she didn't bristle. In the months of training together, they might have become good friends, but she hadn't let that happen. The same was true of Rawley, Bell, and the rest. Instead of listening to them and cultivating the relationships, she had allowed her competitive nature and her ambition to isolate her.

"Give me your key."

"What?" She stared at him.

"I think I can open your box. Come on." He held out his hand.

She hesitated, and then she dropped the key head in it. He stooped and fitted the broken end against the piece in the slot. Rachel held her breath as he gently jiggled it and the door swung open.

"Wow! Thanks a lot, White."

He shrugged and dropped it back in her hand with a grin. "Didn't want you to stay mad."

"That's something I do too often. It doesn't help anything, though." She bent to look into the box.

A small white envelope beckoned her, and she snatched it and tore it open.

Rachel, come home! We miss you.

A moment later she looked up and saw White studying her face. "Well?"

She smiled. "It's from my mother. She wants me to go home for my leave."

"Great. Are you going?"

She nodded, making the decision as she spoke. "Yeah, I'm definitely going. It may be a long time before I have another chance."

"Right. We'll be scattered all over after this."

"Yeah. I hope you get the assignment you want." Rachel glanced back along the hallway as they walked. "Rawley's going to be really upset if she doesn't get DC."

"I know. I hope she gets it."

"Really?"

"Well, sure." White opened the classroom door and let Rachel precede him. "If she doesn't get what she wants, they might send her to Alaska instead, and then where will I be?"

Rachel nodded. "Yeah, I see what you mean. There's only one opening where you want to be. Same here. But do you think they really care where we want to go?"

They sat down at two of the simulator consoles where they'd trained for weeks.

"I sure hope so." White laid his mail on the desk. "I mean, passion counts, doesn't it?"

Rachel swallowed hard and tried to push down a wrinkle in her khaki uniform slacks. "I'm so on edge, even breathing hurts. I know I can do the job wherever they send me, but I really, *really* want Frasier."

"How come you want it so much?"

"Two reasons. It's the smallest operating naval base right now. If you make good there, you're a cinch for a promotion when you leave the island."

"I don't know about that. Seems to me, in a small unit like that you'd be under the microscope every minute. What else?"

He watched her with avid blue eyes, and Rachel felt for the first time that she could open up to him without fearing ridicule.

"I'd give anything to serve with George Hudson." She squeezed her lips together, watching his face.

White nodded, and she let her breath out in a puff. He was taking her seriously.

"I can understand that. They say he's the best. And he helped build the system on Frasier Island. I hear he knows more about defensive missiles than just about anyone else."

She nodded, feeling her excitement build. "He's legendary."

"I don't know as I'd go that far."

"Oh, yeah? He's made Frasier's defensive missile system what it is, and the big brass listens to him, even though he's only a lieutenant. The man has got to be a genius. And somehow he's convinced them to keep him there for three years, even though the tours of duty on Frasier are supposed to be only six months."

"Didn't they say you could request twelve?"

"Yeah. I put in for two tours there. If Lieutenant Hudson stays there and I get the assignment…"

"What, you think you can pick his brain and come out knowing everything he knows?"

"Why not?"

White smiled. "I guess you're smart enough."

Rachel stared at him, wondering anew what she'd missed out on by avoiding friendships. "Thanks, White."

"You're welcome. And I hope you get it."

She sat back with a sigh.

Other people filed into the room, and Rachel caught Monica's eye.

"Good luck."

Her roommate nodded but said nothing.

As Captain Wanamaker entered carrying a leather case, they all stood at attention and saluted. He returned the salute. "At ease. Sit."

They all sat with straight shoulders, facing front. He unzipped the folder on the instructor's desk and took out a stack of large yellow envelopes. After a quick roll call, he looked around the room, meeting the eyes of each ensign in turn.

"Good afternoon. Your training is at an end, and I'm sure you're all happy to know that. This class has done extremely well in all components, and I would like to congratulate you." His dark eyes scanned the room, and his gaze settled on Rachel. "Ensign Whitney, stand up."

Rachel's knees felt like rubber as she pushed to her feet.

"Top honors in this module go to Ensign Rachel Whitney. Congratulations, Whitney!"

Rachel managed a shaky smile as the others began to clap.

"Good job." Wanamaker smiled as she approached. "Here are your orders."

She accepted an envelope from him and saluted. Then she stepped back and turned toward her seat with shaking knees.

She heard no more as he distributed the rest, but sat staring down at the envelope that held her future.

When he was finished, the captain faced them again and said, "Congratulations to all of you. Now, go out there and do us proud."

They stood at attention as he left the room, and then they tore open their orders. Rachel's fingers shook as she extracted her papers and stared at them.

"Hey! I got Alaska," Bill White said. "What'd you get?"

She pulled in a breath and looked up at him.

"Guam!" Monica Rawley wailed. "They're sending me to stinkin' Guam!"

Bill's eyebrows arched. "Did you get what you wanted?"

Rachel nodded and exhaled slowly, closing her eyes. "Frasier Island."

ONE

April 20

"Are you sure this is right?" George asked, frowning as he scanned the form on the clipboard. The young ensign in charge of the resupply detail stood watching him.

"Yes, Lieutenant. Absolutely." Ensign Carver grinned, and George signed the form with a scrawl, not meeting his eyes.

Ron Davidson, one of Hudson's two subordinates on the island, was leaving today. He and the three sailors who had accompanied the ensign to shore had already begun lugging boxes of provisions and new equipment from the ship's boat up to the house that served as an observation station on Frasier Island. The sooner they got the supplies unloaded and stowed, the sooner they could leave.

A uniformed girl stood waiting, shivering in her wool pea jacket. She looked about sixteen, with the wind tugging tendrils of hair from her pinned-up braid. He could hardly believe she was old enough to have completed officers' training. Her bag of personal gear sat on the rocks beside her, and she held the cord, working it nervously through her chilled fingers. His first glance had told George she was strikingly pretty. After that he had deliberately ignored her.

Now he looked her way. "Take your gear topside, Ensign."

She looked as if she were about to salute, and he turned away. Handing the clipboard back, he muttered, "Don't s'pose you'd trade me for one of your men?"

Carver chuckled. "You'll get used to it, Lieutenant."

George turned and picked up a crate of provisions. "As soon as we stow this stuff, we need to clear the helicopter pad."

"You had to drop a windmill on the only flat spot on this island, didn't you?" Carver asked as he hefted a box.

"Had to put it up where it would catch the wind."

"Well, the boat ride in here is a real treat, I'll tell you."

"I've done it a couple of times," George acknowledged. "Thanks for making the effort. We've had to run everything off the generators for the past four days, and the solar collectors are at an all-time low."

They toiled up the slope. The house was perched on a bluff at the highest point of the island, near its western tip, and was built to withstand storms like the one that had buffeted them for the last week, toppling the windmill. It squatted on the hilltop overlooking an expanse of ocean that was empty, except for the five ships of the battle group standing by a quarter mile offshore. As soon as Carver and his men returned, those ships would leave.

Davidson and the sailors passed them on the trail.

"I showed Whitney where to stow her gear," Davidson called.

George scowled. A girl in Ron's place.

❧

Rachel swung her canvas sea bag onto the cot and looked around the tiny bare room. As long as she had privacy, it would do. There was a small dresser and a crate on end for a nightstand. No closet, just a row of hooks on one wall. A small mirror hung over the dresser, and a folding camp chair stood in one corner. This was home for the next year.

She would unpack later. The last thing she wanted was for the lieutenant to think she was shirking her duties while the men unloaded, but she couldn't resist taking a peek out the little window. A heavy wooden storm shutter hung below it, allowing the occupants to secure the window from the inside. She opened the sash and stuck her head out. The window faced westward, over the sea, and beneath it was a sheer drop of several yards to a ledge of volcanic rock that made the foundation of the house.

She swallowed hard. It was a far cry from the lush fields, peach orchard, and distant buttes that she could view from her bedroom window in western Oregon. She felt vulnerable and alone.

"Well, Lord, it's You and me," she whispered.

It still felt strange to talk to God. A week ago she would have scoffed at the idea. Her faith was still untried, but she had no question it was real. Despite her nervousness at meeting the renowned George Hudson and taking up her new post in an alien setting, she felt an overriding calm that had never been there before.

She went to the cot and opened her bag, taking out the top item, a small paperback Bible, and set it on the upended crate. Knowing that God was with her, she could stand whatever came her way here. Even the shock that struck her when she saw arrogant hostility in her new superior officer's eyes.

As she hurried to the boat landing, she steeled herself to meet Hudson again. All through her four years at the Naval Academy, followed by special training, she'd had trouble submitting to authority, but with great effort she had kept her quick temper in check. She could easily ruin her chances for a challenging Navy career, and succeeding was very important to her. She'd never enjoyed failure, and in order to avoid it, she had conformed to the rigid discipline of the military life.

Now that was behind her, and she was beginning the exciting part, the special assignment she had worked for so hard. She had the training, and she was ready.

Hudson fascinated her. When she'd heard about him at the high security training center back in Seattle, she had built up a respect for him. At first glimpse she'd known he was all she'd imaged: handsome, stalwart, heroic. His dark hair and gray eyes were very appealing. But he scared her a little. *If only he would smile*, she thought.

She was the first woman to qualify for the highly classified detail, but her pride in that had crumbled under Hudson's baleful stare. He measured her against some unknown standard, and she obviously fell short.

She was resolved to make good on Frasier Island, and to leave in a year with a clean record and a recommendation for promotion. If Hudson was disappointed in his new subordinate, he'd soon change his mind. Her father called her stubborn. Rachel preferred the designation of tenacious. She would teach the handsome lieutenant what tenacity meant.

Pierre Belanger sat dutifully at his console in the control room, deep in the volcanic rock beneath the house. Months of isolation and forced quietude on Frasier had taught him patience. A couple of sailors poked their heads in for a moment and yelled a friendly greeting, but he couldn't give them his attention. Ron Davidson was supervising the unloading of the supplies, and George was no doubt down on the rocks signing the manifest and greeting Ron's replacement.

One of the sailors came down the stairs with a crate. He set it gently on the floor before coming up behind Pierre and clapping him on the shoulder. Pierre recognized Misner from six months ago.

"Well, Belanger, things are gonna change around here, hey?"

Pierre shot him a quick glance and then looked back at his console. "Happens every six months or so."

"Not like this." Misner went away laughing.

Pierre was intrigued, but he sat silent, looking from one screen to the next. Camera monitors, sonar, radar. Eight hours a day, with a couple of short breaks. The three men spelled each other around the clock. He could hear footsteps, distant voices, and thumps as crates were set down heavily in the storeroom overhead. Then it grew very quiet.

At last George came down the stairs. Pierre could always tell when George entered the room. He made almost no noise, but went straight to his station, not like Davidson, who talked to anyone whether they were listening or not. This time George came and stood beside his chair without speaking.

"What's up?" Pierre asked.

"New recruit's here."

"C'est la vie."

"Oui, mais…elle est une femme."

Pierre sat without moving, staring at the passive sonar display without seeing it, for ten seconds. Ron's replacement was a woman. *"Elle parle français?"* he asked softly.

"Sais pas." George was quiet for a moment. *"Elle est trop jeune."*

"Magnifique." She was too young—but by whose standard? George always thought the recruits were too young.

Pierre and George had often spoken French in the past six months when they didn't want Ron Davidson to understand them. They had formed an unspoken bond that excluded the third man long ago. George had been here six tours now, three years since the day the program was instituted. He should have gone off the island long ago, but every time his relief came due, he requested another tour on Frasier, and so far his requests had been granted.

Now Pierre's own year was up, but he had decided that another six months wouldn't kill him. He liked being here with George, knowing the two of them were the ablest sentinels in the world, the only ones who could possibly do this job this well. In a spurt of patriotism and loyalty to George, he had offered to let Davidson go, and through some machinations that were hazy to Pierre, the switch was approved.

Ron had jumped at it. He'd hated the island from the day he stepped out of the helicopter. Of course, he came at the worst time of year in the North Pacific, during typhoon season, and he had faced long odds of breaking into the established friendship. Pierre felt a flash of shame for having treated him coldly. It wasn't in his nature to freeze a man out, but Davidson was an odd bird. Or maybe it was he and George who were the odd ones, and Ron was too normal to let them feel comfortable. Whatever it was, Davidson's constant carping and fastidious habits had nearly driven George insane. Pierre had been able to keep his sense of humor most of the time, but he knew he could never leave George here with Ron and some new man, an unknown quantity who might be worse even than Ron.

And now George had dropped the bombshell. Ron's replacement was a woman, a very young woman. Pierre knew the odd feelings of apprehension, wonder, and chagrin that coursed through him were mild compared to what George must be feeling. George had hardly stepped off this rock for three years. He thrived on the solitude, or at least he thought he did. Pierre wasn't so sure.

But he knew George would not voluntarily leave the island now. Until the Navy forced him to, he would stay and stand watch for his country. America…all those people. Men, women, and children that George had never seen and didn't want to see. He would willingly give his life for them, but could he go back and live in his beloved country when the time came?

"You stay here," George said. "We're going to clear the helo pad."

"Send Ron down. I'll help you."

"No, he's already charged up to leave. You can concentrate better than him."

Pierre shrugged. "All right."

It was his regular shift, and when he'd sighted the ships on his monitors, Davidson and George had left him alone in the building while they tended to business outside.

"You putting the new recruit on duty today?" Pierre asked.

"She might as well get a running start. If we mollycoddle her today, she'll expect it."

Pierre nodded. "Okay. If you need me to stay on a while with her, I will."

"It's my job to train her. But I might send her down here while we finish up outside. I don't think she'd be much help with the heavy work. I was hoping they'd send us a man who could pull his own weight."

"Perhaps she has other skills," Pierre said gently.

George looked toward the doorway. "There's a lot she doesn't know."

"They're still not telling the recruits what we really do?" Pierre shook his head, remembering his own shock when George had clued him in on their mission a year ago. "You going to tell her first thing?"

"We'll see. Might let her settle in a little first."

Pierre nodded. "I'll leave that to you."

"All right." George moved quietly toward the stairs.

"Hey!" Pierre called. "Did they bring coffee?"

"Plenty, unless *mademoiselle* is a caffeine addict like you."

Pierre smiled. His glance swept over the monitors on the console, and then he focused for twenty seconds on the aircraft identification chart that hung on the side wall.

✒

The wind seemed mild after the gale they had endured over the past week. George and Carver passed the sailors again on the narrow path as they went back down for more supplies. Davidson nodded at him, his eyes eager despite the weight of the crate he carried. When they reached the landing, George looked over the few boxes that were left.

"We'd have brought you more if we could have landed a Seahawk today," Carver shouted.

"Well, you brought the new equipment and coffee in."

"Not to mention Davidson's replacement." Carver laughed at his grimace. "Yes, well, you fellows have to eat. We left some frozen food and a crate of cookies and popcorn on the ship. Maybe we'll be able to stop by again in a few weeks. Don't want you to run short on rations."

As he lifted the box containing Pierre's precious coffee, George saw the girl coming cautiously down the steep path.

"Can I help, sir?" she yelled against the wind. He pointed to a box he thought she could wrestle up the trail. He didn't watch to see if she could lift it, but seized another carton and turned away.

When all the supplies were inside, George gathered the men around him.

"The crucial thing is to clear the debris of the windmill off the chopper pad." He looked intently at each of them. "You can't stay here long enough to repair it. This weather's too unpredictable. Belanger and I will have to work on it ourselves when the wind drops. But we need to be able to get helos in here in case we have an emergency, so we'll just drag the pieces off to the side and leave them there. Got it?"

Rachel Whitney's solemn blue eyes were huge as she nodded.

"Not you," he said quickly, and she winced.

"I'd like to help." Her voice was quiet and earnest, but George shook his head.

"Davidson will take you down to the control room. Belanger is on duty now, and he can show you the basics of the monitoring job while the rest of us take care of this detail."

"Yes, sir." She looked disappointed, and her dark lashes lowered, hiding her expressive eyes. He'd never seen eyes quite like that. George found himself watching, waiting for her to look up again, and he looked hastily away. Trouble. Nothing but trouble.

It was a relief when Ron led her to the stairway that went below, to the control room. But George knew the relief would be short-lived. Rachel Whitney was here to stay.

TWO

"You boys want some coffee?" George asked when the heavy components of the fallen windmill had been moved.

"The seas are pretty heavy. I think we'd better head out ASAP, but thanks just the same," Carver replied.

"Right."

They tramped down to the boat landing, and the sailors prepared the boat for the difficult launch. Davidson stuck his hand out, and George took it reluctantly. The man had been his constant companion for six months. They didn't get along very well, but it was hitting him full force that Ron was leaving for good, and his replacement was a female—a green ensign straight out of training. He dreaded facing her again. In his mind he saw her standing on the rocks, her hair whipped by the wind, and those wide blue eyes holding a look of terror masked by determination. It was going to be a long six months.

"You sure you want to leave?" he asked Ron, without real hope. "We could send that girl back—"

Ron laughed. "You should have taken your chance to get off here, George. You're stuck with her now." He heaved his sea bag into the launch.

George turned to Carver. "See you next time."

"Maybe not. I'm getting out in July." Carver grinned and raised one eyebrow.

George took a deep breath. Things continued to change in the outside world too. He extended his hand. "Nice knowing you." It seemed a little flat.

He and Carver had seen each other several times in three years. Once George had gone out to the ship in the helicopter for a brief meeting with Commander Norton, who supervised him long-distance from Pearl Harbor, and Carver had shared twenty minutes of coffee and conversation with him afterward. It wasn't exactly a deep friendship, but his job didn't allow for friendships. He had fellow workers that he lived with twenty-four hours a day, and he had acquaintances in the outside world. That was it.

Carver clambered into the boat, and Davidson and the three sailors shoved it into the surf and scrambled over the gunwales. Carver manned a pair of oars, steadying the boat in the waves.

Pierre came scrambling down the path as they pushed away from shore.

"*Bon voyage,* Ron," he called, waving.

"Who's on duty?" George snapped.

"Ensign Whitney."

"She's been here two hours and you left her alone in the control room?" He didn't try to keep the edge from his voice.

The young Frenchman smiled. "She knows her stuff, George."

"She may be smart, but she's still a rookie."

Pierre shrugged. "Give her a chance. You didn't tell me she's a knockout."

George refused to acknowledge that comment. He stood watching silently until the boat was past the worst rocks, beyond the jagged inlet, and Carver started the motor. The only landing place on Frasier Island was hardly worthy of the name. In good weather, they used helicopters. But they'd almost lost a Seahawk in high winds during George's first tour, and the captain was reluctant to risk his men and equipment.

If the weather was too rough when supply ships came, they wouldn't even try to land a helo or a boat, but would drop a few critical items, go on to other business, and come back—when? A month later…two…six? George was glad they had made it in today. Supplies had been running low.

He saw that the launch had reached the side of the ship, and raised his arm to wave. A scrap of white flapped from the deck, and he knew a man was watching them through a telescope. It would be their last contact with the outside world, other than by radio, for some time.

Pierre said, "You must have realized how pretty she is, George. She's smart too. Eager to learn. You had to notice that."

"Okay, so I noticed. But I can't think about stuff like that. You know it's impossible."

"Stuff like what?"

George didn't know why he let Pierre goad him. Maybe it was the ensign's innocent demeanor. Or maybe it was just that George liked him. Pierre was the closest friend he'd had in years, and George let him say things no one else could get away with.

He had let Pierre see his hurts and fears. Maybe that was a mistake. It seemed Pierre was becoming the conscience George had tried to leave behind.

He couldn't stall any longer. It was time to deal with Rachel Whitney's orientation. Until Pierre had voiced it, he'd almost been able to classify her mentally as a sailor, a rookie, a trainee—not a disturbingly beautiful young woman. He turned resolutely to the steep, rocky path.

<hr />

Rachel glanced at her watch. Pierre had been gone nearly half an hour. She didn't mind. It gave her a chance to get used to the equipment and the depressingly plain room. She focused on the monitors, trying not to remember how far underground she was. A twinge of nervousness startled her. It wasn't claustrophobia exactly, but it was the same uneasy feeling that had steered her away from submarine training.

She hadn't expected it to hit her here. She set her teeth and determined to overcome it quickly. If George Hudson had an inkling that she had qualms about being fathoms underground or beneath the water, he'd find a way to get rid of her. She sent a mental prayer upward. Her friend Heidi, on the USS *George H.W. Bush,* had assured her that she could pray anytime, anyplace, without making a sound.

She gazed at the monitor that showed the battle group standing by in the choppy seas. That was better. Almost like having a window.

Footsteps sounded on the stairway behind her, and she glanced over her shoulder and then back to the radar screen. Belanger entered whistling, and her spirits lifted. He had changed out of his uniform into faded jeans and a gray T-shirt.

"How's everything, Rachel?"

"Couldn't be more peaceful."

"Terrific. George says for you to go on upstairs for lunch."

Her stomach began churning again, and she relinquished her post to him reluctantly. Pierre settled into the padded swivel chair. As she hesitated, he glanced up at her and winked.

"He doesn't bite."

She managed a smile and headed for the stairs. When she reached the top of the second flight, she paused and took a deep breath. She had come here expecting to serve under a hero, but her first meeting with Lieutenant Hudson had left her wondering if he were truly as smart and noble as he was rumored to be. She hated to think it, but already he seemed to have something against her. Or had she imagined it? Maybe she had overestimated his antagonism. *Help me keep my cool, Lord,* she thought, and she wondered if Heidi was right—that her silent prayer really went straight from Frasier Island to God's throne.

Hudson was standing over the gas stove in the kitchen, tending a skillet of sizzling pork chops. The table was set for two, and sliced tomatoes and rolls were set out.

"We don't get fresh meat and produce very often." He turned to the table and slid a chop onto each plate, leaving one in the skillet.

"You cook lunch every day?" Rachel asked warily.

"No. I'm usually sleeping now. I get up around this time and eat, and then Pierre and I get supper later. If you like to cook, I won't say no."

She smiled weakly. "Maybe we could take turns?"

He shrugged. "We'll work something out. It's hard because we can never all three sit down together and hash things out. One of us has to be on watch constantly. Every second. You understand?"

She nodded, pushing back a lock of hair that rebelliously fell forward again. "Why don't they have a fourth man here for relief? I mean, what if something happened? What if one of us is sick?"

"Then we do twelve-hour shifts. It's hard enough for them to bring on the supplies required for three of us. We're so isolated, and the landing place is nearly inaccessible."

"But they built this place…" She let it trail off, assessing the thick walls of concrete and stone. It was crude, but solid. She hoped the plumbing was modern.

"It leaves a lot to be desired," George admitted. "They had to bring all the lumber and pipe and wire in by helo. It could be worse."

Rachel wanted to ask more questions during the meal, but George's perpetual frown silenced her. When they had finished eating, she took her dishes to the sink and reached for the bottle of soap on the drain board.

"Leave those. Pierre can do them after he eats."

She eyed George in surprise. "It won't take a minute."

"Fine." He took two mugs from a shelf and filled them with black coffee. Rachel quickly washed their plates and silverware and rinsed them with warm water from the sluggish tap. She wondered if she'd just made a big mistake, voluntarily taking on KP duty. George sized up the packaged snacks that had arrived that morning and selected a box of cookies.

"Come on. You're up. We try to keep the schedule out of courtesy for each other." He headed for the door, carrying his coffee mug and a handful of gingersnaps.

She snatched up her mug, not daring to take a few seconds to add milk to her coffee, and followed him down the two flights of stairs.

Belanger sat with his back to them and didn't look up as they approached.

"Pierre, Ensign Whitney thinks she's ready to take over."

"Hello again." She stepped closer to Pierre, beside the console with its monitors.

He threw her a magnificent smile. "Welcome back, Rachel."

Relief flashed through her. At least one of them was friendly. She glanced around the room and took in anew the windowless walls, the complicated electronics that comprised their ocean surveillance equipment, navigational charts, wall charts depicting aircraft silhouettes, and a detailed map of the island.

"Sit down." Pierre nodded at a chair on the other side of him. Rachel walked behind him and sat. "Now watch the screens."

She let her eyes go deliberately from one monitor to the next. She would watch for eight hours a day. Suddenly the weeks of training seemed ridiculous. This was it. Straining their eyes for nothing. Empty ocean.

"Every few minutes, you look up," Pierre reminded her. It annoyed her slightly, but she didn't say anything. If she just did the job, they would see that she knew how.

She glanced toward the monitor that showed the view captured by the camera mounted above the boat landing and caught her breath. The carrier battle group was gone.

During her first visit to the control room, the *Bush* had been clearly, reassuringly visible on the screen. *I can still catch Ensign Carver*, she'd thought. That chance was gone now.

But she wasn't sorry. She'd even feared for a few moments, when she'd climbed out of the launch on the rocky shore, that Lieutenant Hudson would send her back to the ship. His quick visual appraisal had seemed to end in disappointment, and his silence during lunch hadn't reassured her.

She tore her gaze away and looked at the other monitors. One, two, three. The radar screens, and the sonar. Again.

"I'll stay with her a while," George said.

Pierre stood up, stretching. "How was lunch?"

George grunted and took his chair.

"It was very good," Rachel said, not looking away from the screens. "Yours is in the kitchen."

"Galley," said George.

"Sorry."

Pierre laughed. "We get mostly Navy men here. Call it whatever you want."

"I'm Navy," she said defensively.

"Bien sur." Pierre was out the door.

"What did he say?" she asked.

"Loosely translated?" George shrugged. "Of course."

She looked at him. "He speaks French."

"Watch the screens."

She turned quickly back to the console, feeling her face flush.

"This job isn't conducive to conversation," Hudson said after a moment. "You can't drop your guard. Ever."

She nodded. It would be easy to forget, she knew. During training, the instructors had warned them. *It will seem like such a simple job, so boring, a waste of time, even. But you must always be vigilant.*

The silence grew, and she wished Hudson would leave. She could handle this alone much better than with him brooding beside her.

"Why did they pick you for this, anyway?"

She was startled at his question. "I guess they felt I was the best."

He snorted. "Better than us?"

She felt a flush washing up her neck to her face. "Lieutenant Hudson, I have great respect for you and the others who serve here. I know you are the absolute best in the world. I should have said, I was the best in my class."

His lips twisted in a wry grimace. "What did you take, Missile Monitoring 101?"

"Something like that."

Hudson shook his head. "Well, I guess we have to get replacements from somewhere."

Rachel decided to ignore him.

George had thought she would break the silence, but she had more patience than he'd given her credit for. He watched her carefully, just waiting for her to make a mistake, but she didn't. He knew he shouldn't have spoken so disparagingly to her, but he didn't care. She was turning his small, well-ordered world on its ear.

After twenty minutes, he said, "It takes a few weeks to settle in here."

She continued watching the monitors. "Yes, sir."

He laughed shortly. "You can cut the *sir* around here when it's just the three of us. That would get really old in six months."

"I'm here for a year."

"Really? Davidson thought he was too."

Her face went scarlet, and George felt a tiny stab of guilt. If he didn't control his anger, she'd be filing a harassment complaint on him. But the color in her cheeks made her look suddenly alive and intriguing.

"Look up now," he said softly. She immediately obeyed his voice, but she focused on the distant map of Frasier Island for ten seconds, studiously avoiding his face.

"You have to save your eyes. They're vital to this job." He told himself he was trying to be patient. This was a new recruit, like any other. He needed to be careful and treat her the same way he'd treated the others who had come to the island, even though just sitting beside her had set his adrenaline flowing.

"Do you ever get a vessel in these waters, other than Navy?" There was an almost imperceptible tremor in her voice, and he knew she was fighting to keep her serenity.

"It happens."

"How often?"

He didn't answer for a long time. She went back to her silent vigil. At last he said, "Five times, that we know of."

"That you know of?"

George sighed, trying not to think about the time on his first tour when the kid, Carlton, had broken his leg, and he and Matt Rubin had stood twelve-hour shifts for days. He had fallen asleep at his post one night in the wee hours and awakened in panic. What if a Chinese ship had come while he slept? What if a plane…? He had never told anyone, not even Matt, and they were like brothers back then.

"Yeah, five vessels in three years. Two tankers, a Filipino cruiser off course, a Japanese trawler, and a yacht that got caught in a storm and was dismasted."

"Wow."

"We tried to signal the yacht, but we never saw a sign of life on board."

"How close were they?"

"Really close."

She shuddered. "Couldn't you go out and try to help them?"

He shook his head. "It takes four men to launch a boat from our cove. This island is one of the worst I know of for landing a boat or launching one. Second only to Pitcairn. Even if you could do it with three people, which I doubt, someone has to stay on watch."

"But…" She glanced at him briefly, her eyes troubled. "You might have saved some lives."

"Or lost some trying. We regretted not being able to help them. We hoped they'd run up on the island, but they didn't. They missed the point, and the yacht just drifted away."

The feelings of helplessness that George hated returned. Matt Rubin had been on duty when he spotted the yacht. He'd pushed the alarm button, and George had hurried to the control room.

"Look out there!" Matt's agitation had been evident, but he had kept his post. George had peered at the monitor and then dashed up three flights of stairs to the roof, where they kept a high-powered telescope, and gazed out at the drifting boat that rose awkwardly on the crest of each swell.

The third man came up and stood beside him. "They're drifting. They need help."

"Not from us," George said. "We can't get to them."

He radioed a distress signal, but the nearest American vessel was hours away. When they finally heard planes whining over, the yacht was long gone to the south. They had given the best guess they could on its whereabouts, but it had never been found. Probably it swamped and sank. Maybe the crew had been washed overboard. There had been a violent storm the night before.

"Is Pierre sleeping now?"

Rachel's question brought him back to the present.

"Maybe, but I doubt it. He usually sleeps when I'm on duty. So should you. He's probably unpacking supplies."

"So, you both sleep when the other's on watch, and have your free time together, while I'm on duty?" she asked.

George swallowed and looked away. He'd developed the schedule to avoid Davidson, but he couldn't say that. "Well, Pierre and I usually spend some time together in the evening, making repairs and such, before I go on watch."

She nodded soberly, and he thought she might be looking down the months ahead at a rather bleak existence. Did he really want to crush her spirit? His impulse was to treat her coldly, just within the limits of regulations, until she decided this detail was for men and begged for a transfer. The realization startled him. When had he stopped being decent to people?

"Bring any books?" he asked.

"A couple. They wouldn't let me pack much when they found out they had to use the boat. I left a box on the ship in care of a friend."

He nodded, glad he had made the effort to change the tone of the exchange. He didn't care whether she liked him or not, but he didn't want her to hate him.

"We've got a small library. Most guys bring a few books and leave them." He wondered what Rachel had brought. Maybe something new. That would be nice. Or maybe a classic he hadn't read in years. But he didn't ask. Better to have the anticipation. He knew Carver had brought half a dozen volumes he had ordered. They were still in a carton in his room. He would open them later, with his slim packet of mail, when he was alone. He pushed away the twinge of guilt that came as he realized that his books may have edged out some of Whitney's personal belongings.

He sat watching her, periodically checking the screens himself to be sure she wasn't missing anything. He ought to leave her alone. She obviously knew the drill. He told himself it was because she was new and unproven, but deep down something whispered that it was her femininity that kept him in the chair.

He leaned back and studied her profile. Her hair glistened where it was pulled back behind her delicately sculpted ear. She wasn't wearing makeup, and her skin had a healthy sheen. Her chin had a determined set to it, until she bit her bottom lip with even, white teeth, and it struck him that he was making her nervous. She probably felt the way he would if an admiral sat looking over his shoulder while he was on duty.

Time to tell her about the true nature of their mission. He straightened and cleared his throat. "Listen, what we do is vital to the security of the United States of America. You'll never be famous for doing this job, and you'll never get a medal or be written up in *Time* magazine."

"I understand."

"Believe me, whatever they put you on for a simulator back home, it was nothing like this."

She eyed the console screens dubiously. "It was exactly like this."

"Yeah." He hesitated, and then he decided he wasn't ready to disillusion her. Did she really need to know there was more to it than the missile silos beneath the waves? Pierre would say he should tell her, but he needed to know he could trust her first, and he didn't know that yet. He made the easy decision. He would wait.

"Okay, Whitney. You ready to fly solo? You know what to do if you spot something."

Her hand moved toward the alarm switches. "I assume you'll come running as I radio in the news."

"Before you radio in," he corrected her. "No offense, but let Pierre or me take a look before you make contact."

She eyed him uncertainly, just for an instant. "Yes, sir."

"It's George." He wondered if he would regret making that concession so early. He stood up and headed resolutely for the stairs.

Why did she make him feel guilty? For three years he'd done the job here without his conscience bothering him.

But Rachel Whitney's huge blue eyes made him think of his sister, although Judy's eyes were a warm mocha. For some reason Rachel, like Judy, brought on the feeling that he'd neglected a vast area of responsibility. He wasn't here on Frasier Island just to stand watch. He'd come to carry out his duty, but he'd also come here to escape his personal life. Up until now, it had worked. But Rachel's arrival brought back a flood of memories. Another life, a happier time, torn from him.

He remembered that final week he'd spent at the ranch with Judy and Jason and the kids. He'd known when he said goodbye that he would stay away as long as possible, though Judy's pleas heaped on the guilt, and the two little girls did their best to break his heart.

Judy meant well, trying to force him to face his apathy and his spiritual emptiness. But he'd left them behind, seeking a time of oblivion, of numbness, waiting for the massive pain of his grief to ease. He'd told himself it would fade slowly, and one day he'd be able to feel things other than sorrow.

Was today that day?

As George climbed the two flights of stairs from the control room to the galley, the intervening three years skimmed through his mind. Somehow Rachel Whitney had stirred his memories, reminding him that his life touched those of others, causing them to have feelings too. Maybe it was the dogged resolution in her eyes that brought back such clear images of another face. He put his hand to his chest for a moment and felt the ring through the fabric of his shirt. He could remember, but with less pain now. Maybe it was an acceptable compromise.

THREE

Rachel thought she could hear their voices occasionally, far away and quiet. Once she was sure she heard a door close, but she was deep in the rock, and sounds were muffled. At suppertime Pierre brought her a tray with a sandwich and a cup of coffee, spelled her for a short break, and then left her alone again. The fatigue of the trip began to assail her as the evening advanced. She'd been sending up mental prayers all day for the stamina she needed to face this new situation. Now the prayers changed. *Lord, just help me stay awake until the shift ends.*

When George came back at 2200, she was nearly overcome with sleepiness. She jumped when he spoke, close beside her.

"Anything interesting?"

"Oh, uh, no, not really. An hour or so ago the sonobuoys picked up some movement, but I'm pretty sure it was a school of porpoise."

"I'll take over."

"Thanks."

She stood up, watching the screens until she was sure he was in place. "Do I smell popcorn?"

"Pierre's bedtime snack. He'll make enough for you too."

She stood uncertainly. "Well, good night."

He nodded almost imperceptibly. "Be sure to ask him to show you how the shower works."

"Right." Was he saying she needed a shower? She looked down

at her crumpled uniform. *Quit analyzing everything,* she warned herself.

She climbed the stairs, through the first basement and up to the sitting room. She went to one of the windows. Darkness had fallen, and clouds scudded across the star-strewn sky. When she entered the galley yawning, Pierre jumped from his chair.

"Rachel! How did it go?"

"Fine. Kind of boring."

He smiled. "That is usually the case. We try not to disturb each other so we don't break concentration."

"I'll get used to it."

"Not like training?" he suggested.

"You're right. There were always a lot of people in the room during training. I think I'll send Captain Hedges a suggestion. He needs to give trainees practice in monitoring alone for hours at a time."

"Hedges? I remember him. Dark hair, quick temper." Pierre filled a cereal bowl with popcorn and handed it to her.

"That's him," Rachel sat down and ate a handful of popcorn. She smiled at Pierre. "This is like home. My dad always makes popcorn on Saturday night."

"Homesick already?"

"No. Well, just a little. It's going to be really different here."

"Like being in prison at first," Pierre agreed. "But then…I don't know. After a while, you realize how free we are."

"Free?" The thought challenged her ideas of life on the small island.

"Sure. We do our job faithfully, but there's no one standing over us. And when we're off duty, we can do whatever we want."

"Except leave."

"Well, of course. We couldn't leave if we wanted to."

"Is there even a boat?"

"There is, but it's useless without more people to launch it. It's too heavy for us, but anything lighter would capsize immediately in our water. You have to have something heavy to get through the surf and beyond."

"So boats are only used when a ship's crew comes in."

"Right. We're marooned for sure."

She considered that. "They told me before I came, but I didn't understand what it would be like. They were talking for a while about adding another man out here, so I was hoping there would be four—"

"They were?" Pierre was clearly startled, and she noted how clear and bright his wide brown eyes were. He was too good-looking and gregarious to be out here in oblivion for more than a year. He couldn't be single, could he? But if he had someone back home, why would he volunteer to stay? It was only people as determined as she was to make good, and loners like George Hudson, who really wanted isolation.

"I guess the budget was too tight. But if this detail is so important, you'd think they wouldn't scrimp on it."

"The people back home, they think the Cold War is over, but it's not," Pierre said carefully.

"That's why we're here, right? So the Chinese or the Koreans can't slip a missile past us."

Pierre licked his fingers, eyeing her uneasily. "Well," he said with his dazzling smile, "one can always hope."

"You…you think it could happen?"

"Mademoiselle, if it could not happen, would we be here?" He rose and took his bowl to the sink. "And now, it is my curfew. I'm on watch at 0600."

Rachel rose quickly. "Oh, the shower. George said you could show me, if it's not too much trouble."

"Right this way."

He took her down the concrete steps into the basement. Bare lightbulbs glowed above them. Rachel didn't especially like the dingy, closed-in feeling. At least the control room was well lit, and she could see outside via the monitors there.

She had been in the basement before but had not paused to learn the layout. Pierre led her past the stacked crates of fresh provisions.

"The storage areas here are for food and supplies. The generators are here. They did train you on maintaining them, didn't they?"

"Yes."

"Of course, the windmills are running all the time and putting amps into the storage batteries, but during typhoon season, we're bound to have some problems with them. The solar collectors are also a big help, but again, when it's cloudy, the way it was this week, no power. The computers have battery backup, but so much of the equipment needs power, we have to make sure we keep the generators up."

"I could see the windmill from the ship."

"Well, one is down right now, thanks to the storm we just came through. When they built this place, they used the generators all the time, but during his first tour, George figured it would be a lot more efficient to use wind and solar power. He sent the commander his designs, and the next ship brought the windmill parts. He and his buddy Matt Rubin built them. I helped him construct the solar collectors last summer."

"I'm impressed."

"Well, it beats trying to ferry big tanks of fuel in. Fire extinguisher here." He pointed it out. "First aid kit. Stronger drugs are locked in this cabinet. Rifles over here."

Pierre walked on past a workbench, a small chest freezer, and an old wringer washing machine.

"Fancy laundry," Rachel noted. In a new house so full of the latest technology, the outmoded appliance was incongruous.

"It's simpler than the modern ones," Pierre explained. "If it breaks down, we can fix it and not have to send out for new parts."

"Makes sense. Otherwise we could go for months with no washer."

"Exactly. And we can't spare power for a dryer, so we use the solar version."

"Clothesline?"

He tilted one eyebrow as he nodded with a grin. "The shower is here. Remember, the water heater is small. We have to pace ourselves on laundry and doing dishes and showers."

"I can wash my clothes in cold water."

He smiled. "That will help. George used to get furious at Ron. He'd get up in the afternoon and want a shower, and Ron would be doing laundry. I finally worked out a schedule for hot water use, but George never got over it."

"Whatever works for you guys, just let me know. Give me Ron's schedule, if that will help."

"Okay. Soap and towels are here."

"Community linens?"

"Right. I think they gave us some new sheets. We asked for some and another blanket."

"I brought a quilt."

"An honest-to-goodness quilt?" Pierre's features softened with a wistfulness that touched her.

"My grandmother made it. I'll show you."

"I'd like to see it."

"How long have you been here, Pierre?"

"A year."

"Wasn't it your turn to leave?"

He looked away for an instant. "I couldn't leave them together, you know? George would have gone nuts."

"Why didn't George leave?"

"He likes it here."

"Everyone talks about him at the training center. They say nothing can entice him off this island."

"He thinks of it as home now."

Rachel frowned. "How could someone call this home? I mean, doesn't he have a family?"

Pierre shrugged. "His folks are gone. He has a sister. He usually hears from her when the ship comes."

"What about you?" she asked softly. "Where's home?"

He cocked his head to one side. "Maine."

"Maine? The state of Maine?"

"*Bien sur.* Where did you think?"

"I don't know. Louisiana, maybe."

He laughed. "My grandfather came down from Quebec after the war. World War II, that is. He always called it The War. There were jobs. He went to work in a woolen mill."

"So you were born in the States?"

"Oh, yes. Me and eight other kids."

She arched her eyebrows, and he laughed again. "I have the early watch, so I need to sleep now."

"Of course. I'm sorry I kept you up so late."

"*Ce n'est rien*—it's nothing." He bounded up the steps.

Rachel peeked into the dismal shower. At least the concrete walls had been painted. She supposed she should be thankful there was fresh water on Frasier, and a pump to bring it to the house. A flush toilet, a water heater, a shower, and a wringer washer. It was enough. She went upstairs to fetch a change of clothes.

ఴ

The smell of coffee lured Rachel out of bed in the morning. She surveyed the clothing in her compact dresser. She had been told the men on Frasier wore comfortable work uniforms or civilian clothes, which had prompted her to stuff a pair of jeans and a couple of extra tops into her sea bag, but she wondered if she should attempt to look a bit professional. Still, George and Pierre had changed into civvies yesterday the minute the men from the *Bush* left the island. She decided jeans were in order, at least for her off-duty hours. She pulled a bright pink blouse on with them and brushed her hair before putting it into a conservative braid.

It probably doesn't matter what I wear. The way things are going, I may not see George all day.

Her observations and Pierre's meager confidences left her with the impression that, no matter how glowing George Hudson's military record was, he was a bit of a misanthrope and would avoid her at all cost. He would come to relieve her at the end of her shift, but beyond that she might never see him. She quickly squelched the thought that she would be missing something. Time to put aside the fantasies about the hero.

Oh, well. She would do her best not to upset him and would concentrate on befriending Pierre. He seemed open to it, and she wanted to change her track record for getting along with people. If George were sleeping all morning, it would be up to her to provide lunch for herself and Pierre, and she was sure she could easily win over the sanguine young man with a little of the culinary skill her mother had taught her.

Rifling the cupboards, she rejected cereal for her breakfast. She wasn't desperate enough to eat it with powdered milk yet. She'd seen granola bars in a crate she'd helped unpack. She located them at last and headed outside with her sketch pad.

Following the path that led to the boat landing, she looked out over the surf. The tide was low, and she could see the jagged rocks that made beaching a boat so treacherous. The sea beyond the inlet caught the sun's glare, and the long, rolling swells threw back a dazzling reflection. She knew the island was west of Wake, east of the Marianas. For some reason, she had pictured a tropical island. Their latitude wasn't much north of Hawaii's. She had read everything she could about Frasier, which wasn't much. It was as though the United States government wanted to keep the tiny island a secret, which she supposed they did.

A few minutes after noon she descended to the control room, carefully balancing the lunch tray she had prepared for Pierre, planting her feet precisely on each step to avoid spilling his coffee.

"Hi. I didn't know if you'd want your lunch down here, or if I should step in for you while you went up, so I brought a tray."

He didn't look up until she was standing beside him with his meal.

"Hey, that looks good. Thanks."

He removed headphones as his eyes roved from screen to screen once more. Rachel set the tray down on a desk to one side.

"Fancy headphones. Those aren't the ones I used last night."

"They sent us some new hydrophones. They're more sensitive, so we can hear what's going on underwater up to a hundred miles away now. George and I installed them yesterday."

"While I was on duty? I didn't see you."

"We went down the cliff path. The cameras don't cover it."

"So, you put new sensors down in the silo area?"

"George did the diving, and I spotted for him. The array is in sixty feet of water."

"Terrific." She picked up the headset and examined it. "I think this is just like what I trained on in Seattle."

"Really?" Pierre's eyes widened.

"Sure. They had state-of-the-art equipment for us to work with. And they tested us on motor sounds—ships, submarines, you know— and whale songs, lots of noises. We spent a lot of time on interpreting the passive sonar."

"Wow. Sounds like your training was more comprehensive than mine."

She studied the displays before them. "Do you think anyone's going to come in here with a submarine? I mean, if the Reds come after the missile silos, it'll be by plane, right?"

"You never know. A sub could get in here and do some major damage. Or a diver could come in from a boat a couple of miles away."

"You really think so?"

"Well, they know we're here, that's for sure. They've got satellite photos, just like us. I'm sure they saw the construction job when this complex was built."

She took his place at the console, and he left the room for a few minutes. She searched the monitors diligently, but her thoughts were on the missile silos off the west end of the island. The massive building job had been difficult, even in the comparatively calm summer seas, and had taken most of two construction seasons. When the missiles were at last in place, the house for the watchers, with its control post beneath it, had been hastily erected. The project had been shrouded in secrecy, and the Navy had succeeded in keeping it from becoming public knowledge in the United States, but authorities were certain the intelligence contingents of many foreign nations had watched with great interest.

Pierre came back and sat down at the desk to eat.

"So, do you eat down here?" Rachel asked.

"I usually go up, but it's okay." She glanced his way and saw him inspecting the food.

"It's beef stew."

"Thought so."

"Is that all right? I found the meat in the freezer."

"Sure."

"I didn't know if you guys had a meal plan."

"This is great."

When she glanced over again, he was crossing himself, and she suppressed a smile. Was he thanking God for his meal or praying that she wouldn't poison him?

"Good biscuits," came his muffled comment a few seconds later. She forced herself not to look his way. "Better than Ron's."

"Thank you. There are more upstairs. I left things out in the galley in case you were still hungry. When you're finished, I'll put the rest away for George."

"Is that cake?" Pierre asked. "I thought I smelled something good, but I didn't want to hope."

She laughed then. "It's a walnut cake."

"We have walnuts?"

"I brought them. Just a couple pounds. My grandfather has a

walnut orchard, and I thought they might be a treat for you out here."

"Yeah, we've never had walnuts since I've been here," Pierre admitted.

"But you don't hate them or anything? I mean, can't you order what you want?" She focused on the camera monitors and then back to the radar screen.

"Well, to some extent, but it's hard knowing what to ask for six months in advance. We can't get much fresh stuff because we can't keep it, and I would never think to ask for something like walnuts."

"Mm-hmm. I saw what you got yesterday. Lots of Spam and canned chili."

"We also get frozen meat and vegetables. You gotta eat vegetables." Pierre was a little defensive.

Rachel said hastily, "Of course."

"We take vitamins too, though."

She nodded. "They had to leave some stuff behind yesterday. I hope you guys don't suffer too much because of that."

"Well, you'll suffer with us, I guess."

She smiled. "I don't mind cooking lunch. I guess you and George take care of supper?"

"Yeah. Breakfast is every man for himself."

"That's fine."

"Maybe you can help us make the list next time we order. This is really good. Thanks, Rachel."

"Did I forget anything?"

"Uh, maybe I'll go get more coffee. You want some?"

When she left Pierre to his duty later and took the tray of dirty dishes to the galley, she found George peering skeptically into the stew pot.

She stopped in the doorway. "Pierre ate it and survived."

"Hmm." It was a noncommittal sound, but George reached for a bowl and spoon.

"Biscuits are here." She removed the clean towel she had laid over them to keep them warm. "There's cake over there." She ran water into the sink and began washing the dishes. George ate in silence. *Well, this is going to be jolly,* she thought sourly.

When he rose and filled a water glass, she turned toward him.

"Pierre said you installed new hydrophones yesterday. I had training on that technology."

He eyed her testily. "So?"

"So, maybe I can help you guys with it, if there's anything you don't understand."

He shrugged. "The book and audiotapes are self-explanatory." He frowned, and she thought he was staring at her shoulder. She looked down self-consciously, but saw nothing unusual.

"I took a little walk outside this morning."

His eyebrows arched, but he said nothing.

"I was wondering if it's all right for me to explore the island. Can I just ramble?"

He carried his glass to the table and sat down again. She noticed with satisfaction that he was on his second biscuit.

"Sure. Just take your radio and don't go falling off a cliff. I don't want to have to come rescue you."

"I'll do my best not to put you through that." She turned back to the sink to hide her discomfiture. As little as she had seen him so far, George Hudson was getting under her skin. So he was the senior man here. That didn't give him license to be rude.

When she turned around again, he was helping himself to a generous slice of cake. She hesitated, wishing she could say something to bridge the chasm between them, but she gave up. She would take her sketch pad and see if she could find the cliff path Pierre had mentioned.

She was nearly to the galley doorway when George spoke.

"If you're going outside, put something dark on."

She turned in surprise. He was staring at her blouse again. She felt uncomfortable under his scrutiny but decided to keep the tone light.

"Low-flying aircraft?"

"You never know." He pulled the cake pan closer to him. "And be back on time to relieve Pierre."

She smiled. He couldn't resist giving orders, could he? "Just cover what's left of the cake when you're done, okay? If there's any left." She ducked out the doorway and headed for her room to get her black sweatshirt.

FOUR

"She's a nice girl, George." Pierre sat on a folding canvas chair in the sitting room, eating the last piece of Rachel's walnut cake.

"Another infant to babysit," George muttered, flipping through the handbook for the underwater listening system.

"She's smart," Pierre insisted. "She knows this technology. She even earned the Underwater Surveillance badge. You gotta be pretty good for that. And it'll make things easy on you. You don't have to train her on it."

"Right. She wants to train us."

"Would that be so bad?"

George scowled. "We can figure this out without her help. It's not that big a change."

"I dunno. Can you tell a baleen whale from a dolphin?"

"Well, yeah. Can't you?"

Pierre shrugged. "Well, dolphins, yes, but not all signatures are as easy to interpret. Rachel says she can tell a Japanese commercial ship's engine from an American oil tanker. And sometimes I know we've got a whale out there, but I don't know what kind it is. Some of them click, and some of them sing, you know?"

"It's not the fish I'm worried about."

"They're mammals."

"Don't start, Pierre. Just put some extra time in with the training tapes. You'll be fine with this new equipment." George stretched his legs, wishing they had a sofa, or at least a comfortable armchair, but space in the helicopter that landed every few months was too valuable. They were lucky to have cots.

"Yeah, well, I think we should tell her everything."

"What for? Ignorance is bliss."

Pierre's eyes were troubled. "Don't your orders tell you to brief new personnel as soon as they arrive? If you'd give her a chance, she might be an asset to this operation."

George sighed. He didn't want to be unfair, but he couldn't see the necessity of bringing another person in on the most dangerous secret in the world. "Look, you think she doesn't have enough to worry about? She's got missiles and potential enemy craft on her mind. Why bother her with the rest?"

"She's here to help us protect it, George. If she doesn't know it's there, she could unintentionally make a mistake."

"Davidson did fine without knowing."

Pierre shook his head. "That was wrong. We were supposed to tell him. You know that. What do you suppose is going to happen when the Pentagon debriefs Ron, and he can't tell them anything about their most valuable possession?"

"They haven't complained yet. I'm telling you, a secret is safer if you don't tell it. They send us these raw recruits, and they can do just as good a surveillance job thinking it's only half a dozen warheads they're sitting on."

"How do you explain all the new equipment?"

George laughed. "It's just updating our old technology. She said herself the new hydrophones are the standard now. So we're installing new underwater cameras next. Big deal. She doesn't suspect a thing."

Pierre shifted uneasily. "She's smart, George."

"So? The story is, they're coming in July to inspect the silos and do some minor repairs. The cameras will help us monitor the job."

"Except the cameras won't be trained on the silos."

George pressed his lips together. Pierre's logic was sound, and the guilt he'd been trying to ignore was pushing itself forward. He hadn't

considered his briefing policy to be deceit. Wasn't national security
a higher priority than strict truth? Even as he tried to justify it, he
knew better, and that made him angry. "We'll worry about that when
the time comes. For now, we're just testing the camera system and
watching for approaching subs. That's plausible. She doesn't need to
be in on every little detail."

Pierre shook his head. "She should know. What if we have an
emergency?"

"No!" Pierre flinched, and George winced. "I'm sorry, but I have
to use my own judgment. You know as well as I do that Ron would
have blabbed. He was a talker. I don't know why they ever screened
him for this detail. He was a security risk."

Pierre sighed. "Maybe. I don't know."

"Well, I do. If we'd told him everything, they'd have had trouble
when he went back. Just like with Carlton. They had to shut that
kid up."

"You make it sound sinister."

"Well, let's just say they had to make him understand it was critical
for him to keep his mouth shut. He almost spilled the whole thing.
The fewer people who know, the better."

"Do you think the staff at the training center even knows?"

George laughed. "Not a chance. They're training these kids in
classified missile monitoring. Only a handful of top brass in the
Pentagon knows the whole story."

"Well, don't forget that not so long ago I was one of those high-
risk kids they sent you, and you told me."

George allowed himself to smile. "I know better now."

"What? If I came now, you'd keep me in the dark?"

"I don't know." It was the truth, and it troubled him. Was he stepping over a line into paranoia? Maybe they were right, and he'd been
out here too long. He was tired, he knew that. He'd been shortchanged
on sleep the last few days, getting his detailed reports and outgoing
mail ready, and then unloading and working on the new equipment.
But it wasn't just that. Somehow, over the months of monotonous

duty, his former standards of right and wrong had blurred. Keeping an official secret was one thing, but lying to Rachel Whitney about the purpose of the equipment? He looked at Pierre uneasily.

"You gotta admit, she's a good cook," Pierre said.

"What does the food matter?"

"Best meal I've had in a year. That stew was thick and the meat was tender. And the biscuits—"

"Yeah, yeah," George said dismissively. "She wore pink today."

"I saw that. Kind of strange, huh?"

"Pink." George sighed. "Do you know how long it's been since I've seen anything pink?"

"There were some flowers last summer, down near the spring," Pierre said thoughtfully. "Some kind of hibiscus, I think."

George shook his head. "They were redder. Her shirt was the same color as…"

"As what?" Pierre was watching him closely.

George shrugged. "I don't understand it. Why am I so attracted to her?" Pierre's grin only added to his irritation. "You think it's funny."

"No, I don't think it's funny. I think it's wonderful."

George glared at him. "Idiot. I can't even consider something like that. And besides, she's nothing like…" He reached for the tape recorder. "Come on, let's get to work."

Pierre smiled. "Right. We need to learn to separate the manatees from the buoys."

❧

Rachel took her sketchbook the next morning and headed out along the ridge, beyond the steel tower that supported the whirling windmill, past its fallen counterpart, lying in pieces, along the path that led past solar panels anchored to the rocks, and down into a declivity where the spring bubbled out of the rocks. If not for the rivulet of fresh water, Frasier Island would not be habitable, and the missile complex would have been built elsewhere, perhaps nearer to population centers. It made the difficult boat landing acceptable, and the trouble of construction bearable. She dabbled her fingers in the cool, sweet water and wondered what tortured course it followed, through the volcanic rock, to surface here.

All around her the foliage was straining into fullness, and blossoms were beginning to splash the bushes with white, gold, purple, and red. She went on, toward the far end of the island, along a faint path. Frasier was less than a mile long, and she had no fear of losing her bearings. The house and the windmills stood on the western end, where the land humped up before falling away abruptly in sheer cliffs like a miniature Gibraltar. At the far end of the island, grasses and palms grew nearer the shore, but there was no beach, only more of the jagged black rocks that would pulverize a boat.

She pocketed the leaves of several plants to take back to the house. She was sure she had seen a book on Pacific flora on the shelf that held their small library. One bush she thought might possibly be a coffee plant. Was it possible at this latitude? Surely Pierre would have noticed it last summer, when the beans matured.

She stood for a long time on a ledge, looking down at a flock of birds that swirled about the face of the rock. She spotted several nests and realized it was hatching time here, just as it was at home in Oregon. Eagerly she began to sketch the scene, wishing she had brought binoculars. The birds were smaller than gulls. She drew them carefully, catching the bend of their wings and the markings on their heads and breasts. There was a bird book too.

When she went back to the house she began her lunch preparations, still thinking about the birds. She took the leaves from her pocket, laid them on top of her sketchbook, and then began scrubbing potatoes. The boat had brought a meager stock of fresh vegetables and fruits, and she was determined none would go to waste. Soon they would be surviving on the likes of Spam and canned green beans. She hoped there would be lots of fruit growing here by summer. There would be coconuts, for sure. Could they have a garden? She thought volcanic soil was good for gardens. She had brought a few seeds, hoping.

At lunchtime Pierre praised her culinary efforts so highly she was embarrassed.

"Poor boy. You've really been hungry, haven't you?"

"Not hungry, exactly, but those instant potatoes are terrible. And sometimes I think I'd just about die for a piece of my mother's *tourtières*."

"And what is that?"

"Pork pie."

"Hmm. I don't think we've got any pork, have we?" Already Rachel's mind was spinning. She could improvise a gravy. Pie crust was easy enough. Maybe she could contrive a passable *tourtière* from Spam. Wasn't there a bit of sausage in the freezer? And surely she could spice up the instant mashed potatoes when the supply of fresh ones ran out.

She went to the galley and immersed herself in experimental cooking. *Funny. I came here to protect the world, and instead I'm trying to invent Spam Surprise.*

An hour later, George came in silently. His quizzical look made her wonder how much flour was on her face.

"What's for lunch?"

"Today, steak and potatoes. Tomorrow, *tourtières*."

"You're making tomorrow's lunch today?"

"Just getting the crust ready. I'll chill it overnight. Your plate's in the fridge. You can microwave it."

He opened the door of the compact refrigerator and took out the plate. His gray eyes brightened when he took off the covering of plastic wrap, but he said nothing. He leaned on the counter and waited while his dinner went round in the microwave.

As she washed her hands, Rachel saw him observing the leaves on her sketchbook.

"I see you found the coffee bush," he said.

"Did I? I hoped that was what it was. Are there any more?"

He shook his head. "Just the one. Pierre was hoping for a coffee plantation. He took a few beans off it last fall and roasted them."

"How was it?"

"Awful."

She laughed. "Have you tried gardening?"

"Thought about it. There are some places the soil is deep enough. But it would be on a steep slope. We've used every flat spot for equipment."

"What do we have for fruit?"

"Bananas on the south side of the path and breadfruit, but I don't know anyone who likes that."

"I'd like to try it."

"Of course you would," he said, retrieving his plate.

Rachel didn't know whether to feel hurt or not. She decided it would be a waste of time.

"Those birds that are nesting on the rocks…" she began.

"Plovers. The eggs aren't bad."

"You *eat* them?"

His gray eyes were placid as he sipped his coffee, saying nothing.

She left him to his lunch and took her sketchbook and the leaves into the sitting room. *I could just ask him about these others. He obviously knows everything there is to know about Frasier.*

The little library was an odd assortment of volumes—novels, biographies, a handful of reference books and technical manuals, and a lone volume of poetry. She wondered who had chosen them. Stubbornly, she pulled the botany book from the shelf. She wouldn't ask him for help when he so plainly wished he had never laid eyes on her.

George Hudson was clearly not the man she'd imagined him to be when she heard about him at the training center. She had eagerly anticipated working with him and learning from him. To hear the instructors tell it, George was the most dedicated, patriotic man in the universe, and the most knowledgeable about this project, although perhaps a bit eccentric. *Ha! If they only knew! I was really stupid to think he'd be a mentor.* She felt a pang of regret, knowing that there was much he could teach her if he were willing.

By the time she had identified her leaves, she had to rush to put her things away before going on duty. She hurried to the tiny bathroom and then her bedroom. She didn't want the men to have any reason to complain about her performance. So far she felt she wasn't being much help on the mission. Pierre appreciated her cooking, but other than that she was just the other person who could watch the monitors. And George? She was less than nothing to him, a negative mark. She knew he would replace her in a minute, given the chance.

He was opening a crate when she went through the sitting room and didn't look up. She wanted to stop and see what was inside, but she sensed he wouldn't like that, and it was 1400 on the nose. She hurried down the stairs.

❧

"What's going on up there?" she asked when Pierre came four hours later to give her a break.

"We've been unpacking new equipment."

"What kind?"

"Cameras, mostly. We'll be installing them tomorrow if the weather's good."

"Terrific. Can I help?"

"Well…" Pierre refused to meet her eyes. "I think George wants to do it during your shift. He has to sleep in the morning, you know."

Rachel didn't say anything. She was furious, but she knew it wasn't Pierre's fault.

"I'll be back in fifteen minutes."

"Take your time."

She went swiftly up the two flights of stairs. George was examining a sophisticated camera and had a manual open on the floor beside him.

"New cameras," Rachel said brightly.

He glanced up and then turned his attention back to the device.

She determined not to give up. "So, Pierre says you're installing them tomorrow."

"That's right."

"I want to help, George."

"Pierre will help me. He's a good diver."

"Diver? You mean they're underwater cameras?"

"The latest technology."

She stepped closer. "May I look?"

He handed her a bundle wrapped in bubble plastic, and she carefully opened it.

"Oh, these are nice! I can dive, George. I had—"

"I know, I know. You had the training."

"Well, yes. I feel as if I haven't done anything yet. I want to be part of the team."

"You're still getting acclimated, and besides, our water's pretty rough. I wouldn't want you to risk it."

"You have the expertise to show me what to do to be safe in this water. I'm a seasoned diver, and I want experience in every phase of the operation."

He said nothing as he focused his attention on the camera. Rachel felt a simmering sense of injustice that threatened to boil over into rage. *He's my supervisor,* she reminded herself, *and he has the capability of making my life miserable for the next year.* She set the camera carefully back in the crate and turned without another word and left the room.

Rachel's days blended into a blur of alternating shifts in the control room, hours spent inventing new recipes, and mornings outside in the lovely paradise. The new cameras were installed without her assistance. George and Pierre positioned a small satellite dish on the roof, near the shelter that housed the three standard surface-to-air missile launchers and the telescope, and then they repaired the windmill. Rachel fumed inwardly, but she gave up asking for responsibility. George had won this round, and it didn't sit well.

At last she remembered the counsel Heidi had given her on the *Bush,* and she turned to God with pleas for composure and acceptance.

God was not part of Rachel's plan when she entered the Naval Academy. She had managed to get through her undergraduate work and advanced training by focusing on her long-range goals, but even so, she chafed under the strict discipline. She was impatient with the other women in her unit and anticipated the day when she would be the one giving orders.

She had unexpectedly been confronted by her own spiritual condition on the ship during the tedious voyage out from Seattle. The storm that blew George's windmill down had delayed their arrival at Frasier Island, and she had vented her anger in the cabin she shared with Heidi Taber.

"You can't blow your top every five minutes and do your job well," Heidi had said gently.

Rachel turned on her. "That's none of your business."

Heidi shrugged. "It's everyone's business when you're confined to a ship."

Rachel thought about that a lot. Frasier Island was small enough to be even more constricting than the huge ship, and with only two other people at hand, chances were good that she would make trouble if she let her temper flare during her new assignment.

Later she apologized to Heidi and hesitantly asked her how she stayed so calm under stress. They shared long conversations about God and human nature over the next two days, and at last Rachel admitted she needed a relationship with God. In the little time they had left, Heidi had encouraged her and given her a Bible, with a promise to pray for her after Rachel left the *Bush* for her new duties.

Rachel was determined to do justice to that promise. Every day she read a little more in the Bible and attempted to voice her feelings to God.

When she was out in the tiny jungle or sitting on the unforgiving rocks, she could forget the missiles poised to deal destruction and the conflict that festered between her and George. The island bloomed around her, violently beautiful, in extremes of soft blossoms and jagged cliffs. Birds she had never seen before visited the isolated patch of ground on their way to the arctic for the season. Shimmering butterflies hovered on full-blown flowers, so brilliant they seemed artificial until they whirred off in the light breeze. There was always a breeze that kept the day from becoming stifling. Rachel began to feel more serene, and to see God's presence in the beauty around her.

In her ramblings, she discovered a spot on the north shore where she could climb down between the rocks and then wade in a gravel-bottomed pool between rough black boulders without cutting her feet on lava rock. Sometimes she followed the stream down from the spring and sat on its bank with her bare feet in the water, her sketchbook open on her knees.

She sat drawing a bird that clung to a swaying taro plant one morning early in May, and wished Pierre were there to see it. But she and Pierre were never free together during the daytime. If George spelled her for her supper break, she could steal a few minutes to eat with Pierre and share bits and pieces of her life with him, but they never had time to take a leisurely walk together. Every day when his lunch was ready, she excitedly told him what she had seen that morning. The evening before, he had described for her a breaching whale he had spotted off the east end of the island while he was fishing. But there was never a companion with her when she searched the waves for a thrilling sight like that. Would it mean as much to see it alone?

"Not bad."

She jumped.

George was standing just behind her, and his shadow darkened the white paper she'd been drawing on. He had crept up softly enough that her bird, across the stream, had not flown away.

"What is it?" she asked.

"You got me. Some kind of a warbler, I'd say." He dropped to the ground beside her. "May I?"

She hesitated and then put her sketchbook in his hands. "It passes the time."

"Hmm." He turned the pages back, one by one, pausing at the drawing of Pierre wearing the earphones, hunched over the sonar display. Rachel watched his face, but George showed no emotion. She swallowed, realizing it was important to her that he didn't disdain her work. She felt vulnerable as he scanned each drawing—the rocky east shore, the cliff with the plover nests. He was seeing life on the island through her eyes, and he might not like her slant.

When he reached the beginning, where she had drawn a hasty impression of Frasier Island from the deck of the ship that had brought her, he frowned, studying the scene carefully.

"The windmill's too conspicuous."

"They're pretty hard to camouflage."

"True. It's a trade-off." He handed the sketchbook back to her, and she was disappointed that he didn't comment on the quality of her drawings. She wanted his approval, but even his scorn would have been better than indifference. "The Navy's participating in a joint exercise over the next ten days. There may be some activity in the area."

"What kind of activity?" she asked.

"Well, we're out of the shipping lanes, and they plan to keep the forces away from us, but we could spot some planes or ships. Just remember, if you see activity, it's probably from the allied naval exercise, but you can't assume that it is."

"No?"

"Absolutely not. It's unlikely a hostile government would send a crew out during a show of allied force, but it's just possible they might see it as the perfect camouflage."

"So, the Koreans might sneak a bomber past the allied fleet and tiptoe in here."

"I'm just saying it could happen." George's gray eyes were sober as he studied her face. "If anything shows up within two hundred miles, you call me. I don't care if you're positive it's one of ours, you call me."

Arrogant. But she said, "All right."

He nodded. "If it *is* one of ours, it's off course. And if it's not…well, we just need to know."

"What if I get a pod of migrating whales?"

"Call me." He rose and walked up the stream bank without another word.

Rachel exhaled in exasperation. As if she couldn't handle a situation like that. She knew the drill for making contact with a vessel or aircraft of unknown origin. George didn't have to micromanage everything. She supposed it was ages since they'd had any action in the vicinity of Frasier, and he was bored and restless. If anything *did* happen, George Hudson had to be the one in charge.

The warbler had abandoned her, and she stuck her drawing pencil in her shirt pocket. She didn't feel like drawing anymore. Somehow George had ruined whatever contentment she had managed to find that morning.

He could be attractive if he weren't so self-important. On impulse, she flipped to a new page of the sketchbook and drew quickly. The lines came from her memory and her imagination.

When she had finished, she held the pad away from her and studied her creation. George Hudson, smiling winsomely. The gray eyes almost glittered. He was incredibly good looking in her fantasy portrait, much more handsome than his normal gravity allowed. It was the George she had hoped would befriend her. For a moment, when he'd asked politely to see her drawings, she'd almost regained her belief that they could break through the hostility between them and have a normal relationship, even if it never went beyond the usual fraternity in a military unit. But George was determined not to step over an invisible line, that was plain. And it wasn't the line that separated officers from their subordinates. It was something else.

She studied the portrait, knowing she was missing out on something valuable. *That's the way I wish he'd look at me,* she realized. *Just once. It would be worth all this grief he's giving me.*

She sighed and closed the sketchbook.

FIVE

George stooped and looked over Rachel's shoulder at the monitors. "You didn't call me."

She jumped. "You said if they came within two hundred miles. We're getting radio signals, and everything's fine. They're off Wake, well out of that range."

He frowned at her defensiveness. It was true. The fleet was far beyond the limits he had set for her. "Nothing closer?"

"Not so far. They seem to be fanning out toward the Northern Marianas."

"Okay, I'll take over." He waited impatiently while she took off the headphones and vacated the swivel chair.

"Everything's going the way it should, George." There was an edge of stubbornness in her voice.

"Okay. Get some sleep." He focused on the radar, then the sonar, then the monitors connected to the land and underwater cameras. He could sense her still standing a little behind him, aft of his right elbow, but he ignored her.

She was hard to ignore, and under other circumstances he might have welcomed her presence. But not here.

Finally she broke the silence.

"Is it just because I'm a woman? Or do you treat all newcomers this way?"

"What way is that?" he asked carefully. The last thing he wanted was a messy confrontation with her.

She gave an unladylike snort. "You're the ranking officer here. All right, I can follow orders. I *have* followed your orders. But I can contribute a lot more to this project than you've let me. I have skills. I have intensive training, much as you disdain it. I can handle most situations as well as you can. And I know when I can't, and that's when I ask for assistance."

He took a deep breath, not looking up at her. "All right, Ensign. I hear what you're saying."

"Do you?" Her voice rose, and she moved impatiently.

George sighed. This was what he hated most about the change of personnel every six months. It took weeks for a new recruit to sort out his role in the tedious surveillance operation. Pierre had settled in quicker than most and was comfortable here. Ron had never felt at ease on the island. Rachel Whitney might be that way too. Some of them just couldn't fit in. The fact that he was also having trouble defining her role wasn't helping, but it was paramount that he maintain a distance between them. He had to. Even if she was so wholesomely gorgeous it made his heart ache.

"I understand how difficult it is to be thrown into a new situation where you're not in control."

She laughed outright. "Oh, sure. You've never been out of control in your life, George. You wouldn't allow that to happen. All I'm saying is, look at me. See me as an intelligent person. Respect me."

The trap was closing. If he didn't meet her eyes she would feel she had cause to resent him. But looking at Rachel Whitney, seeing her for what she was…he'd decided days ago that could be dangerous.

Modern women didn't want you to see them as feminine. They wanted to be viewed as equals. Military women were worse than civilians. They expected to be one of the men. Equal assignments, equal responsibility. He'd tried, but she definitely was not one of the men. If Rachel knew how he saw her when his guard was down, she'd be shocked.

His reaction to her femininity rattled him, and lately unexpected feelings had been sneaking up on him. When he saw her drawing beside the brook, for instance. He'd come close to seeing her as a person then, perilously close. It wouldn't have been difficult to drop the reserved air and talk to her about her art. She was very good. But then he would have wanted to talk to her about other things, more personal things, maybe. Something inside him yearned to get closer to her. But that wasn't going to happen. He wouldn't let it.

His best defense so far had been ignoring her. Short of that, he could be distantly cordial. But he couldn't treat her the same easy way he did Pierre. Never.

Slowly, he raised his eyes from the monitor and looked up at her, concentrating on her eyes. She was trying to be firm, but in a flash he saw that she was close to tears.

Terrific. *Respect me or I'll cry.* The trouble was, he didn't blame her.

"I run things around here the way I think is best." He looked away first, but the guilt pressed down on him. He didn't enjoy hurting her.

She took a deep breath, and he thought she would protest further, but suddenly she turned and walked out the door.

❧

She met Pierre in the sitting room and tried to duck past him into the hallway, avoiding his eyes.

"Hey, Rachel, want a bedtime snack?"

"I don't think so," she choked.

He caught her arm and swung her gently toward him. "Are you okay? What's up?"

"I'm fine." *I will not cry.*

Pierre cocked his head toward his left shoulder. "George been barking at you?"

"I'm okay, really." The tears spilled over.

Pierre draped his arm loosely over her shoulders. "Hey, don't let him get you down."

She shook her head helplessly. "I'm sorry. It's just…he thinks I'm an imbecile. He won't let me do anything but stand watch and bake cookies."

Pierre smiled. "And exquisite cookies they are."

Rachel glared at him. "I came here to serve my country."

"You do. Your performance has been exemplary for the past four weeks."

"Tell that to George."

"I have. We were talking about it this evening."

Rachel blinked, trying to stem the flow of tears. "Really?"

"Yes. I told George they sent us a good recruit this time."

"What did he say?"

"Not much."

Rachel's hope plummeted.

"But that's good," Pierre said hastily. "If he thought you weren't doing the job, he would have said so."

"Right." She sighed. So long as George thought she could handle the job, what did it matter whether he liked her or not? But it did matter.

"Come on," Pierre said. "I think we need cinnamon toast and chocolate milk tonight."

"How can you drink that powdered stuff? It makes me gag."

Pierre laughed. "Chocolate syrup does wonders." He steered her toward the galley.

"I'd rather have a cup of tea." Rachel sank into one of the straight chairs.

"Tea it is." He took a mug from the cupboard, filled it with water, and placed it in the microwave.

Rachel watched him fretfully, wishing she could confide in him. They were becoming friends, but his first allegiance was still to George, and she couldn't forget that. Still, she couldn't go a year without anyone to share her intense feelings.

"Pierre, do you have a girlfriend at home?"

He carefully punched the buttons on the keypad before he answered. When he looked at her, his eyes were eager and shy at the same time.

"Marie," he said softly.

She smiled, happy to know he had someone he could feel that deeply about. "Don't you miss her?"

"*Certainment.*"

"And she's waiting for you?"

His deep brown eyes clouded. "Well, I…" He shrugged.

"Did you get mail from her when I came?"

"*Oui. Beaucoup des lettres. Mais…*" he smiled apologetically. "*Pardon.* I forgot your education is lacking. In Oregon they teach you Spanish, *n'est-ce pas?*"

Rachel smiled. "French seems very exotic where I come from."

"Well, you see, she expected me to come home last month. I sent a letter out with the boat, explaining the situation, but…"

"You haven't heard from her since."

"No, of course not." He took her mug from the microwave and passed it to her.

"You'd think we could call home once in a while since we got that satellite dish."

"Well, we could, but, of course, we don't want to draw attention to this installation. Perhaps, if I tell George how much I long to speak to Marie…"

"I should have known it was George's fault." Rachel sighed. "He has no heart, and he thinks everyone else should be able to live without human contact the way he does."

Pierre frowned as he mixed his chocolate milk. "George is a complex man."

"He's arrogant."

"No, I don't think that is it."

"Are you blind?"

Pierre's pleading eyes confused her. "He holds this mission to-gether."

She shook her head. "He doesn't do a solitary thing you and I couldn't do in his absence."

"I think he does."

She sipped her tea, still baffled by the young man's loyalty to George. She admitted to herself that she felt drawn to the pensive lieutenant, but every time she thought she saw an admirable trait in George Hudson, he did something that made her feel practically homicidal. Her morning prayer times were growing longer, and sometimes she felt they were the only thing that calmed her and kept her from expressing her frustration.

"I guess I expected too much," she said at last.

"And what did you expect?"

"Well…" She thought about that. "I'd heard so much about George. Nothing concrete, but—"

He nodded, smiling. "I heard the stories too. How he rescued one of his shipmates way back. And how he knew this system inside out, and even made design changes to improve the facility."

"Right. I guess I thought he was perfect. And…and nicer, somehow."

Pierre popped two slices of bread into the toaster. "Perhaps in time you will see that other side of George. It's not a myth."

"Then why is he so hostile toward me?"

"Perhaps time will also reveal the answer to that. But, come. What about yourself? Do you have someone at home?"

Rachel shook her head. "My folks," she amended. "Two brothers. Nobody special. I mean, like you do."

"Well, I am hoping Marie has not given up on me. I told her one year, you see. And now…well, I hope she is being patient."

"I still don't understand that. Why would you choose George over Marie?"

He chuckled. "It wasn't like that."

"Wasn't it?"

"No. It seemed, at the time, that things were at a crisis here. George and Ron, they fought all the time. We didn't know who would come in to replace me. If you had been here with them, I don't think you would have been able to keep them calm. I don't say that because of any fault in you, but I know from experience how hard it was. And there are things George…should not have to bear alone."

She nodded slowly, not certain she understood. "So you sent Marie a letter and packed Ron off."

"Yes. And I will say that we got a good bargain in you." His dazzling smile was irresistible.

"Thank you, Pierre, but George does not share your opinion."

"Don't be hasty in judging him. As he sees how steady and consistent your work is, he will come around."

Rachel shook her head. "He's so stubborn. I'm thinking maybe I should go on strike and refuse to cook until he lets me take an equal share in the official work."

"Oh, no, no, please, don't do that! I have not eaten so well in a year."

Rachel smiled. "You're very kind. I hope Marie appreciates you."

SIX

"You're too hard on her," Pierre insisted as he helped George overhaul one of the generators. Rachel was on duty a flight of stairs below them, and he knew it was safe to speak candidly to the lieutenant.

"What, you want me to treat her special?"

"No. Just stop treating her like dirt."

George winced, but maybe it was because he'd yanked the flywheel off and pinched his finger.

"Listen, I've come to a conclusion about Ensign Whitney, and nothing you say will change that."

Pierre sat back on his heels. "Really? I've got to hear this."

George scowled and wiped his greasy hands on a rag. "I've decided not to fall in love with her."

"Ha!"

"You find that amusing?"

"The fact that you're even talking about it amazes me."

"I just don't want you getting ideas. She's attractive, she's courageous…"

"But not someone you could love."

"I didn't say that. I said I won't."

Pierre couldn't hold back a grin. "You can't just decide something like that, you fool."

George's resolute glare confirmed his suspicions.

"What?" George demanded.

"She thinks you hate her. You've worked hard to keep your feelings at bay, haven't you?"

"Like I said, I've made my decision."

"You've decided not to love Rachel."

"That's right."

Pierre shook his head. "How sad."

George threw his wrench to the concrete floor with a clank. "You know I can't even think about having a personal relationship right now."

Pierre shrugged. "Perhaps the timing is not the best for you and Rachel, but she won't always be under your supervision."

"It's not just her. It's any woman. I can't get involved right now."

"Why ever not?"

George was silent for a moment, and then he picked up the wrench and attacked the generator with new energy.

"She wouldn't expect you to grieve forever, my friend."

George slapped his hand to his forehead. "Let's change the subject. Please."

"Fine."

They worked in silence for a few minutes, but Pierre guardedly watched his friend.

George looked him in the eye suddenly. "It's not just Pam. It's her family and…I don't know. I'm just not ready. But it's impossible, anyway. You know she and I would both be disciplined. I don't need to ruin my career after all these years, and she doesn't, either. She's just starting out. When she leaves Frasier, she needs to go with a clean record."

"And a glowing recommendation from her CO?"

"You're pushing it."

"Fine. But you admit you're attracted to her."

"Excessively. That's the problem."

"So stop treating her like an idiot. Let her use her knowledge and training."

George reached for a different wrench. "I'm trying to keep my sanity. The best way for me to do that is to have as little contact with her as possible."

Pierre smiled. "You're in deep, aren't you?"

George's frown spoke volumes. "If you say one word to her—"

"I won't."

"Good. Tell her—oh, I don't know. Tell her she can maintain the solar collectors. I just can't work with her yet. Closely, I mean. She wanted me to take her diving, and I turned her down flat. No way. Maybe later, after I get used to her."

Pierre nodded. "Sure, George. It wouldn't hurt you to be civil, though."

"That's what you think."

❦

Rachel performed her duties conscientiously and tried to ignore George's coolness. They settled into a truce in which they rarely spoke to each other, but she never felt at ease when he was nearby. Her sorrow grew as she realized how badly she wanted his friendship.

The island burgeoned into lush summer. Pierre showed her where to fish, and she spent hours dangling a line off the eastern point of land. During those hours, her thoughts drifted to home, to the mission they performed, and occasionally to her hopes for the future, beyond her stint on Frasier Island.

She was beginning to wonder what God had in store for her once her tour of duty was completed. She had planned on a straight course to becoming a top naval officer. She had dreamed of it for years, and since high school had planned accordingly. At Annapolis, her goals had become grim resolution: She *would* succeed in this challenging field, and no man would stop her. But now her ambitions seemed less urgent than they once were.

For the first time, she tried to see her life from God's point of view, and an excitement began to grow in her. He forgave all her past wrongs, and He could lift her from the dark guilt that had surrounded her for the last few years. That knowledge was liberating. Knowing He could lead her anywhere in the future frightened and at the same time thrilled her. She began to mark passages in her Bible that assured her of God's leading. *Find rest, O my soul, in God alone; my hope comes from him (Psalm 62:5). This is what the Lord says—your Redeemer, the Holy One of Israel: "I am the Lord your God, who teaches you what is best for you, who directs you in the way you should go" (Isaiah 48:17).*

Whenever her thoughts strayed to George, she reined them in sharply, although sometimes it seemed he was invading her conscious mind in spite of her will. She decided that if he could ignore her with impunity, she would not give him the satisfaction of brooding about him. In her hesitant prayers, she asked God to help her overcome her anger at his attitude. To her surprise, she couldn't completely get rid of the latent admiration she'd felt for him from the first. He was good at his job, that was certain. Every day she saw the results of his consistent hard work. And he had nerves of steel. If she were ever in danger, she knew she would want a man like George at her back. She told herself it didn't go beyond that, yet she found herself speculating that he could make a woman feel precious beyond everything if he wanted to.

They were nearing the end of June when Pierre greeted her announcement of lunch with an enthusiastic grin.

"Did he tell you?"

"Tell me what?" Rachel asked uneasily.

"We're calling home."

She stopped in her tracks. "Really? George said that?"

Pierre nodded happily. "One phone call, ten minutes."

"When?"

"This afternoon."

She smiled slowly. "Thanks for letting me know. George probably wouldn't have told me. He'd have let you call Marie and forgotten I miss people too."

"You underestimate him."

"Do I?"

She sat down at the console and watched the screens while Pierre went to eat his lunch, but already she was planning what she would say to her parents. They didn't even know where she was and were probably worried, although she had told them she might not be able to contact them for a while.

She began a mental list of questions to ask. George would probably insist she tell them nothing about their top secret life on Frasier.

Pierre came back carrying his coffee mug.

"George is up. He says you can make your call now, and I'll make mine when you relieve me at 1400."

"I can't believe it."

Pierre smiled. "It's true."

She raced up the stairs and into the galley. George was starting a fresh pot of coffee. Rachel stopped in the doorway and said to his ramrod straight back, "Is it true? You're going to let me call home?"

He turned slowly, a thoughtful look on his face.

Rachel swallowed. *What if he was yanking my chain? I wouldn't put it past him.*

"Sure, you can call if you want. But I'll have to monitor your conversation."

"What?" She felt her face flushing. "That's ludicrous."

"The security of our nation is not ludicrous."

He carefully measured the coffee into the filter, and Rachel felt her fury mount.

"You're actually going to stand over me while I call my parents? You're a pompous tyrant."

He raised his eyebrows.

"Who monitors you when you call home?" she asked bitterly. Her anger threatened to explode, and her hands began to shake. She grasped the back of the chair in front of her.

Watch yourself. She stood still, clutching the chair, appalled at her own words. She had let his coldness affect her more than she realized, and now she was overreacting in a big way. That and the informal atmosphere in the small unit had made her forget that one couldn't be rude to an officer, and she had allowed her suppressed resentment to ferment. She gulped, wondering if she had pushed him too far. Would he deny her the chance to call in punishment for her outburst? *He might,* she thought guiltily. *Insubordination. I've really got to watch my tongue.*

"I'm sorry." She blinked, trying to sort the feelings that raged through her. *Lord, help me out here.* She'd pleaded for divine guidance, and now she'd thrown everything she'd learned from Scripture out the window. She needed more help where George was concerned. Had she thought she could work through this thorny relationship on her own? She had let the phone call be more important to her than anything else, that was all. And now she'd shown her immaturity. Just when she'd thought she was making progress in her spiritual walk, she'd committed a huge offense.

Find rest, O my soul, in God alone.

She closed her eyes for a moment. *Lord, forgive me. How can I undo this? I don't deserve the respect I want from him.*

A sardonic smile touched George's lips as he slid the hopper into the coffee maker, and she swallowed hard. She knew there was more she needed to discuss with God, but that private conversation would have to wait.

"Just keep in mind our status and the importance of this mission. You will give no indication of your location or your duties."

"I understand," she faltered.

He nodded. "You want to call now?"

She looked around uncertainly. He had a plate of food on the counter. "You haven't eaten."

"I can eat while you talk."

A wave of shame swept over her. Her own behavior was far worse than his. She wondered if he had even considered revoking her privilege. Maybe Pierre was right, and she was too hard on him.

"If you don't mind."

"Come on in the other room." George carried his plate and mug, and she followed him meekly. He set his meal down in the sitting room and went to the radio that was the counterpart of the one in the control room below.

"Why don't they just give us a cell phone?" she asked.

George shook his head, smiling. "Now, *that's* ludicrous."

"Oh." She had shown her ignorance, confirming his low opinion of her. She eyed him as he lifted the handset. "Can I ask you something?"

"Sure." As usual, his eyes avoided hers.

"Were you thinking of not letting me call?"

"When?"

"Ever."

He met her look then. "What are you talking about?"

She gulped. He seemed slightly amused. Maybe it was all in her mind.

"I…thought maybe you'd say I couldn't call because I was…insubordinate."

He laughed, shaking his head. "Am I such a strict disciplinarian?"

"Well…"

"Come on, Rachel. Do I make you check in and out around here? Require you to tell me where you're going when you go out the door with your sketch pad?"

She looked down at the floor. What he said made sense, but he still made her feel that he despised her, that he didn't trust her or her abilities. Part of her brain was urging her to apologize again. Another part still wanted to pound the stuffing out of him.

Lord, please help me keep my temper in check. She licked her windchapped lips and looked up at him, but he was immersed in readying the equipment. He didn't expect an answer. *Typical. He made his point, and any response from me would be superfluous.*

"Calling Oregon?" he asked.

"Yes."

He nodded. "It's calm today. We should be able to get through."

Rachel sat on the edge of a chair and tried not to wriggle while she waited. George relayed her parents' phone number to someone at the naval base in Pearl Harbor. The storm of feelings he had set off inside her subsided slowly, and anticipation took over. Suddenly, her mother's voice came into the room.

"Hello, Whitneys'."

"Mom!" Rachel jumped up and grabbed the microphone from George's hand so fast he took an unsteady step backward. "Mom, it's me! Can you hear me?"

"Rachel?"

"Yes!"

"Oh, sweetheart, where are you?"

"I can't tell you. I'm a long ways away, but I love you, Mom."

"I love you too. Let me get your father. Harry! Harry! Come quick. Rachel's on the phone."

George chuckled and smiled at her. She found herself smiling back. That was the look she had despaired of ever seeing on his face—one of friendship and amiability. He was incredibly handsome in that moment.

"Hey, pumpkin!"

"Daddy!" She felt her face go red even as she said it. She'd think later about whether she cared if George knew she called her father *Daddy*.

"Well, it's the world traveler. Have you been getting our letters?"

"Not yet. We don't get mail very often here."

"Where's here? Timbuktu?"

"Can't tell you, Daddy."

"All right. Are you okay?"

"I'm fine. Just great. How about you and Mom?"

"We're good. I skinned my knuckles at work yesterday, but we're fine."

Her mother's voice came again, breathless. "Rachel, your cousin Marcia had her baby."

"Really? Boy or girl?"

"It's a boy this time. Justin Tyler."

"Great. Tell Marcia I sent a hug. How are Ted and Joe?"

"Good. Joe's got a new girlfriend."

"What's her name?"

"He hasn't told us yet."

"Then how do you know he has one?"

"Oh, it's obvious," her mother assured her. "He goes out every Friday night dressed to the nines." Her voice faded in and out, and Rachel squeezed the microphone, willing it to keep the connection.

"Mom, I can't talk long. I just wanted to tell you I'm all right, and I love my assignment, and I miss you and Daddy."

Her father's voice came very faint. "We love you, pumpkin."

"Frasier 130?" The Navy man's voice was stronger.

"I'm here," Rachel responded.

"We lost your connection."

"Ten-four. It's all right." She handed the microphone to George and stood still for a moment. It was over so fast, but she knew she would go over and over it in the days to come. There was so much more she had wanted to say. When she glanced up, George was watching her keenly.

"Thank you," she whispered. "My brother has a new girlfriend."

George shrugged a little, smiling. "There you go. News from home is great, isn't it?"

"So, did you call home?"

He shook his head. "I don't exactly have a home anymore." He picked up his plate and settled into a chair. "Pierre wants to call later, when he gets off duty. He thinks his fiancée will be home."

"I hope he gets through." Even though she knew it wouldn't happen, Rachel wished George would continue the conversation. They'd proven they could talk like two civilized people, and it wasn't torture.

She was still slightly aggrieved that he had required her to make the call with him present, but at least she'd had the brief contact with her parents, and she hadn't said anything to make him sorry he'd allowed her to call. Her resentment was overshadowed now by her desire to hear George laugh again, to see his eyes glitter with eagerness. But he had begun to eat, and the indifference that was worse than open dislike had returned to his expression. The intangible barrier was there again between them.

Rachel went to the galley and began cleaning up the lunch dishes, fully aware of the subtle shift in her relationship with George. She'd lashed out at him, yet he had stayed calm and professional. He'd far outshined her in this encounter, and her heart was heavy. She'd given him plenty of cause to dislike her, even to discipline her, but he'd looked beyond her petty rage and seen her isolation and homesickness. Was it possible that he understood her inner turmoil better than she did?

She threw the sponge into the dishwater, and soapsuds splattered her shirt. It was no longer enough that George didn't despise her. She wanted much, much more.

"Help me, Lord," she whispered. "I think I may be in over my head."

❧

When her shift ended that evening, Pierre met her on the stairs with gleaming eyes.

"You talked to Marie!" she cried.

"*Oui, mon amie.* Ten glorious minutes." His even white teeth flashed in a smile.

"She's not mad at you?"

He shrugged. "She was very disappointed when I did not come home, but…"

"She's waiting for you."

He nodded. "I told her to go ahead and buy her wedding dress."

"Fantastic! I'm so happy for you!" She threw her arms around him and he laughed, returning her embrace.

"So, you talked to your parents."

"Yes, but we lost the connection after a couple of minutes. But it was worth it, anyway." They walked toward the galley together. "Did George already tell you everything?"

"Pretty much, I guess."

"Figures. Doesn't he believe in privacy?"

"Does that bother you?"

She smiled up at him. "Since it's you, I don't mind, but the fact that he blabbed to anyone is annoying. My brother has a new girlfriend, and my cousin had a baby boy."

Pierre's face sobered. "George said you told them you love it here."

"I do."

"I thought you were having a rough time adjusting."

"You did?" She punched his arm playfully. "Want coffee?"

"Not this late. I'm headed for bed. How about some popcorn, though?"

"All right. You make it." Rachel opened the cupboard for glasses while Pierre got out the popcorn. "You know, if it weren't for George, this would be the ideal assignment."

Pierre shrugged. "It takes a special person to like it in such a remote spot."

"Yes. But it's beautiful. I have lots of time in the mornings to think and draw and write."

"It's very different from most naval installations. It helps a lot if you like the people you're with."

She nodded. "I like you. And I guess I like some things about George."

Pierre feigned shock. "Tell me quick, before you change your mind."

Rachel smiled. "He knows when to relax regulations. He could make us miserable if he wanted."

"I shudder to think what will happen if he leaves and a new commanding officer comes in."

"He's not thinking of leaving?"

"Oh, no. He'll stay until they force him to go."

"Well, let's talk about something more pleasant than Lieutenant Hudson. Did you and Marie set a date?"

"Not yet. I don't know how long debriefing and all that will take. But I know one thing: We'll be married by Thanksgiving."

Rachel sighed. "That's great. I'll miss you. Do you realize it's less than four months before you go?"

"I'm counting the days." He put the bag of popcorn in the microwave. "I told her we're a small unit, and that we have a female ensign here."

"You told her about me?"

"*Bien sur.* She asked if you were pretty. You see, Marie can be a little jealous at times."

"What did you say?"

He hung his head. "I told her you are very plain. It's the only time I've ever lied to her."

Rachel smiled. "You should be a diplomat. Does she know where you are?"

"She knows I'm in the Pacific. That's about it."

"George stood over me like a hawk to make sure I wouldn't tip my parents to any military secrets."

"Well, he's a careful man. That's an asset to the Navy."

"Did he stand over you?"

"Well, no, but—"

"I knew it! He trusts you, but not me. He stood right there and listened to every word."

"He called his sister," Pierre said.

"He did?" She was ambushed by the gladness that shot through her. "So he doesn't hate all women. Just me."

"Don't think that."

"It's true. No matter what I do, it's not good enough. No matter what I say, he turns it around and makes me feel stupid."

"It's important to you that George like you?"

"Crazy, isn't it?"

"Not at all."

Rachel turned away, her shoulders sagging. "Why should I care what he thinks of me? If he thinks of me at all."

"I told you, *cherie*, he is a complex man. I'll also tell you this: He admires your artistic nature."

"You're joking."

"No, I'm not. I understand you let him see your sketches."

"He didn't say a word about them."

"He thought they were good. He told me so."

She watched him, trying to discern whether he was telling the truth or trying to be kind. At last she asked in a small voice, "Why would he tell you that and not say anything to me?"

Pierre hesitated, and then he opened the microwave and took out the popcorn. "Perhaps it is better not to speculate."

SEVEN

A week later, when George came to the control room to relieve Rachel at 2200, he found Pierre sitting next to her, chatting with animation.

"What are you so happy about?" George growled.

"It's the Fourth of July," Pierre grinned. "Guess what Rachel has?"

"A brass band, fireworks, and a cannon?"

"No, just the fireworks."

"I brought a little box of sparklers," Rachel said.

"Sparklers?" George muttered. She stood to relinquish her post to him, and as she turned to face him, he couldn't help shaking his head at her childlike eagerness. He'd tried to ignore her unsuccessfully. She seemed determined to come up with new ways to draw his attention. "You can't light them after dark."

"Oh, come on, George. They're *sparklers*. We'll check the radar first to make sure there are no ships or planes in the vicinity." Her lips took on an attractive poutiness. He turned quickly to the console and reached for the headphones.

"Take them down in the hollow, by the spring. That's an order."

Pierre shot him a bewildered look, and George realized it had been more than a year since he'd issued an official order to Pierre. He was getting lax, that was certain. Still, his camaraderie with Pierre had been so easy and natural, he felt guilty pulling rank now. If only Rachel didn't throw him off balance.

"Just use common sense," he relented.

"We will, George," Pierre said stiffly.

"Aw, rats." Rachel put on a petulant whine. "I was hoping you'd let us set off a missile. Just a little one."

George scowled at the nearest monitor in deadly silence.

"It's a joke, George," Pierre prompted.

"That kind of joke is not funny. It's like getting on a plane and saying, *I have a bomb in my briefcase. Just kidding.*"

Rachel sighed. "Come on, Pierre. This guy doesn't know how to have fun."

Pierre threw a worried glance in George's direction. "We'll be careful."

"Want us to save you one?" Rachel asked gaily.

"No, thank you."

❧

Rachel ran to her room for the box of sparklers and met Pierre in the sitting room.

"Come on, I've got the matches." He grabbed her hand as they ran down the path toward the spring laughing.

"I wanted to stand up on the edge of the cliff and light them." Rachel opened the box and handed Pierre one of the little metal wands.

"We'll have to watch the sparks," he cautioned. "Maybe we should get in under the trees in case a plane comes over."

"If a plane comes within five hundred miles of here, George will call an emergency." She held up her sparkler, and Pierre lit the end of it and then his own.

"Hooray!" Rachel shouted, whirling the sparkler through the air. "Happy Independence Day, Pierre! Too bad we don't have a bell to ring." She could see the orange sparks reflected in his dark eyes as he inscribed circles in the air above his head.

"How long since you heard 'The Star-Spangled Banner'?" she asked.

"Long time ago. Before I came here."

"Well, that's unpatriotic! Military personnel are the most patriotic Americans there are, and we ought to sing it once in a while."

"Are you serious?"

"Sure. Come on." She started in somberly, her clear alto ringing out toward the jungle. Pierre joined her after a moment, but they both faltered when the melody ran too high. He dropped the key and they went on, laughing, to *the home of the brave.*

"There!" She dipped her spent sparkler in the spring and shook another from the box. "Now I feel like it's really the Fourth of July. Thanks for celebrating with me. I'd feel stupid doing this alone, and I'd probably wind up homesick and depressed."

He lit the sparkler for her. "What do you do at home on the Fourth?"

"Go to a parade and have a huge family picnic. They have fireworks at night, over the Willamette. It's beautiful."

"We have them too." Pierre's sparkler hissed and spurted into a fiery glow. "I took Marie the last time I was home on the Fourth."

"You'll be home in October. She's waiting."

He nodded soberly, and Rachel felt a pall of loneliness threatening them.

"Look at the moon." She pointed her sparkler toward the three-quarter globe rising above the trees. "Marie can see it, *cheri.*"

"Think so?"

"Know so."

He sighed. "Of course, it's 0500 in Maine. She's sound asleep."

"And dreaming of you."

He smiled bleakly. "You don't give up, do you?"

"Never."

"Good. Because I've been wondering lately what it's going to be like for you and George when I'm gone."

"I've tried not to think about that."

"Just keep your chin up. Sooner or later he'll realize what a good scout you are."

She laughed. "Maybe the new guy will be a real jerk, and I'll look better by comparison."

"Maybe the new guy will be a woman. Ever think of that?"

"Say, wouldn't that drive George insane? It would push him over the edge to be left on his island with two women."

Pierre was silent, still watching the moon as his sparkler fizzled into smoking darkness.

"It is, you know," Rachel said.

"Is what?"

"*His* island."

Pierre sighed. "It's true he loves this place. He's putting all his energy into protecting what's here."

"The missiles?"

Pierre was silent.

"I thought he was protecting the U.S. of A."

"Well, he is. Indirectly."

She frowned, trying to read his face in the moonlight. "It seems pretty direct to me. China launches a missile at Los Angeles, and we launch ours at Beijing. What could be more direct than that?"

Pierre reached for the box of sparklers. "I was thinking of something else. So, you think they should rename this rock Hudson Island?"

"That would be appropriate. But people would think it was named for Henry Hudson."

"A tenacious fellow." He lit another wand and handed it to her.

"Probably a direct ancestor of George's."

"Did he have descendants?" Pierre asked. "I seem to remember his crew mutinied and set him and his son adrift in Hudson Bay."

"Hey, now there's an idea." She raised her eyebrows and tried to form a sinister grin.

"Watch yourself, girl. You're wicked tonight."

"We could dump him off the cliff path."

"Nah. We'd have to stand twelve-hour shifts then."

Rachel laughed. "You're right. And who would fix the windmills when the next typhoon knocks them down?"

"Not me." Pierre took the last two sparklers from the box. "This is it."

Rachel took one. "Let's light them in honor of George. In memory of his inner child, whom he's made stand in a corner for forty years."

Pierre struck the match and held it to her sparkler. "He's only thirty-seven."

"There, you see? He was cranky before he was born."

They both laughed and held their sparklers high.

EIGHT

In mid-July an aircraft carrier group stood off Frasier, and inspection of the submerged missile silos began. Rachel noted the underwater cameras were turned by the divers to cover the silo area while they worked and then returned to their original positions, pointing outward toward a rocky ridge and beyond, westward. The inspection seemed brief to her, but perhaps there was more activity during Pierre's shift.

With the ships ready to take their outgoing mail, she labored over her letters home, praying considerably over the wording. She loved her family, but she knew she'd been at the heart of a lot of conflict before she left home. Her Bible study was doing its work, and she didn't want to wait until her year on Frasier was up to tell her parents she was a Christian, and to apologize for past behavior she knew had upset them. Her two younger brothers deserved a sincere apology too, and she worked on notes for them for hours, tearing up several false starts. Still not entirely satisfied, she dropped her letters at the last minute into the outgoing bag.

The ships lay off the point for three days. The first night George informed her that officers would come ashore the next day. She fixed lunch for ten, but only four men came from the ship in a Seahawk. It landed on the ridge, beyond the second windmill.

She was startled when George prepared to meet the visitors in his white summer uniform. She was used to seeing him in T-shirts and camouflage pants. It struck her that the lieutenant cut a very handsome figure. She peeked into the control room and saw that Pierre was also wearing a uniform, and hurried to her room to change out of her cutoffs, although George had said nothing to her.

It was like Christmas in July. The captain handed George a bag of incoming mail, and the seamen unloaded several crates of produce, frozen food, and pastries.

Rachel hurried downstairs to tell Pierre of their bounty.

"Doughnuts!" His bliss was contagious.

"Chocolate bars too. I hid them for later."

Heavy footsteps came down the stairs toward the security door they seldom closed. George was bringing the captain down for a tour of the control room.

Rachel took over for Pierre at the console so he would have a chance to talk to the outsiders.

"George seems a little nervous," she whispered as he rose from the observation station.

"Well, we don't get brass very often."

Pierre waited up for her that night, and they sat on the rocks by the landing place, eating doughnuts and reading their mail by flashlight while George, back in his comfortable civvies, kept the unending vigil. Rachel's letters from home warmed her heart. It seemed as if everyone missed her and forgave her, although they hadn't yet received her contrite letters. The next day the ships left, and the horizon was empty once more.

In late August the rains began. Monitoring weather forecasts became a critical part of their duties. Rachel checked their weather instruments on the roof each morning and kept a meticulous log. After each tropical storm, George made a minute inspection of the windmills, the missile launchers, and all the other equipment. Twice he and Pierre went diving to inspect the submerged missile silos and cameras. Rachel's anger at being excluded had mellowed during her four months on Frasier.

Gradually she was learning to turn her discontent in that area over to God. She still wanted to be in on more of the action, but she also wanted to be faithful in her position, and slowly she was accepting the diminished role George had handed her. Whenever he provoked her, she retreated to her room and prayed for wisdom and serenity, spent some time reading her Bible, and then took out her sketchbook.

Between storms, the island steamed. She took to wearing shorts and a baseball cap on her rambles. Pierre risked life and limb climbing a tree to bring her some breadfruit. She tried baking it, stewing it, and frying it, and decided she agreed with George about its taste.

When her sketchbook was full, she began hoarding paper to draw on. Pierre donated a pad of unlined stationery. In exchange, she drew him a detailed sketch of the house perched on the bluff.

"For a souvenir. You can show it to Marie when you go home."

"It's great. I'll have it framed."

"Just don't tell George. He'd say it was a security risk."

She had called home two more times, and she was thankful George had let her, but she didn't see much of him, other than his arrival in the control room each evening at the start of his shift. It was easy for them to avoid each other. He stayed out of the galley until she went on duty, and she pretended he didn't exist. It was simpler that way.

One morning as she sat on the rocks near the boat landing reading her Bible, she glanced up to see George standing on the path above her, but as soon as she looked his way, he turned and walked toward the house. She was struck by the conviction they had both missed out on something. Tears filled her eyes as she turned back to her reading, and she knew she was still carrying shreds of her old anger and hurt.

When she went off duty on clear nights, she went outside to look at the stars. Meteor showers thrilled her. After mulling it over for a week, she approached George for permission to use the telescope on the roof. She'd had a bit of astronomy in high school and again in her navigation courses during training. To her surprise, he agreed without warning her not to abuse the equipment.

The stars hung so low and bright over Frasier, she could almost believe they were closer than the mainland. She stayed on the roof for more than two hours, until she was so sleepy she couldn't focus. When she came down the stairs after midnight, George was taking his break, getting a cup of coffee in the galley.

"See anything exciting?" he asked without turning.

"Nothing that would show up on the radar. But I found Saturn tonight."

"There's a book of astronomy charts in the other room if you want to use it."

Rachel stared at his back as he replaced the coffee carafe. She hadn't seen an astronomy book in the four months she'd been on the island. He must have had it in his room.

"Thanks."

She found it near the radio set in the sitting room. It was a well-worn paperback, ten years old. She turned to a dog-eared page and studied the sky chart. It was the winter sky over Frasier Island, she realized. How many times had George sat on the roof, looking up at those stars before his shift began?

She pulled in a shaky breath. She wanted more than George's approval now, and that could be heartbreaking. They had a lot in common, if he would only admit it. But they'd started out on the wrong foot, and more than once she'd let her anger show. She couldn't hope for more than his tolerance. That hurt.

❧

Rachel had already begun a list of supplies to order. George would relay it to his superiors three weeks before the end of the tour. If they were lucky, they would get most of the provisions they requested for the next six months. *Sunscreen,* she wrote on the list, and then, *Christmas decorations.* George would scoff, but they would be ready for some frivolity by December. She felt a sharp pang of regret that Pierre would not be there to wish her a *joyeux Noel*.

They would have to order any gifts they wanted to give. She couldn't survive Christmas without giving presents. But how could she come up with a suitable gift for George? She'd better order something generic for the new guy too.

She wandered toward the banana grove in the bright, steamy morning. It was going to be hot again. She'd found a place where orchids grew, delicate, ethereal wisps of color in the green. Drawing them in gray was not satisfactory. She would order a large box of colored pencils, she decided. The good ones, artist quality, with many shades of green. It would be her Christmas gift to herself.

She sat on a log in the comparative coolness of the grove and took her pencil from her breast pocket. An orchid vine twined around the stem of the bush it clung to, dependent on its sturdy support. She began to draw, striving to capture the blossom's fragility.

A low whine suddenly became audible, sending her heart pounding and adrenaline pumping through her. It was what they listened for constantly but rarely heard: an approaching aircraft.

She ran out of the shelter of the trees, searching the sky. It was still a ways out, and to the west, she thought, beyond the house and the cliff, over the sea. She couldn't see it, but she ran toward the house, scanning the horizon. She was panting as she climbed the steep slope from the spring toward the windmills on the ridge.

The whine became a rumble, and she knew the plane was a jet. Surely Pierre had caught it on radar long before she had heard it. She wished she could see inside the control room, and wondered if George was there. Of course he was. Pierre would follow the protocol and call George as soon as he became aware of the aircraft. Her hand went to her radio, but she decided that Pierre didn't need an interruption from her.

Maybe it's a Navy plane out on a test run. But they should have been notified in advance if that were the case.

As she ran past the first windmill she saw a flash in the azure sky, racing out from the cliff on Frasier to meet an unseen projectile in the sky. She saw the explosion as the two missiles collided and disintegrated into white smoke, and heard a *whooshhhh—crump!*

She stood stock still at the base of the second windmill and stared upward. She saw the plane then, at eleven o'clock, coming out of the west-southwest, straight toward Frasier Island, and the rumble became a roar. It was coming fast and low. She clamped her hands over her ears and froze, pressing against one of the windmill's angle iron supports to make herself less visible from above. *It's targeting us!* Her prayer was wordless.

There was another *whoosh* overhead, and a second missile zipped out from Frasier, in a clean trajectory, from the launcher on the cliff to the moving aircraft.

Rachel stifled a scream as the jet fragmented in a flash, and pieces fell to the sea, trailing smoke that hung in the air in faint wisps, dissipating even as she forced herself to push away from the windmill and run beyond the house to the head of the cliff.

She stared out over the sea where the plane had disappeared. The waves gently licked the rocks below, as though denying their part in the violence. She squinted against the glare of sunlight on water, looking for anything. There had been no parachute, she was certain of that. There was no raft. She thought she saw a piece of debris lifted on a distant swell.

She turned away and walked quickly into the house and down the stairs. Her legs were shaking, and she paused to lean on the railing for a moment and take deep breaths. *Dear Lord, this can't be happening. Give me strength!*

She could hear voices. George was on the radio, communicating with Navy officials, describing the incident. She pushed herself down the remaining steps and into the control room.

Pierre was staring at one of the camera monitors. George, as she had expected, was huddled over the radio. She walked up behind Pierre and put her trembling hand on his shoulder. His eyes were dark and troubled as he glanced up at her and then back at his console.

"I saw it," she said.

"They were going to strike."

"They fired a missile at us." She hated the tremor in her voice.

Pierre reached up briefly and squeezed her hand. "Yes."

"Whose was it?"

"Don't know yet. But it wasn't one of ours."

George stood up. "They're sending a cruiser out for recovery. If they can salvage any debris, it will tell us a lot."

"I thought I saw something floating," Rachel choked.

He nodded. "Well, we can't get out there. We'll just have to wait and hope something's recovered."

"They wanted to destroy the missile installation," Rachel said, looking George in the eye.

He took a deep breath. "Maybe."

"What else? It looked like a suicide mission to me, they were so low. But the warheads wouldn't have gone off, even with a direct hit, would they? That's what they taught us in training."

"No, that can't happen."

She saw a look pass between George and Pierre.

"What?" she asked, tension making her voice rise. "What am I missing?"

"You've got to tell her," Pierre said softly, looking at the underwater camera monitors, but the rocky ledge beneath the waves on the western perimeter of the island was peaceful.

"Tell me what?" She looked from him to George.

George seemed to be backpedaling, trying to decide what to say. The radio set crackled.

"Frasier 130, do you read me?"

He turned and lifted the handset. "Frasier 130, go ahead."

"ETA for recovery helos four hours, fifteen minutes."

"There won't be anything left by then," Pierre muttered.

"I copy," George said.

"We're sending a couple of F-14s for a flyby to see if they spot anything."

"What's their ETA?"

"Twenty minutes."

"Pierre, tell me," Rachel whispered urgently.

Pierre glanced uneasily toward the lieutenant. "I can't. I'm sorry."

She rounded on George then. "What is going on? This was a security breach of major proportions, and I go on duty soon. You need to tell me everything."

George swallowed. "You all set, Pierre?"

"Yes, sir."

"Be alert for those Tomcats."

"Yes, sir."

Rachel stared at Pierre numbly. The mood had changed. The two men were all business, and Pierre was in the subordinate seaman mode.

George faced her. "Ensign Whitney," he began and then he dropped his gaze. "Rachel."

Even George was having trouble sorting out the ramifications of the incident, she realized, and it disturbed her.

"We almost bought it, didn't we?"

He nodded.

"They were targeting the house?"

"We're not sure."

"But you just told me they couldn't ignite the warheads."

"That's right."

"Because if they could, Frasier Island would blow up, and us with it."

"But they couldn't."

She eyed him distrustfully. "So the only danger was if they'd fired a missile at the house or wrecked some of our equipment."

"Not exactly."

She waited, adrenaline coursing through her body. "What's going on? Other than us sitting on half a dozen A-bombs?"

"We're not."

Rachel gulped. "We're not?"

He ran a hand through his hair. "Look, I was supposed to brief you when you came, but…" He glanced at her and then toward Pierre. "I really messed up. I'm sorry."

Rachel couldn't believe what she was hearing. George was apologizing. It wasn't possible.

"I don't understand."

He grimaced. "Look, I could be in a lot of trouble here. It's up to you, I guess. See, the warheads have been disarmed."

"What?" She shook her head in disbelief. Without the warheads, the nation's defense system was crippled. Their reason for holding vigil on Frasier was nonexistent.

George raised one hand beseechingly. "They had to do it. If anything had happened, it could have destroyed the firene." He walked across the room and stood with his back to her.

Rachel stood dumbstruck, trying to make sense of what he had said.

"Destroyed the…?"

"We couldn't take that chance." He turned back toward her. "Listen, I know you're upset, but I truly thought it was in the best interest of security not to tell you."

She whirled toward Pierre, but he was refusing to look at her. "You were supposed to brief me on this and you didn't? And what's this firene business?" Rachel found it hard to breathe. "You and Pierre could never disarm live nuclear warheads. Could you?"

"No, no, we didn't do it. The Navy did. It was all done properly and safely."

"When?"

"About a year and a half ago. Before Pierre came."

She shook her head. "And the reason we're still guarding these useless missiles is…?" Surely the Navy wasn't bluffing the world, hoping to stave off nuclear war by pretending it had warheads at the ready when it didn't.

"The firene. That's what we're protecting now." He stepped toward her. "It's the most valuable material on earth, and our engineers discovered it by accident when they started construction on the missile silos more than four years ago. They had no idea what it was at first, but now they're starting to believe it's the most precious resource the United States has."

"George...how could you not tell me this?"

"I...just..." He looked helplessly toward Pierre, but he was studiously watching the monitors.

Rachel felt her fear peak and anger take over. "You are something else. You decide you don't like me on first sight, so you disobey orders and neglect to tell me the vital details of our mission. Where do you get off deciding when to obey orders from the Pentagon?"

George swallowed. "I thought..."

"You thought!" She shook her head. "You really enjoy running your little kingdom here, don't you, George? You run things the way you think is best. That's what you told me last spring. Because you know better than anyone else what's best for Frasier Island and the world, don't you? Better than the chiefs of staff, better than the president, certainly better than some wet-behind-the-ears female ensign. We had a very real emergency here today—"

"But we did exactly what we would have if you'd known," George insisted. "We had to stop that bomber. It didn't matter whether he thought he was destroying nuclear warheads or firene, we had to take him out."

"Which you did brilliantly," Rachel said sardonically. "You are out of line, Lieutenant. It's time you realized that."

She turned and marched up the stairs and to her bedroom, where she collapsed, shaking, on her cot. She lay there for several minutes, staring at the ceiling and pulling in deep breaths. Her fury ebbed. The crisis was past. Should she go back and offer to help reload the equipment? Another enemy aircraft could appear at any moment, and two of the three standard missile launchers were empty now. But she couldn't face George again yet. She had to face God first and get rid of this anger.

NINE

A soft knock came at the door.

"Go away!"

"Rachel," Pierre called softly.

She pulled herself up and opened the door.

"Rachel, try to understand."

"I'm trying, but I can't. You both knew, and you were supposed to tell me in April."

Pierre ducked his head. "I asked him to tell you, but I couldn't go behind his back."

"I figured that. King George. He's treated me like a leper since the day I came." She heard a low whine, and cocked her head. "What's that?"

"The Tomcats, looking for flotsam."

She nodded. "Does George need you below?"

"No. He reloaded the missile launchers. He went to check them, and then he came back to the control room. He asked me to come talk to you. Do you have any questions?"

"Oh, *now* I'm allowed to ask questions."

"Ask anything you want, *mon amie.*"

She stamped her foot in frustration. "I'm *not* your *amie.* Do you think I can trust either of you now?"

"I'm sorry."

A great sadness welled up inside her. "Pierre, he should have told me."

"Yes, he should have." He held his arms out, and Rachel sank into them and let the tears flow. "Sit down, *cherie*." He guided her toward the cot, and she sat on the edge, sniffing. Pierre brought her a box of tissues, and she blew her nose.

"I'm sorry," she whispered. "This whole business has been a bit unnerving."

"I understand."

"Do you?"

"I think I do."

"Don't tell George I cried. Please?"

"I won't."

"He'd say it was a typically feminine reaction, and he'd use it to justify not having women in combat situations."

"Give him an opportunity to learn from this."

Rachel dabbed at her eyes with the tissue and took a deep breath. "So, George got to test the reloading machinery for real."

"Yes. Everything went like clockwork."

She looked him full in the eyes. "What is this firene stuff we're sitting on?"

"We don't know exactly. It's some kind of rock or metal that no one had ever seen before."

"What, it only grows on Frasier?" she asked with a shaky smile.

"They believe it's a meteorite that hit the water a hundred years or so ago and lodged against the base of the island."

Rachel caught her breath. "It's space junk?"

He nodded. "That seems to be the best explanation. When they started building the installation, they thought it was just a ledge of rock."

"That ledge! That's what we see with the submerged cameras."

"We put those in so we can actually see it. If someone sends in a sub or a diver, we can see them now."

"But why is it so valuable, other than being scarce?"

Pierre sat down on the floor and took her hand. "They're testing it. They took a small sample back from that first expedition. One of the divers thought it was funny-looking and scraped off a chunk. It sat on some commander's desk for months, and then somebody sent it to a lab in Pearl Harbor. They freaked and sent it to Washington."

"So, what is it?"

"They still don't know. It's an element unknown on earth. But it's stable, at least under the present circumstances. They're trying different things, and they believe it has great potential as an energy source."

"You mean…fuel?"

He nodded. "A small piece of firene, under compression, could produce more energy than fifty tons of coal. That's why they call it firene. But they don't want to start heating houses with it, for several reasons."

"It could be dangerous." She fingered a seam of the patchwork quilt, imagining what this discovery could mean.

"Right. It doesn't seem to be radioactive, but they're trying to make sure burning it won't be noxious. And then, someone got the idea of using it as a weapon."

Rachel's eyes snapped to his. "A weapon?"

"Yes. They're testing its reactions to different elements. Combined with a small amount of sulfur, it burns quickly and is extremely hot. If they can find a way to contain and detonate it, it may make weapons as powerful as A-bombs without the aftereffects of radiation."

"No fallout. No wonder it's such a big secret."

Pierre nodded. "Our government doesn't want anyone else to know what we've got until *we* know what we've got. They're testing it in dozens of ways. It may even have some medical applications. We just don't know yet."

"It's too big to cart off to Washington," she said.

"Yes, but it's too small to parcel out to the world. There's only so much of it, so our scientists are trying to discover the best way to use it. When we know, they'll start mining it. Remember when they came to inspect the missiles in July?"

"There were no missiles to inspect down there."

"Right. They were taking more samples."

She took a slow, deep breath. "And we have to make sure nobody else starts chipping away at it while we wait for them to analyze it."

"Exactly. It could be used against us."

"That plane," she said uneasily. "Does someone else know it's here?"

"Maybe. There could be a leak. You're one of a handful of people who know this stuff exists, but somehow another government could have gotten wind of it."

She cradled her face in her hands. "That's why George is so paranoid. He wanted to be sure, if there was a leak, it didn't come from here."

"Right. He takes this very seriously."

"So, we don't know if that bomber was out to destroy our mythical missile site or blow the firene out of the water."

Pierre shrugged. "Perhaps he was going to hit the house. Get rid of the sentinels and then send in a cleanup crew to take over the base."

She looked into his eyes. "Is the naval command checking to see if any foreign aircraft are hovering?"

"Absolutely. They've got AWACS doing top-level reconnaissance right now. If there's even one ship or plane out of place within a thousand miles, we'll know it soon."

"Japan owns Marcus Island now," Rachel mused. "You don't think Japan would do this, do you?"

"After Hiroshima? I have my doubts. But North Korea is another story, or even China."

"Yes. What would have happened if they had dropped a bomb on the firene?"

"A direct hit?"

She nodded.

"We don't know for sure. Probably nothing, except to pulverize it. But…we just don't know. It might have gone up in a mushroom cloud, and we'd be gone. That's why they took the nukes out of here, Rachel. We just don't know, and it was too dangerous to leave nuclear material here, where it might be targeted by accident."

She reached to squeeze his fingers. "So what will George do to me now?"

Pierre smiled. "I think he's more concerned right now about what *you* will do to *him*."

"How do you mean?"

"He disobeyed orders in not filling you in on the situation. He could be severely reprimanded."

"I wouldn't report him for this."

"Are you sure? Think carefully."

"I'm sure. He saved our lives when he intercepted that missile."

Pierre looked off toward the small window, smiling. "Actually, I did that."

"You? Bravo! Then I must thank you."

"It is nothing. Part of the job." But his smile didn't leave his lips.

"Did George take over and hit the plane?"

"No. He stood there watching and said, *Just don't wait too long, mon ami.* I think it went rather well, don't you?"

"Like an exercise on the simulator," she admitted. "Is this the first time you've hit a real target?"

"Yes. I was nervous."

She squeezed his hand. "I'll make you a pie tomorrow. There's no time now. It's almost my shift."

"Thank you, *cherie,* but you must make amends with George, or we will not be able to function as a team. We need that badly now."

Rachel considered that. "Yes, but still…you believe his intentions were good, don't you?"

"I do. And he knew you would be just as vigilant not knowing. He never would have kept it from you if he'd thought it would jeopardize the mission. I say that with certainty."

She sighed. "I was insubordinate again, wasn't I?"

Pierre chuckled. "Just between you and me, I'm glad I got to see that performance. It could have been better. Maybe you should have slapped him."

She laughed ruefully. "Assaulting an officer. That would have been the icing on the cake. Pierre, if he dislikes me so much, why doesn't he just ask for a replacement? I was surprised he didn't after the first time I blew up at him. They could have brought someone on that ship that was here in July. They could even replace me today, I suppose."

"He doesn't dislike you, *ma cherie*."

"Right. He's just scared I'm going to report him." She shook her head. "I was wrong to get so angry. I'm sorry. If he weren't so bullheaded…"

"What?"

"No, that's not right. I can't blame him for everything. I know better than to explode at my superior officer." She smiled at Pierre. "I haven't been fair to George, have I? I've been angry with myself because I like him, even though I've tried not to."

"How well do you like him?"

"Very well. Much better than I did yesterday. I think I understand some things now that had me stymied before. But liking him is useless, it seems. I've sabotaged any chance I might have had to gain his respect by letting my temper get out of hand. Pierre, what am I going to do?"

She stood up slowly and walked to the window. A column of smoke hung between sea and sky a half mile away. "They've put out a flare."

Pierre came and stood behind her. "That's good. They've spotted some debris. Let's go get an update from George."

"You go. I think it might be dangerous for me to see him again this soon."

"He won't discipline you. He's feeling too guilty right now."

"Go. I'll be down when it's time for my shift."

Pierre went out, and she took her Bible and sketchbook from her dresser and sat down wearily on her cot. *When will I learn, Lord? Seems I still can't keep this temper in check.* She turned to the book of Psalms and read mechanically at first, her heart still thumping, but eventually she was able to focus on the soothing words.

The LORD is my light and my salvation—whom shall I fear? The LORD is the stronghold of my life—of whom shall I be afraid? (Psalm 27:1)

Forgive me, Lord. It's more than just a bad temper. I guess it's time I admitted that. Her sobs shook the cot. *You know I've let the past anger me and control my attitude toward other people. When I feel threatened, I fight back. George has taken the brunt of that, and it's not his fault. I deserve to be transferred out of here and demoted, but You've let me stay and given me time to learn. All right, I see the problem. I've got to get beyond the fear and leave that part of my life behind. But I've proven I can't do it alone. You say in Your Word that You'll give me strength. Well, I need it, Father.*

It was far tougher than she'd expected, being out here where Sunday was like every other day and no one spoke of God. Her time on the ship with Heidi, the only Christian she'd ever listened to, had been too short. There was so much she had yet to discover about this new life! Time and again she'd failed to rely on God, and now she'd shown her worst side to both the men. They'd almost been killed, but instead of being thankful, she'd let her fear and anger take over again.

It wasn't just Pierre's good aim that saved us, Lord. You were watching over us today. Thank You. Help me make peace with George.

She flipped the sketchbook open to the drawing of George, smiling at her with no trace of sarcasm or ridicule. Could she start over with him somehow? With her index finger, she traced the line of his jaw. She didn't feel worthy of his friendship anymore, and she couldn't blame him for not offering it.

"I'm sorry, George," she whispered.

TEN

George stayed in the control room through most of Rachel's shift, keeping in close radio contact with Commander Norton in Pearl Harbor, and later with the recovery vessels. As the hours passed and lines of fatigue etched deeper at the corners of his eyes, Rachel wondered how long he could go without sleep.

She had hoped to have a chance to speak to him about their fight, but he was busy with his duties, so she determined to stick to hers and do everything right.

Her routine watch became a video game whirl of images on her screens as jets, and then helicopters and boats, entered their monitoring zone. When the noise of multiple engines became too confusing, she discarded the hydrophone headset, but with George's coaching, she managed to keep track of each component in the search for debris from the downed plane.

Pierre came to relieve her for supper, but George refused to leave his post. Rachel went up to the galley and ate a sandwich, and then she put George's plate on a tray with a pot of coffee and three mugs. He wolfed the sandwich between calls, and Pierre hovered, not wanting to miss any action.

"It'll be dark soon," George said an hour later, leaning back in his chair. "They're calling off the search for tonight."

"Have they got anything?" Pierre's pacing had taken him from the radio to the navigational charts and back countless times.

"A good-sized sheet of metal off the fuselage, and a piece of fabric. They think it's from one of the seats."

"And?" Pierre's face was intent, more grave than Rachel had ever seen it.

"They're thinking Iranian."

Pierre swore softly under his breath, and George shrugged.

"Iranian?" Rachel protested. "How can Iran have planes in the North Pacific? Do they have a ship within ten thousand miles of here? This is crazy!"

George frowned. "They're not sure yet, but that's what they think. It could be North Korean. That particular aircraft...well, like I said, they *think*. They're still working on it."

Rachel thought that one over as she studied the radar screen and then the submerged camera monitors.

"What do *you* think?" she asked at last in the stillness.

George rubbed his chin where whiskers darkened his jawline. "I don't know. Maybe Iran is in cahoots with someone else. Someone with a bigger navy."

"Someone with interests in the Pacific," Pierre said.

George nodded thoughtfully. "In the past they've stuck pretty close to home, but who knows? Some of their people have held a grudge against us. There could be a covert element that's been negotiating with factions in other states. The terrorist network is huge and it's global. I don't pretend to be an expert."

"Iran could be supplying planes and men for this mission, with someone else floating the transport," Pierre suggested.

George stretched. "Take a nap, *mon ami*. I may need you in the night."

❦

When Rachel climbed the stairs at 2200, leaving George to his quiet vigil, she was surprised to find Pierre hunched over a book in the sitting room.

"You should be sleeping," she scolded.

He straightened with a sigh. "I tried, but I kept thinking about that plane."

She walked over to his chair and took the book from his hand. "Trying to make a positive ID?"

Pierre nodded. "If it's the plane they think, there were two men in it." He raised his eyes bleakly to meet hers. "I killed two men today."

She laid the book down and sat down beside him.

"You had to do it. We'd all be dead if you hadn't. It's war."

"With whom?"

She patted his shoulder, not knowing what to say.

Pierre leaned back in his chair and closed his eyes. "I don't get it. They came out of nowhere. Reconnaissance still can't tell us where they launched from."

"Iran has formed a secret alliance with some Far Eastern country," she guessed.

"Maybe. We've been monitoring North Korea for a long time now. And there's always China."

"Afghanistan, Pakistan, Cambodia…" She sighed. "Maybe even Russia."

"I wonder if the public knows about this attack."

His suggestion troubled her. "We've always announced it when we've had a strike made on us. We even tell the world when we've decided to strike another country. Libya, Iraq…"

"How do you know there weren't other times? In a remote spot like this, there are no civilians, no witnesses except us, no cameras but ours. You don't think the Pentagon would hush it up?"

"Why would they?" she asked.

"The firene. If the world hears that Frasier was attacked, they'll want to know why, and the government does not want to reveal that just yet."

"Couldn't they just put out the word that one of our naval installations was attacked? A defensive missile base, even."

He shrugged. "Then the media would ask a lot of questions. Reporters would be wanting to come out here on ships for a look-see. I guess it's up to the president."

"Don't you think the firene would be safer if everyone knew?" she asked. "Then we could protect it openly, and any potential enemies would beware."

He was silent for a few seconds, and then he said wearily, "Perhaps."

Rachel reached up and tousled his fluffy dark hair. "You need to sleep, *mon ami*."

His endearing smile burst out. "Does this mean you trust me again?"

She shook her head in chagrin. "I don't think I ever really stopped trusting you. You could be a proven spy, and I would still put my life in your hands."

"And George?"

She frowned. "I want to strangle him, but…it wasn't all his fault."

Pierre laughed. "Ah, *cherie*, someday you will open your eyes. And now, *au lit*."

"Which means?"

"Go to bed. We don't know what tomorrow brings."

"You too. You're exhausted."

He replaced the aircraft manual in the bookshelf. "I will just step down and see if George is all right first. He has been up all day."

"I can get up in a couple of hours and give him a break," she offered.

"No need. I will be there." He gave her braid a gentle tug and headed for the stairs.

"Pierre," she called softly.

He turned at the door to the stairway.

"It's not your fault. About those men in the plane."

His charming smile was not convincing. "*Merci, ma petite. Bon nuit.*"

❧

At 0230 George heard Pierre coming down the stairway. He glanced at him, taking in his stocking feet and sweats, and the fresh pot of coffee he carried.

"*Comment ça va, Georges?*" Pierre said, setting the coffeepot on the desk near the radio.

"*Tout est bien. C'est calme sur la mer.*"

"*Bon.*" Pierre filled their mugs and pulled the second chair close to George's.

"What am I going to do without you?" George sighed, reaching for his cup.

"*C'est vrai.* You need to make a new friend."

George snorted. "Who knows what they'll bring me in October? Some MIT twit, more than likely."

"No, MIT grads are making too much money in civilian life now. The military can't entice them anymore."

"If word gets out about the firene, every science nerd in the country will want to be out here."

Pierre sipped his coffee. "That may be, but I was thinking of someone closer to home. It's time you two put the animosity to rest."

George eyed him testily. "You know we're oil and water."

"Or gunpowder and a spark."

"Yeah, she went off with a kaboom today, didn't she?" George chuckled.

"You're not one bit sorry you provoked her, are you?"

He tried unsuccessfully not to smile. "I've got to admit, I've wondered what would happen if she got good and mad. It wasn't intentional, honestly. Little spitfire, isn't she?"

"Méchant, Georges!"

"Wicked? Me?"

"She had good reason to be angry with you, and you know it."

"All right, all right. I was wrong. And I said so. You don't think she'll change her mind and file a complaint?"

"No, I don't, but it would serve you right. You bait her constantly."

"That's not true." George felt a little hurt by his friend's opposition. "I've tried to keep things peaceful around here, which is more than I can say for Rachel. I've left her totally alone, haven't I?"

"I guess you have." Pierre's eyes flicked to the monitors. "But you could have made things easier for her."

"Easier? She has the same shifts we have, and she cooks one meal a day. What's easier than that?"

"You blind fool," Pierre said. "Rachel does laundry. She cleans up the kitchen. She checks the solar collectors when she goes out in the morning. She even cleans the bathroom. Who do you think sweeps and dusts around here?"

"Nobody."

Pierre shook his head. "Idiot. That's who did it before I came: nobody. This place was a mess when I landed. I've done my humble part, but Rachel is a workhorse. I found her scrubbing the shower with bleach yesterday. She doesn't complain about mildew and dust. She gets rid of it."

"I haven't complained."

"Of course not. You ignore it. Your surroundings are incidental to you." Pierre smiled and drained his mug. "I think you're part machine. Comfort and cleanliness mean nothing to you. But if you think hard, you'll see that you haven't had as much to ignore since Rachel came, and the machinery is running a little better."

"All right. To be honest, I have noticed what she's doing, although I've tried not to."

"And why is that?"

George shrugged.

"Oh, yes. Your momentous decision. You ordered yourself not to fall in love. But then, we all know how good you are at obeying orders."

George stared at the surface camera screen and set his jaw like iron.

"Rachel came here with some maturing to do," Pierre said, "but she is well on her way now. Perhaps you should reconsider your opinion."

"I don't see why," George said. "She's still a stick of dynamite waiting to go off."

"Today's events were extraordinary. She's been doing much better lately, you'll have to admit."

George scowled at the passive sonar display. He'd also thought Rachel had improved at keeping her volatile emotions in check, but he wasn't about to give Pierre more ammunition.

"Do you think she's pretty?" Pierre asked.

"What kind of question is that?"

"If you say no, I'll know you're lying."

"All right, I won't say no. What do you think?"

Pierre's eyes narrowed. *"Naturellement! Elle est très jolie! Mais…"*

"What?" George asked sourly. "Not pretty enough to make you forget about Marie, is she?"

"You wound me, George. You know where my affections lie."

"Still, you've grown close to Rachel. Does she know about Marie?"

"Of course. And I know where her heart lies." Pierre turned to watch his face.

"And where is that? I suppose she's got a sweetheart pining back in Oregon."

"No, she does not, not in Oregon. But her affections are engaged, I assure you."

"Well, that's a relief," George growled, but something twisted inside him. So Rachel did have a man in her life. He had assumed she must, a girl who looked like that and was smarter than most of the men in the chain of command above her. It didn't matter to him, or it shouldn't. He would have to try harder to ignore her. Why should that be depressing? But it was.

Pierre rose and refilled his mug. "You told me the day she came that she was too young."

"I meant too young for the job."

"Do you still think so?"

George shrugged. "She's done all right. And she's older than I thought at first. She's twenty-five. I figured her for eighteen, right out of high school."

"She had a year of college before she went to Annapolis. She told me some about it."

"University of Oregon," George conceded.

Pierre eyed him speculatively. "So, you've been reading her personnel record."

"I'm her CO. I'm supposed to know what's in her file."

"Hmm. What color are her eyes?"

"Blue."

"Would you say baby blue or azure or slate blue? Steel blue, perhaps?"

"Delft." George didn't look up from the radar screen.

"You surprise me. When did you look at her long enough to discover this?"

"This morning, when she dressed me down royally."

"It took you four months to notice her lovely eyes?"

"They're not always that shade. Sometimes they're grayer. Do you think it's the light in here? Or maybe it was just because she was furious."

"Perhaps there is hope for you yet, my friend."

❧

When Rachel rose the next morning, the house was quiet. She

made coffee and carried two cups down to the control room. Pierre glanced up at her and reached for his mug with a weary smile.

"*Bon matin, cherie.* You see, they are out there again already." He nodded toward the camera monitors.

Rachel scanned the images on the screens. "Still looking for debris?"

"It's unlikely they'll find any more, but they don't want to overlook anything."

"Is George sleeping?"

"Yes. They're coming for him later. Commander Norton is flying out from Pearl Harbor to meet with him on the command ship."

"They're taking George off the island?" An emptiness settled in her stomach.

"Only for a few hours." Pierre sipped his coffee, watching the radar screen. "They've got small boats out in the drift area, and two choppers." He glanced up at her. "Don't worry. The commander wants a personal briefing, is all. They'll bring him right back."

"Why don't they take you? You shot the plane down."

"I'm just a cog in the wheel. George is the driving force here, and he will speak for me. I'm glad, really. He'll put in a good word for me, and I don't have to face the brass."

"Don't you want to see the ship?"

"What for?"

"I don't know. You've been here so long. Aren't you tired of seeing no one but me and George, day in and day out?"

"Are you tired of it?"

"No, not really. But I haven't been here nearly as long as you."

"I find the longer I'm here, the less I want to interact with the outside world," Pierre admitted.

"George seems that way too."

"Perhaps. I'm not sure it's good for us."

"But you want to go home and be with Marie again."

"Of course. When the time comes. Right now we have a job to do."

She smiled. "I got to thinking last night. It was pretty exciting to be here when the first international incident occurred."

"That's right. Until yesterday, Frasier Island has been a humdrum assignment."

"Now it's the hottest spot in the world."

"Yes, but our moment in the limelight is going fast. I assume the rush of reconnaissance and recovery has driven off the enemy."

She nodded, thinking about the change the last twenty-four hours had brought. The entire mission hadn't seemed quite real until yesterday. "So now we know we're not useless. There really is a threat."

Pierre buzzed George when he saw a Seahawk leave the aircraft carrier and head for the island. Rachel hurried upstairs and poured coffee for him. She took out a mixing bowl and was about to pour pancake mix into it when George entered the galley, clean shaven and wearing his uniform.

"Hi. I was going to make you some pancakes."

"No time. The copter's landing. This for me?" He nodded at the mug of steaming coffee. She thought he seemed a little groggy, and his eyelids were heavy.

"Yes. Can I get you something to eat quick?"

"This is fine, thanks."

He left the galley, carrying the mug, and she followed. She hovered uncertainly in the doorway to the sitting room as he put on his hat and picked up the metal-covered notebook he kept his paperwork in. He glanced at her, and she spoke up quickly.

"Is it all right if I come out to the helo pad?"

George shrugged. "No need. They're just touching down to get me." His cool gray eyes ran over her, and she flushed under his scrutiny. It seemed he rarely looked at her, but when he did, he missed nothing. She had pulled on denim cutoffs and a U of O Ducks T-shirt that morning and plaited her hair in two braids. If she'd known the helicopter was coming, she certainly would have dressed differently.

"All right," she said.

"You want anything off the ship?"

"Sunscreen?"

"I'll ask the doc." George shook his head, smiling faintly. "Don't you know the sun is bad for you?" The mocking tone she'd grown to anticipate wasn't there.

"Yes, well, I've tried to ration my Coppertone, but I can't stay inside when it's nice out."

"Children don't know when to come in out of the sun." He turned away. "I'll see what I can do."

Ah, yes, there it was. Rachel stood wondering whether to laugh or explode, but she knew now what she ought to do. She took a deep breath. "George, I'm sorry about yesterday. The things I said."

He looked at her quizzically, his hand on the doorknob. "I was at fault."

She swallowed. "Maybe we both were, but even so, I shouldn't have blown up like that. It was unprofessional and…just plain wrong."

She heard the big Seahawk helicopter close overhead and knew the pilot was ready to settle it on the flat patch of turf that was the landing pad.

George handed her his coffee mug and stood for a moment, holding her gaze.

"Don't worry about it. I'll see you later, Ensign." He went out.

Rachel crossed the room to the narrow stairway that led up to the roof. She stood leaning on the low wall that bordered the flat deck where the standard missile launchers were housed and watched as the chopper's blades beat the air. It lifted slowly from the island, turned, and headed straight for the ship. In her hand, George's half-empty mug of coffee was still warm.

She took a deep breath and went down the stairs. She dropped the cup off in the kitchen and went down to the control room. Pierre was sitting slouched in the swivel chair before the console when she entered.

"George get off all right?" he asked.

"Yes. He wouldn't eat breakfast."

"Don't mother hen him."

"I was not being a mother hen!"

"Ouch. If you're mad at George, don't take it out on me."

She scowled and stamped her foot. Pierre laughed.

"He called me a child."

"And you're so, so mature."

"You're as bad as he is." Rachel flung herself down in the chair near the radio desk, knowing that her good intentions had once more failed her.

"Come on, *cherie*. You know I love you." He smiled beguilingly, and she laughed.

"Marie would throttle you if she could hear the way you carry on."

Pierre shrugged. "I have four sisters. I count you as number five."

"That's really nice. I've got to say, you're better to me than my real brothers ever were."

"That's what's so great about friends."

"Maybe you're right."

Pierre glanced toward her and then back at the monitors. "Why do you get so angry?"

"I don't know. I've just always had a bad temper."

"Always?"

She hesitated. "Maybe not always. But…for the last three years or so."

"Why?"

"You don't want to know."

"Yes, I do."

She sat looking at him as he watched the screens, and a wave of sick dread hit her. Whenever she thought back to that time, she felt ill and depressed for days. She didn't want to go there again. Frasier Island held enough upheaval. Dealing with the present—the enemy attack, Pierre's remorse at killing the pilots, and George's antagonism—was enough. The past could stay in the box to which she'd relegated it long ago.

"Rachel?"

She flinched. Her name was tender on Pierre's lips. He had stood by her through her bouts of loneliness and insecurity. He hadn't rejected her even when she'd spouted to him her rage and frustration over George. He was the best friend she'd ever had, she realized. He was the only one, except Heidi, that she'd let come close since her last year at the Naval Academy.

He met her gaze for an instant, and the glacier in her heart began to melt. In an instant she felt she could confide even this to him.

She sat up straighter and struggled for the right words. "Something happened to me. I've always been a little touchy, I guess. Having two brothers and no sisters can do that. But then, just when I thought I was on the verge of reaching my goals, everything fell apart."

Pierre shot another glance her way, and she blinked at the tears swamping her eyes.

"I…had a month's leave the summer before my last year. I had everything planned and was making those plans come true. My degree, my career in the Navy. I had it all mapped out, and nothing was going to stop me."

She was silent for a moment, thinking about how nearly she had been stopped.

"Then…"

A wave of nausea hit her, and tears spilled down her cheeks.

"You don't have to tell me," Pierre said gently.

She wiped her face with her sleeve. "I think I want to. If you don't mind."

He nodded, watching the camera screens. "I don't mind."

"I was keeping in shape while I was at home on leave. Swimming and…" She swallowed hard. "Running."

"Sounds like you were always as persistent as you are now."

"Yeah, I guess I was. I didn't want to lose any ground while I was on leave." She crinkled a smile at him. "Our muscles are atrophying here, you know. They need to give us a weight bench or something."

They sat in silence for a few seconds, and she studied his profile. Her old distrust and uncertainty made her question whether to go on. For three years she'd kept silent about the one event in her life that had hurt her deepest. Even when she'd opened her heart to God a few months ago, she hadn't discussed this one thing with anyone. Not even Heidi. If there had been more time on the ship, perhaps. And as she thought about it, Rachel knew she hadn't thoroughly hashed the matter out with God, either.

She rolled the fringe of her cutoffs between her fingers.

"Pierre, I never told anyone this before."

"Nobody?"

She shook her head. "I couldn't tell my parents. It would have hurt them so. And my friends wouldn't have understood. They'd have wanted me to..." She stared at him, and Pierre glanced over at her, frowning.

"To do what, *cherie?*"

"To file a police report."

He was silent a moment, and then he asked softly, "Why didn't you?"

Pain and shame swept over her. "I couldn't. I just couldn't. There was no way to find out who he was. I'd gone out alone, early in the morning, to run before breakfast. There was a trail through the woods between our house and a big peach orchard. It came out near an industrial complex. The area had been developed a lot since I was a kid, but I'd always thought I was safe there. I mean, I'd had self-defense training, and I thought if anything ever happened..." She exhaled and shook her head. "He was so quick and so strong!"

"Rachel, I'm sorry," Pierre whispered.

She swallowed the bitter taste in her mouth. "Watch your screens, buddy."

He turned back toward the console. "Maybe the police could have caught him."

"I did think about it, but at the time, I figured there was a pretty small chance. I didn't see his face, and…well, it was only a matter of a couple of weeks until my final year at the Academy started. I didn't want anything to keep me from going back. I also sort of thought that if I filed a report, the Navy would look at that and…and maybe think I was a troublemaker."

"Oh, no, Rachel."

She slumped in her chair. "You're probably right, but do you really think they'd have assigned me to this post if they knew I'd once filed a sexual assault complaint? The only woman at a small outpost?"

Pierre shrugged. "I don't know."

"Well, I wasn't taking any chances. I didn't want to start my official military career with a handicap or get hauled home from Annapolis to testify."

"And so you just kept quiet?"

"Yeah." She sat still for a moment, but a painful doubt settled in her chest, and she sobbed. "I was wrong, wasn't I? I kept telling myself it was better if nobody knew."

Pierre grimaced. "I know it's hard to think about, but that guy…he may still be out there hurting other women."

Her breath came in shaky spasms. "I don't think so."

"You don't?"

Rachel rested her forehead in her hands, with her elbows on the desk. "A few weeks later, my parents told me another girl was assaulted in the same place. They didn't know what had happened to me. They were just telling me the shocking local news."

"And?"

"She…" The pain in Rachel's chest tightened, and she cleared her throat. "She had a gun in her purse."

Pierre made no pretense of watching the console. "She killed him?"

Rachel nodded.

"And you think it's the same man who hurt you?"

"It's pretty likely." She sucked in a breath, feeling a hopeless revulsion toward herself. "I went on the Internet and read all the news reports. Yeah, I'm ninety-nine percent sure. And I was glad she did it. I figured it was over."

"Rachel, Rachel." He sighed and turned back to his post. "These things don't go away so easily."

"I know that now. But at the time, I thought that if I didn't say anything, my life could go on, and I could still meet those goals I'd set. If I told, then everything would have been disrupted." She wiped her tears away once more and sat in silence, wondering if Pierre despised her.

"Are you okay with it now?"

"I'm better. I've been praying lately."

He nodded. "Prayer is good."

"I…saw it as an obstacle to overcome. I was out to prove myself, that I wasn't weakened by it. And I thought I was doing pretty well."

"You did well in your advanced training, I know that."

"Yeah. But…I don't think I've been a very nice person since it happened."

"In what way?"

"For one thing, I haven't made many friends. I…wouldn't let people get close to me. And I started getting mad at the least little thing."

"You could get counseling."

"Maybe. But not now."

"When you leave here."

She thought about that and nodded.

"Because you know you've brought your anger here and transferred it to George."

"Do you think so?"

"Don't you? George tends to be a bit, shall we say, *controlling?*"

"Huh. We could say that."

Pierre shrugged. "You weren't about to let another man make you feel powerless. I think that explains a lot."

She sighed. "George has not made himself easy to get along with."

"So, what do you expect from him? He can't look at you as a woman. He'd like to see you as a seaman, but he finds that impossible, so he compromises by viewing you as a child."

She couldn't help smiling. "What have you been reading, Freud?"

He chuckled but kept his eyes on his screens, moving steadily from one to another.

"And where do you get off saying he can't see me as a woman?" She rested her chin on her fist.

"I didn't say it. The regulation book did. He's your CO."

"Oh, like we can't fraternize! Three people on an island for six months, and King George can't socialize with us?"

Pierre said nothing, and Rachel felt the steam building up inside her.

"And who says I *want* him to see me as a woman? I'd settle for him seeing me as a person!"

"Relax, *mon enfant*. It is not me you are fighting here."

She glared at him. "You just called me a baby, didn't you?"

"No, I said *my child*."

She leaned toward him, feeling her anger bubble but determined to stay calm this time. "You're just like him! You know that, don't you? You're becoming a George clone. You'd better leave this place as fast as you can, or pretty soon you won't want to go." She took a deep breath. "I'm not going to yell and scream at you, though."

"That is good, very good. It's progress." Pierre smiled gently. "Lunchtime is approaching, *cherie*. Perhaps you could redirect your energy there."

ELEVEN

Rachel paced the upper rooms while Pierre kept watch below. Hours passed. She went to her room and opened her sketchbook to the portrait of George. Was he really keeping his distance out of duty? She changed into khaki slacks and shirt, and then she unbraided her hair, frowning at herself in the mirror as she brushed it out. It was getting long. Maybe she should cut it. She sighed and laid the brush down. Did it matter, if he was determined to keep her at arm's length?

It surprised her how deeply she wanted George's affection. An hour ago her anger toward him had once more simmered, almost to a boil, and Pierre had taken the heat. Even so, her admiration for George was growing, along with her desire to gain his approval. The more she learned about him, the more she wanted to know. She hadn't thought it possible, but she was beginning to understand why George acted the way he did, why it was important to him to control the mission, even though he didn't find strict discipline necessary. He'd been out here almost alone for three years, holding things together for America.

She took the paperback Bible and sat down on the canvas chair, near her window that overlooked the sea.

As usual, I've made a mess of things, Lord. Pierre did nothing to deserve some of the things I said to him, and George...

She sobbed and bowed her head. *This is too hard, Lord. I can see now that I didn't do the right thing three years ago. But I want to start* over. *Take the anger away, Lord. Give me a new heart. And the guilt I've been feeling…I should have been braver and filed that report, but I didn't, and now I can't undo it. So, if it's possible, could You please help me to quit feeling guilty over that?*

She turned to a verse Heidi had marked for her in the Bible.

Create in me a pure heart, O God, and renew a steadfast spirit within me (Psalm 51:10).

She sat still and felt hope snowballing in her heart. God would help her deal with all the conflicts she'd been battling. And if she kept listening to Him, maybe He would shape her into the woman He wanted her to be. He could take away her doubts and guilt and fear.

Thank You, Lord! Don't ever let me lose sight of You again. Teach me, because I'm really ignorant. I just wanted to come here and do a job. After I met You on the way, I hoped I'd have a chance to learn more about You and grow. But I feel so alone. Thank You for bringing me a true friend like Pierre. And George…well, Lord, I never expected to fall in love with a man who despises me. Is it wrong for me to feel this way about him?

She pondered her attraction to the lieutenant but came to no firm conclusion as to how God might view her feelings. *I know I'm supposed to follow regulations, and they say I can't have a personal relationship with my superior. I suppose You would want me to just accept that.*

She sighed and let the tears flow unheeded down her face. She couldn't just erase what she felt. But what did her chaotic feelings matter, anyway, when George had barely looked at her in four months?

❧

"No word?" she asked anxiously as she entered the control room.

Pierre removed his headphones. "They called a few minutes ago. George had lunch with Norton. It may be a while."

"Is anything wrong?"

He shrugged. "I don't think so."

Rachel gripped his shoulder. "They will bring him back, won't they?"

"Why wouldn't they?"

"You know they sometimes relieve an officer after an incident while they investigate."

Pierre took a deep breath. "That's not going to happen. We went by the book. If anyone's in trouble, it should be me."

"Pierre!" Her voice cracked, and she swallowed hard. "I'm sorry I got mad at you before. I've asked God to help me with my temper, but I seem to be a slow learner. But you've been great, ever since I came. And if anything goes wrong with George—"

He reached up and pried loose the fingers she had unconsciously dug into his shoulder. "Nothing will go wrong, sweet Rachel. He'll be back soon."

"But still—they could bring in a replacement for him."

"Then we will hang together, won't we? But I tell you, it's not going to happen. Sit down. It's time for your shift."

He left her alone in the control room, and Rachel brooded as she kept watch. Again and again she turned her malevolent gaze to the monitor that showed the ship where George was. Her vivid imagination conjured up sinister and sordid images. George was being held prisoner and interrogated mercilessly. Or he was celebrating Pierre's kill with the officers on the ship, wallowing in champagne. Or he was being stripped of his rank and sent to San Diego for menial duty. Or the record of the time he had spent on Frasier Island was being reviewed with a microscope as the authorities searched for unbecoming conduct. Or the commander was preparing to court-martial Pierre, and George was pleading his cause.

She realized it was fruitless to worry about George and began to pray, never relaxing her watch. She was still tense with anxiety, but reminded herself that even the Navy's hierarchy was controlled by a higher power. God was with her, no matter what the next few hours brought her way.

It was 1600 before the helicopter lifted from the USS *Bush*. Rachel called Pierre on the short-range radio.

"Helo headed our way."

"Got it."

She fidgeted in her chair, but kept her post, knowing Pierre would go out to the landing pad.

George climbed down from the Seahawk and thrust a box into Pierre's arms before lifting out three more boxes and stacking them on the ground. He waved to the pilot, the rotors accelerated, and the craft lifted slowly. George and Pierre carried the boxes toward the house.

"Are we in trouble?" Pierre asked, as the wind and noise from the aircraft diminished.

"No."

"*Bien*. What took so long?"

George frowned. "They made me spend some time with the shrink."

Pierre's eyes flared. "They think we're going loony out here?"

"Something like that. Norton's working out a new schedule. He and the doc think we ought to have shorter tours." He tried not to remember Norton's tone as he'd said, *George, I never should have left you out here so long. I like you, and I listened to you. You've been with this operation from the start, and you're right that no one else could do the job like you do, but you need a change.*

"Will they transfer you out?" Pierre asked anxiously.

"I hope not. He's talking about taking us off for a month after every six-month tour."

"Will they do that? They don't usually like to visit so often."

"Well, Norton's thoughts on that are changing, now that we've been noticed by the world. They won't upset the routine immediately, but it could happen soon."

"Let's go downstairs, so you can tell Rachel too. She's a nervous wreck."

"All right. But we'd better get that frozen stuff put away." George set his boxes down in the sitting room and opened the top one.

Pierre peeked in one of his boxes. "Ice cream!"

George smiled. "For the sweet tooth."

"*C'est moi*," Pierre admitted shamelessly.

They went down the stairs, stopping in the basement storage room to unload the frozen food. When they entered the control room, Rachel turned quickly to look at them over her shoulder before immediately turning back.

"George!"

"You were expecting maybe Commander Norton?"

"Well, you never know."

George dangled a bottle of sunscreen over her shoulder where she could see it. "This what you wanted?"

"Oh, thank you!" Her sidelong glance held a hint of shyness.

He smiled. "I thought you could use this too." He set a new sketch pad on the edge of the desk. Rachel glanced down at it, and her eyes widened. She looked up at him and then quickly back to her radar screen.

"Thank you! How did you get that?"

He shrugged. "You can find just about anything on a ship that big." He slapped a parcel wrapped in brown paper into Pierre's hands. "That's for you."

"What is it?" Rachel asked. He could almost feel her desire to look again, but she kept her eyes on the screens.

George said, "I think it's a videotape. From Maine."

"It's from Marie," Pierre said joyfully, but then his expression clouded. "We don't have a VCR."

"We do now."

"Movies?" Rachel squealed. "You don't think it will spoil the primitive Frasier ambiance?"

"As long as the windmills are running, I don't care," George said. "But we've only got six tapes, not counting Marie's."

"What are they?" Pierre asked eagerly.

"I don't know. Old ones they'd watched a million times on the ship. They're upstairs. Your mail's up there too."

"We got mail?" Rachel's voice caught, and George looked over at her, but she had turned her face toward the sonar display.

"Yes, you got mail." Rachel still wasn't looking his way, and George wondered if her incoming packet held any love letters. She was homesick, he was sure. Maybe he should have put his own selfishness aside and requested that Norton replace her immediately. When she first arrived, he'd have done that in a second, but not now.

No, he didn't want to see Rachel leave yet, and he knew she was determined to stay here for a year. He'd stuck up for her today, telling Norton she was an efficient part of the team. And it was the truth, he realized. Pierre was leaving him soon. No, he couldn't lose Rachel too. He wanted a chance to start over with her, whatever the consequences.

Pierre was examining his package, running his fingers over the handwritten address.

"Okay, let's talk," George said.

He sat in the second chair, and Pierre dropped to the floor between him and Rachel.

"They think there may have been a leak about the firene. Someone from the lab might have told someone. It's all tentative, but the Pentagon is nervous about it. Commander Norton briefed me. It's still very hush-hush, though. The captain of the *Bush* doesn't even know yet. Recovery mission only, as far as the *Bush* group is concerned, but a big covert investigation has been launched from Washington."

"So, someone in the lab may have sold the information," Pierre said. "Whoever bought it came after us, wanting a piece of the pie."

"It's a theory," George agreed. "And the White House announced the air strike this morning."

"They held a press conference?" Rachel asked.

"Yes. Norton said they can't be sure word won't get out some other way, not after this. A whole lot of sailors were in on this recovery op. So it looks better if it comes from the top."

Pierre nodded, his brown eyes intent. "How much did they tell the media?"

"That a small naval installation in the Pacific was attacked yesterday, and one of our finest shot the missile and the plane out of the air." He nodded at Pierre. "Don't get a swelled head, but I told Norton you ought to be decorated, and he didn't argue."

"What happens now?" Rachel asked.

"For us? Business as usual. They're pulling out tonight. Nothing's been made public about the firene, but we need to be extra alert now."

❧

When Rachel's shift ended she went upstairs and found Pierre sitting on the floor in the sitting room, his eyes riveted on the screen of a small monitor.

"You got the VCR hooked up!" Rachel sat down beside him.

He hit the pause button on the remote control. "Let me rewind." He shot an apologetic glance at her. "You can't watch it all because… well, you just can't, but there's a part I want you to see."

"I'd love to."

She settled back, resting on her elbows while he found the spot and began running the tape again. A pretty dark-haired girl was smiling at them flirtatiously from her perch on a swing.

"Everybody's excited about the wedding," she said happily. "I got the wedding dress, but I'm not going to show it to you. But it's, *wow!* And Lisa's going to be my maid of honor, and Nicole, Jane, and Paula are my bridesmaids. I saw your brother Matthieu the other day, and he says he will kill you if you don't have him as your best man." She giggled. "*Viens vite, mon cheri.*"

"She's beautiful," Rachel breathed, "but she's so young!"

Pierre's smile was irrepressible. "She was seventeen when I left."

"Seventeen!" Rachel stared at him.

"She'll be nineteen next week. I wish I could have sent her a present. But George took a letter out for me this morning."

"She was seventeen when you proposed?" Rachel tried to modulate the incredulity in her voice.

He nodded soberly. "You know, I've been thinking lately, wondering...you know, if she had changed."

"Of course she's changed, Pierre."

"Well, yes, some, but...I thought once or twice, what if she hasn't grown up? Because I knew I had. But what if she hadn't? What if she was still immature? I don't want to outgrow her." He glanced at Rachel. "I'm really glad she sent me this tape because..."

"You know better what to expect," she said softly.

"Yes. I can see that she's still my Marie, the woman I love, and she's still as caring and bubbly as I knew her to be, but she's...she's more now. She understands the agony of the separation, but she's been faithful to me, and..." He looked at Rachel with a longing. "I want you to know how I feel."

"I think I understand."

He nodded. "Because being here with you...I've never been this close to a woman before, you know? I've had friends who were girls, but this is different. We live in the same house and eat the same food. You told me...things that were very personal."

She nodded.

"I was beginning to think, *Hey, I know Rachel better than I know Marie.*"

"No, no," she protested.

"Well, I thought maybe. But then I saw this, and I could see that she is still the same. She's the girl I fell so madly for. She's...everything I want, Rachel."

"Of course."

"I think I love her more than I did an hour ago."

"I think so too. I'm glad you got this."

"George got the VCR for me. I know he did. The movies are just an excuse. He saw the package, and he knew what it would mean to me. He said the ship got new DVD players ages ago, and the VCRs were just sitting in storage. So he got one. For me." Pierre swiped at a tear that ran down his cheek.

Rachel smiled. "He's been a really good friend to you. He's been awful to me, but he thinks you're special, and he's right." She put her arms around Pierre's neck and kissed him on the cheek. "Thank you for listening to me earlier. And for encouraging me. I talked to God some more too."

"Are you okay?"

"Yeah, I think so. Better than I've been in a long while. But you should go to bed now."

His boyish smile burst out. "No, let's watch something else. Come on, you pick."

She reached into the box he indicated and pulled the tapes out, one at a time.

"*It's a Wonderful Life.*"

"Hey, I haven't seen that in years!" Pierre snatched it from her.

"You haven't seen anything in years."

"We used to watch it every Christmas."

"So did we." She held up the next one. "*Saving Private Ryan.* Let's keep that one for later. I'm not in the mood for a war movie tonight."

"What else is there?"

"Hmm, *North by Northwest.*"

"Alfred Hitchcock!" Pierre's eyes sparkled.

"Now, listen," Rachel said sternly, "we are not going to sit here all night and watch these in one session. Let's make them last. One a night, okay?"

"Okay, and I won't watch without you."

"Great." She hesitated. "But what if George wants to watch too?"

"I'll watch them again with him during your shift. But only the ones you and I have already watched."

"It's a deal. Hey, how about this one? Nelson Eddie and Jeanette MacDonald, *The Girl of the Golden West.*"

"No, this one. *Blue Hawaii.*"

"You want Elvis tonight?"

"Whatever you want."

"Okay, there's one more." She pulled it out. "*Toy Story.*"

"My favorite!"

"Mine too," she laughed.

TWELVE

With September came more storms. George prowled the island when he was off duty, checking all the equipment. Rachel hardly saw him except for the brief moments when they changed shifts.

She spent rainy mornings reading. Her packet of mail had included three loving letters from her parents, and she cherished them. Her study of the New Testament deepened, and she wished she had some books that would help her. Pierre had told her they could order specific books, but she didn't know what to ask for. As she prayed one morning, she remembered Heidi's help when she had first believed in Christ. If Heidi were still on the *Bush,* she might be able to get a message to her and ask her to recommend some titles.

The first serious typhoon hit violently in the early afternoon, and Rachel stared in dismay at her monitors. She couldn't see anything on the surface camera screens, although the cameras themselves were hooded. The pelting rain reduced visibility to a hundred yards. By contrast, the submersibles continued to show the peaceful ledge of firene, shrouded in twilight. The usual marine mammals seemed to have disappeared, gone south to evade the storm, she guessed. Her sonar and radar displays showed no unusual activity, and the wind worried the house above her, rattling the shutters.

The windmills withstood the storm, with only one blade coming loose. The wind flung it off the ridge to the rocks near the boat landing. When the storm ended, George and Pierre retrieved it with great difficulty, and George spent hours bending it back into shape and reinstalling it on the tower. Rachel spent two mornings clearing branches from the paths and replacing cracked Plexiglas panes in the solar collectors.

They settled into an uneasy calm. The searing heat eased, and they all knew the idyllic, lazy summer was past. Rachel quit wading in the tide pool and began pulling on a sweatshirt for her morning rambles. She spent a lot of time compiling the "wish list" of provisions, and at last handed it to George.

"Wow." He slowly leafed through the five pages of items she had cataloged. "It will take me an hour to relay this."

"I'll do it if you like. Then you won't know what your Christmas present is."

She expected him to object to the notion of Christmas gifts, but instead he said pensively, "I suppose we ought to give Pierre some sort of a send-off."

"Definitely. We're low on sugar, but I'm hoarding enough for a cake. And I was thinking we should give him something for a wedding present. Maybe we could kick in together."

"What, order a toaster? When they deliver it, he'll be getting on the helo to leave."

"How about money? Help him and Marie finance their honeymoon."

George shrugged. "Whatever."

Rachel sighed. "We'll miss him so much!"

George took a bite of the chili she had heated for lunch. They were down to canned goods and whatever she could contrive from the remaining staples. "For once I agree with you. We'll probably get some chowderhead from Annapolis in here, and I'll have to babysit him."

"The training is comprehensive," Rachel reminded him.

"I don't care. They can bring us some new kid and call it a replacement, but Pierre is irreplaceable."

Rachel frowned at him. "Look at me, George."

He started guiltily and raised his chin. "What?"

"If you do anything to keep Pierre from leaving here in three weeks, I will—" She turned away, shaking her head.

"You'll what?" He stood up, towering over her, and Rachel sensed a challenge. She drew herself up to her full five feet, four inches.

"I will personally tear you limb from limb." She stared balefully into his hard gray eyes. George stared back. *I will not back down.* George's self-confident stare made her feel as though she were shrinking, but she stood her ground.

Suddenly, he threw back his head and laughed. "Okay, pumpkin."

"*What* did you say?"

"Isn't that what your father calls you?" George put the list in her hands. "Call Pearl and give them your shopping list."

Rachel's face went scarlet. "Do you think that's appropriate?"

"What, you making the call? You know how to use the radio."

"No, I mean for a lieutenant to call his subordinates pet names."

"*Pet* names?" He was laughing so hard, she thought he might choke. "I'm not sure pumpkin is a *pet* name. Kitten or lamb, those would be pet names."

"You're insufferable."

She stormed out of the galley and down to the control room.

Pierre called out, "Rachel, you're early."

"How did you know it was me?"

"Because you stamped down those stairs like a herd of elephants. George moves on cat feet."

"Like the fog," she said with a grimace.

"*Précisement.* I take it he has made you angry again."

"Me? Angry? Why would you think that?" she asked bitterly. "He heard my father call me pumpkin, and he threw that at me. He'd been saving it for months, just waiting for the right moment. He was mocking me." She laid the provisions list on the radio desk.

"It's been ages since you let loose like this."

Contrition swept over her, and she sank into the wheeled chair.

"I'm sorry, Pierre. Thanks for making me accountable. I…I'm trying to do better."

"He thinks you have a boyfriend at home."

She turned and stared at him. "What does that have to do with anything?"

"Nothing, I suppose."

"That's stupid. Why would he even think that?"

Pierre grinned. "I can't imagine." He nodded toward the monitor. "Come take a look at this whale."

"We've got a whale? I haven't seen one in weeks." She moved in behind him and peered over his shoulder, looking at the waterfall display of the passive sonar monitor.

"I can't actually see it," Pierre said. "He's out of visual range, but I've been tracking him on sonar for a while and hearing his song. It must be a bull humpback migrating, and he decided to pay us a visit."

Rachel shook her head. "He's not moving?"

"He was. Now he seems to be just sitting there."

"That's odd. How long since he surfaced? Whales usually come up every five or ten minutes." Rachel felt her pulse accelerate. She scrutinized the sonar again. The array of hydrophones in deep water off the west end of the island allowed them to gauge the range and depth of approaching objects. "I'd say he's a big one."

"I'm thinking at least sixty feet long," Pierre agreed. "I wish he'd come closer so we could eyeball him on the cameras."

The whale lay a quarter mile beyond the ledge of firene, far beyond the range of the underwater cameras. Rachel straightened. "What are you hearing on the hydrophones?"

"The usual whale songs. He's been at it for twenty minutes, and he's loud."

"Let me listen."

He peeled off the headset, and she put it on, smoothing her hair back behind her ears.

"So?" Pierre asked after a few seconds.

"Shh."

He frowned.

"Call George," Rachel said.

Pierre's eyes widened at her urgency, but he put the call in. George was down the stairs within seconds.

"What have you got?"

"A whale," Pierre said.

"Let me see."

Pierre stood up, and George took his seat, staring at the camera monitors and then the sonar display. Rachel strained her ears. The song was not hard to hear, and it was sending up red flags in her brain.

"You tracked him coming in?" George asked.

"Yeah," Pierre replied.

"Where from? What direction?" George probed.

"Out of the west. I could hear his song a long ways away."

"Sperm whales usually come down from the Arctic this time of year," George said.

"It's not a sperm whale." Rachel frowned, listening for the faintest nuance.

Pierre said, "No, it's a humpback, right, Rachel? Just like on the tapes."

She nodded, still focusing on what she heard. "It's a humpback song, all right."

"He's not moving much." George frowned.

"He kind of glided in and settled there," Pierre said.

"How long's he been sitting?"

"Ten minutes at least."

"They usually surface pretty often," Rachel put in.

"Just out of our camera range," George said thoughtfully. "I haven't seen any movement at all in the last three minutes. Wish we had another camera, farther out." He glared at the sonar screen. "Something's not right with the way that's registering. I can't put my finger on it."

Pierre shrugged. "Well, you know what they say. If it looks like a duck and quacks like a duck…"

Rachel looked at him sharply. "Except this doesn't have the signature of a duck."

George raised his eyebrows and swiveled to look at her. "May I?"

She removed the earphones and handed them to him. "When he pauses and starts to repeat, see if you can't hear another noise behind it. It's faint, but I'm sure I caught something."

She and Pierre stood silent as George listened intently. A wicked smile spread over George's face.

"He's got an electric motor. What do you know?"

Pierre's incredulous expression would have made Rachel laugh if the situation had not been so serious. "A submarine?" he asked.

"A sub with the song of a humpback and an ultraquiet motor," Rachel confirmed. "That's why they're standing off so far. They're not taking a chance that we'll actually catch them on our monitors."

George jumped and his eyebrows furrowed. "Oh, boy. That sound I just heard had to be an airlock hatch cover closing."

"They're putting divers out," Pierre said.

"Or taking them in."

Rachel felt adrenaline surge through her. "What do we do, George?"

"Go whale hunting."

"Wait." She put her hand on his shoulder. "If you just blow it out of the water, we'll have a repeat of the plane incident. We can't recover anything ourselves, and there might be survivors. Shouldn't we call in a recovery team first?"

George frowned. "They won't stick around. If we wait for reinforcements, they'll be long gone. I suspect their divers are taking samples from the ledge, down low where we can't see them. I wish they were closer, but there shouldn't be a problem locking on to that sub."

As if to confirm his theory, the feedback on the sonar display began to change.

"I should have fired while they were immobile," George moaned, hastily flipping the alert switch on the torpedo launching device. "Rats, I'm going to lose them!"

"They're not leaving yet." Rachel held her breath as the display indicated the object was moving slowly around the firene ledge, toward the southern side of the island's tip. She glanced toward the camera monitors and saw a blur of movement at the extreme range of one lens. "Look!"

"Call it in," George snapped at Pierre and then he sat deathly still, watching the sonar screen as Pierre hastened to make radio contact.

"They're settling on the bottom," Rachel said. "More samples?"

"Maybe. They're hiding from the cameras, with the firene between us and them." George sat motionless.

"They can't possibly know that we've seen through the ruse," she insisted. "Sooner or later they've got to move out away from the ledge."

"Yes, and when they do, I'll get them."

Rachel bent close to watch over his shoulder, scanning first the camera monitors and then the sonar display.

"Here," George growled, stripping off the headphones. "The noise is driving me nuts. They must figure we're idiots if they think we wouldn't see through that."

"I don't know. The humpback has a very complicated song compared to most other whales. They may have chosen it because it camouflaged the mechanical sounds best, and hoped we wouldn't listen too closely. It's bought them time, which is what they needed."

He nodded. "Hey, they're moving again."

"I can't see them."

"No, but the sonar's got them. As soon as they're out beyond the ledge and I've got a clear shot, that's it."

"Yes, sir," she said fervently.

At the next desk, Pierre said urgently to Norton's radio operator in Pearl Harbor, "This is critical. Get Commander Norton immediately. We need AWACS and recovery again."

Rachel squinted at the camera monitor. Far out, at the extremity of the available light, she thought there was movement, but she wasn't certain. She opened her mouth to speak, but before a sound came out, George had made his move. At the instant it registered in her brain that a torpedo was speeding toward the submarine, the water began to churn, and a mass of bubbles erupted where a dark bulk had been.

THIRTEEN

"Bingo," George said under his breath. "Pierre, get over here. I'll talk to Norton. Rachel, go up to the roof and use the telescope. Look for survivors."

She ran for the doorway.

"Wait!" George cried. "Better take your weapon."

Startled, she gave him a nod and then hurried to her room. Her pistol had stayed in the bottom of her sea bag for more than five months, with her survival pack. She pulled it out, shoved in the clip, and then strapped on the holster and dashed for the roof stairway.

She trained the telescope to the west, but even without its aid she saw several dark shapes in the water about a quarter mile offshore. She wondered how many men the submarine had held, and if it were possible any had escaped.

She focused in on each fragment deliberately, looking for signs of life. It was impossible to identify anything. They were just…pieces. Zeroing in on one large item, she gasped as color came into focus. Orange. She peered intently through the telescope, but no human presence appeared. Could someone be in the water beside it, hanging on to it? It was drifting slowly toward the southeast. She was reasonably sure it wouldn't beach on Frasier.

Pulling back from the eyepiece, she took one more sweeping survey of the water and was about to turn away when her attention was snagged by an irregular movement amid the steady motion of the waves. A bobbing black object moved closer to the rocky shoreline.

She raised her radio and signaled George. "There's a swimmer heading for the west point."

"How far out?"

"Not that far. Two hundred yards, maybe."

"Swimming strongly?"

"Not really, but making progress."

"I'm coming up."

A minute later he joined her on the roof.

"I lost track of him." Rachel pulled back from the telescope's eyepiece. "He may have landed, out there." She pointed, and George looked through the scope.

"Did he have diving gear?"

"I couldn't tell."

"I closed the security doors," he said. "Pierre is calling the *Bush* to tell them we've got at least one survivor. They'll need to put a helo down ASAP."

She knew that when George shut the steel door at the bottom of the stairs, only Pierre could open it, from the inside, unless George used his key. All of them had keys to the upper door, opening into the basement storage room, but only the commanding officer held the key to the lower door.

"There's something," he said, training the telescope on the far rocks. "Could be a person between those big slabs out there." He pulled his Beretta from its holster. "I'll head out there. Stay here and direct me."

Rachel looked through the telescope again, shivering in the sharp wind. "I see it. You think that's a man?"

"Maybe. Here." George peeled off his gray sweatshirt. "Put this on."

"All right. But I saw something else earlier. A partly inflated life raft, I think. It was drifting southeast. I couldn't see anyone on it or in the water near it."

He nodded grimly. "Tell Pierre." He turned and went lightly down the stairs.

Rachel went to the south edge of the roof and leaned on the low wall, letting her gaze rove over the rocky shore, looking for movement as she gave Pierre a quick update by radio. She scanned the waves again. Maybe the nondescript lump George had spotted with the telescope wasn't a man. Maybe the swimmer hadn't made it.

The roaring of the surf rushed up to her, and her complete isolation bore down on her. George came into view below her, walking rapidly toward the head of the narrow cliff path. He looked up and stopped, raising his radio.

"See anything else?"

"Negative."

He waved and headed for the shore, his pistol at the ready in front of him.

She went back to the telescope and studied the motionless object again. It was lighter than the black volcanic rocks, but impossible to identify. She scanned the shore again, willing her eyes to pick up an image that didn't belong on Frasier. The wind tore at her hair, pushing it back from her face.

George signaled her again. "Keep going," she told him. "Straight out toward the sea." She went to the west wall and looked down. It would be so easy for a man to hide down there between the jagged slabs and chunks of stone, but it was high tide. The surf broke over them, rushing toward the base of the bluff on which the house stood. The waves crashed against the face of the cliff again and again.

❧

Far out on the point, George stood on a large boulder looking warily around him. The man from the submarine could not have survived, he told himself. It wasn't possible to come ashore there without being tossed against the rocks and pulled under by the next inundating breaker.

He looked out over the waves, shivering. The wind seemed to drain his body heat. He ought to have sent Rachel to get her jacket instead of giving her his sweatshirt.

His radio blipped.

"Come toward me a few yards," Rachel said.

He hopped to the next rock, holding his pistol carefully, but he didn't really believe he would need it. It was probably a piece of debris. He hadn't seen any living thing on his monitors after the explosion. Of course, the cameras weren't as high as the telescope, and his sonar wouldn't pick up a swimmer close to shore, below the cliff. He kept turning, searching, then descended from his rock and clambered to the top of another, closer to the water.

He glanced up toward the house again. Rachel was visible on the roof, but wearing his gray sweatshirt, she was not as good a target as she would have been in the bright pink blouse that always drew his unwilling eye. The sweatshirt hung nearly to her knees, over her faded jeans. He remembered the first time he'd seen her, standing by the boat landing waiting for his orders, scared but resolute. Slowly, over the months she had inched into his heart, and he couldn't decide whether that was good or bad.

"You're almost there," she said over the radio. He waved and moved with caution over the huge, algae-slick stones. He bent down, his pistol leading, to look into the tide pools between the boulders. A slab of rock nearly covered with barnacles lay beneath him.

He signaled Rachel on the radio. "Is that it?"

"Yes, right below you."

"It's a rock. I'm not finding anything. Go relieve Pierre and send him out here. The two of us will have to extend the search."

"I can join you."

"Negative. I want you on the monitors."

Rachel disappeared from the rooftop.

George continued his wary quest while he waited for Pierre, but it seemed next to hopeless. There were so many potential hiding places. The two of them couldn't search them all thoroughly in a day, and the search itself was dangerous.

Had Rachel really seen a swimmer? He believed she had. Her eyes were sharp, and she was quick at synthesizing sensory data. He almost wished she hadn't seen it. He was damp from the spume, and the enervating wind tore at him.

His heart hammered, but whether from exertion or from thinking about Rachel, he couldn't tell. He made himself breathe slowly. He needed a clear head at times like this.

A big nuisance, Rachel Whitney was, but one he didn't want to do without. He felt somehow that he had lost a round, just by admitting his growing regard for her. His resolve had slowly crumbled, and he knew his rash declaration to Pierre that he would not love Rachel had been premature. Even so, he couldn't act on his feelings. That would mean disaster for them both.

At last Pierre appeared on the cliff path, hurrying toward him, a bundle under his arm. George stood up and waved, watching his progress anxiously. Binoculars hung around Pierre's neck, bumping against the front of his sweatshirt. By the time his friend neared him, George could hear a faint rumble over the wind. He knew it was an Airborne Warning and Control System jet, and he automatically turned his eyes skyward.

Pierre tossed his bundle onto the rock and then climbed up and opened it, disclosing a thirty-foot nylon rope and a first aid kit, wrapped in George's camouflage jacket.

George seized the coat gratefully and pulled it on, then picked up the rope. "You get the first aid kit," he yelled. "The tide's turning, but the rocks are slippery."

"We can't search the whole perimeter."

"If he made it ashore, which I'm starting to doubt, he'll be on this end of the island," George said. "He could be holed up some-where along this stretch, but I doubt he'd have the energy to move far inland."

"Right. I asked for a landing team."

George nodded. "Good. Let's go."

They separated but stayed in touch with each other and Rachel by radio. It was a tiring, fruitless job. The sun fell toward the horizon, and George was so tired he was afraid he'd make a costly mistake on the rough terrain. They couldn't afford an injury now. At last he called to Pierre to meet him back at the house.

"Let's get some rest and wait for the landing party. We've done all we can for now."

❧

Rachel kept her post, and it seemed hours before the men returned. Pierre had insisted on closing the security door when he left her, in case any of the enemy had made it ashore.

"George?" she called as she heard the door open behind her.

"Yes. What's the word?" He came to stand beside her.

"The *Bush* carrier group is on the way. I guess you saw the recon planes."

"Yes. Will the ships make it by dark?"

"No. Captain Gallant advises us to secure the house for the night. They'll arrive about 0200 and land a Seahawk at dawn."

"Pierre's putting the shutters up now."

"Did you find anything?"

"Not really. A couple of small pieces of debris. Intelligence has their work cut out for them on identifying the origin of the submarine. Any reports on that raft you saw?"

"None." She glanced up at him. His face was gray and careworn. "Are you all right?"

"I'm fine. Just a little tired, is all." He sat down in the second chair and put his feet up on the radio desk. Water dripped from his boots.

"You're soaking wet."

"Guess I ought to change."

He seemed lethargic in comparison to his usually high energy. Rachel knew he'd been out in the wind for at least a half hour without his jacket, and he had apparently been drenched while searching all the crannies near the water line.

"Go take a hot shower and drink some coffee. When you feel better, come back, and I'll go up and cook something."

"Sounds good." He unbuttoned his jacket slowly, and she felt that he was watching her. At last he said, "Pierre's taking this hard."

"Why?"

"He totally misjudged things with that so-called whale. Missed all the warning signs."

Rachel glanced at him. "It was a clever ploy. The passive sonar is tricky, and we're all inexperienced at identifying real targets."

"I suppose. And we haven't had the new noise detectors and underwater cameras that long."

"Those new hydrophones are supersensitive. If you hadn't installed them last spring, we might never have known that sub was there."

"Now that's scary," George admitted.

"They would have been in and out, and us none the wiser, just thinking a humpback had paid us a visit."

"I guess you're right. Still, he should have called me as soon as he saw that whale coming from the west, straight for us. I'm not even mentioning the little lullaby camouflage."

"The new subs are really quiet," Rachel said.

"I know, but still…I'm not sure I'd have picked up on it as quickly as you did—" He broke off, and Rachel shot a quick look across at him. His eyes were droopy with exhaustion. "You did a great job today," he said.

A shot of exhilaration flashed through her. George giving praise was new and gratifying. She had finally met his standard, and that thrilled her, although she wished it weren't at Pierre's expense.

"Thank you, Lieutenant," she said softly. "I think our teamwork was pretty good." She smiled over at him, and saw that the chain with his dog tags hung down against his black T-shirt. She caught

her breath and realized she was staring. Even as George's fist closed
on the dog tags, she snapped her gaze back to the monitors. When
she glanced over again cautiously, he had dropped them down the
neckband of his T-shirt. She looked over at the aircraft chart, trying
to reconcile the new affinity she felt for George with the keen disappointment that assailed her.

The radio crackled. "Frasier 130, this is the USS *Bush*."

Rachel reached for the microphone. "Please go take care of yourself, George. I can't concentrate with you sitting there about to pass
out on me."

FOURTEEN

The next morning Rachel stood anxiously beside George, watching the big chopper descend. She had braided her hair snugly, but the wind from the rotors threatened to dishevel it anyway. Her uniform felt strange and restrictive, but she was glad she had worn it when Captain Gallant stepped down from the Seahawk, followed by half a dozen sailors.

"Lieutenant Hudson," Gallant said warmly. "And Ensign Whitney, isn't it?" he asked, returning Rachel's salute.

"Yes, sir. Welcome ashore."

"Thank you. I thought I'd better oversee things myself today."

"Right this way, sir," George said. "I'll brief you and your men on the situation."

Rachel led the way up the path, trying to walk briskly and confidently, not looking back at the captain and the men who followed him.

"I think my men should make a sweep of the island," Gallant said when George had detailed the search he and Pierre had conducted the previous afternoon. "Even though you found no survivors yesterday, we'd best do everything we can to make sure there's no one out there needing help, and that there are no enemies on shore."

"Yes, sir. I highly doubt that the person Ensign Whitney saw made it through the surf, but it's remotely possible," George conceded. "I don't think we'll find anything, but it's advisable to go over the entire island while we have the men available. However, our terrain is pretty rugged. I wouldn't want one of your men to be injured."

"I won't feel you're secure if we don't do it," Gallant insisted.

George sighed, looking at Rachel. She knew she would feel safer too, but she managed to keep an impassive expression.

"Yes, sir. Thank you," George said.

"I've detailed one helicopter to circle your perimeter looking for any survivors or debris. Of course, if someone were hiding…"

"Yes. There are lots of crevices a man could hide in, and a patch of jungle. And there are one or two barely accessible places I'd like to check myself. I can get to them safely," George said.

"Since you and Whitney know the island so well, perhaps you would like to direct the search in two groups," Gallant suggested. "I'll go with Ensign Whitney's group."

George turned to Rachel. "Ensign, would you step downstairs and fill Belanger in on the plan?"

She went quickly down the stairs. Pierre would want to help with the search, but she was glad it was his turn at the monitors. Even though it would be a rough job, it would be interesting, and she would have a chance to talk to outsiders. Perhaps she could find out if Heidi was still with the *Bush* and send the message she'd prepared with one of the sailors.

       ❦

As soon as Rachel had left the room, Gallant turned to George. "There's something I need to speak to you about privately, Lieutenant."

George tried not to show his surprise as he stepped to the far side of the room with the captain.

Gallant lowered his voice. "Commander Norton requests that you accompany us back to Pearl Harbor for debriefing, and possibly go on from there to Washington."

"Washington?" George's stomach lurched.

"This is serious business. The Pentagon will want a full report."

"But I can't leave now. Things have become very sensitive here."

Gallant shook his head regretfully. "Norton thinks you can. He says you're overdue for leave and could take a couple of weeks off afterward. Visit your family. Have a little R and R." His eyes never left George's face.

George tried to frame his reply, but words eluded him.

"We brought Belanger's replacement," Gallant went on. "It's a little early, but we had to come anyway, so we pushed through the paperwork. That man beside the door, Chadwick, will be staying. But now that Norton is so anxious to see you, I thought we could take you off instead, and leave Belanger."

George swallowed hard. "We can't do that. Belanger's getting married, sir. He has to get home."

"We're three weeks early," Gallant pointed out. "Chances are, we'll be back with supplies before too long."

George's glance flicked to the sailor standing near the door, staring into space with a bored air.

"I—no, Captain. That's not acceptable."

Gallant sighed. "I won't force you, but we could get an alternate in here pretty quickly, I think."

"What do you mean, sir?"

"Two new men, and we'll take you and Belanger off together. Tomorrow, perhaps."

George considered what that would mean. Leave Rachel here alone with two new recruits. He hated that idea.

"Would Ensign Whitney be in charge?"

"Well, yes, I suppose so. Chadwick doesn't outrank her, and I don't think there's another officer ready for this duty."

"She hasn't got a lot of experience."

"As much as anyone will have here. Norton told me they'll be curtailing the tours here. Twelve months max. With half that under her belt, Whitney's a seasoned hand."

George swallowed. "Does this mean I won't be back? You said you could leave Belanger while I go make my reports."

Gallant shrugged. "It's not up to me, Hudson. Norton hasn't said outright he'll transfer you."

"But he's implied it."

"It's not my decision. I know Norton has great respect for you and your work. Perhaps a stint away from here would satisfy him, and you could come back."

"I can't leave so suddenly. I need a day at least. There are things I'll need to discuss with Ensign Whitney about the operation here." George saw that one of the sailors was looking at him and realized the conversation was no longer private.

Gallant looked around at the men. Rachel was emerging from the stairway. "All right, we'll come back for you tomorrow. I don't dare wait any longer than that. There's bad weather brewing. If they can get another trained man out here by then, I'll send him, and you bring Belanger with you. If not, well, if I can only get one of you off this little paradise, it will be you, Hudson. Do you understand?"

"Yes, sir." George glanced toward Rachel. She had stopped in her tracks at the top of the stairs, her eyelids lowered.

"And Chadwick stays," Gallant added.

"Now?"

"He's got his gear and his orders. He's staying."

It was final, no mistake. George met Gallant's eyes. "Yes, sir. But…"

"What?" Gallant snapped. His amiability was wearing a little thin.

"We don't even have a bed for him," George said.

"Yes, well, I assumed he'd be sleeping in your bed tonight, Lieutenant." The captain frowned and lowered his voice. "I'm making a concession here, Hudson. I have to answer for my decisions. Please don't make me regret this one."

"No, sir."

Gallant turned to Rachel, smiling. "Ensign Whitney. Ready to lead our expedition?"

"Yes, sir." She stepped forward, smiling brightly.

"You take this part of the island, and we'll take the east end," George said to Rachel. "Cover everything this side of the spring."

She nodded, and George determined not to worry about her. Neither half of the island search would be easier than the other, and he had his own reasons for picking the east end for himself.

It was too bad he and Pierre couldn't execute the comprehensive search on their own. He didn't want the captain's men to risk their necks, and he didn't want to reveal all his secrets to them. But there was just too much ground to cover, and they really needed the extra manpower to get the search done properly before dark.

He would set the sailors to searching the jungle while he made a quick trip to a small cave he knew. If a desperate man approaching from the sea happened upon his emergency stash at the opposite extremity of the island, the installation would be in danger. But he didn't want to reveal that hideaway to anyone, even American sailors.

❦

Rachel had the captain, Chadwick, and two other men to direct, and she laid out her plan as it formed in her mind, trying to keep her nerves in check.

"We'll begin here in the immediate area of the house," she said to Gallant. "Then two can search the boat landing area and the others take the cliff path on the south side of the house. There's a large, rocky area along the shore that will be difficult to search. It may take several hours."

Gallant looked up at the thickening clouds. "We'd better get at it. I don't like the way the wind has picked up."

"Yes, sir. Ensign Belanger tells me we're in for a storm tonight."

She checked her pistol and radio, and fastened the collar button of her wool jacket. When they had searched every conceivable hiding place around the building, she sent the captain and two men around toward the descent along the cliff.

"The submarine was there, due west of the point. Lieutenant Hudson found small pieces of debris on the shore there. We'll check the boat landing and the windmill area, sir, and then come around to meet you on the rocks."

"Can you get around there?" Gallant asked with concern. "It looks treacherous from the sea."

"The tide's more than half out. It's rough, but we can do it. Take care on the rocks. Those below the high water line tend to be slippery."

They separated, and she led Chadwick to the head of the steep path that led down to the cove.

"I'll check the rocks along there," she said, pointing to the other side of the path. "You take this side, and beat those bushes between the path and the windmills. We don't go over there much. Watch for flattened grass. There aren't any large animals on the island, so if it looks like something's been there, it was a human. And there's a small shelter down there at the shore, where our boat is housed. Make sure you look inside."

Chadwick nodded and left her halfway down the path to carry out her instructions. As he worked his way across the rocky slope toward the green area, Rachel rounded the shore of the cove, peering between the slabs of rock.

After twenty minutes, she was on her way back, higher up, but the slope was so steep she couldn't imagine a waterlogged man who had survived an explosion dragging himself up there. If anyone made it this far, he'd stick to the path or just hole up above the tide line.

"Anything?" she asked, as Chadwick rejoined her.

He shook his head.

"All right, let's go this way, and we'll meet up with the captain. Follow me for this first part. It's tricky, and I don't want you breaking your leg." She smiled inwardly, remembering how offended she'd been when George had said much the same to her on her arrival. She tried to push from her mind what she had heard inside and the devastating knowledge that George would be leaving within hours.

Chadwick scrambled doggedly after her, around the bottom of the bluff. She stopped periodically to scan the terrain and examine niches capable of concealing a body, and she saw that Chadwick was panting.

After they had negotiated a rough stretch, she thought he needed a breather, and she sat down on a rock. "So, you're staying with us."

"That's right. Sounds like you'll be giving the orders around here after tomorrow."

Rachel wasn't sure how to answer that. If she assured him things were very informal on Frasier, he might take it as license to be lax or aggressive, and she didn't want to be taken advantage of because of her inexperience or her gender. This was no time for meekness, she decided. "If things go that way, I'll be showing you the ropes."

"First name basis," Chadwick said.

Rachel gazed at him, trying to project coolness. "That's a privilege that comes with friendship."

"I heard you wear civilian clothes a lot of the time." His eyes raked her from head to toe, and she was glad for her jacket. Unwelcome memories flew into her mind.

"We make exceptions when we have company." She got to her feet. "Come on. The wind's picking up."

By the time they worked their way around the shore beneath the house, the tide was nearing its lowest ebb. Skirting a treacherous jumble of rocks that was normally underwater at the base of the cliff, she saw Captain Gallant far out on the rocky shore. The wind was strong and gusty now. There was little vegetation on this barren end of the island, making the landscape bleak against the roiling sea.

She turned to Chadwick and saw that he was limping slightly. "You okay?"

"Roger. Just slipped a little."

"Looks like the storm's coming in."

He scanned the sky. Off to the west and south helicopters passed slowly over the water, and Rachel could make out two boats patrolling the area where debris was most likely to be found.

"They'll call this off," Chadwick guessed.

"Probably. Come on. We've got a lot more ground to cover."

⇛

She was exhausted when they toiled back to the house three hours later. George and his crew were not in evidence, and she called him on her radio.

"We're ending our search, Lieutenant. The captain doesn't want to risk delaying the chopper any longer in this weather."

"Affirmative," George replied. "We'll be there in ten minutes."

She turned to Gallant. "Come on in, Captain. I'll put some coffee on."

The four men followed her into the galley.

"Make yourselves at home," she invited as she removed her jacket. "The head's that way."

She started the coffeemaker and opened a cupboard door, frowning at the meager supply of crackers and canned goods.

"Can I feed you gentlemen?"

"We'll need to get off as soon as possible," Gallant said. "This wind is getting dangerous."

"Going to be a real howler," she agreed. Chadwick was watching her, and his direct stare made her uneasy. The other men were looking around, and that wasn't any better. She felt exposed as one of them squinted at the note she'd left Pierre on the refrigerator the previous night: *Mon ami,* North by Northwest *again tonight? R.* Good grief, they could certainly speculate on what that meant!

She set a box of crackers on the table and got out mugs, powdered milk, and a bit of the precious sugar.

"If you'll excuse me, I'll take Belanger a cup of coffee." She made her escape and hurried down the stairs with a covered mug.

"At last!" Pierre cried. "I was getting cabin fever."

"Sorry we were so long." She put the mug in his hand.

"Any survivors?"

"Not that we know of. We found one unrecognizable piece of plastic that may or may not have come from the sub. Gallant's taking it with him. Pierre, please let me stay down here. I can't stand being under the captain's scrutiny any longer."

"What's wrong?"

"They're taking George off the island." She gripped his shoulder. "What will I do without either of you?"

"Are you sure?" He darted a glance at her before looking back to the console.

"Positive. Gallant brought us a new guy—Chadwick. He's staying here tonight, and tomorrow they're coming back for you and George. Another man's supposed to be coming out from Hawaii."

"What's Chadwick like?"

She shrugged. "First impressions?"

"Yes."

"Predatory."

Pierre's injured look stabbed her. "*Cherie,* they mustn't do this to you."

She raised her chin. "It's part of the assignment. This is normal. We've lost sight of that, Pierre. We don't know what normal is anymore."

"I've never seen you like this before, wanting to hide in the basement."

"It's almost time for my regular shift," she said.

Pierre's intent gaze pierced her. Those soft brown eyes could look deep into her heart now, he knew her so well. She sighed. "You're right. I was uncomfortable up there."

"Are you scared of him?"

"I don't know yet. He just seemed…well, it's hard to say. He's not as tall as you, but he's got twenty pounds on you." She grimaced. "I don't know why George wanted me up there instead of you."

"Perhaps he was preparing you for leadership, duckling."

She winced. "Oh, please. Don't *you* start on the pet names."

Pierre's eyes widened. "*Pardonnez moi.*"

She waved one hand in dismissal. "Sorry. It started with the *pumpkin* thing."

"You prefer vegetable names?"

Her laugh turned into a marginally hysterical giggle. "Don't call me your little cabbage. This isn't funny."

"You're right."

She sighed. "Captain Gallant kept looking at me like he was sizing me up, wondering if I could handle being the senior officer here."

"Is George in yet?"

"He wasn't when I came down."

Pierre stood up. "You take over the watch. I'll go up and see what I can learn. I didn't expect to be leaving so soon."

"The captain wanted to take George immediately, I'm sure of it. They were discussing it when I went upstairs earlier. George told him he needed time to brief me, so they're coming back tomorrow to get you both."

"Not if this storm keeps moving in its current direction." Pierre took a last glance at the radar. "I'd better get up there."

"Hey, wait!" Rachel scooped up the forgotten provisions list. "Take this to Gallant. It will save me trying to put it through by radio in the middle of a typhoon."

FIFTEEN

Pierre came down the stairs an hour later. Rachel had seen the helicopter leave on her screen. She heard him talking to Chadwick as he approached and knew she would have to wait until later for another private talk.

"I'll get you set up here. There shouldn't be many surprises." Pierre walked up behind Rachel. "How we doing? Everything under control?"

"Yes. All vessels are standing off. The *Bush* radioed a few minutes ago that they have to abandon the air and sea search."

"The captain told us they'd probably head for shelter at Wake," Pierre said. "They'll be back as soon as possible, but it may be several days."

Rachel sighed. "The sentence is deferred."

"Why don't you run upstairs and eat something?" Pierre suggested.

"I'm good for a few more hours here," she protested. "You've had a long day."

"No, it's okay. George needs to go over some things with you. I'll run through the routine with Chadwick."

She stood up reluctantly. As much as she wanted George to stay on the island, she wasn't sure she was ready to go one-on-one with him. She was tired and hungry, and she knew it wouldn't take much for him to set off her anger and frustration again. But she also knew she would risk that to spend time with him.

"You've met Chadwick," Pierre said as she turned toward them.

"Yes. Hello again."

"It's Brian." He smiled, and he wasn't so bad-looking, she thought. Sandy hair, straight nose, broad shoulders. Was there such a thing as too friendly? No, Pierre had welcomed her wholeheartedly, and she hadn't felt this way.

She nodded. "See you later."

When she reached the main level, George was coming down the hall from his room wearing a black T-shirt and his favorite camo pants.

"Rachel, we need to talk."

"Sure. Can I just get out of this uniform?"

"Fine. I'll fry some Spam. You hungry?"

"Starving." She walked briskly to her room. Funny how a man could make every nerve more sensitive. Chadwick's presence had brought on a wary uneasiness. Being in the same room with George used to make her bristle, but now it filled her with anticipation. What made the difference? They both were dangerous, she supposed, but she trusted George. Was it just because she didn't know Chadwick?

George was an enigma. She was still finding out how little she knew about him. Even though he could make her furious without even trying, she was drawn to him as she'd never been drawn to a man before. His stubbornness and confidence could drive her crazy, but gradually she was beginning to see those qualities as tenacity and leadership. The desire to be near him increased inexorably. She found herself hurrying to get back to the galley, even if they ended up doing battle royal.

She reached for her pink blouse, but thought better of it. That particular shirt seemed to guarantee a frown from George. She pulled on a navy blue knit top and soft jeans. The knees were so thin she was sure the threads would give way soon, but nothing else she owned was as comfortable. She took out her braid and brushed her hair smooth. Even as she worked, she hoped George would see her intense desire to contribute to the operation for what it was, not the selfish ambition he seemed to imagine. And she thought he was avoiding her less. He had even praised her once yesterday. It was precious little, but precious indeed.

❧

The food was nearly ready when George heard Rachel approaching. Inside him a warm satisfaction battled with regret. He turned from the stove as she entered the galley. She looked so normal. What would it be like to come home from a nine-to-five job to Rachel?

"Long day," he said as their gaze met. Her eyes were a soft gray-blue in the subdued light.

Rachel smiled grimly. "It sure has been. What do we need? Two plates and forks? How about Pierre and Chadwick?"

"They ate while I was closing the storm shutters."

"Big gale tonight." Rachel opened the silverware drawer.

"Maybe big enough to keep me here a few days."

She turned toward him, and they looked at each other.

"George, I—"

"What? Don't tell me you'll miss me."

"Maybe I will."

"Sure. You'll miss arguing with me."

She eyed him narrowly. "Are you trying to make me mad again?"

He held her gaze for a moment and then shook his head. "No." He turned the slabs of meat in the frying pan. "Guess I'm just getting a little apprehensive. This may be my last couple of days here. Ever."

Rachel drew a ragged breath. "I'm sorry."

He shrugged but didn't look at her. It would be foolish to try to get close to her now, but the desire was greater than ever. "Norton and I understand each other, but we don't see eye to eye on this isolation thing."

"It sounded to me like they'll let you come back after you take a leave. A few weeks, maybe."

George opened his mouth and closed it again, and then he turned toward her. The knowledge that he would be leaving her, along with the island that was now part of him, filled him with sorrow. At that moment he couldn't imagine life off Frasier, and the prospect of life without Rachel was even more bleak. "I think I'd better fill you in on a few things, just in case."

"You mean there's more I don't know?" Rachel's eyes widened. She seemed ready to prickle or relax, depending on the cues he gave her.

"Just a couple small things." He turned off the burner and brought the frying pan to the table. "There's the paperwork. You'll have to keep the log and check in with Pearl once a week."

She nodded. "Can you show me the log later? I want to do it right."

"Sure. Look, if there are going to be four of us here for a few days, we ought to change the schedule. It will give us a break, and Chadwick can work in slowly."

"That sounds good. Six-hour shifts?"

"Why not?" He sat down and lifted two slabs of Spam and some brown rice onto her plate. "I'll take my regular shift tonight, and when Pierre relieves me at 0600, we'll start the new schedule. Chadwick can take over at noon, and you at 1800."

"Do you realize what that will mean?" she asked.

George paused with the spatula in midair. "What?"

"You and Pierre and I can sit down like a family at this table tomorrow at noon, provided you guys haven't left yet."

He smiled. "That will be strange. But good, I think."

She nodded. "I wish we could have done it before. The only place all three of us have been together is in the control room."

He laid the spatula down and reached for his fork. "Well, it looks like you'll be in charge when we go."

Rachel sighed, and he caught a glimpse of apprehension in her features. Her uneasiness about the coming changes in personnel was sparking protectiveness in him, and he wasn't used to that. He hadn't felt this custodial since his sister, Judy, had been attacked by a vicious dog and he'd had to beat it off with a big stick.

"Chadwick and I are the same rank," Rachel said.

"But you've got seniority. Don't let him put anything over on you."

"I…I can handle it, George."

"He doesn't strike me as the meek type." He looked deep into her eyes. She had a determination that he admired, but sheer willpower couldn't withstand a stronger force, any more than his windmills could outlast a typhoon. He couldn't let go of the fear that she wouldn't be strong enough. He ran a hand through his hair. "I hate this."

Her eyes darkened. "If *you* don't think I can do it—"

"It isn't that," he said quickly.

"No? Then what is it? You've never thought I was officer material."

George struggled with that, wondering if he was being fair in his assessment. "That's not so. It's the situation." Ordinarily, Rachel would do just fine in a position of command, he was certain. She was clever and able to think ahead. But isolated, beyond the reach of support, where she could be overpowered…

He remembered being threatened by an older boy when he was in middle school. It had taken weeks of frightened fumbling to realize he could stop the intimidation by not reacting to it outwardly. Slowly he had groped his way into confidence. That lesson had stood him in good stead as a naval officer.

He saw that Rachel was waiting anxiously to hear what he would say. "You need to project authority from the start and expect them to respond. After that, it all depends on the men."

She nodded. "If they can accept the situation and make an effort to get along, everything will be great."

He lowered his eyelids as guilt washed over him. "Rachel, I haven't exactly tried to get along with you. I'm sorry about that."

She sat staring at him for a moment and then looked down at the rice cooling on her plate. "I knew you didn't like me from day one, but…I've tried, George. I'm sorry if I didn't meet your expectations of a good team member."

The regret was enormous. What had he thrown away? For almost six months, she'd been right here in the house with him, and he'd insulated himself from her warmth and friendship. He was jealous of Pierre, no question about that. Pierre was so comfortable with her. They got along like two happy children who hadn't learned to worry yet or analyze the way other people made you feel. They simply enjoyed each other. He sat alone in the control room nights, knowing they were upstairs throwing popcorn at each other and watching *Toy Story* over and over.

Pierre had told him all the intimate things Rachel had done for him. *She's enslaved you,* George had growled when Pierre related how he'd sung "The Star-Spangled Banner" with her. She even cut his hair now. So what if she did a better job than he could? That wasn't the point. He didn't know how Pierre could sit there cracking jokes while Rachel stood close to him with her hands in his hair. Just thinking about it made him want to get up and leave the room—or kiss her.

He realized he'd been staring at her mouth and looked away. "I was an idiot."

She started to protest, but he waved his hand to stop her. "You were right when you said I didn't respect you at first, but that was foolish of me. You've done well. I should have accepted you and prepared you for this moment." She stared at him, and her obvious shock made him feel even more guilty. He shook his head. "I was kidding myself not to think one of my subordinates would take over my job someday. I regret not helping you and teaching you every aspect of this command. Don't be like me, Rachel. Look at the new personnel as skilled people who are here to help you do the job. Make sure Chadwick's ready when you leave next spring."

She nodded slowly, her eyes riveted on his. *She's taking everything*

I say at face value. The thought shocked him. She used to pick everything he said to pieces, looking for ulterior motives, but somewhere in the past five months that had changed. He wasn't sure when, but her irritability had softened and evaporated.

He wished he'd done things differently. At least he had the chance to give her a few words of advice. "You might want to start out with discipline a little tighter than we're used to. You don't want them to think they can wipe their feet on you."

"What if they won't listen to me?"

"I don't know. Call Norton, I guess." But it wasn't whether they would listen that had him worried. He'd seen Chadwick look Rachel over with great interest. She was too young and beautiful to be put in command of a couple of louts like Chadwick on this remote post, even for a short time. He sighed and filled his coffee mug.

They both knew that if she had to resort to calling the commander, her Navy career would stall. Wariness was written all over her face. George tried not to think that Chadwick might get out of line and try to bully her.

"I never expected to be the senior person here." She stared down at her slender hands.

George nodded soberly. "It's quite a shock, isn't it?"

She took a deep breath. "You and Pierre should pack tonight, in case they come back tomorrow."

"They're halfway to Wake. This storm means business."

"So, you'll have three or four days?"

"At the most. Time enough for me to size up this new man, and for you to write some nice, long letters to the people you love."

Rachel nodded. "Will you take a letter to my friend on the *Bush?* Ensign Taber."

George swallowed. So there it was. Her heartthrob who wasn't in Oregon was right there on the ship that would take him away from her. The spark of hope he had tried not to nurture dimmed. "Sure."

She bit her lip. "Look, is there anything I can do to help you get ready? Do you need laundry done?"

"I'll take care of it." The thought of her handling his clothing was unsettling.

"No, seriously. Just give it to me tonight."

George shook his head. "It's going to be too wet to dry clothes for the next few days. I can do it on the ship."

"All right. If there's anything else…"

"I can't think of anything." George ran his hand through his hair. He knew his nerves were showing, and he didn't like that, but he couldn't help it. He was losing her. Her and Pierre at the same time.

"You need a haircut," she suggested.

"I—" He picked up his fork and stabbed a bite of Spam. "No, thanks. That's…that's good of you to offer, but—"

"But what? I saw the hatchet job Pierre did on you the last time."

He couldn't look at her, but looked past her, and realized he was holding his breath. He exhaled with a sigh.

"Did I say the wrong thing?" she asked softly. "I mean no disrespect, sir."

He couldn't help smiling. "Since when?"

Her face flushed, and she ducked her head. "I'm sorry, George. Really. I know I've said some things in the past that I had no call to say. Under other circumstances, I'd have been busted for saying those things to my CO."

George's lips twitched. "That day Pierre shot down the plane."

"Yes. That's an example."

He laughed. "Well, if it helps, you're not the only one who thinks I'm a megalomaniac. That's part of why they're making me leave, although Gallant didn't come out and say it."

"Great. You have to leave because you're too authoritative, and I'll have to if I'm too soft." Her plaintive expression shredded his heart.

"Maybe we'll meet up at some shrink's office in San Diego," he said with a smile, and then he sobered. "Rachel, I'm concerned about this whole thing, about leaving you here with two new men. We've always brought one new recruit on at a time. You need to have one old hand here to give you support."

She eyed him from beneath lowered lashes, and he wondered what she was thinking.

"I'll have to take it as it comes. Get tough if the situation calls for it. What else can I do?"

He leaned back in his chair. "Gallant did mention the possibility of leaving Pierre here until I came back."

"Really?" She sat up in an eager jolt and then grimaced in dismay. "No, we can't ask him to do that! I mean, the wedding. Marie's got it all planned."

"And you'd have to tear me limb from limb," George said with another smile.

"Well, yes. There is that."

He pressed his lips together, still smiling, and the glitter in her eyes made his heart lurch. "If you stand up to these guys like you did to me, you'll be okay, Ensign."

"Really?"

"Really. You could bring a rampaging Hun to his knees when you're angry."

❧

George was uneasy as he went to take up watch. He'd left Rachel smiling, but he still didn't like the prospect of leaving her vulnerable. It was true she had cowed him once or twice, but his surrender had been willing. He hadn't had a meanness in him that wanted to crush her.

He wondered about Chadwick. Beneath his outward cockiness, there had to be a decent man. The Navy considered him officer material. Surely Chadwick and Rachel could find some level of professional courtesy that would let them work together without the friction he and Rachel had experienced.

He thought back to that day when she'd confronted him in the control room after Pierre's kill. More than anything, he'd been ashamed of himself for giving her cause to despise him. He'd fought his attraction to her since she came and had thought he was successful. Now he knew that wasn't true. He wanted her to look up to him, not just because of his rank, but because she found him worthy of her respect. He couldn't expect more than that, if she'd lost her heart to another man. That knowledge brought on a bleak regret that caused his spirits to dive to a new depth.

It's bad enough I have to leave here with my future up in the air. I have to go away knowing she'll never feel about me the way I feel about her. He inhaled deeply and determined to put all thoughts of her aside for the next few hours.

"How's it going?" he asked when he hit the bottom of the stairs. Chadwick was wearing the hydrophone headset, and Pierre was sitting beside him.

"The last we heard, the *Bush* will be back Thursday if at all possible. And other than Typhoon Gabriella, all is calm."

"Two days."

Pierre nodded.

"All right, you guys get some sleep. Chadwick, I'm sorry, but you're going to have to sleep on the floor tonight. I put some blankets on a chair in the sitting room."

"No problem. And it's Brian."

George nodded curtly.

As Pierre and Chadwick headed for the stairs, George settled at the monitoring station. Pierre hung back.

"Go ahead up, Brian. I'll be right there. Maybe we'll make some popcorn."

When Chadwick was out of earshot, he looked expectantly at George.

"You, me, and Rachel, noon tomorrow in the galley," George said. "Chadwick gets the 1200 to 1800 shift."

"Sounds good. You think we can do anything about this?"

"I don't have a choice." George looked up at his friend.

"She's afraid of him, George."

"She can handle it."

Pierre hesitated. "That depends on him and the other new man, doesn't it?"

George winced. "I hate this." He considered refusing to leave Frasier, but that wouldn't help. They would all think he'd tipped over the edge of sanity because he'd been on Frasier too long. If he disobeyed Norton's orders, his career would be over. How would that help Rachel?

Rachel was wiping the last dish when she heard movement in the sitting room. She looked through the doorway and saw Chadwick spreading a blanket on the rug. She ducked back before he saw her and put the plate in the cupboard.

She decided to breeze on through to the hallway and go straight to her room. If he said anything, she'd call "good night" and keep going.

It wasn't the way she had hoped the evening would end. She'd been longing all day for a heart-to-heart with Pierre, but she didn't want to stay up and socialize with Chadwick hovering. She took a deep breath and walked through the doorway.

Chadwick looked her way. "Hey, Ensign. Is there a place to get a shower?"

She broke stride. "Sure. It's downstairs. Uh, is Pierre coming up? Maybe he could show you."

"No problem," Pierre said heartily from the stairway door, and Rachel could have kissed him.

"Your timing is a beautiful thing," she whispered, her back to Chadwick, and Pierre gave her his killer smile.

"Grab your stuff, Brian. We may not have hot water by morning.

If we have to use the generators, the water heater is one of the first things we shut down."

Rachel fled to her room before either man could speak to her again. She ought to sleep, she knew, but her stomach was churning. She picked up the sketchbook George had brought her a few weeks earlier and opened to the first blank page. Sitting on the edge of her cot, she began to draw with firm strokes.

A knock on the door startled her. She jumped, holding the sketchbook close to her chest.

"Who is it?"

"C'est moi!"

She opened the door. "Come on in."

Pierre stepped over the threshold and looked around warily. "Are you hiding?"

"Yes."

He laughed. "Well, Brian's in the shower. We ought to have a few minutes' peace."

"I don't like him."

Pierre shrugged. "I know, but you have no choice."

She nodded. "I know that, and I'll deal with it, but…you're a person I can be honest with, and I wanted to register that."

He came a step toward her. "I understand."

"You didn't tell George, did you?"

"You mean…"

"What I told you while he was gone."

"No. I will never tell anyone."

"Thank you." She turned toward the window. "We can't watch movies with Chadwick sleeping out there."

"Well, I'm beat tonight, anyway."

"Me too," she admitted. "There was one thing I wanted to ask you, though."

"What is that?"

"Pierre, we're good friends."

"Very good friends."

"Sit down, please." She sat on the cot, and he pulled her folding chair over beside it, facing her. She looked at him long and hard and then swallowed. "If you fell wildly, deeply in love with an acquaintance of mine, and there was something about her that I thought might affect your feelings for her, I would tell you."

Pierre stared at her in bewilderment. "Yes, I suppose so."

"Wouldn't you do the same?"

His eyebrows lowered. "Are we talking about George?"

"Who else?"

"Your feelings are that definite?"

"Seems crazy, doesn't it?"

"No, not really."

She rested her hand lightly on his shoulder. "Thank you. I hoped you would understand."

"I didn't tell him."

"Not that. It's something else. Something about him."

"All right," Pierre said slowly. "What is it you want to know?"

"Look at me."

"I'm looking." Their eyes locked.

"Is George married?"

"Married?" Relief flooded his face. "Of course not. What made you ask?"

Rachel hesitated. "He...he wears a ring with his dog tags. It looks like a wedding ring."

She waited silently, afraid she would cry if she said another word. The wind howled around the house, whistling at the shutter that covered her window.

Pierre's brown eyes were sad, like a bassett hound's, she thought. Was she intruding where she shouldn't?

"You need to know this?"

"I...thought I did. What do you think?"

"I think..." He studied her for a moment. "*Cherie,* I think that you will not be hurt by not knowing. Unless he wishes to speak of it, of course."

"But…I can't ask him."

"Why not?"

"I don't know him well enough. We don't discuss personal things like that."

"Perhaps, when you know him better…" Pierre said gently.

"But he's leaving. I may never see him again." She felt tears welling up in her eyes. Exasperated, she laid the sketchbook down and reached for the tissues on the crate that was her nightstand.

"Then I ask you, how would it benefit you to know this private thing about him? Any more than he would benefit by knowing your secret?"

She pulled in a choppy breath, unable to answer.

Pierre picked up the sketchbook and turned it toward him. Rachel started to reach for it but stayed her hand. Pierre was nodding as he studied her new drawing of George in his uniform, his hat brim shadowing his brow. She'd given him a haircut on paper, so he wouldn't look shaggy, and a smile that was only for her.

"It's a good likeness," Pierre murmured, "and it reveals much." He looked up and grinned. "About you, *cherie*."

"Perhaps I'd better destroy it."

"Will it bring you comfort while he is gone?"

"I don't know."

"Best keep it."

The wind's steady accompaniment to their conversation was interrupted by a loud, rattling crash that shook the house, making Rachel jump up.

"What was that?"

"Windmill number one, I'd say."

SIXTEEN

"Macaroni again?" Pierre carried a chair from the sitting room into the galley so they could all sit around the small table.

"Sorry. Our options are limited." Rachel drained the canned beets and set the dish on the table. George turned on the light that hung low over the dining corner. Rain pelted against the storm shutter.

"The worst part is, we're left with all the things we don't like," Pierre complained.

"That's because you ate what you did like first," she pointed out.

"Children, children," George intoned, taking his seat. "Be thankful we haven't run out of toilet paper. May I remind you, Pierre, that you did the ordering last spring?"

"Well, I sure didn't order three cases of beets."

Rachel touched Pierre's sleeve. "I think you're a bit nervous, am I right? Heading back to civilization. Maybe even prenuptial jitters?"

He looked from her to George and then reached for the pan of macaroni. "*Je le regrette.* It isn't that, but…may I speak freely?"

Rachel glanced toward the doorway. "I think you can."

"George has no choice about leaving."

"That's true," the lieutenant said impassively, but Rachel thought she detected sorrow or regret in his eyes. Maybe he was just tired.

He'd had less than six hours of sleep, but he insisted on being on time for this meeting.

"I refuse to leave." Pierre dipped the spoon into the macaroni Rachel had prepared with powdered cheese mix, dry milk, and margarine. She watched him heap his plate, unable to believe what she'd just heard.

"You can't."

"I can. I do."

She turned to George. "Say something."

George looked across at Pierre. "Thank you, my friend."

Rachel's jaw dropped as Pierre nodded and went on calmly preparing his plate. "No. You can't do this, Pierre. You *need* to go home. And you!" She rounded on George, her hands clenching. "You promised me!"

"I did no such thing." His injured tone made her look away and catch her breath.

"Well, you should have!"

"It's only for a short time," Pierre insisted.

"You don't know that. They might keep George away for months!" *Or forever*, she thought bleakly, but she wouldn't say that in front of George. She knew how deep his attachment to Frasier was.

"I'm not leaving you here alone," Pierre said.

George sat silent, staring at his empty plate.

"I won't be alone," Rachel choked.

"I stand corrected," Pierre said. "But that, after all, is the point. If you could do this job single-handedly, there would be no problem."

"You think these men would jeopardize their careers by intimidating me?"

"Chadwick does that already," Pierre replied. "He's not even trying, and you shake like a leaf when he's near."

Rachel stood up. "I won't let you do this. It's not fair to...anyone!"

"Sit down," George said.

Rachel glared at him.

"Come on, this isn't going to turn into a shouting match. If you want to prove you're a rational adult and can run this place, sit down and make your point logically."

His condescension infuriated her, but she knew that storming out of the galley would only confirm his suspicions that she was a spoiled child. She stood for ten seconds, glowering malevolently at him.

Pierre swallowed and touched her hand. "*Viens, mignon!* I'm the one who has upset you. Don't be angry with George."

She plunked down into her chair, and George picked up the serving spoon.

"Macaroni and cheese?"

Rachel closed her eyes, trying to bring the riot of emotion under control.

"This is your fault," she said between her teeth.

"How can you say that?" Pierre cried. "George has not—"

George silenced him with a small gesture. He leaned toward Rachel and said softly, "You said it's not fair. To whom?"

She drew a deep breath. "Well, Pierre, for starters. He's delayed his marriage six months already. I don't want to be the cause of another postponement. Then there's Marie. I wouldn't blame her if she couldn't understand this."

"Who said life has to be fair?" Pierre said lightly.

George frowned at him. "Go on, I'm listening."

Rachel sent up a quick prayer. *Lord, help me to speak to him wisely for once!* She looked into George's eyes. "It's not fair to me, either. It's special treatment. The Navy doesn't make special allowances like that for women. We've screamed and fought to be treated equally. You're saying I can't handle this."

George sighed. "I don't mean to disparage you, Rachel, but it scares the daylights out of me when I think of the regrets I could have if Pierre and I both leave here tomorrow."

She swallowed. "These guys have had training in human relations." She wiggled her fingers to make quotation marks in the air. "If they get out of line, I'll just have to remind them of that."

"What if it's too late?"

She pushed away the misgiving that said he was right. What if one of the new men became too aggressive and her fear took over? "Do you really think they'd do something blatant?"

"Who knows, if there's no man who outranks them?" George asked. "You hear things about men who take advantage of a situation. I don't like to think it would happen here, but I just don't know."

Apprehension had been nibbling at her confidence already, and George's words were feeding that. His gray eyes seemed to see the fear inside her. She glanced at Pierre, and he looked down at his plate. He wouldn't reveal her past wound, but she could tell he was thinking about it.

"If I'm going to be afraid of sailors, I've chosen the wrong career," she said.

"Do you *want* to be the top-rated person on this island?" George asked.

She pushed a beet slice around her plate with her fork. "If they brought another woman…"

"I asked Chadwick," Pierre said. "There were no women in his class for special training. Just six other men."

She raised her eyebrows. "Well, there was another woman in my class."

"She's on another assignment now. They won't fetch her to keep you company, *ma cherie.*"

"I can handle it." She turned toward George again, more confident. "Maybe it's a test for me."

George shook his head. "No, this wasn't planned. The submarine took everyone by surprise. If that hadn't happened, they'd have left me alone for a while."

"But I can do this. I know I can. Please don't tell me I can't."

George leaned toward her. "You're a competent woman, Rachel, and I think you'll do fine. But you've got to admit, this is an extraordinary situation. I feel Pierre's decision is a good one. It will give you a respite while you get to know the new personnel, whether I'm able to return or not. When Pierre goes, if you're the one in charge, you'll be ready."

"Fine." Rachel sighed. "Who ordered these stupid beets, anyway?"

The rain continued throughout the afternoon. George wandered restlessly through the house, going several times to the control room to check in with Chadwick, study the weather indicators, and test the radio. There were no incoming calls. The Navy was battened down in ports dotting the larger islands across the Pacific.

At 1500, Pierre corralled him and Rachel for a final screening of *Toy Story*. Rachel sat between them on the rug, alternately cheerful and despondent. She jumped up half an hour into the movie to remove her *bon voyage* cake from the oven.

Pierre cajoled her into a smile on her return. "You are the queen of cuisine, little cabbage. The smell of your creation is driving me wild."

"Doofus." She shoved him playfully and nestled in between him and George again.

"I speak the truth. George, back me up."

"No one else can do so much with so little," George said with a smile.

Her lip trembled, and he looked away. She sat quietly while the film lasted, bantering occasionally with Pierre, seeming content. George closed his eyes and leaned back against the wall, very aware of her sitting beside him, her shoulder not quite touching his.

When the movie ended, she stood up. "Guess we'd better get something to eat. I'm on duty in an hour."

"Rewind, please, Pierre." George got up and followed her to the galley.

She had the can opener out and had chosen corned beef hash and spinach for their supper.

"Wish we had something more festive," she sighed when George entered.

"Maybe they'll bring you some fresh fruit this time."

"Wouldn't that be great?"

"They know you'll be needing supplies soon." He leaned against the doorjamb, watching her. "They won't leave you here for months with nothing but rice and macaroni."

"I can't make frosting, but I think I can manage a weak glaze." She sniffed. "This cake was supposed to be for Pierre."

She turned away from him and spread the hash out in a skillet. George didn't dare think she was grieving over him. The possibility of her staying with no senior officer to keep discipline had her on edge, that was all. And there was the unknown man in her life. Pierre had said as much. *Her affections are engaged.* Maybe she was wondering how long it would be before she saw him again.

"So, is your outgoing mail ready?" he asked at last.

Her hands stilled, and it was a moment before she answered. "Yes, it's over here. I've been writing a rambling letter to my folks, but I sealed it this afternoon." She took two envelopes from on top of the microwave and held them out to him.

He couldn't help glancing down at them. *Ensign Heidi Taber.* His heart raced. "Anything else?"

She shook her head. "No. My mother will share the news with the rest of the family."

He stepped closer to her and put his hand to her chin, turning her head up so she would look at him. Was it possible? Had Pierre misunderstood? Her eyes met his for an instant, and she caught her breath and then looked away.

George stood very still, looking down at her as a tidal wave of emotion crashed over him. He wished he could tell her how hard leaving was going to be, because he was leaving her as well, not just the island. If he knew she had feelings for him… But, no. Her animosity was gone, but he couldn't hope for more.

He smiled ruefully. "I guess if Pierre were the one leaving, you'd be crying buckets."

"George, don't. I don't want to be all puffy-eyed when I go down there to relieve Chadwick, okay?" Her gaze flickered to his and slid away again.

"Sure. Just trying to lighten the mood."

Tears ran down her cheeks then. He watched her uncertainly as she grabbed a dish towel and wiped her eyes with it.

He bit his lip. How much of this turmoil was for him, and how much was for Pierre, he wondered. "Rachel, I didn't ask Pierre to do this."

She picked up the can opener and sank the blade violently into the rim of the can of spinach.

"It was his idea."

She didn't speak or look at him. He waited, expecting her to explode, maybe to accuse him of lying. Her shoulders trembled.

He took a deep breath. "Look, this may be the last chance we have to talk, and I don't want to go away with you angry."

"Fine."

He felt helpless, but he plunged on. "There's one more thing I need to tell you. There's an emergency stash at the other end of the island, in a little cave above the high water mark. Matt Rubin and I made it the first month we were here, but we never had to use it. The entrance is kind of hard to find until you're right on top of it. It's down between some rocks. I checked it yesterday when we made the sweep, and everything was intact."

"You think we'll need it?" She still didn't turn toward him, but he had her attention now. He could tell by the way she raised her head when he mentioned the cave.

"I hope not, but the way things have heated up lately, I wanted you and Pierre to know it's there." *And if I never come back, the secret won't go with me.*

"Pierre doesn't know?"

"No. You're the only person I've told."

She was silent for the space of two breaths, and then she asked, "How do we find it?"

"Go to the coffee bush and sight straight east. You have to climb around on the seaward side, below it. It's rough, especially at high tide, but you can make it."

She nodded. "Thanks. I'll remember."

"Rachel."

She turned slowly toward him then, and a pang of anguish struck him. He would carry the image of her innocent, stricken face with him. If only he had made peace with her sooner! It was too little, too late.

She reached out and touched his forearm lightly, and he felt as if his skin were on fire.

Her eyes were dark with sorrow. "Midnight blue," he said almost inaudibly. He bent toward her, thinking all the while, *I can't do this.*

Her eyes flared in surprise, and her long lashes came down to veil them as his lips touched hers. He stood there motionless for an instant, willing himself to end it quickly, but when he felt her hands settle tenderly on his upper arms, he pulled her swiftly to him.

I can't do this, he told himself again, but the kiss lengthened, and her hands crept up to his neck. Her warm fingers twined in the back of his hair, where it was too long. He pulled away at last, still shocked that he had let it happen, and that she had too. She buried her face in the front of his camouflage T-shirt.

"I'm sorry," he said hoarsely. "I shouldn't—" He cleared his throat. "I shouldn't have done that." But he held her firmly against him, stroking her hair. The rich brown locks ran like silk through his fingers. "I'm sorry."

She drew a deep, ragged breath and pushed away from him, stepping back. "Listen, I need to do a couple of things before I go on duty." She dashed away a tear with the back of her hand. "Can you guys heat your own supper?"

"Sure." A great sadness was settling over him. "Go ahead. We'll be fine."

Rachel went quickly through the sitting room to the hallway. Pierre's door was open, but she didn't stop there. She went into the bathroom and ran cold water in the sink, blotting her face with a wet cloth. Her watch told her she had twenty minutes, and she despaired of looking normal when she faced Chadwick.

"Lord, help me," she whispered. "I've got to show my strength now, before George leaves. I can't let Chadwick see me as the weak link in this mission."

There was a lot more she wanted to talk over with God, but she didn't know where to start. Her heart hammered as the memory of George's kiss resurged. Had he instigated that or had she? It had come out of nowhere, or so it seemed. But in an instant that kiss had crystallized her fluid feelings for George. She would never be ambivalent toward him again.

She went to her room and pulled on a sweater. The sketchbook lay on top of the small pine dresser, and she opened it to the new picture of George. In the drawing he looked hopeful and confident that they could be happy together. The George in the picture wanted to be with her, to stay here with her and build a future.

But that wasn't the real George Hudson. The real George had kissed her on impulse and immediately regretted it.

"Are you truly sorry?" she whispered. "I don't think I can bear it if you are."

SEVENTEEN

It was another day and a half before the storm abated and the *Bush* was able to return. Rachel longed to talk to George, but he avoided her all day, or so it seemed to her. He'd slept through the morning and went directly to the basement when he got up, to make sure the generators were in top form. They were never alone together during that intervening day, and Rachel thought it was by design.

Late in the afternoon she put rice on to boil for their supper and sat at the table in the galley with her Bible. The wind still raged outside, and the rain beat on the shutters.

She couldn't keep her mind on her reading, and at last she gave it up. It was impossible not to think about George.

She tried to rationalize the kiss. He had reached out to her because he was nervous about leaving the familiar. Or maybe he had sensed her sadness and simply felt a need to comfort her. He certainly hadn't given any indication since it happened that it meant anything more personal than that.

He didn't come upstairs before she began her shift, and when she passed through the basement he looked up from his work just for a moment and nodded. She alternately brooded and prayed as she kept watch.

When he came to relieve her at midnight she searched his face. There was nothing there that said things had changed. He was his usual competent, taciturn self.

"George—" He already had the headphones on, and she hesitated beside his chair as he settled down for his watch.

He glanced up at her. "Get some sleep, Rachel," he said with a tight smile.

She waited only another instant. What was there to say, when he obviously didn't want to talk?

She lay awake for hours that night, knowing George was alert in the control room. Was he thinking about her?

She tossed fitfully, listening to the howling wind. Before dawn, she fell into a sleep of exhaustion. When windmill number two crashed to the earth in the early hours, she stirred and moaned, but didn't wake.

❦

The lights in the control room flickered and went out. The computers, radar, and sonar hummed on uninterrupted, and the battery-powered emergency lights came on, dim but steady.

George watched the monitors stolidly, refusing to think about kissing Rachel. It had been an error in judgment, no matter how glorious the moment had been. No way on earth was he going to repeat that blunder. It could mean his career, not to mention the consequences Rachel would bear if word got out. She must be thinking about that too. She certainly hadn't looked happy since it happened.

Pierre padded down the stairs a few minutes later.

"Everything all right down here?"

George stretched. "Yeah, we're fine. Better start the first generator if you want coffee."

"Heard from the *Bush?*"

"They're headed this way, although the seas are still high. They expect to be here by 1600 hours. I think Gallant's getting antsy."

"I hoped we'd come through with one windmill standing," Pierre said.

George frowned. "I thought it was letting up, but we must have had some big gusts. I'd better get out there this morning and see if they'll be able to put a helo down."

"With Chadwick, we ought to be able to clear the pad."

"I won't be here to help you make repairs." George scowled. "Maybe you should just leave the windmills down until I get back."

"They might use one of the helicopters to help us lift them today."

"If they're not in a hurry, sure. I'll ask Gallant."

Pierre nodded, looking over George's shoulder at the monitor that showed the boat landing. "They can't bring a boat in today. Not unless things calm down in a hurry."

"They want me out of here. If there's any way Gallant can put a Seahawk down, he will."

"It's not you personally. The Pentagon wants to know everything they can about that sub."

"Maybe." George wished he could read Earl Norton's mind.

Pierre straightened. "So, this is it. Your last shift."

"Looks like it."

"You talked to Chadwick?"

George nodded. "I told him to make the Navy proud and remember his training. You know, he doesn't seem like that bad a kid. A little cocky. If Rachel wasn't so edgy, I'd think everything would be all right."

"Are you sure it's not you who's edgy?"

George drew a deep breath. His chest hurt a little, thinking about Rachel and what the kiss had or hadn't meant to her. Should he take Pierre into his confidence on that? No. The fewer people who knew, the less chance for trouble.

"Maybe when she gets to know Chadwick a little better, she'll feel more comfortable," Pierre said.

"Let's hope so."

"George, I'm going to call Marie as soon as I can get clearance, but that may take several days. You won't forget to call her for me?"

"I'll try as soon as I reach Pearl."

"Thanks. I know she's going to be disappointed."

"I can never repay you for this," George said.

"Don't even think of it." Pierre shrugged. "Rachel probably doesn't need me. I think she's going to land on her feet."

George nodded. "In which case, your sacrifice is for nothing."

"It's good insurance, and it's only for a little while." Pierre smiled, and George almost believed that he'd be back on Frasier in a matter of weeks.

"I wish I could talk to her the way you do."

"What, stupid jokes and what kind of pizza we wish we had?"

"You know what I mean. You two are so comfortable together. No tension."

"Rachel makes you tense?" Pierre laughed and sat down on the edge of the radio desk.

"As if you didn't notice."

"She told me she offered to cut your hair, but you wouldn't let her."

George shifted in his chair, watching the radar screen. "That would be a little much."

"Well, you do need a haircut. Want me to do the job? You don't want to face Gallant looking like that."

"Sure. As soon as you get off today."

Pierre said softly, "She also told me you kissed her."

George sat still for a moment, allowing himself to think about it. It had been thirty-six hours, and he'd done his best to forget it, but he couldn't. It intruded on his thoughts over and over, especially during the tedious hours of the night watch. "That was a mistake."

Pierre folded his arms across his chest and cocked his head to one side. "A mistake? Want to rephrase that?"

George gritted his teeth. "I can't get involved with her. You know I can't."

"Whoa. At first you were certain she hated you. Now you know she doesn't, so you have to dredge up some other excuse to keep your distance."

"Come off it. You know I can't."

"Why not?"

"You know. Ethics, regulations, the whole nine yards." George glanced at his friend and then at the sonar. "There's Pam too."

Pierre shook his head. "Pam is gone, George. And she would want you to be happy."

⌒

Lieutenant Ellis frowned at his clipboard. "I'm supposed to leave a man and bring two back."

"Things have changed," George said. "Belanger's staying until I return. Captain Gallant and I discussed the possibility when he was here three days ago."

"I don't know," Ellis said doubtfully.

The new man, Greene, stood behind him, waiting to learn his fate. George appraised him. He was in his late twenties, small-framed and wiry, with glasses and coffee-colored skin.

"You've had the advanced training for this assignment?"

Greene met his eyes. "Yes, sir."

"You want to stay?"

"Yes, *sir*."

Ellis set his jaw. "I'm not taking him back."

"Hey, that's up to you," George said, "but Ensign Belanger isn't leaving today. Did you bring enough rations for four people for a month?"

"I…think so. The helo was loaded to capacity. Gallant had us pack a lot of food and medical supplies, and all the other things you asked for that we had on board. The rest will come out from Pearl in three weeks."

"When I come back," George said firmly.

"That's more than I can say, but Captain Gallant told me we were taking you and Belanger to Pearl and would be back here in three weeks. That's all I know."

George grunted. "All right. You go ahead and supervise the unloading. I'd like a few minutes to say goodbye to my staff."

Ellis snapped the case of the clipboard shut and adjusted his hat before he headed out into the drizzle. George went quickly down the stairs to the control room.

"Good luck, Brian. Looks like you are keeping the fourth man. Andrew Greene. You know him?"

"Yes, sir. We trained together." Brian started to rise.

"Don't get up," George said. "Keep your post."

"Yes, sir."

George shook his hand and went upstairs. Pierre and Rachel were waiting in the galley. He looked at their somber faces.

"Hey, don't look so happy. You get to keep your six-hour shifts."

Pierre grasped his hand. "I'll move into your room, George. Then you can have it again when you come back."

"Merci, mon ami." He was leaving a lot of personal gear behind, and he found the thought of Chadwick touching his things offensive.

"Chadwick can have my room, and we can partition off a corner of the sitting room for Greene," Pierre said. "The bedrooms are too small for two, but that will give him some privacy."

"It's that or the storage room, I guess."

"Right." Pierre glanced at Rachel, who was twisting the chain her dog tags hung from. Her tan was fading, and her face was pale.

"Use the books in my room," George said. "There should be a couple of new ones too, somewhere in the supplies they're unloading."

Pierre nodded. "I'll carry your gear out."

George waited until he had gone and a contingent of sailors had passed through the sitting room to go for another load of supplies.

"Guess this is it," he said softly.

Rachel raised her chin. "This isn't about you. It's about the mission. Remember that."

He nodded, unconvinced. "I'll tell them whatever they ask me about the operation."

"You're representing all of us." She smiled tremulously.

It wasn't at all what he wanted to talk about now, the debriefing and the operation. "Listen, I'll try to call you guys when I get a chance."

"Please do." She looked businesslike and untouchable in her crisp white uniform. Only her eyes gave her away, until she whispered, "We'll miss you."

"You'll be fine," he said.

"So will you. They don't know how strong you are, George. This island hasn't taken anything from you. It's made you better."

He looked off out the window. The storm shutters were down for the first time in days, and the daylight that streamed in seemed too bright. "You didn't know me before."

"No, but…there's nothing wrong with you, I know that. No matter how many psychologists they make you see, remember that."

"Thanks. That means a lot." He reached out tentatively, and touched her smooth cheek with his fingertips. She seemed to freeze, breathless, and he dared to run his fingers along her jaw, toward her ear, wondering if he could kiss her one more time. He hadn't planned to. Regulations were clear, and he might never see her again. But he wanted to, more than anything.

"Sir, Lieutenant Ellis says we're ready to take off."

George spun around and frowned at the sailor in the doorway. "Right with you."

The man looked at him, then at Rachel, nodded, and disappeared.

"He won't raise the windmills?" she asked.

"It's still too windy. And, anyway, there's a lot of welding to do. I gathered up all the small parts I could find this morning, but there was one component I couldn't locate." He realized he was rambling and staring into her eyes.

"You should go."

He nodded. "Yeah. I don't want Ellis on my case. Gallant will be bad enough, when I show up minus Pierre."

"Do you think they'll come back for him today?"

Her eyes were huge, and George thought she must be envisioning herself, Greene, and Chadwick alone on the island.

"No. Ellis has probably radioed the ship and told Gallant already."

She nodded. "I guess we'd know it by now if Pierre had been ordered to go. He'd have been in here getting his gear."

"As long as I leave, Gallant will be happy." He almost had his nerve up to kiss her when she stepped away.

"Goodbye, George. I…I won't go outside."

His regret became an ache. "So long." Her lower lip trembled, and he knew he couldn't linger or he'd have her in his arms when Ellis stormed into the room. He smiled ruefully and walked out.

⁂

The door to Rachel's room opened a crack, and she jumped and whirled toward it. Pierre was peeking in at her, where she lay on her stomach on her cot.

"Oh, it's you. You scared me."

"I'm sorry. I just wanted to see if you were all right. The Seahawk is on the ship."

She took a deep, shaky breath.

"I'm going to move into George's room now, and Chadwick can have mine, since he was here before Greene," Pierre said.

"All right, I'll help you. Is Greene going to sleep on the floor?" She pushed herself up and sat on the cot, brushing her hair back.

"They brought an air mattress. He can use that. We'll hang up a couple of blankets for now, and see if we can scare up anything to build a partition later."

"Whatever you think. Did you get mail?"

"No. You?"

She shook her head.

"We've got chocolate." His eyes glittered.

She tried to smile but couldn't. "What else?"

"Tomatoes and pineapple. New movies. The Three Stooges, John Wayne, and *Hello, Dolly.*"

She made a face. "No cartoons?"

"*Ma petite,* we got the Stooges. What more do you want?" Pierre's aggrieved look succeeded in drawing a smile.

"I'm so glad you stayed," she admitted.

"These guys may not be so bad. I think we should have a film festival tonight."

"All right." She sat on the edge of the cot and fumbled for her shoes. "We'll plan it around the end of my shift. We can watch one movie with Greene, and you can watch another with Chadwick when he gets off."

"Except that I'm taking over the graveyard shift. George suggested it."

"Do you think you should? You're not exactly a night owl."

"I'll get used to it."

"When things have happened around here, it's been during the morning shift," she said.

"That's why you're taking the 0600 to noon watch. Your eyes and ears are the best."

"You spotted that plane."

"And you unmasked the whale."

"Right. You work out the schedule and tell me when I'm up. I think I saw some Kool-Aid mix. I'll make cookies too."

"Paradise regained," Pierre sighed.

EIGHTEEN

Rachel kept busy through the early evening, baking cookies and taking a few hours in the control room to help make Pierre's adjustments in the schedule work. She was glad when he took charge of introducing Greene to the system.

"I'll get out and check all the solar collectors tomorrow," she told him that evening as he set up the first movie.

"Good. I think the rain's letting up," Pierre said.

"Are we supposed to brief these two on the firene?"

Pierre frowned. "George said to wait."

Rachel took a slow, deep breath. "I don't want to keep them in the dark."

"If George comes back, he'll do whatever Commander Norton tells him. He promised me that. And if not, then the new senior officer will receive orders on the issue. That may be you."

She nodded but couldn't return his smile.

Greene carried the tray of glasses and Kool-Aid in from the galley.

"What are we watching?" he asked.

"The Three Stooges." Pierre punched the play button and sat beside Rachel on the floor, with his back to the wall. Greene settled on her other side. He had a pleasant manner, but seemed still a little nervous, as if he was not sure where he fit in.

Rachel passed him the plate of oatmeal cookies. "I don't think we can get the windmills up without a helicopter."

"We can run off the generators for a few weeks," Pierre said.

"How does that affect the routine?" Greene asked.

Pierre shrugged. "No hot water. And we'll have to keep servicing the generators."

Rachel tried to give her attention to the movie, but her heart wasn't in it. Even with the two new men, the house seemed empty. Pierre and Greene guffawed at the Three Stooges' antics, but she wrapped her arms around her knees and sank into reverie. Her sense of loss was overwhelming. Pierre convulsed with laughter and threw her a sidelong glance. She quickly brushed away a telltale tear. He slid closer to her and draped his arm across her shoulders.

"He'll come back," he whispered in her ear.

She nodded and sat up straighter, trying to focus on Curly Joe.

When the video ended, Pierre pushed the rewind button. "Almost time for me to spell Brian."

Rachel jumped up. "I'll put some coffee in the thermos for you." She hurried to the galley, thankful to be out from under Greene's speculative eye. She fixed the thermos for Pierre and tidied the galley a bit, but her mind was on the ship bearing George farther and farther away. She knew she had to make the best of her new circumstances, so she pushed him out of her mind and went back to the sitting room.

"It's cold in here." She handed Pierre the thermos and a chocolate bar.

"Can we get more heat?" Greene asked.

"Better get another sweater," Pierre recommended. "We have a space heater, but with the windmills down and the sun hiding, we need to conserve fuel for the generators."

"Why can't we be warm all the time like Hawaii?" Rachel knew the bitterness in her voice had nothing to do with the weather.

Greene looked from her to Pierre. "We're north of there," he said hesitantly, as if he couldn't believe she didn't know that.

"Right." Rachel managed to regain her businesslike tone. "Take care, *mon ami*. Call me if you need anything."

Pierre bestowed one of his dazzling smiles on her. *"Bon nuit, mignon."*

He headed for the stairs, and Rachel went to her room for her U of O sweatshirt. The silence when she reentered the sitting room was thick.

"So, *Yellow Rose of Texas?*" Greene asked at last.

"Sure. Whatever you guys want. I don't think I'll watch it all. I need to be up early."

The machine clicked off, and Greene ejected the Three Stooges tape. "Are you and Belanger an item or what?"

Rachel felt hysteria threatening. Before she had formed a reply, Chadwick came out of the stairway.

"All right! Cookies and TV!" He plucked the video case from Greene's hand. "Oh, man. I was hoping they'd give us *Splash!*"

"You don't like Westerns?" Rachel asked brightly.

He turned, and she felt his look boring into her.

"I like whatever you like, Rachel." His smile was a challenge.

No, she couldn't sit down for an hour and a half with these two. "Hey, it's midnight, and I'm on duty in six hours. I'm going to get some sleep. Good night, fellas."

As she stepped into the hallway, she heard Chadwick say petulantly, "Some party."

❧

At 0530 Rachel left her cot and dressed quickly. She had the shutter open, but she could barely see in the gray light of dawn.

"Keep him safe, Lord," she whispered. She inhaled deeply and went on with her prayer. "Help me not to make any mistakes today. Please, Lord, I need to make good decisions, and sometimes I forget that."

She unlocked her door and tiptoed toward the galley. She'd never locked her door at night before Chadwick came, but now it was automatic.

Greene's privacy curtains partitioned his corner in the sitting room, and she thought she caught a faint snore. She rummaged quietly in the galley while the coffee brewed, and then she carried a laden tray below with her.

"Ah, sweet Rachel! Is that a grapefruit I spy?"

"Yes, and I commandeered the last two doughnuts. Stay and eat breakfast with me?"

"It will be a pleasure." Pierre slid the headphones down around his neck and eyed her critically. "How are you doing?

"I'm fine."

"You look awful."

"Thank you very much." She held out a plate with his half of the grapefruit.

"Go ahead," he said. "I'll keep watching while you eat."

"I guess *eating together* was a misnomer." Her first bite of the tart fruit was heaven. "They've got to find a way to resupply us more often."

"Maybe we could have a greenhouse."

"That's a great idea. Because without the vitamin tablets, we'd all have scurvy by now."

"What do you make of Greene?" Pierre asked.

She spooned out another section of grapefruit. "He's all right. Smart, observant. He thinks we're 'an item.' His words, not mine."

Pierre chuckled. "Well, that could come in useful."

"What do you mean?"

"If they think you are the love of my life, they won't mess with you."

"No!" she protested. "I'm not getting into one of those role-playing situations."

"No need. We're good friends. We'll just keep them guessing."

"I think Chadwick knows better, and Greene will ask him."

Pierre kept watching the screens, but his eyebrows arched. "You think Brian knows about you and George?"

"What about me and George? There's nothing between us."

Pierre let that pass. "Does Brian still get your hackles up?"

"Yes. Not the way George did. George used to make me livid. Brian just makes me...squirm."

Pierre nodded. "I think maybe a little romance developing between us would protect you."

"Absolutely not."

"For appearances, *mon enfant*. Nothing serious."

"What we have now is enough," she insisted. Pierre's occasional touches and terms of endearment must appear romantic to the outsiders. She didn't want to play games, and she didn't want anything to happen that Pierre would regret when he at last left the island. She touched his hand. "You need to keep Marie uppermost in your heart, dear friend."

He inhaled sharply. "It's been so long."

"I know. You should have gone yesterday."

"Too late to think about that, but...no, I'm sure I did the right thing. Marie will understand."

"Well, she wouldn't understand it if you pretended to be in love with me."

"All right," he conceded as she stood in preparation to swap places with him. "But if I let Bozo lay a hand on you before George gets back, what do you think my life is worth?"

"You make it sound as if he's commissioned you to be my bodyguard."

"Why else am I still here?"

"Pierre, look at me."

He stood up and reached for her hand. "*Ma petite,* you understand, don't you? If George comes back and I've let something happen to you, I'm a dead man."

"He told me he didn't ask you to stay. He knew you needed to go home! It's nice to think he cares about me, but how can you let him run your life like this?"

"No, no, *cherie.* I volunteered because I knew he would feel easier if I stayed here with you."

"I knew it. You don't think I'm fit for command."

"That's not true." Pierre sighed. "It was the look in your eyes when Chadwick came on to you. I couldn't help thinking, *If he looked at Marie like that…* And I knew you must be remembering what happened to you before. That is the only reason I'm here. It's not because of anything George said."

She sighed and sat down, reaching for the earphones. "It's probably all in my head. I'll look back on this later and see how foolish I was to be afraid of the new guy. But he was practically salivating last night, Pierre. I couldn't stay in the same room with him."

Pierre squeezed her shoulder. "It will be fine."

"I've got to stop being afraid." She studied his face for an instant. "I knew there could be personality clashes when I came here, but I never expected this. If they send in a new officer instead of George, what will I do?"

"You'll rise to your duty and perform it with excellence."

"Ah, *mon ami*, when you are gone…"

"You won't be alone. He'll be back."

Rachel sat still for a moment considering. "First you without George, then George without you. Do you think he and I can survive without you as a buffer between us? We'll destroy each other."

"I think that is past, *cherie*."

"He's always been so antagonistic. Until the last. I hoped he felt something for me. Besides antipathy, I mean."

Pierre patted her shoulder. "You were not mistaken."

Rachel found it hard to take a deep breath. "If I could just be sure. Because he seemed like he wished he hadn't kissed me."

Pierre smiled. "Trust me on this one. He cares. And you…you have loved him since before you came."

She bit her lip. "You've known all along."

"Yes. For you and George, it's just a matter of time."

"But if they won't bring him back—"

"Where is your faith? He is returning."

NINETEEN

"Here are your orders." Gallant handed George the packet. "Norton's not happy that I left you out there Tuesday and had to go back for you. When we arrive in Pearl, an escort will take you straight to the airfield. You'll be flying to San Diego, then Atlanta and DC. When you get to Washington, they'll give you a few hours to sleep off the jet lag, and then they'll have you in the Pentagon."

Things were moving too fast. George hadn't had time to locate his sleeping quarters on the ship, and he was already on the bridge with Gallant.

"So, I won't be seeing Commander Norton?"

"The brass wants you in Washington yesterday. North Korea is screaming about that sub."

"Korea?"

"It was theirs. You blew a hole the size of Texas in the hull, but the crew on the *Simpson* located the wreckage before we had to pull out Tuesday evening. There's already talk of salvaging it. The Korean government wants her heroes back for burial."

"But they decided the plane we shot down last month was a Russian-built Iranian jet," George said.

"What can I say?"

George's brain went into overdrive. "Are Korea and Iran working together? Does the whole world know our secret?"

"Your speculation is as good as the next man's." Gallant seemed a bit put out that he had been kept out of the loop on the firene mission.

George nodded. "So, will I be riding back with you in a few weeks?"

"You got me. All I know is that I go back with the unit's supplies and a salvage rig, and bring Belanger off. And no excuses this time." Gallant eyed him testily. "You boys are mavericks. Norton shouldn't be letting you call the shots."

"Long-distance management is always difficult. The commander realizes we're closer to the situation and understand better what's needed."

Gallant shook his head in exasperation. "I can't help liking you, Hudson, and I know you were in on this from the beginning, but still…"

George shrugged. "Just trying to do my duty to the best of my ability."

"Well, Commander Norton thinks a lot of you. He asked me to make sure you're comfortable." The captain smiled. "I put you in the VIP quarters. Hope it suits you."

George raised his eyebrows. Gallant outranked Norton, yet he was bowing to the commander's wishes. "Norton and I go back a long way," George admitted.

"You were his aide, weren't you, before…?"

"Yes, sir."

"Mmm. Well, Earl and I are old friends too. We don't actually see each other often, but we keep contact. We go back all the way to the Naval Academy."

"I didn't know. He's been good to me and my unit."

"He's concerned about you."

George hesitated, then he said, "I've gone by the book, sir."

"Oh, he doesn't question your performance or doubt your abilities. It's these new studies on solitude and confinement."

"Sir?"

Gallant shook his head. "They never used to worry about social issues, but now it's different. Anyway, you'll get in some socialization on this trip. Maybe you'll get extra points for that."

"I think having the extra man on Frasier will be good," George said. "For the last few days we worked out a new schedule, and the pressure was less with four people."

"Well, if hostile nations are going to keep targeting Frasier Island, we may have to scale up the personnel there."

"It would be hard to supply many more," George said, "and it's a small piece of real estate. You can't put too many people on Frasier without seeing the effects of overcrowding."

"Next they'll be studying that," Gallant said in despair. "For every active operation, it seems like they've got four studies under way."

George smiled. "Yeah. Well, thank you, Captain. Oh, and I have a piece of mail here for an Ensign Taber. I believe she's on duty on this vessel."

"Fine. Just give it to the lieutenant here. I'll have someone take you to your quarters."

⸎

Rachel missed her early morning hikes, but it felt good to have her official duties behind her by noon. The worst part of her day was when Brian came to relieve her at midday. Evenings she could avoid him, but when she was on duty in the control room, she couldn't escape him.

The day after George left she was tracking a school of dolphins when he came down the stairs at ten minutes to twelve.

"This is pretty neat, Chadwick," she said, determined to be civil. "There are about a dozen animals, and they're about two miles out. You can hear them calling to each other."

"It's Brian."

She ignored that. He said it every time she addressed him by his last name. She'd been able to begin calling Greene "Andy," but

"Brian" still stuck in her throat. Her strategy with him was to keep the tone light but impersonal. "So, what's for lunch?"

"Chicken pie."

"Sounds good."

"Don't expect too much," he chuckled. "It came frozen."

"Hey, after what we've been eating for the last few weeks, I'm sure it will be divine."

"You should smile more."

She froze, not able to come up with a quick comeback. He bent down close to her, and she could smell him and feel the warmth of him.

"What are you doing?" she snapped.

"Looking at the monitor. Can you see the dolphins?"

She leaned away from him. "Just on the sonar. Look, are you ready to take over?"

"Yes, ma'am," he said silkily, too close to her ear. "Are you ready to let me?"

She stood up, putting the chair between them, and shoving it toward him a little with her legs.

"You're out of line."

His eyes widened. "Aren't you being a little sensitive?"

She took off the headset and laid it on the desk. Without a word, she turned and left the room.

Was she letting her fear and memories of the past affect her interaction with Chadwick, or was he really crossing the line? She couldn't answer the question, but she was determined to make sure she didn't make the problem worse without cause.

The rain had stopped, and that afternoon she, Pierre, and Andy spent an hour sorting the parts that had broken off the windmills and dragging them into position. Pierre wanted to get the welding done and have the two towers ready to raise when the *Bush* returned. They carried the smaller pieces to the house and down to the basement workbench where he could work on them.

When that task was finished, Rachel took her sketch pad and

circled the house, searching out the best place for her imaginary greenhouse, and then she sat down to draw it. She would send her plan to Commander Norton with the next ship. The greenhouse might never materialize, but it was satisfying to see her plan develop on paper.

When it was finished she walked toward the spring, stopping to check each of the solar collectors. She kept a tally on the back of her sketch pad, telling her how many panels needed replacement.

The spring was down in the hollow below the ridge where the windmills were, and the wind usually skimmed over the depression. It was a sheltered spot, and it was pleasant to be out of the breeze. The grass and weeds were drying quickly, and Rachel sat down on the stream bank in the late afternoon sun. She felt protected and safe, especially with Chadwick buttoned down in the control room. Some ruptured seed pods appealed to her artist's eye, and she took out her pencil once more. Birds called to one another, and she felt at ease in the serene hollow. Her drawing took shape quickly, and she was pleased with it.

Suddenly she realized the birds were silent, and she sat rigid in the stillness. She lifted her head and peered toward the small patch of jungle. Adrenaline shot through her, and she realized she was in danger of breaking her pencil, she clutched it so tightly. She made her fingers relax. It was silly. Brian was on duty. Nothing else on Frasier could hurt her.

She made herself resume drawing, but her contentment was shattered. After a moment she stood up and started swiftly up the path to the ridge, shooting frequent glances over her shoulder. The sun was below the treetops now, and the hollow near the spring was in shadow.

When she got to the house the sitting room was empty, and she closed the door behind her and leaned against it, her heart still tripping.

Calm down. Everything's fine.

She could hear Pierre banging away at the windmill parts in the basement. The urge to dash down the stairs and tell him about her experience was strong, but instead she made herself go into the galley and put potatoes on to boil for their supper. She had to get over this nervousness or she'd be useless to the mission.

She put frozen hot dogs in a pan of water and set the burner on low heat. By then her hands had stopped shaking. She went down the stairs and over to the workbench.

"Hey, *cherie*," Pierre called cheerfully as she approached. Andy smiled at her.

"Hi, guys. I went out to check the solar panels, and I'll need to replace a few tomorrow."

"I could help you," Andy offered.

She shrugged. "If Pierre doesn't need you, but it won't take me long."

"Well, if the weather's good tomorrow I'm going to try to get the windmill rotors back together," Pierre said.

Rachel went back upstairs and finished the meal preparations. The evening ahead, when Chadwick would be off duty, hung over her. She didn't like the tension between the two of them, and she didn't want to have to hide in her room every night to avoid him. She dreaded every meeting with him, and his attempts to impress her hadn't made her dislike him any less.

Six months! she cried inwardly. *I can't take this for six months!* She knew she had to find a way to make Chadwick curb his behavior.

As she headed toward her room, Pierre came up from the basement.

"Hey," she called. "Is this a good time for me to look at George's books?"

"You can look anytime. I've only been keeping the door locked out of deference to George, not to keep you out." He dropped his voice, glancing down the hall. "He wouldn't want just anyone in there, you understand."

He went with her to his room, and Rachel eagerly knelt by the small bookcase fashioned from a wooden crate.

"George likes mysteries!"

Pierre smiled. "He donated the ones in the sitting room. These are the new ones he hasn't read yet."

Rachel ran her fingers over the spines of his books. "He's into history too. I didn't know that." She laughed suddenly. "Peanuts cartoons?"

"That is mine."

She glanced up at Pierre. "Oh, sorry."

"I think I hear Brian out there. Maybe I will just go get a bite to eat with him while you—"

"Hey, what's this?" She pulled a thick hardcover from the shelf.

"I think it's some sort of dictionary."

Rachel opened it. "No, it's not."

He shrugged. "George has an eclectic taste."

She caught her breath as the tiny numbers and abbreviations suddenly made sense, and turned quickly to the title page. "Pierre! This is a book that tells you where things are in the Bible."

He frowned and leaned closer. "Really? That's odd."

"No. It's wonderful!"

"But…" Pierre swiftly looked over the shelves again. "There's no Bible. And I've never seen George with one. Why would he want that?"

"I don't know. Unless…" She felt a sudden wave of hope. "Unless he took his Bible with him."

❦

George climbed into the car with Warrant Officer Shaw.

"Commander Norton asked me to greet you personally and tell you he regrets not seeing you tonight," Shaw said. "He had an engagement, and our orders are to send you on to Washington immediately.

"That's fine," George said. "Maybe I'll see him on my next trip through."

"I'm in charge of the supplies for the Frasier unit," Shaw told him, as the car sped toward the airfield.

"Any problems there?"

"No, I've been adjusting the quantities of provisions for four men, instead of three."

"You think they'll leave the fourth man there?"

"The commander thinks it would be prudent at this point."

"So do I."

Shaw cleared his throat. "He, uh, did question the need for Christmas ornaments, Lieutenant."

George chuckled. "That's Rachel. Ensign Whitney. She's big on celebrating. It's good for morale."

"Yes, sir, but space is at a premium. If she wants to substitute that for some of the other personal items she requested—"

"Put it on my account," George said gruffly. "Send them in place of the new boots I ordered."

"If you're sure, sir."

"I am." He could get a new pair of boots in Washington and wear them back.

Rachel, sweet, Rachel. What are you up to tonight?

He pictured her on the roof, staring up through the telescope. The sky was clear tonight, at least in Hawaii. She ought to have a great opportunity for stargazing. He leaned against the frame of the car door and glimpsed the Little Dipper. Darkness would just be falling on Frasier. *Venus. She can see Venus right now.*

⌘

Rachel made a minute adjustment in the telescope's focus. The jewel-sprinkled sky was breathtaking. She wondered if George was still on the *Bush* or if he was at Pearl Harbor. Maybe he was already aloft, winging toward the mainland. She stiffened as she heard the door to the roof creak open behind her. Andy was on watch. That had better be Pierre.

The silvery gleam of Chadwick's light hair sent a wave of dread through her. She turned away and sat still as he came toward her.

"Moonlight becomes you," he said.

"You want to use the telescope?" she asked briskly.

"No. There are more beautiful things to look at than the sky."

Her upper lip curled. "That's supposed to turn me to jelly?"

"You don't know a good thing when you see it." He hadn't given up the coaxing tone yet.

"Leave me alone, Chadwick."

He laughed. "I can see this is going to be a long process, but that's okay. Getting there is half the fun."

"Excuse me?" She hated the snarling sound of her own voice.

"Frenchie let slip that he's getting married soon. You're going to need a shoulder to cry on when he leaves."

"Drop dead." She stood up and turned toward the stairway, but Chadwick grasped her wrist and pulled her back toward him. Her heart raced as her fear escalated.

TWENTY

Pierre knocked on Rachel's door, but there was no answer. He opened it a crack and peeked in, but she wasn't there. He went to the sitting room and then checked the galley. She wouldn't go outside alone this late, would she? It struck him that Chadwick wasn't in evidence, either. Maybe he'd gone down to chat with Andy in the control room.

He heard footsteps overhead. Of course. Rachel was on the roof, using the telescope. Another sound came—a thud. He strode up the stairs. The door at the top flew open just as he reached it, and Rachel charged through, colliding with him so hard she almost sent him flying backward. He held on to her and slammed back against the side wall, one hand groping for the railing as he struggled to keep his balance.

"Pierre! Sorry!" she gasped.

"Are you all right?"

She pulled away from him and ran down the stairs and into the hallway. The roof door was still open. Pierre went up the remaining steps and looked out. Brian was sitting on the low wall at the edge of the roof beyond the telescope, swearing and rubbing his shin. Pierre stepped out onto the roof and walked toward him.

"Problem here, Brian?"

Chadwick eyed him uncertainly and then laughed. "Oh, no. She made herself quite clear."

"You sure?" Pierre stepped closer. "Because if it's not clear, I can draw you a diagram. Leave her alone."

Chadwick stood up and winced as he tested his weight on his right leg. "Capricious little fury."

"Yeah, well, some women just like to be treated with respect."

"Maybe. But some women want to be pursued too."

"Rachel doesn't. You crossed the line, Ensign. Do I need to file a complaint?"

"No way. I got the message. Loud and clear."

"So we'll never have to repeat this conversation, right?"

Chadwick turned and limped toward the door. "Right."

When Chadwick was clear of the stairway, Pierre went straight to Rachel's door. It was locked this time. When he knocked and called to her, she opened it and flung herself into his arms.

"Did he hurt you?"

"No," she choked. "He grabbed me and I—I threw the book at him. George's astronomy book. It went over the wall. Then I kicked him."

"I think you got the better of him."

"This time."

"You should report this," Pierre said.

"No, I can't. Norton will say this outpost is too isolated for men and women to serve together, and guess which gender they'll remove?"

"Hmm. I don't suppose they'll replace us guys with three women."

"You got that right. Pierre, I don't want any black marks on my record. When I leave here, I want them to say I did a good job and performed my duties well, with no problems."

"But he's harassing you. This isn't the first time, is it?"

She hesitated. "He's always been bold, but when he heard you're marrying someone else... I guess you were right about that, *cheri.* He and Greene thought you were my boyfriend. Now they know better."

"Andy hasn't bothered you, has he?"

"No, he's just curious. I think he's all right. A little owlish, but he seems like a decent sort."

Pierre sighed. "I kind of like him. I told him about Marie yesterday. I guess that was a mistake. I figured it didn't matter, since you'd told me you didn't want to pretend we had a romance."

"They thought that anyway, and you were right. It acted as a deterrent."

"Well, I had a little chat with Brian. He knows I won't let this type of behavior pass."

"I didn't think he'd go that far. Do you suppose he'll shape up now?" she asked.

"He says so. I'll talk to Andy too. If Brian sees that all three of us think he's a jerk, maybe it will shame him into good behavior."

"I don't know," Rachel said wearily. "They were in training together, but Andy seems nice enough. Talk to him, if you want. It will be embarrassing, but if you think it will help…"

"I'm Brian's supervisor. I've got to come down on him for this. It's important that he knows every one of us finds his conduct despicable."

"Do you think he'll come after me again?"

"I don't. He seemed sincere. But don't go wandering off alone at night, *ma petite*. If you want to look at the stars, tell me, and I'll accompany you."

"I'd better see if I can retrieve George's book."

"If it went over the side, I'll get it. I don't want you out there alone. The south wall?"

She nodded and reached for her sketchbook, the way she always did when she was troubled.

"Pierre! Oh, no!"

He was at her side instantly. "What is it?"

"He's been in my room."

"How can you tell?"

"I left the sketchbook closed, but it's open now, to the greenhouse plan I made."

"Are you sure?"

"Positive. I always close it, and Andy's been on duty for four hours. It couldn't have been him. It wasn't you—"

"No."

"Then Brian must have come in here tonight and looked at my sketchbook. I guess I forgot to lock the door when I went up to the roof this time. Oh, man, what else did he do?" She looked around frantically and then she dashed to the dresser and began pulling open and slamming the drawers.

"Easy, easy, *mon amie*." Pierre put a hand on her arm, and she looked up at him in anguish.

"I can't take much more of this."

"Can you tell that he's touched anything else?"

"Not for sure. I'm not the neatest housekeeper, but I'm certain about the sketchbook."

"All right. There's no proof. I suggest you lock your door all the time, whether you're in this room or not. I'll have another talk with him."

"Pierre, I've been so scared."

"That's understandable, with what you've been through."

She turned away, hiding her face. "I haven't taken a shower for two days because of him."

"You should have told me. Come on, get your things. I'll stand watch in the storage room while you get your shower."

She inhaled shakily. "George's nightmare is coming true. You're having to babysit me."

∽

George's mind was spinning with all he had learned that day. After his extensive debriefing, he'd received a tour of the laboratory where top secret experiments were conducted on firene samples.

"It's a very interesting element," Commander Marston told him.

"Under the right circumstances, it reacts violently. Perfectly stable otherwise, you understand, but with sulfur it's volatile, and a touch of zinc makes the explosion twenty times as powerful."

"Twenty times?" George blinked.

"At least. It's definitely the weapon of the future."

"With sulfur and zinc. But with the limited quantity..." George began.

"It takes such a small amount, Lieutenant! We can make a million missiles, easily, with what's in that meteorite. And we're already searching for more in other parts of the world. We're even discussing a plan with NASA that would send robots to search for firene on the surface of the moon."

"You think there might be some there?"

"Who knows? Mars, even. It would be worth developing robots to retrieve it from Mars."

"That's amazing. Just thinking about it—"

Marston smiled. "Mind-boggling, isn't it? It would take time, but this discovery is vastly important. If we found another source, we could consider using it for fuel, perhaps, or other nonmilitary uses."

"I was told the mining at Frasier Island will begin in the spring."

"Yes, as soon as the typhoon season is over. We'll have ships out there all next summer, no doubt. It will be an interesting phase of the operation."

George looked at his watch. "Thank you, Commander. It's been very educational to see all this. I've got to get over to Admiral Truax to discuss operations at Frasier."

He hurried to the admiral's office with some trepidation. The normal part of his debriefing was over, but they were keeping him in Washington. How long was this going to go on?

"Hudson, come in."

He sat opposite Truax, trying to calm his jitters.

"I have some disturbing news for you," the admiral told him. "As you know, word has leaked out about the firene you've been guarding so diligently, and foreign powers have made at least two attempts to get at it."

"Yes," George said, his apprehension rising.

"We thought the leak must have come from the laboratory, but it seems we were wrong." Truax threw him a look of sympathy. "I'm sorry to have to tell you this, but we've put out a warrant on a man previously on duty at Frasier Island."

Carlton. That clumsy kid who broke his leg out there!

"It's very difficult when an old colleague betrays the cause," Truax went on, shaking his head. "I'm so sorry about Rubin."

"Rubin!" George exclaimed. "Matt Rubin?"

"Yes. This coalition of rogue states got to him, Hudson."

"I don't believe it."

"It's true, I'm afraid."

"No. Matt was going to retire in Montana."

"Oh, he's retiring, all right. They gave him a villa outside Havana. I'm afraid he's already fled the country. We can't touch him in Cuba."

George felt as if a horse had kicked him in the chest. *We were like brothers!*

"We'll try to keep the firene under wraps until we mine it," the admiral said. "We'll continue to man Frasier Island with four men until the weather settles down, and we'll have subs patrolling the area continuously. I'm meeting with the president this evening to decide how much to make public. We'll start mining in April or May. And of course, we'll need a battle group to defend the divers during the operation."

"Yes, sir," George replied. "Will I be able to go back now?"

"We'll see." Truax stood up and offered his hand to George. "There's another meeting tomorrow. One more thing to discuss. I'll send a car for you at 0900."

"Yes, sir." George left the office with misgiving.

❧

Although Chadwick stopped annoying her, Rachel still arranged her life around his schedule. When he relieved her in the control room at noon each day, she kept communication to a minimum as she turned the work station over to him.

The afternoons, while he was on watch, were her times of freedom. She hung out laundry then, checked the equipment, fished, and sketched. But she always made sure she came in early, before dark. She usually fixed supper and ate hers alone. When Brian came up-stairs, she left him and Pierre in the galley to eat together while she escaped to her room.

She stayed there most evenings now. She read her Bible vora-ciously, using George's concordance to chase the answers to dozens of questions sparked by her reading.

The book was in good condition, and she wondered how often George had used it. Did he believe in God? His manner when she arrived at Frasier would have made her guess he did not. He didn't believe in anyone but George Hudson—and maybe Uncle Sam. But now she wasn't so sure. He certainly cared about Pierre, and he seemed to have some concern for her too. He thought about profound subjects, that was certain. If she learned he had a deep personal religious belief, it wouldn't shock her now.

Occasionally Pierre would coax her out in the evening for a game of rummy, and once they watched *Hello, Dolly!* Brian joined them, but Pierre sat between them. Even so, she was uncomfortable. Instead of attempting to flirt with her, Brian watched her dolefully.

"What am I going to do?" she asked Pierre, before he left her at her door that night. "Am I paranoid, or does he stare at me?"

"He stares at you. I'm sorry. Maybe I should talk to him again."

She grimaced. "No, this is between me and him. I appreciate what you did before, but somehow I've got to patch things up with him myself without letting him think I'm open to advances." She put her hand to Pierre's cheek. "Not all men are like you. If they were, the world would be a better place."

"I will annihilate him if he touches you again."

"No, *cheri*. This is something I have to deal with myself."

Pierre started to speak, and then he shook his head.

"I know," she said. "I'll never be able to handle it unless I can control my nerves. I hate being a helpless female."

"You're not helpless."

"Ha. I wouldn't have thought so. He came at the wrong time, Pierre. My defenses are down."

He nodded. "You've got to stop feeling inadequate, *ma belle*. I know you are a courageous woman, but you haven't let Brian see that. When he does, he will know you are a force to reckon with, and his respect for you will keep him in line."

"That's pretty much what George told me about authority. But I let Chadwick scare me so badly, I couldn't command respect."

"You can if you try. But—"

"But?"

"But don't take any chances."

TWENTY-ONE

George sat in an anteroom at the Pentagon, waiting to be called before a panel of officers. He'd given his reports on the submarine incident, the firene, the garrison at Frasier Island. What more was there to talk about? Ill at ease, he stood and began pacing.

"Would you like coffee, Lieutenant?" the ensign at the reception desk asked.

"No, thank you."

She turned back to her computer.

At last a commander came to the door and beckoned to him. "Hudson, this way, please."

He was ushered to a seat midway along one long side of a conference table. Two admirals, four captains, and the commander watched him take his seat.

"Lieutenant Hudson, it's a pleasure to see you again," began gray-haired Admiral Truax. "We'd like to ask you some questions today about your—hmm—forty-two months on Frasier Island."

"Yes, sir."

"Your three-man unit is the smallest we've maintained for any length of time in the twenty-first century. Your reports indicate that it's worked well and been an efficient use of personnel."

George nodded. "Yes, sir. It's gone smoothly for the most part."

"Have there been any problems?"

"There have been a few rough spots," George said, "most notably when one of our men broke his leg and needed to be evacuated. I understand the present experiment with a four-man team is going to be extended, and I think that's wise."

Truax nodded. "Considering the value of the firene and the interest that has recently been shown in it, I believe the larger contingent is needed. Our ships have been out to Frasier twice in a month's time for reconnaissance and recovery."

"Yes, sir," George conceded. "It's impossible to predict what's going to happen next out there. The nature of the mission is obviously no longer a secret in all quarters. But the automated reloading machinery has made it possible to defend the installation with minimum personnel."

Admiral Quinn broke in, with a deferential glance at Truax. "I believe we've settled the future plans for the mission. We know the tremendous potential the firene has for our national defense. We'll be sending crews of engineers out to mine it as soon as possible. By May for certain, perhaps as early as April, if the weather cooperates. After that, the nuclear warheads on Frasier will be rearmed."

George nodded. This news had been broken to him in an earlier meeting.

Quinn went on. "What we're mainly concerned with right now, Hudson, is the emotional effect of this type of duty on men and women."

George blinked. "Well, it gets boring at times. Some people get lonely. I've got an ensign right now who is anticipating his upcoming wedding. He's ready for a new assignment, you might say."

The men laughed.

"Hudson, you've had one woman on the island for the past six months," Truax said.

"Yes, sir. She's been a fine addition to the unit. Very dedicated and efficient."

"And having a female there hasn't caused any friction?"

"I don't believe so, sir."

"So, you approve assigning mixed crews to this type of duty?"

"Well," George said slowly, "I would recommend screening the candidates—male and female—closely." The discussion was too close to what he feared Rachel was dealing with, and George fell silent.

"Were you uncomfortable when you were told a woman was coming into your unit last spring?" Captain Bainbridge asked.

George glanced down the table toward him.

"I'll be honest, sir, I wasn't thrilled initially. I had some of the same concerns this panel evidently has. But Ensign Whitney's conduct has been exemplary, and I'm proud that I can serve with her."

Bainbridge nodded and seemed to be encouraging him to elaborate.

George cleared his throat. "Change is always unsettling, gentlemen. Whenever we get a new crew member, it takes a few weeks to settle back into a comfortable pattern. The new personnel take a while to find their niche in the operation. I found that Whitney was well trained and able to carry her weight, and the mission went forward without disruption."

"Did you ever feel it was a mistake to mix gender in such a small operation?" asked Bainbridge.

George felt torn. If he said no, it wouldn't be the truth. "At first, I thought there might be problems. Personality clashes are always magnified in a small group. But I saw it working on Frasier. I think it depends on the person's character, not on gender."

"So, now you've swung around and are in favor of mixed operations."

He hesitated. It might not always work. Was Rachel having trouble right now, even as he spoke to defend her right to be there?

"As I said, I think it depends on the character of those involved. If the men and women respect each other and behave in a manner becoming to U.S. military personnel, then I don't see a problem."

Captain Bainbridge leaned back in his chair and looked up at the ceiling. "I'm satisfied."

"Same here," offered another captain. He had been staring at a sheaf of papers in front of him throughout the interview, and George had thought he wasn't listening.

"Very well," said Truax. He briefly polled the others. "Lieutenant Hudson, will you stay, please? Gentlemen, this meeting is adjourned."

George rose as the officers prepared to leave. Several of them approached him and offered their hands. Admiral Quinn said, "Good work out there, Hudson. Too bad these foreigners got onto it. Not your fault."

"Thank you, sir."

When the room had emptied, Truax said, "Sit down, please, Hudson."

George sat. He met the admiral's steely gaze, fighting a twinge of nervousness.

"We've discussed a new assignment for you, and the panel seems to agree you're ideal for it."

"Sir, I..."

"Yes?"

"I beg your pardon, sir. I was hoping I could keep my position at Frasier Island until the firene is collected."

"Hmm, well, let me just outline this option for you."

"Yes, sir."

"Congress has directed us to do a study on the effects of gender mix in remote operations. With the recent cutbacks we don't have many officers to spare, but with your experience and background, the panel agrees with me that you'd be just the man to head this thing up."

George felt his eyes must be glazing over. For ten minutes he managed to sit still and appear calm as Truax droned on. Finally he had to speak.

"Well, Admiral, I can see you've given this a lot of thought, and I appreciate your thinking of me, but I'd really like to see the Frasier operation to its conclusion."

"There's a promotion in it, Hudson. You'll have an office in this building and a staff of four."

"That's...that's very tempting, sir. May I ask you something?"

Truax sat back. "Feel free."

"Do you think I'm unfit for field work any longer, sir?"

"Certainly not. We just thought your expertise would be helpful in this."

"Why weren't there any women on this panel?"

The admiral's brow creased.

"You must have a female officer who could take this assignment and run with it. There was a Lieutenant Anne Rogers I worked with for a while in San Diego some years ago. She's probably a captain by now. If she hasn't retired, she'd be great. Meanwhile, sir, I'm the most knowledgeable man you have when it comes to Frasier Island. We've got a coalition of hostile nations trying to steal the firene from under our noses, and I feel my place in all of this is right there on Frasier, protecting it until our engineers can safely remove it to a new location."

Truax inhaled slowly. "I guessed you'd feel that way. The truth is, we're being pressured on this study thing. Congress has tied some funding to it."

They would. "Well, sir, no offense, but I don't think I'd do so well at pushing paper. Do I have a choice in this matter?"

"The orders haven't been issued. Your personal feelings will be considered, I give you my word. But don't be hasty, Hudson. Take some time to think about this. You have some leave coming, I believe."

"Yes, sir. They gave me two weeks, starting tomorrow."

"You'll be visiting family?"

"I thought I'd go see my sister in California."

"Let me know, Hudson. You can contact my office here, or pass the word through your supervisor, but I'd like to know soon. Meanwhile, something tells me it won't hurt to look up this Anne Rogers you mentioned."

At precisely 0600 on Frasier Island, George's radio call went through, and Pierre's voice was clear over the airwaves.

"Frasier 130."

"Pierre, mon copain, comment ça va?"

"Georges! Ça va bien, mon ami! Où es-tu?"

"I'm at my sister's, in California. Did you get through to Marie?"

"Yes, last night, finally. She told me you called her."

"I had to wait until I got to DC. There wasn't any time at Pearl. But I told her I was optimistic you'd be home by the end of the month."

"Have they told you that?"

"Not officially. I'm on two weeks' forced leave, but it was my impression the *Bush* will be back then."

"With you on it?"

"No promises yet. They want to put me behind a desk in Washington."

"George! No!" Pierre's shock registered across thousands of miles. "They can't do that to you!"

"Take it easy, buddy. It's not final yet. I'm kicking and screaming. Is Ensign Whitney there?"

"Oui, monsieur. She just came on watch. I'll take over for her, so she can give her full attention to you."

"C'est bon." He waited impatiently until Rachel's voice came, distant and breathless.

"George!"

"Rachel," he said softly. Even across the miles, her voice thrilled him. "How's it going?"

"I'm coping, George. We miss you."

He wasn't sure what else to say on this very public call, but he wanted to hear her talk some more. "What do you want for Christmas?"

"I want *you,* back in time for Halloween."

"What, no nylons or perfume?"

"Ha! What would I do with that stuff here?"

"Seriously," George persisted, "how about art supplies?"

"George, just come home!"

His heart lurched, and he tried not to think what the radio operator in Pearl was making of this conversation. "I'll see what I can do. How are the recruits doing?"

She was cautious. "It's a mixed bag."

"Somebody giving you a bad time?"

"Well…I'm learning to handle it. Things are a bit strained at times, but I think they're improving."

"Rachel, listen to me. Let Pierre help you if you need it."

"I will. I am. Hey, I sort of ruined your astronomy book."

"What did you do, leave it out in the rain?"

"Not exactly. I'm sorry. If you want to pick out a new one, I'll pay for it."

"Forget it."

There was no response.

"Rachel?" he asked sharply.

"Sorry, sir. We lost your connection."

TWENTY-TWO

Three days later George stood leaning on the corral fence at the J & J ranch. His two nieces sat on the top rail, watching their father put a registered quarter horse mare through her paces. George had fretted through the first days at the ranch, but riding good horses and prolonged contact with his sister and her family had gradually calmed him.

Judy Martin came out of the barn and stood next to him, watching with satisfaction.

"Nice mare," George said.

"Isn't she beautiful? I wish we could keep her. But if we kept them all, none of us would eat. Her new owner is picking her up tomorrow."

He swung around to look at her. Judy was three years his junior, but she looked even younger to him. Her chestnut ponytail and worn denims gave her a tomboy look. "You're happy, aren't you?"

"Very." Her satisfied smile faded. "Are you?"

He took a deep breath, looking off toward the mountains. "Right now, I'm not sure."

"George," she said urgently, taking his arm and pulling him toward the ranch house, "you can't go on like this forever."

"Like what?"

"You know. Shutting yourself off from everyone. I don't mean the island. That's symbolic, certainly, but it's not your main problem. Those admirals have no idea what they're talking about."

"And you do?"

"Well, sure. You're not loony because you've been isolated so long. It's the other way around."

"I've isolated myself because I'm crazy?"

She arched her eyebrows and pushed him into a kitchen chair. "Tell me you haven't been on the edge a few times." She turned away from him to pour coffee for them both, but an almost fearful concern lay beneath her light tone.

"Judy, I'm fine."

When she came to him with the two coffee mugs, her eyes glistened. "I've been so worried about you. I know you don't want to be smothered, but…George! We've had two phone calls and a few notes in three years. That's not normal."

Tears streamed down her cheeks, and she snatched a tissue before she sat down, pulling her steaming mug to her. The heavy guilt that had dogged him so long was back, and George stirred his coffee, watching her uneasily.

"I'm sorry. I couldn't write for a long time. I feel bad because I know it worried you and disappointed the girls. But I just…needed time to deal with things."

"Have you?"

He shrugged. "It's been tough."

She nodded. "I know you had to get away from Earl. He has a very strong personality, and you couldn't stay too close to that, not after what happened."

"Earl and I get along fine."

"Sure, when you're thousands of miles apart."

He laid his spoon down and took a sip of coffee. "Things are better now."

"Good. That's really good. Because I've been concerned. You were out there with guns and cliffs and things."

He barked a short laugh. "You think I'm suicidal?"

"I've prayed for you every day, George."

He swallowed hard. "Thanks." He avoided Judy's intent gaze, not wanting her to see the truth. He couldn't count the times he had stood on the cliff on the west end of Frasier, staring down at the crashing waves. He'd told himself it was duty and the Navy that kept him from doing anything rash. His country needed him. He hadn't considered how his sister would feel.

"How are things between you and God?" she asked softly.

He winced and took another sip.

Judy said quickly, "I know you can't go to church or anything. Have you had anyone out there to talk to? Spiritually, I mean."

"No, not really." *And that suited me just fine.*

She leaned toward him and clasped his hand. "We love having you here, George. Please don't leave us for so long again."

He squeezed her fingers. "I'm sorry. I've missed you, and I can't believe how grown up the girls are. I really didn't mean to drop out of the family, Judy."

"Just don't forget that when you go back."

He nodded. "When I got the picture of Abbey last spring, it brought me up short. I know I've missed out on a lot. She looked so mature holding that trophy. And I can't believe she was riding the foal that was born the last time I was here!"

"We'll have to send pictures more often, I guess."

"Do that. And we should be getting mail more often now. I ought to be able to call out more frequently too. The project I'm on will end next summer, and there'll be a lot of activity back and forth between us and Pearl after April."

"That's good. Try to keep in touch." She stood up. "I need to go help Jason. You still look tired. Maybe you should take a nap."

She left him, and George wandered to his room. His niece Cassie had given it up for him and moved in with her sister temporarily. He went to the window and looked out at the superb horses grazing in the pasture. He'd thought he didn't miss riding until yesterday, when Jason had put him on a frisky bay gelding and led the whole family on a wild trek into the foothills. That was something he would never have on Frasier Island. It was the first time he'd admitted it felt good to be back in the real world. Judy was right about the family. She was right about a lot of things.

He opened the closet and took out his duffel bag, feeling deep inside, to the very bottom, and pulled out a small, leather-covered Bible. It was ages since he'd opened it, but something had made him drop it in the bag when he began packing. Was it because it had been a gift from Judy years ago, and he was afraid she would ask him what became of it? Telling her he was carrying it with him all over the world might soothe her fears, but it wouldn't ease his guilty conscience.

He sat down on the twin bed with the ruffled pink bedspread and opened the pocket-sized Bible to the psalms. He read for a long time. Finally he lay back, exhausted, on the pillow. *I give up, Lord. I'm tired of trying to make sense out of this life. You take over, please.*

∽

Judy's hands were immersed in dishwater the next morning when George pulled a dish towel from the rack and began drying the silverware and cereal bowls.

"Wow! A lieutenant doing KP."

He laughed. "Come Christmas shopping with me, Judy."

She blinked up at him. "You can't do that yourself?"

"I'm leaving in a few days, and I need your input. I'd like to get gifts for you and Jason and the girls before I leave, and...there's something else I need help with."

"What sort of thing?"

"Well, it's kind of...it's confidential."

"Now I'm curious."

Two hours later they were wandering through a mall, laden with packages.

"Let's put these in the truck and grab some lunch," George suggested.

"My brother buying me lunch. I think that's a first."

"Jason and the girls can fend for themselves once, can't they?"

"Sure." She pulled out her cell phone and called Jason to tell him of their change in plans as they headed toward the parking lot. "All right," she said when she'd hung up. "Now tell me the rest of it."

"The rest of what?"

"Something tells me we're not done shopping."

"Well, no. I haven't got your present yet, and I want to get something for...for the people in my unit. Well, actually, I don't even know two of them. I'll take them some books, I guess. It's Ensign Whitney I'm thinking about, though...Rachel."

Judy studied him thoughtfully as he unlocked the cab of the pickup. "This is a bit out of the blue, George."

"Not really."

"Mm-hmm. What does she like?"

"Well, she's artistic."

"So, paints, an easel, something like that?"

"I dunno. I've never seen her paint. She draws. But I know she ordered some pencils and sketch pads for herself."

"Come into the Western wear shop, and I'll show you what I want. Maybe Rachel would like one too."

"Oh, that's nice," he said fifteen minutes later. Judy was trying on a fringed suede jacket. She buttoned it and turned, posing for his inspection. "It's great on you."

"There you go. Buy two and your shopping's done."

"I don't know," George hedged. "It's awfully personal, don't you think? And bulky."

"Bulky?"

"We get one helicopter to transport all our provisions for six months. They're very strict about how much personal stuff we bring."

"You couldn't fit this in?"

"Maybe, if I left my dress blues and the Halloween candy behind. She'd look cute in it, though." His eyes met Judy's suddenly, and he shrugged.

"Why don't you just buy her a ring?" Judy asked.

"A—oh, no, no, we're not ready for that."

"You sure?"

He hesitated.

"George! You're blushing!"

He looked around quickly and leaned toward his sister. "Things are a little complicated right now."

"How complicated?"

"Well, I…"

"Have you told her how you feel about her?"

"Not yet," he admitted.

"Do you think she reciprocates?"

"I'd like to think so. Pierre says she does."

"Pierre? Your second in command?" Judy put her hands on her hips and scowled at him. "Can't you speak for yourself, George?"

"Very funny. Come on, take that off so I can pay for it. I'm starved."

"All right, but after lunch I think we should take a peek in the jewelry store."

"I told you, no rings."

"Yet."

"Yet," he agreed.

"When the time comes, you won't be near a jewelry store."

"I can't, Judy." The idea of buying an engagement ring at this stage of the relationship seemed ludicrous. If Rachel rejected him, having it with him would be a constant reminder of his splintered dreams. "We're light years from that kind of commitment."

"Well, then, something less permanent," Judy said.

He frowned, pulling out his wallet.

"What's the matter, George? You said it has to be small. Does she wear earrings?"

"No. Do you think a pendant is too personal?"

"As opposed to what? Lingerie?"

"Judy!" He looked apologetically at the clerk, who was smiling as she swiped his credit card.

"Just giving you a little perspective," Judy said. "Silver or gold? What's her coloring?"

George could picture Rachel without any prompting. Her rich brown hair and blue, blue eyes. "Are sapphires expensive?" he asked.

Judy leaned on the counter and said conspiratorially to the clerk, "My brother. He's got it bad."

"Sapphires are nice," the clerk said. "Better than a box of choco-lates."

"She likes books," George mused. "I'm thinking maybe a diary. One of those nice leather-covered ones. Hey, she needs an astronomy book."

"Too bulky," Judy said firmly. "Sapphires would be much better. Compact. Expressive. Significant but not binding."

"Do you really think so?"

"I'd better get you to the jewelry store fast." Judy picked up the bag with the jacket in it and herded him toward the door.

❦

Rachel meandered along the ridge path, avoiding the area where the fallen windmills sprawled. She briefly checked the solar collectors along the way, satisfied that all had been repaired. It was nice to have a warm day again. The forecast for the next few days was calm, and she was looking forward to a quiet afternoon in the sun, when she could settle down on the rocks to read her Bible and draw.

The grasses and weeds on the island had matured, and the dried weed stalks and fall blossoms gave her some new subjects to sketch. New birds were paying visits as well, on their way south from the Arctic. Rachel had equipped her backpack with binoculars, camera, sketchbook and pencils, and her radio was strapped to her belt. She breathed in the clean, fresh sea air with pleasure. Maybe she would go all the way to the eastern point today and watch for whales.

She stopped for a moment at the spring, remembering how George had interrupted her artwork there last summer. Memories of George were everywhere on Frasier. Thinking about him made her heart beat faster, and she wondered when and if he would return.

She turned toward the faint path that led past the jungle toward the rocky eastern end of the island, praying silently as she went. For George she pleaded for safety, comfort, and contentment. She knew now that beneath his calm, almost cold demeanor a torrent of opinions and passions raged. *No matter what they do to him, Lord, give him peace.* For days now she'd been begging for his return. Was that appropriate? How could she know if that was what God wanted for George and for herself? She couldn't know until the USS *George H. W. Bush* returned. And so she prayed for serenity, for herself, and for him.

A sudden movement beside her startled Rachel, and she whirled toward it, but as she turned a man seized her wrist and yanked her off the path. She screamed and twisted, pulling as hard as she could.

No, Lord! Not again! Help me!

It registered in a flash that he was a stranger, a thin man in tattered, muddy brown trousers and a ragged undershirt. Middle Eastern, perhaps, or eastern European? His chin was covered with dark stubble, and his dark eyes were desperate. And he was very strong. Her pistol! She had stopped carrying it after the sailors searched the island. She kicked at his knee, fumbling with her free hand, straining to reach her radio. She yanked away and fell hard in the brush. Only then did she realize he held a metal rod. He raised it as he stepped toward her.

TWENTY-THREE

Pierre was jerked from sleep by a piercing alarm. He slapped at his clock and then realized it was the emergency alarm. He had used it to call George when the enemy plane and submarine approached Frasier, but he'd never been upstairs to hear how annoyingly penetrating that sound was. He jumped up and shut it off. Then he grabbed his portable radio from the crate beside the cot.

"What, Brian?"

"It's Andy. Brian's taking his break, and I'm down here."

Pierre shook his head, still feeling sluggish. "Okay, what's up?"

"I just got a radio call on the short-range, but then nothing. I called Brian, and he's on the roof."

"It wasn't me." Brian's voice came, strong and close. "It must have been Rachel. I'm coming down."

"Where is she?" Pierre began to pull his pants on as he spoke.

"She was near the windmills a minute ago," Brian said. "Thought I'd just go up to the roof and get some fresh air, and I saw her. She was walking toward the spring."

Pierre fumbled for his boots and dropped the radio. He picked it up quickly. "Where are you now?"

"Heading for the spring."

"I'm right behind you. Got your weapon?"

"No. Should I?"

"Go," Pierre said. "Andy, stand by and try to call her again."

"Aye, aye."

Pierre jammed his feet into the boots and grabbed his holster and radio. He ran down the hallway and out the door. Brian was just visible, nearly to the helicopter pad. Raising his radio, Pierre pushed the call signal.

"Rachel, *cherie*, where are you?"

There was no reply for a moment, and then Brian's voice came. "I'm almost at the spring. I don't see her." His panting was audible. Pierre kept running, up the ridge. He'd reached the top of the descent to the spring when Brian spoke again. "She dropped her backpack."

"Where?"

"Almost to the jungle."

Pierre bolted down the slope.

~

Rachel scrambled to her feet and ran. The man was between her and the spring, so she sprinted for the jungle, trying to think where she could find safety. If this man had been hiding out on Frasier for almost two weeks, since the submarine was destroyed, he probably knew the jungle better than she did with her occasional forays.

She reached for her radio again, and knew instantly that she had lost it. Terror gripped her, squeezing the air from her lungs. She had pushed the call button once, she was certain. Somehow she had to circle and head back toward the house. Even as the thought came, she felt the man's hand close on the back of her shirt and pull her backward.

He shoved her against a large palm trunk and held her there, gasping, his face only inches from hers. Rachel's pulse thudded in her temples.

"What do you want?" she choked.

He stared at her, and she doubted he understood a word of English. He leaned back a bit and she saw that he still had the metal bar. A piece of angle iron from one of the windmill mechanisms, perhaps. Before he left, George had mentioned a missing component. It seemed years ago.

Rachel watched him warily, wondering if death was near. She couldn't ward off many blows from the two-foot bar.

"What do you want?" she asked again. "You must be hungry. We can feed you." She rubbed her stomach, and his eyes flickered. "I don't have a gun," she said. "If you're after weapons, you picked the wrong person. I don't even have a pocket knife on me."

He stood irresolute for an instant, and she thought perhaps he did understand, after all. But then he raised the iron stick and brought it down so swiftly she barely had time to reach out and grasp it, deadening the blow. The end of it grazed her forehead, and she felt it slice the skin as her forearm absorbed the shock.

She grappled for the bar with all her strength, and they circled slowly, staring into each other's eyes. *He must be weak from lack of food.* Unless he'd stolen from their supplies, and she would know if he had, he must have survived on coconuts and shriveled breadfruit.

The panic was dissipating. A burning determination replaced her fear. This was for her life.

Her thorough training in merciless self-defense edged into the fringes of her mind. Yes, it had been a while, but it was part of her now. If only her head didn't hurt so badly! She timed her move carefully and jerked the iron rod in close, throwing the man off balance, and then kicked as hard as she could. He recoiled, but held on to the bar, pulling her with him.

"Rachel!"

At the sound of her name she froze, determined not to look away from her enemy, but the man turned toward the path. Rachel shoved him, and he fell, but her push had made her loosen her grip, and the iron bar went with him. Involuntarily she put her hands to her head. The pain was excruciating.

"Get back!" Brian charged toward her, and she leaned against the palm tree, dizzy and weak.

Instead of leveling a weapon at the intruder, Brian leaped on the man. Rachel watched in horror as the tussle over the iron was renewed.

"Where's your gun?" She screamed.

"Rachel!"

She whirled toward the voice this time, as Pierre ran toward her.

"Your gun, your gun," she cried, and saw with relief that Pierre was carrying his pistol.

As he approached the wrestling men, she saw the enemy wrench free from Brian's grip and shove him to the ground. He raised his makeshift weapon.

"Drop it," Pierre yelled, but the intruder brought the bar down with all his remaining strength.

Rachel screamed as Pierre's weapon fired.

They stood in silence watching the man crumple to the turf beside Brian. Then Brian moaned, and Rachel made herself inhale.

"Are you all right?" Pierre called to her.

"Yes." She ran to Brian and knelt beside him. He was gritting his teeth and panting.

"He broke my kneecap!" A spate of vile language followed.

"Lie still," Rachel said. Blood oozed through Brian's right pant leg, and a contusion was already discoloring his forearm.

"Hold still," Pierre commanded. Gingerly he touched the injured leg, and Brian screamed.

"Sorry," he gasped. His pale hair was plastered to his brow with sweat.

"We'll get you back to the house," Pierre said. He looked at Rachel. "You sure you're all right? You look awful."

She felt the wound on her forehead. Her fingertips came away sticky with blood. "I'm a little shaky, but I'll be okay. What do you want me to do?"

Pierre handed her his radio. "Call Andy. Then I want you to go back and relieve him, if you're up to it. Have him bring the first aid kit and the stretcher."

"What about him?" She nodded toward the fallen stranger.

"Is he alive?" Brian asked.

"Don't know," Pierre said.

"Check him. I'm good."

"Okay." Pierre turned toward the other man, and Rachel waited breathless as he cautiously approached her fallen adversary and felt for a pulse.

"He's breathing."

"We'd better put pressure on the wound," Rachel said.

"Abdominal wound," Pierre muttered, and she wondered if he wished he'd killed him outright.

"He's worse off than me," Brian said. "Take him first. I mean it."

"No, we'll take you," Pierre said.

"Don't be stupid." Brian shifted his position slightly and groaned. "We need him for intelligence. Take him first."

❧

Rachel hurried along the path as she signaled on the radio. Her head wound throbbed savagely, but she didn't dare stop for fear she'd collapse. "Andy, this is Rachel."

"Thank God! What's going on out there?"

"We have company. I'm coming to relieve you so you can help Pierre."

"Where's Brian?"

"He's injured. I think he'll be okay, but you need to call Pearl Harbor immediately." Near where the man had first attacked her she found her radio, and a few steps farther on was her backpack.

She staggered a bit in the hollow and stopped to catch her breath. Blood trickled down her cheek and soaked her collar. She stooped and splashed cold water from the spring on her face, and the pain in her head seared as she bent over. She straightened and went on, climbing the steep path to the ridge with faltering steps.

By the time she entered the house, she felt nauseous and dizzy again, but she dragged herself to the stairway and went down, clutching the railing.

"Rachel?" Andy called, before she was through the storage area in the first basement.

"Yes," she replied, but it came out in a little puff. She went on, down the next flight of stairs.

"You're injured," Andy cried.

"Keep your post." Shades of George's stern perfectionism. She almost laughed.

"Get over here, then," Andy said. "If you can't get yourself over here, I'm coming to get you."

"I'm coming."

She leaned on the door frame for a second before launching herself into the control room. She made it to the extra chair in four steps and sank into it, leaning forward with her arms on the radio desk.

Andy glanced over at her and swore. "What happened out there?"

"There's a man."

"I guessed that much. Where'd he come from?"

"The submarine, I guess."

"No way. He's been out there more than a week?"

She shrugged helplessly. "Must have been. He looked like he'd been sleeping out in the weather for days."

"I thought there was a thorough search that first day."

"There was, but…there are just too many hiding places on this island."

Andy nodded, looking at the monitors. "Maybe he sneaked around and watched you searching, then hid in one of the spots you checked first."

"Could be. Anyway, Pierre shot him."

Andy stared at her, making no pretense of watching his console screens. "For real?"

"Yes. Brian got there first, but he didn't have his gun, so he tackled him and got a broken leg and who knows what else for his trouble. The guy was pounding him when Pierre got there, so Pierre took him down. But he's still alive, so you need to get out there and help Pierre bring him and Brian back here."

"That's not going to be easy."

"Right. Take the stretcher and the first aid kit from the storage area."

"I'd better get you a bandage for that gash first."

"No, this is already taking too long. The prisoner could die on us. Get going."

"Call Pearl again."

"Didn't you tell them we need support?"

"Yes, but I didn't have any details. They told me to report in ASAP."

"All right," she said.

"Are you sure you can stand watch in your condition?"

"Yes. Go!"

She heard him bound up the stairs. Cautiously she raised herself from the chair and shifted into the one before the monitors. Nothing but water, sky, and a small but dense school of fish. Good old empty ocean.

She knew it might be an hour or two before the men could relieve her. It was up to her to stand watch and make sure medical help was on the way. She pressed her sleeve against her throbbing wound and made herself look at each of the camera monitors, the sonar, and the radar. She started to put on the headphones, but it hurt too much.

Lord, help me, she prayed as she reached toward the long-range radio. *Just let me stay conscious.*

TWENTY-FOUR

Pierre left Andy in Brian's room to watch him while he went to the locked drug cabinet in the storage room. Rachel had been alone in the control room for more than an hour while they brought the prisoner in, dressed his wound as best they could with a pressure bandage of gauze, dosed him with morphine, and went back out for Brian.

Once they had Brian in bed, Andy had cut off Brian's pant leg and put an ice pack on his swollen, purple knee while Pierre got on the radio in the sitting room and consulted Commander Norton's aide and a doctor in Pearl Harbor. The advice he got wasn't encouraging. Stop the bleeding if possible, and sedate both patients until help arrived.

Pierre took the second dose of morphine out of the cabinet and locked the door. He could hear Brian's groaning, but decided to check in with Rachel first. He looked down at his clothes. He'd stumbled and ripped his jeans, and one knee was scraped and bloody, but he decided he was probably the least battered of them all, except Andy. The blood on his sweatshirt was probably the prisoner's. He peeled the sweatshirt off, dropped it near the wringer washer, and then went on down the stairs.

"You okay, *cherie?*" he called as he entered the room.

Rachel jumped and turned to face him.

"I'm sorry." Pierre advanced slowly. "I didn't mean to startle you."

She took a shaky breath and rubbed her temple.

"Rachel, it's all right." Pierre rested his hand lightly on her shoulder. "The prisoner is incapacitated."

He wheeled the second chair over and sat down next to her. "You want to tell me about it?" The blood had congealed on her face and in her hairline on the left side, and an ugly welt had formed around the cut. He noticed purple bruises that had formed on her forearms, but he didn't mention them.

"He popped up out of nowhere. I was distracted, I guess. It was the last thing I expected. With Brian on watch, I figured there was nothing out there that could hurt me on a beautiful day like this."

"Once things settle down, Andy and I will go out and look around, see if we can backtrack him and find out where he's been hiding."

She nodded. "I still can't believe he's been here all this time. Do you think it's possible there are more?"

"No. If there were, they'd have teamed up by now and you wouldn't be alive."

"I think he wanted weapons."

"Maybe he was hoping to pick us off one by one," Pierre suggested.

"Yes, but we haven't been out much all week because of the rain. And when we were, we usually went in a group to work on the windmills."

"Right."

"You know, I thought I heard something once, and the birds went all quiet near the spring, but I put it down to paranoia about Brian." She looked over at him and then back at her radar. "Say, do you think that rod he was brandishing came from the windmills?"

"The missing part that's been giving me a headache."

She nodded. "If George had had an inkling—" She broke off and shrugged in apology. "Sorry. I've got to quit thinking about how different things would be if George were here. We're on our own now."

Pierre was silent for a moment. Were they both losing confidence in the likelihood of George's return? "Are you all right here for a little while longer? I need to give Brian some morphine. Then I'll come back and look at that cut."

She looked at the ampule in his hand and then back at the monitors. "I'm all right now, but I could use some aspirin. What happened to you?"

"I slipped on the trail. Anything happening out there?" He nodded toward the console.

"No, nothing. Just fish."

"Are you sure you're okay? Because I can send Andy down while I do this…"

"No, really."

"Rachel, I'm sorry I couldn't get there faster."

She blinked but didn't respond.

"I'll come back in a little while. You need some rest."

She nodded.

It took twenty minutes for the morphine to ease Brian into sleep. Pierre watched him anxiously, wondering if they could cut the dosage or hold it back longer than four hours per shot.

"The *Bush* can't be here for another forty-eight hours," he told Andy, when Brian's moans had subsided and he breathed evenly.

"What are we going to do?"

Pierre shrugged. "Keep him drugged, I guess. If his patella's broken, we can't do much. Try to keep the swelling down, keep checking for circulation to his foot, and when he's awake we check for sensation and movement. That's what they told me."

"Maybe the joint's just wrenched."

"I don't think he'd have screamed like that." Pierre shook his head in self-recrimination. "How could we have missed that guy? George and I looked for several hours that first day, then Gallant and his men helped go over the whole island."

"Is Rachel okay?" Andy asked. "She had a bad cut on her forehead."

"It seems to have stopped bleeding. When you go down to take over for her I'll clean it up and get a butterfly bandage on it."

"I like her," Andy said. "She seemed a little standoffish at first, but I like her. And she didn't complain when she came in a while ago. Just told me what to do and got on with the job."

"She's a terrific girl and a good sailor," Pierre said. "I'll miss her."

"You think they're taking you away this time?"

"I know they are. And I need to go." Pierre stared down at Brian's knee. It was swollen and discolored with pooled blood. "We'll need to change the ice pack."

"One of us had probably better stay with him and the prisoner, don't you think?" Andy asked.

"Well, within earshot, anyway. That morphine should keep them out for three or four hours. But we only have six more doses for the two of them to share, so we've got to make it last as long as we can."

Andy nodded. "How do you want to divide up the duties until the ship gets here?"

Pierre checked his watch. "It's another hour until your regular shift. But if you go on now and do seven hours…"

"Right. You can relieve me at the usual time, and Rachel can go on at 0800 for eight hours."

Pierre nodded. "She needs some rest."

"She looked wild when she came in, but she seemed rational. Do you think she's really all right?"

"I'll feel better when a doctor looks her over."

Andy looked down at Brian. "Quite a turnaround in their relationship."

"Yeah, if he hadn't gotten there when he did, it might be Rachel we're sending out for treatment. It would have been better for him if he'd had his gun, but…well, no use having regrets. He got there in time to save her."

Andy eyed Pierre thoughtfully. "He told me the other night he wished he'd started out on a different tack with her. He was attracted to her, but I think he looks at her differently now."

"She certainly won't have to worry about him bothering her anymore." Pierre frowned, wondering how Rachel's frayed nerves were taking this latest assault. What would life be like for her if George didn't return? He said, "If George Hudson comes back, everything will be fine."

"If not?"

"Then you and whoever else they bring will have to work with Rachel. Andy, she's been traumatized. It may take her a while to get her confidence back. She was brutally attacked."

Andy looked down at Brian's injuries. "Yeah. Maybe she should be replaced too."

"No, she doesn't want that, and she's a great worker. You'll like her a lot when you get to know her better. She's like a sister to me. And she has a right to be here and do her job without being afraid."

"She doesn't have to be afraid of me."

Pierre nodded. His instincts told him he could trust Andy. He had to. Andy had come through today, signaling him immediately when Rachel didn't answer his call. Andy would have to be Rachel's friend and ally.

"I'll go down now and relieve her," Andy said.

"I'd better come with you, in case she's still wobbly."

"Think Brian will be okay alone?" Andy asked.

Pierre studied Brian's face. "He's definitely out. Come on. Just let me check the prisoner." They had put the stranger in Pierre's cot and restrained him by tying him to the frame, in case he tried to escape while they brought Brian in. Pierre went in and stared at the unconscious man for a moment. The prisoner's breathing was shallow but steady.

They went down the two flights of stairs, and as they approached the bottom, Pierre called, "We're back, *cherie*. Andy's going to take over now."

She didn't turn toward them, but slowly removed the headset and laid it on the desk. Pierre saw Andy appraising her bloody face, the purple splotch beside her left eye, and the bruises on her arms.

"Come on, let's go upstairs," Pierre said. "I'll take care of that cut, and then you can get some rest."

"I'll fix something for all of us to eat first," she said, darting a glance at Andy.

"No big rush," he said with a smile.

She got up soberly and went with Pierre up the stairs.

⁓

"Earl, thanks for seeing me."

"I'm glad you came in, George. Sit down." Commander Norton looked him over critically. "You look well."

"Thank you, sir." George balanced his uniform hat on his knee.

"So, you're heading back to the island."

"Yes, sir. For now."

"There's some question as to whether we'll man that outpost once the firene is removed."

George nodded. "I'd like to see the operation through that phase. Then I think I'll be ready for a change."

"You turned down a good offer."

"I'm glad it was an offer and not an order, sir."

Norton nodded. "I doubted you'd want to be confined like that. I'm glad we were able to connect today. I was hoping I'd have a chance to tell you personally that you're taking a new man out with you."

"Another new man?" George asked.

"Yes, there's been some action on the island. Your crew has a prisoner to be removed, and—"

"A prisoner? How did that happen?"

"It seems there was a survivor from that submarine incident after all. He hid out in the jungle for a week or two and then made himself known. One of your ensigns was injured in the capture and needs immediate medical attention."

"Which one?" George asked with dread.

Norton opened a folder on his desk. "Chadwick. Fractured patella and possibly a couple of cracked ribs, in a lot of pain. Our doctors advised Belanger to ration his morphine. They only have eight doses."

"That won't last them until the ship gets there."

"Especially not if they split it between Chadwick and the prisoner."

George arched his eyebrows.

"Gunshot wound. Abdominal. Belanger's skeptical he'll make it, but they're trying to save him."

George shook his head, aghast at what Pierre, Rachel, and Greene were going through. "That's why you're flying me out now, to join the *Bush*."

"Yes, the group was headed for Guam when the call came from Frasier, and they changed course last night. It will take them another day and a half to get there, at least. The replacement is already on board."

"He's been trained for the detail?"

Norton grimaced. "No, but this is an emergency. We can't wait for a specialist to transfer."

"So, this new recruit doesn't have the advanced training?"

"I'm afraid not all of it. He's an E-5, and was training for submarine duty."

George frowned. "Maybe we should just go with the three-man team a while longer."

Norton shook his head. "Too risky. Another injury and you'd be up a creek. And these attacks on the firene have me thinking it's better to have too many men than too few out there."

"All right, I'll take him. But can you line up a trained replacement soon?"

"I think we could send someone out within a couple of months."

George nodded in resignation.

"I recommended your request be accepted, George. Things are evolving fast at Frasier. We need the stability only you can give to that command right now."

"Thank you. I've been wondering what you think of all this action. And what do you make of this odd alliance?"

"The North Koreans and Iranians?"

"Mmm. It's bizarre."

"So long as they don't hook up with China," Norton said.

George nodded. "Is Belanger's prisoner Korean?"

"No. They're not sure what he is, but Belanger says he's not Asian. Middle Eastern, maybe. They don't think he speaks English, and he's in pretty bad shape."

George sighed. "Well, they'll do the best they can until we get there. Earl, there's something personal I wanted to speak to you about, if we have a minute."

"I wish there was time to have you out to the house for dinner. Camilla would love to see you. But your plane is waiting."

"I'd like to see her again, sir. Maybe next time."

The commander nodded. "What's on your mind?"

"Sir, I know it's a ways away, but I'm giving serious thought to leaving active duty when my twenty years are complete."

Norton's eyebrows rose. "How many years do you have in now, George?"

"Sixteen."

"You've had a good career so far."

"I think so. But I'm starting to feel I need a change of pace. There are some things I want to do, and some of them won't wait until retirement."

"What things?"

George swallowed. "I'm thinking I might want to raise horses."

"No money in that, is there?"

George shrugged. "My brother-in-law's getting a reputation as a trainer. He's offered to let me work with him for a while. And

I've been saving my money the last few years. I think I could buy a modest place of my own."

"You always liked horses." Norton shook his head. "You're a man of rare ability, George. I'd hate to see you leave the Navy."

George drew a deep breath. "Sir, I want to have a family too. I want a chance to raise children while I'm young enough to enjoy it."

Norton looked at him steadily for a long moment before looking away with a sigh. "You deserve that."

"I'm not sure I deserve anything, sir, but…I'm thirty-seven years old. I don't have forever. And if I do have the chance, I want to spend time with my family. I don't want to be out on cruise or stuck in a remote spot while my kids grow up without me. Oh, don't get me wrong," he said hastily as Norton stirred. "I've loved being on Frasier. It was what I needed three years ago, and I daresay the mission needed me. But it's coming to a close, and I'm ready to move on to something more…normal…for the next few years, and then I think I'll be ready for civilian life."

"This longing to raise a family, is this just a general feeling, or do you have someone in mind?"

George swallowed. "I have someone in mind, sir."

"Well. You haven't had much opportunity to meet women lately, so unless you had a whirlwind romance during your leave, I have to assume the lady in question is…Ensign Whitney."

"Yes, sir." He waited for Norton to protest, but the older man sat quietly, staring at the photos of his own family that decorated his desk.

At last he looked George in the eye. "Do you love her?"

"Yes, I do."

Norton nodded slowly. "You're her supervisor, however. Perhaps you should have taken that job in Washington."

"Her tour on Frasier is up in April, sir. I haven't spoken to her yet, and I won't while she's my subordinate. But when the time comes, I hope to marry her, and I hope we wouldn't have to be separated for four more years."

Norton sighed. "She could be reassigned until her obligatory service ends. I'm sure you'd be snapped up for an administrative position, or perhaps for a training instructor."

George smiled. "So long as it's not heading up a sociological study."

Norton leaned back and watched him for a moment, his lips tight. "Why did you tell me this? I shouldn't let you go back there. You know that."

George hesitated. It was true. By all rights, Norton should transfer him as far away from Rachel as possible. "You're more than my CO, Earl. This is family business. I didn't mean to put you in an awkward situation, but I won't embarrass you or the Navy. You have my word on it."

The commander picked up the folder and stared at it, unseeing. After a long moment, he sighed. "I hope it goes well for you, George. I mean that sincerely." Norton rose and extended his hand.

TWENTY-FIVE

They waited for two nightmarish days. Pierre was firm about the drug schedule, although the prisoner thrashed and moaned through the last hour before each dose. They kept him sedated as much as possible, partly to keep him quiet, and partly because they didn't know what else to do for him.

After his second dose, Brian told Pierre to give him the Tylenol with codeine instead.

"I know you're hurting, Brian," Pierre said. "Don't be noble."

"He's worse off than me," Chadwick replied. "Besides, if you can't keep him out of it, he might try to escape."

"I think he's beyond that."

"You can't take the chance."

Pierre gave in and held the morphine back for the prisoner. He sat at the man's bedside for hours, feeling helpless.

"It's not your fault," Rachel told him. She'd come off watch and sought him out to ask him if he was hungry.

"If he dies, they won't get anything out of him." Pierre rubbed his eyes and stretched. "Anyway you look at it, I couldn't do it right."

"What do you mean?"

"I couldn't keep you and Brian from being hurt, and I couldn't capture this guy without hurting him so badly he can't give us information."

"Thank you for doing what you did, anyway," Rachel said. "He almost killed Brian. He would have killed me if you guys had been any slower."

"Let's not think about that, *cherie*."

She managed a little smile. "Come on, let's raid the refrigerator. I'll sit with Brian for a while after that, and you should sleep. You need to be alert when you're on duty."

Pierre consented, and she led him off to the galley. "You and Andy are exhausted," she said as she put their dinner in the microwave. "Last night Andy slept in a chair in Brian's room."

"I know. I think he feels guilty because it was actually Brian's shift. Andy should have been the one to dash to your rescue."

Rachel smiled. "Let's not do that. I'm thankful for all three of you. Andy was giving Brian a break, and he acted quickly to alert you guys. No one could have done more."

She sent Pierre off with an armload of clean linens to sleep in her room, and then she went in to sit by Brian's cot.

"Hey, Rachel," he whispered.

"Hey, yourself. How are you doing?"

"Not good, but I'm trying to preserve my last shred of dignity."

"Hurts a lot?"

"Yeah."

"I'm sorry. I wish I could do more for you."

"Hey, you don't have anything to be sorry about. I was the idiot. Before, I mean."

Rachel touched his hand. "Forget it."

"No, I'm leaving here soon, and I don't want all your memories of me to be unpleasant."

"Well, I didn't exactly give you a cordial welcome."

"Where did that guy come from, anyway?"

Rachel inhaled deeply. "Andy spent all morning trying to find out. He's pretty sure he was hiding out in the boat shelter."

Brian's eyes clouded. "That was part of my detail the day of the search."

"Right, but it's not your fault. He was probably watching us from a distance, and crawled in there as soon as you and I left the area. Figured we'd already looked there, so he'd be safe for a while."

"He was right."

"Yeah." She picked up Pierre's scrawled schedule. "Looks like I can get you some more Tylenol."

"Thanks. I guess it helps some, but it doesn't kill the pain."

"Think how much worse it would be with none."

He fell into a fretful sleep an hour after she dosed him, and Rachel went to the storage room to wash a load of Pierre and Brian's laundry and then up to the galley to start supper preparations. None of them were eating well since the incident, and she was determined to get things back on track. It was late in the afternoon when she hefted the basket of wet clothes up the stairs and took it out to the clothesline. Her head was aching again, and her arms were sore where the man had bruised her, but she stuck it out, hanging all the wet clothes to flap in the constant wind. She couldn't send her two companions home with bags full of dirty clothes.

She sat with Brian again that evening. He was groggy, but he seemed to like having her there, so she took one of George's mystery novels in and read to him until he fell asleep. She checked the prisoner a couple of times, but Pierre insisted on taking care of him when he wasn't on duty. Rachel could tell her friend despaired of the man's surviving.

When she got up for her shift the next morning, the mood had changed. Pierre had dark circles beneath his eyes, but he smiled when she took the headset from him.

"They'll be here later today. The weather looks good. I'm going to sleep, but if I'm not up by 1400, call me."

"Sure. I looked in on our guest, and he's status quo. Brian is still asleep. And I changed my sheets. You can sleep in my bed again if you want."

"*Cherie*, you are the noblest of women."

Rachel took up her post prickling with anticipation. At last the *Bush* and its companion ships were returning. They came onto the radar screen early in her shift. She wanted to call Pierre, but she knew he hadn't been sleeping long, so she waited.

She was tempted to initiate radio contact, but if she learned George was not onboard, her disappointment would be unbearable. She watched the painfully slow progress the carrier group made on her radar, on a straight course to Frasier.

Andy entered the room near noon, peering at her from behind his glasses. "Hey, Rachel, I've got sandwiches ready. You want to go upstairs and eat, or should I bring it down here?"

"Thanks. I'll go up."

She made a quick trip to the bathroom and then peeked in at Brian's door. He was asleep. She paused at the door to Pierre's room and saw that Pierre was in there, wiping the prisoner's brow.

"You're supposed to be sleeping."

"This fellow was groaning, so I came in to give him his meds and see if I could help him. He's quiet now, so I guess the codeine helped some."

"Go back to bed."

Pierre sighed. "All right. I'm not sure I can sleep anymore, though."

Rachel fetched her plate and a tall glass of iced tea and carried it down to the control room.

"I decided to eat down here, Andy. You can go."

"I'll stay while you eat."

"Thanks." She sat down near the radio and picked up half her tuna sandwich.

"I see we're tracking the *Bush* group," Andy said.

"Yeah, I got them on the screen about three hours ago. Didn't see any reason to disturb you guys. They won't be here 'til late this afternoon."

"I wonder if Pierre's all packed."

"Oh, his jeans are still out on the line," Rachel said. "Maybe I should run and take them in."

"I'll get them when I go up."

"Let him sleep," she pleaded.

"I will. He's really tired." Andy had the routine down and methodically checked one monitor after another.

"I hope Marie gives him a terrific homecoming."

"Rachel," Andy said hesitantly, "I'm sorry about what happened."

"Thanks. I'm just glad you were on the ball. I tried to call in, but there wasn't time. All I could do was hit the call button once."

"Well, we have to work together for quite a while yet, and I just want to be sure you know that I'm proud to be serving here with you. Brian told me how you were fighting that guy when he got there. He said you were holding your own."

She lowered her eyes. "Thank you, but I was just about at the end of my rope. If Brian hadn't showed up and taken the worst of it…well, I'm thankful to all of you guys."

"Do you think Lieutenant Hudson is coming back?"

Rachel took a slow, deliberate sip of her tea. "I don't know. He wasn't sure, and we haven't heard yet."

"I only saw him for a few minutes," Andy said. "What's he like? I mean, is he fair? He wasn't about to let that Lieutenant Ellis tell him what to do. I kind of admired him. He was fearless."

Rachel smiled. Fearless. He'd seemed that way to her too, but she knew that deep inside he dealt with fears Andy didn't understand.

"He only worries about things that are important," she said.

"What would he have done if he'd been here when that guy attacked you?"

Rachel didn't have to think about the answer to that question. If George had been here, she might have voiced her uneasiness that day she was sketching near the stream. And George wouldn't have given up looking for that piece of angle iron. He'd have realized they had an intruder long ago. She smiled at Andy. "If he'd been here, it wouldn't have happened."

❦

Pierre made radio contact with the *Bush* soon after he got up.

"They're flying in medics to move Brian and the prisoner first and then they'll bring in another chopper with our supplies and personnel to help us raise the windmills," he reported to Rachel as she kneaded bread in the galley. "For once we've got good flying weather."

"You and Andy need to help them," she said. "Let me stay downstairs while they're here."

"All right."

"And George?"

"I don't know." Pierre smiled ruefully. "I was afraid to ask."

"I know how you feel."

"*Cherie*, if they don't bring him, you'll be all right. Andy is on your side now."

She nodded. "I think I went about it all wrong with Brian. I should have had it out with him right at first. That might have changed things."

"I don't know."

She bit her lip. "I hope he's not crippled for life. He did that for me, Pierre."

"We're not any of us going to feel guilty, remember? Be glad he's alive and leaving honorably."

She nodded, but tears sprang to her eyes. "I didn't have time to think, you know? It was so quick!"

Pierre stepped around the table and held out his arms. "I keep thinking about it too. I had to shoot him. There was no other choice."

"Yes, you did." Rachel hugged him for a second, holding her floury hands carefully away from his clothing, and then pulled away. "Thank you. Leave me alone now, Pierre. I want to get this bread rising before I go downstairs again."

"Right. I'd better check Brian."

He left the galley, and Rachel wished she could take the hollow, grief-stricken look from his eyes. She savagely pounded the lump of dough.

She watched the Seahawk on the monitor as it lifted from the deck and whirred toward Frasier. The medics would be on it. Maybe they would tell Pierre whether or not George was on the ship.

She waited impatiently and was tempted to call Pierre on her portable radio. *No, he'll be down soon to say goodbye. I'll ask him then.*

It was half an hour before Andy came trotting down the stairs. "You need to go up. They're getting Brian and the prisoner ready for transport, and the doctor wants to check your cut."

"Thanks. But I thought you were going to help with the windmills."

"Come tell me when they're ready, and I'll go."

The doctor frowned as he pushed her hair back gently. "That must have hurt like the dickens."

"That's an understatement," Rachel said.

"You should go out to the ship for an X-ray, Ensign."

"No. No, I'm fine."

"The skull is thinnest at the temple."

"If I had a fracture, I'd know it by now, wouldn't I?"

"Not necessarily." He shone a penlight into her eyes and then made her track the light as he moved it from side to side. "I don't like the discoloration around your eye, but there doesn't seem to be any swelling. Is the headache gone?"

"Mostly."

"Hmm. You really need a full evaluation."

"I want to stay here, please."

The doctor sighed. "All right. I'm going to give you a few stitches."

"You can do that now, two days after it happened?"

"It's not fully healed, and this will help pull the skin back together." He turned to his instrument case for the local anesthetic. "It will leave a small scar, but your hair ought to cover most of it if you don't pull it back."

"I don't care about the scar," Rachel said.

"You're an unusual woman, then. Any other injuries?"

"Just bruises."

"I'll take a look at them after I do this." He straightened, holding the sutures and needle.

Rachel bit her lip and looked toward the door. Near it Pierre's gear lay in a neat pile. Close by the blanket walls that concealed Andy's sleeping quarters was a small stack of boards.

"Do you know if Lieutenant Hudson is coming back?" she asked, and immediately wished she hadn't.

"Hudson? Never heard of him."

Rachel swallowed hard.

"But some big shot came aboard yesterday," the doctor said, tilting her chin to just the right angle.

"Like an admiral or something?"

"I don't know. He was important enough that they flew him out in a fighter. Could be he's your new CO."

Rachel sat unflinching, thinking about that. Ten minutes later the doctor was finished. She made a trip to the bathroom and examined his repair job as best she could in the mirror. *Big deal,* she told herself. *That's nothing compared to what Brian's got to live with.* She went to her room for her wool jacket and then went out to the helicopter pad.

The chopper was halfway back to the aircraft carrier, and Pierre stood with two seamen, watching its progress.

"Hey, Rachel," he called. "How'd it go?"

"Not bad." She brushed her hair back with a sheepish smile and showed him the stitches.

"You're a woman of intrigue now," Pierre said, and she laughed. He looked toward the two sailors. "These two guys stayed to help with the unloading and the windmills. The next chopper will be full of our supplies, but they can ride back in it."

"They're not our new crew members?" she asked.

"No," said one with a grin. "We're just muscle. Your two new men are on the next chopper."

Rachel swallowed. Two new men. Did he mean that literally? She looked at Pierre, and he shrugged with an anguished look.

"Maybe I should say goodbye to you now, and then Andy can come help unload and put the windmills up." She stepped closer to him, and Pierre clasped his hands behind her head, resting his wrists on her shoulders.

"You are one tough cookie," he said. "You're going to get through this, no matter what."

She nodded. "I won't cry. No matter what."

"Don't box yourself in," he warned. "Crying's not a crime." He led her away from the others, one arm draped loosely over her shoulders. "*Ma cherie*, I will never forget you."

"Same here. When I get stateside again, I would love to visit you and Marie."

"I'd like that."

She nodded, smiling. "I've always wanted to see New England."

He turned her to face him, his brown eyes deep and serious. "Rachel, be brave."

"I'll try."

"You're going to be an admiral someday, I know it."

She laughed. "You're wrong. I…think I'm getting out as soon as I've done my required time."

"Truly?"

"Yes. I wanted to make a career of the Navy, but things have changed for me. I don't think this is the path I want to take now. I want to complete my tour here and my obligatory service, but after that…well, we'll see."

"You've done so much already. You're fulfilling a very important mission."

"I appreciate that. And I love this place. But…I want something different. I want…"

"What, *ma petite?*"

"What you're giving Marie, I guess. A home. Unconditional love."

He smiled and planted a soft kiss on her forehead. "You shall have it."

"I don't see how, if I stay in the Navy."

"All things are possible."

"Pierre, what I really want is…whatever God wants for me. Do you think that's crazy?"

"No. It's the sanest thing I've heard in a long time. We should have talked more about God, you and me."

"Yes." She could feel tears coming. "I'm sorry we didn't."

"We could have had great theological debates over cocoa and popcorn. Why don't you try that with—with whoever is here to talk to in the evening?"

"I might just do that."

"Chopper's coming!" one of the seamen called.

They turned and stood watching it come closer. The sound increased to a roar as the Seahawk flew directly over them and then settled ponderously on the flat patch of turf.

Rachel held her breath, unable to move until Pierre took her hand and guided her slowly toward the helicopter. The rotors slowed and stopped. A man in khakis hopped out, holding a clipboard.

"Who signs for the cargo?"

As Pierre took a step forward, a strong voice called, "I do!"

George climbed out of the chopper and took the clipboard, signing his name with a flourish. He turned then and looked toward them.

"*Mon ami!*" Pierre cried. He and George met grinning and clasped hands.

George looked past his friend toward Rachel. Their eyes met, and George nodded gravely. "Now, *that's* a shiner." He stepped closer to Rachel and touched her cheekbone with gentle fingertips. "They told me you acquitted yourself well, Ensign."

She could smile then, and he answered her with a smile that very closely resembled the one she had drawn. She felt her heart would burst.

"I'm going to relieve Andy," she whispered.

"All right, but I expect a full report from you later."

She raised her hand in a salute, which he returned smartly. She turned and walked quickly up the path, breaking into a run and dashing away a stray tear as she entered the house. When she reached the bottom of the second stairway, she cried, "Andy, quick! Go help them unload."

"Hudson?" he asked.

"He's back!"

TWENTY-SIX

Rachel sensed George's presence rather than heard him, but she wasn't afraid. She caught her breath and waited, her eyes on the camera monitor that showed the ships beyond the boat landing. He moved up close beside her and laid something on the edge of the desk. The bright color drew her eye.

"Candy corn?" she laughed.

"Happy Halloween."

She wanted to jump up and embrace him, but she couldn't. She shifted her gaze to the radar screen. "Welcome home, George."

His hand rested on her shoulder, and her own flew up to meet it.

"We need to talk," he said softly, stroking her slender fingers with his thumb.

"They've finished unloading?"

"Yes. I'm going to change clothes and see if we can get those windmills up. But as soon as we're done, I'll send Greene and Garcia down—"

"Garcia?"

"The new guy. Then you can come up, and we'll talk."

George was sitting on the floor carefully restocking the first aid kit and the drug box when Rachel came upstairs. Anger and contrition surged inside him when he saw her bruised face again. He ought to have been here for her.

"Hey," she said as their eyes met, and she colored slightly and looked around at the crates and the pile of boards.

"The lumber's for the partition."

She nodded. "I'd better cook something. It's supper time, and you guys have worked hard. Can we talk after we eat?"

"Sure. You had some mail and a box from a friend on the *Bush*. I put it all in your room. Hope you don't mind."

She smiled. "That's great."

He went on with his task, content just to be back in the same house with her. Her quiet movements in the galley were followed by the smells of cooking meat and baking bread.

When she announced that dinner was ready, he took a tray down to Greene and brought Garcia back.

"So, where are you from?" Rachel asked the new man.

"Florida."

George thought his accent was quite thick for a third-generation American.

"I was stationed in Seattle last," Garcia continued.

"He was in the right place at the right time," George said. "We needed an instant replacement."

"I am happy to be here." Garcia was wolfing Rachel's cooking. "This is delicious."

"Thank you. It's not always like this." She smiled. "Fresh meat and veggies today, macaroni and canned beets later."

"I saw them take the two wounded men out of the helicopter," Garcia said. "What happened? They had a fight?"

"Sort of," Rachel said. "We had an incident earlier, and apparently a hostile combatant was on the island for more than a week before we knew it. He…attacked me, and one of our men was injured subduing him."

"This has become a sensitive operation," George said. "I want all personnel to wear their sidearms from now on, and never go out alone without your radio."

Garcia nodded.

After supper, George helped him settle his things in Brian's old room. Andy had seen the lumber for the partition and decided to keep his corner quarters. George gave Garcia a tour of the storage area, laundry, shower area, and the roof. Finally the newcomer retired to his room, eager to catch some sleep.

George found Rachel sitting at the table in the galley with one of her sketchbooks and a new box of colored pencils.

"Great. I was hoping you'd still be up." He looked at his watch. "I've got a couple of hours to kill."

She smiled up at him as he sat down opposite her. He looked at her drawing.

"The banana grove in summer," he said.

She laughed. "I haven't had colors in so long! I had to try out some greens."

He reached for the box of pencils. "Ninety-six colors! May I?"

She nodded, and he slid out several blue pencils and held them up, fanning them out in his hand. He discarded a couple, holding up the last three, and then he looked closely at her eyes.

"This one's too light." He laid down one pencil and held the other two up, next to her temple. "Chin up. Hmm."

Her eyes widened in question.

He smiled. "Oh, yes. This one." He turned the one he had selected, squinting at it. "China blue." He nodded. "Of course."

She smiled and tipped the box of pencils up, extracting three, and then she leaned close, studying his eyes.

"Battleship gray?" he suggested.

"No…" She frowned. "No fair. You've got these hazely flecks in them."

She scribbled on the edge of the pad and then pulled out another pencil to add random dots. "That's it. Gunmetal gray with tawny flecks."

He smiled. "Do you like horses?"

Her obvious astonishment made him laugh with delight. He felt as though he was on his first date ever, just discovering how fascinating a woman could be.

"I love them."

"My brother-in-law trains cutting horses," George said. "I stayed with him and my sister for a few days. They started on a shoestring, but after years of hard work they've got a nice spread, and they're building a clientele. My sister, Judy, trains horses for shows. Western pleasure and trail horse classes. Equitation too."

Rachel's eyes shone. "I used to draw nothing but horses when I was in junior high."

"Ever own one?"

"No, my parents were too poor. How about you?"

"I spent half my life on horseback before I joined the Navy."

"Are you a cowboy? I had no idea."

He laughed again. "Well, I'm sure there's a lot I don't know about you too."

"I have all the Glo Bugs displayed in my room at home. It took me three years to collect them."

"The which?"

She chuckled. "How could I not know you were a horse lover?"

"I wasn't giving up any secrets."

"And now?"

"Ask me anything."

Rachel smiled and leaned back in her chair, and George thought he would be content if time stopped at that moment.

"All right. Are we telling these two guys about the firene?"

"Yes. The official word is that our divers will begin mining it in April or May, as soon as the weather is right."

"What will they do with it?" she asked.

"Stockpile it to be made into new and wondrous weapons."

"The no-fallout kind?"

"Yes." He reached in the pocket of his camouflage pants and

brought out an object the size of a walnut, setting it on the table in front of her.

"What's this?"

"Firene."

"You're joking." She looked up at him quickly. "It's safe to handle? I mean, it's not like mercury or anything?"

"No, our scientists are satisfied that, in its natural state, there are no side effects from contact. But dip it in sulfur and put a match to it, and we'd be gone. Poof. Us and half the island."

"Wow." She picked up the nondescript rock and studied it. "This island was a volcano. If the meteorite had hit it when it was active…"

"I don't want to think about it." She handed him the rock, and he tossed it lightly and caught it. "Next summer, this mission will end."

"What happens to Frasier then?"

"They're kicking it around at the Pentagon. Scuttlebutt is they'll rearm the nukes. Or they may just abandon the post."

"Do you think they'll sell it?"

"I doubt it. It's a good location to have for future purposes. I suppose they could give all the admirals timeshares on this house as a vacation spot."

She laughed. "Right. No swimming. No flat place to play golf or tennis. No access to shopping or medical treatment. No cable TV or telephone. They'll be standing in line."

He smiled. "Say, I brought you a new astronomy book. It's a lot better than the old one."

"Great. I want to pay for it."

"Nope."

"George—" Her attempt at a scowl failed miserably, and his pulse raced.

"So, what *did* you do with the old one?"

"I threw it at Brian, and it flew off the roof and down onto the cliff path. Half the pages fell out and blew away."

He stared at her for a long moment. "Well."

"Yes."

He nodded, watching her china blue eyes. "Are you really all right?"

"Yes."

"Tell me the truth. Did Brian hurt you?"

"No. And we were friends at the end. He saved my life, George. If not for his injuries, I think Brian and I could have worked together with no more problems. At least not major ones."

"Good. I'm glad to hear that. And what about the intruder? That wound looks pretty nasty."

"I'll be fine."

"You sure? Because when I saw you, I felt like pounding someone."

"Pierre did that for you."

George sighed deeply. "I wish I'd had more time with Pierre before he left, but I'm glad he's finally away from here."

"He needs to be with Marie." Rachel began putting the pencils back in the box. "I admit I feel responsible for Brian's injuries. I never should have gone out there alone."

"Why not? You'd been doing it for months."

"I know. I thought I was safe in broad daylight." She looked up at him. "I mean, it was Brian's shift. The one time of day I could feel free. But since the two attacks on the island, we all should have been more cautious."

"One thing I've learned is that you can't go blaming yourself for every bad thing that happens."

"You're right."

He considered carefully what he wanted to say and decided that the time of testing had arrived. If she couldn't accept him the way he was now, then he had no right to pursue her. "Rachel," he said quietly, "you have to leave God some leeway. I refused to do that for a long time."

Her stare was so intense that he closed his eyes for a moment, wondering if he had just torpedoed his own dream. When he opened them, she was smiling.

"Do you think about God, George?"

"Yes."

She swallowed. "Me too."

"I'm sorry you had to ask. I should have told you before."

"I used your concordance. And I was praying for you."

His heart tripped. "I'm glad. I had an interesting conversation on the *Bush* yesterday with your friend, Heidi Taber."

"You did?"

"Yeah. What she said about you made me very happy."

"She helped me a lot. I had no idea what God had done for me, or that I was accountable to anyone but the Navy."

"She's an insightful person."

Rachel nodded. "I can see now that God put me in close quarters with her for a purpose. I'll always be thankful for that."

"For me it was my sister who got me back on track. She nudged me until I couldn't ignore her or God anymore." He smiled. "You'd better get some rest. Your watch follows mine, I understand."

"Yes."

She gathered up her things. George was a little disappointed that the private interview was ending, but he needed some time before his shift. Not time alone, but time to continue the process of sorting things out with God.

"I think I'll sleep tonight," Rachel whispered. "George, I missed you so much."

Their gaze met once more, and he hesitated just long enough to send up a quick prayer. He didn't want to say the wrong thing now, and fulfilling his promise to Earl was crucial.

"Rachel, you have no idea, no idea at all, how much I missed you."

Her lips curved upward. "Maybe sometime you can tell me."

For two weeks George bided his time. The new men settled into the routine, although he found himself coaching Garcia quite a bit. Because of his incomplete training, Garcia called him frequently in the afternoons, when pods of migrating whale and porpoise entered their range.

"There's a lot of activity this time of year," George told him. "They're leaving the Arctic. This is the first year we've had such a sophisticated system, and it picks up things we used to miss."

It kept him busy, but with the submarine still fresh in his memory, he encouraged the others to keep him alerted to mammal activity and to watch closely for irregular movements and sounds, especially of lone animals.

They weathered one storm with the windmills still intact. The subtle change in seasons brought a new beauty to the island. Rachel sketched birds that stopped to rest in their migration. When the men tracked whales close by during daylight hours, she went up to the telescope or hiked to the extremities of the island to catch a glimpse. Whenever he could, George went with her, and they stood side by side, binoculars raised, watching the majestic animals blow and dive.

She came to him one mid-November evening in the galley, where he'd spread out papers on the table to work on his reports.

She slipped into the chair opposite him and waited in silence until he finished writing a sentence and looked up. His pleasure in her presence and the simple fact that she'd sought him out were tempered by the somber set of her mouth and the anxious light in her eyes.

"Can I help you?"

She licked her lips, looked toward the door, and then back at him.

"George, I…"

He waited. This was serious. He tried not to let his imagination run off into grim possibilities.

Her gaze focused on his eyes, and she drew in a breath.

"I need to tell you something."

She ducked her head for a moment, and he wondered if she was praying.

Lord, whatever this is about, help me to make it easier for her.

"I'm listening, Rachel."

"Okay. I should have told you before, but I was sure you wouldn't want me here, and then when Brian came and you thought I wasn't strong enough…" She raised her chin and met his gaze. "As usual, I let my pride interfere. I knew you wouldn't leave me here if you knew my history, and I was being selfish. I wanted to stay, and I wanted to prove to you and the world that I was capable."

He frowned, trying to make sense of this roundabout confession. Her anxiety was causing his own apprehension to rise.

"What is it, Rachel?"

She clasped her hands and stared down at them. "I was assaulted once. Before I came here."

The silence hung between them for a long moment. George felt as though he'd stepped onto a rapidly descending elevator.

She swallowed hard. "I never told anyone—well, except Pierre—and I wouldn't have told you, but now…well, I've been studying Scripture and praying about it and thinking a lot about it, and…I thought you had a right to know." Her forehead wrinkled as she looked up at him and waited.

He drew in a careful breath. "Are you saying it affected your reaction when you were attacked here on Frasier?"

She relaxed and sagged into the chair. "Not just then. It affected all my reactions. To you. To Brian."

He nodded, thinking back to the early days, when she'd chafed under his arbitrary decisions and rebelled at his authority. He was more glad than ever that he hadn't come down hard on her then. He'd considered it, but at the time his own guilt had kept him from doing more than bark at her.

"Is there anything I can do?"

After a pause she whispered, "You're praying for me now, aren't you?"

He nodded. "All the time."

"Don't stop."

He wanted to walk around the table and take her in his arms, but his inner radar told him not to. She'd positioned herself carefully, with the table between them. She wanted him to consider this objectively, as both her commanding officer and her friend, and not turn it into an emotional scene.

"Are you all right?"

"Yes. Now I am."

He frowned at the scar beside her eye. "You're sure? If you need to go stateside…"

"No. Please don't ask me to do that. You, of all people, know that time is a healer. It's taken me a while, but I'm learning how God works. Finally I'm getting to where I can put that incident in perspective." Her earnestness tore at him, but she was more serene than he'd ever seen her. "I'm not telling you this because I want sympathy, George. I just thought you deserved an explanation. It's not an excuse for the way I behaved, but…"

"I've seen a big change in you since I came back."

"Thanks." She smiled and gave a little shrug. "That's all I wanted to say. You're busy."

"Come back anytime. I'm not too busy for you."

She left as quietly as she had come, and he sat for a long time, staring down at his log without seeing it.

"Ah, Rachel," he whispered at last, shaking his head. He'd nurtured his own pain far too long. Why hadn't he seen the struggles of others around him?

Lord, thanks for giving me another chance. Please, do whatever it takes to make me into the man she needs.

❧

A few days later, they stood on a rock high above the northeastern shore, watching a small pod of swimming animals.

"Sei whale?" George hazarded.

"No, the flukes aren't right, and they're too small."

"They're a long ways out."

"Northern bottlenose," she said firmly, as one breached. "Oh, look at that!"

"You may be right. Aren't they rare?"

"Yes. I wish we could hear them."

The whales moved slowly away, and Rachel sighed. She sat down, opened her sketchbook, and began to draw. George crouched at her elbow, watching her swift strokes.

"I can't do them justice," she complained as her soft pencil formed the outline of a bull surfacing.

"Tell me how you're getting along with the men," George said, settling more comfortably beside her on the rock.

"Fine. Garcia seems a little slow, but he's learning."

"I'm still hoping we'll get a replacement for him soon. But he and Greene don't make you uneasy?"

Rachel kept on drawing, frowning as she worked. "Andy's okay. He knows what's what. He looks up to you, and he can see that I'm your favorite. That goes a long way."

She glanced up at him. Her face was serene, and he was thankful for that. His days ended early each morning, when she came down to the monitoring station and greeted him. The first few times, her eyes had held anxiety, as though she didn't feel safe until she had reassured herself that he was still there. But since she'd told him about her painful past, she'd seemed more peaceful, and he knew her faith was doing its work.

He usually made time for a quiet talk with her each evening, and in those times he sensed a new contentment in her. Last night he'd suggested they read a psalm together, and although they hadn't touched, he'd felt the bond between them strengthen, drawing her heart closer to his.

She turned back to her whale drawing with a secret half smile, and he wished he could read her thoughts. The wind lifted her hair a little, pulling tendrils free from her braid. He wanted to curl one around his finger, and he clasped his hands together between his knees to be sure he didn't.

She said, "Garcia is a loner. I try to be friendly, and he responds, but he's not outgoing. Doesn't talk about his family much."

"Mm-hmm." George nodded. "Rachel, have you wondered why I kissed you before I left here but haven't touched you these past two weeks?"

Her pencil stopped its motion for an instant. Then she resumed her strokes, filling in the water around the whale. "Not really. I think I'm finally getting to know you, George."

"And?"

"If you want to, you will."

His heart hammered as he realized how deeply she trusted him.

"No, that's not it. I want to all the time."

She kept drawing without pause that time, but a slow flush stained her cheeks.

"What, then?"

"There are layers of reasons. What you told me the other night is one of them. But even before you told me...well, there was Chadwick."

"I'm not frightened anymore."

"I'm glad." He bowed his head for a moment. "I spoke with Norton last night. Chadwick will probably be discharged soon."

"From the hospital?"

"From the Navy."

Her hands stilled, and she turned to look at him closely. "I didn't file a complaint."

"It's medical. But I think it's for the best."

She opened her mouth but then closed it.

"It's all right, Rachel. It has nothing to do with you, really. His injuries are severe. Don't worry, though. He'll get disability pay until he's sound again."

She looked at him, and her bottom lip trembled. "I still feel bad about what happened between Brian and me."

"It's over."

"Yes. And I don't think something like that will happen again, as far as I'm concerned. I know I'd handle it differently the next time."

"Good. It was a little unnerving to see you in the helpless role."

Just for an instant, the old rebellion threatened in her eyes. Then she looked down at her sketchbook with an ironic smile. "My pride still flares up now and then. I'm praying about that."

"Oh, Rachel." He touched her hair lightly but then immediately pulled his hand back and shifted, moving away from her slightly on the rock. They sat silent for a long minute.

"Will his leg heal all right?" she asked at last.

"Pretty much. But I suspect it will bother him some."

"I feel guilty about that," she admitted.

"Don't."

She stared out over the Pacific. "George, I let you down."

"By being attacked?"

"No. By being afraid." Rachel looked up at him. "I'm leaving in April, you know. And I've decided that I'll leave the Navy as soon as my required stint is over." Tears shone in her eyes, and she laid the sketchbook down, turning her head away from him and drawing up her knees to rest on.

"You've had enough?"

"I want to stay here until my tour of duty is done and complete all my commitments. After that...I'm not sure."

George could barely hear her, with the wind blowing gently and her face turned away from him.

"I am so selfish," she said. "When they came for the prisoner, the doctor wanted me to go out to the ship for medical care, but I was afraid they wouldn't let me come back. I needed to be near you. And I didn't even know for sure yet that you would be here."

Again, the desire to hold her and shelter her in his arms was almost overpowering. "If it helps," he said, "I was desperate to get back here myself, and it wasn't because of my concern for the mission, as important as that is."

She turned her head and looked at him then. The bruise had faded. Her eyes were liquid, and she hugged her knees, pillowing her cheek on her arms.

"Rachel, if you leave in April, the mining crews will be on their way. I'll stay here through that operation, but..." He stopped. The time wasn't right yet, he knew. "Of course, there are layers of protocol too."

"Regulations," she agreed. "I thought that might be part of it."

"Yes. It's a small unit, and we can't get around that. I don't want Andy and Miguel to leave here someday and say I wasn't fair because I was in love or that I let you distract me from my duty."

She said nothing, and he wondered if she was pleased that he found her distracting or alarmed at his indirect declaration of love.

He looked at the horizon and then back at her. "Do you understand? If I let myself kiss you good night, for example..."

"I understand."

"But it doesn't mean I don't want to, or that I don't have feelings for you."

Her long, damp lashes came down to mask her china blue eyes. "I'll keep that in mind."

He smiled at her. "As to Chadwick, leave it to God now."

"Why didn't I know this about you before you went to Washington?"

"What?"

"You know. That you believe in God. You talk to Him. You trust Him."

"Because I wasn't doing any of that back then. I hadn't finished my own rebellion."

"You've made things right, though."

"Yes."

"I thought I was the only one here who believed."

"That was my fault. A lot was my fault. I was angry and stubborn, but then, you already knew that." Regret swept over him, but it wouldn't do any good to wallow in it. "Anyway, I made things difficult for you when you came, and I'm sorry."

She smiled but did not protest.

"I've been thinking about my career too," he said. "Twenty years will be enough for me, I think."

Her eyes held no surprise, only a contemplative empathy.

His radio burbled, and reluctantly he pulled the portable unit from his belt. "Yeah, Miguel?"

"We have a ship off course, a merchantman en route to the Marshall Islands and Japan."

"You have radio contact?"

"Yes, sir. They're a hundred and fifty miles south of here."

"I'll come in and check with you in a few minutes."

"Yes, sir."

She was still watching him in that mournful, wistful way. *I could kiss her this instant. No witnesses but the seabirds. It doesn't have to become a habit.*

But he knew it would.

She reached for her sketchbook, turning away from him a little, and was on her feet before he could offer his hand.

"Come on, Lieutenant. You've got work to do."

TWENTY-SEVEN

Rachel's Thanksgiving dinner was a triumph. Turkey breast, squash and peas from the freezer, gravy, rolls, potatoes she had hoarded, canned cranberry sauce, and dressing from a box. And pies. Pumpkin, pecan, and apple.

She ate with George and Andy in the mid-afternoon, and then Andy carried his pie downstairs and let Miguel come up and eat his dinner while she and George ate dessert.

"I don't think I've eaten this much in twenty years," George moaned, sitting back and staring at the half piece of pecan pie still on his plate.

"What were your last two Thanksgivings like?" Rachel asked, sipping her tea. She had quit eating long before the men did and was anticipating a rich bedtime snack.

George shrugged. "The first year we forgot to order anything special. Matt tried to come up with something. I think he caught some fish. I know it was nothing like this. And last year, Pierre did a ham dinner. It wasn't bad, but he didn't make pies. We had stale little pastries from the freezer."

"It's very good," Miguel said, raising his forkful of turkey vaguely in Rachel's direction.

"Thank you," she said.

George stretched. "I feel as if I've got more to be thankful for this year than I have for a long time."

"Me too," Rachel nodded. "How about you, Miguel?"

He shrugged. "This is not exactly what I had planned for now, but it could be worse."

"I got some word today on the man Pierre shot," George said.

Rachel caught her breath. "Did he make it?"

"Yes. It was touch and go for a while, but he's making slow progress now. They haven't gotten much out of him yet, but they know he's Pakistani, and they've got a translator and are starting to question him."

George's radio trilled, and he answered.

"Friend of yours calling you," Andy said.

George rose and walked quickly into the sitting room. Rachel could hear him tuning in the big radio. "Rachel!" he shouted. "Get in here!"

She rushed out of the galley. "What is it?"

George's boyish grin gave it away.

"Pierre!" she cried.

"Just back from his honeymoon in Quebec."

She grabbed the microphone.

"Quebec, you goose? Why didn't you take her someplace warm?"

"We're going someplace warm, *cherie*. They're shipping me to Japan and Marie is coming with me. Hey! I'm going as a lieutenant JG."

❧

Christmas was approaching, and Rachel was full of secrets. She made their common rooms festive, stretching the decorations Warrant Officer Shaw had grudgingly allowed and making more to supplement them. Andy brought her a small bush for a Christmas tree, and she festooned it with paper chains made from strips of paper she colored in ninety-six colors. The smells of her baking tantalized the men, and to avoid a mutiny she allowed them to sample the sweets she was freezing for the holidays.

She made wrapping paper from waste paper, coloring the backs brightly in reds, greens, and golds, and had her Christmas gifts wrapped and waiting a week in advance. The gray Shaker knit sweater for George seemed inadequate now. She wished she'd known things about him that she knew now when she ordered, but there was no chance to exchange it. In September she had racked her brain and decided to order videos for the two new men, and she thought Andy and Miguel would appreciate them as much as anything. Her candy ration had been cut back, but a box of chocolates and a small one of peanut brittle had made it through.

She waited impatiently for Miguel to relieve her on Christmas Eve. She had a few last touches to put on her table decorations for tomorrow, and more cooking to do. They would have to settle for instant mashed potatoes, but her gravy would cover the pasty taste. She had yeast dough in the refrigerator and wanted to shape the rolls and get them rising.

Miguel arrived on the dot of noon, wearing his jacket and a little out of breath.

"Sorry. I lost track of time."

"You're not late. Say, Miguel, does your family have any special Christmas traditions?"

"No, no, we just…do like everyone else."

She nodded. "I was thinking maybe we could sing some carols tonight. Do you think that's corny?"

"Well…whatever you want, Rachel."

She grinned. "You guys spoil me, I know."

"We appreciate you," he said, taking her place at the console.

"*Adios*," she said gaily, heading for the stairs.

❧

George joined her in the galley at 1430. He was fresh from the shower, wearing a green T-shirt and camouflage pants, with his pistol holstered at his waist.

"What's that smell?" he demanded.

"Hmm. Could be orange rolls. Want one?"

"No, I want two."

She laughed and put two of the glazed crescent rolls on a plate for him as he poured coffee.

"Andy around?" George asked.

"I haven't seen him all day."

"He didn't give you a break this morning?"

"Now that you mention it, no."

George set his mug down and picked up a roll. "I want to climb windmill number two this afternoon. We're in for a storm soon, and I want to make sure everything's ready. It seems to rattle a little when the wind is out of the north."

"They've stayed up a long time."

"Yeah. This is the best year I've had, I think, as windmills go."

"Well, if you can't find Andy, let me know. You need somebody out there spotting for you if you're going to climb."

"Okay. Maybe I'll just give him a call."

"Check his room first," Rachel said.

"I just looked in there. His bed is made."

She frowned. "I didn't see him on my monitors, but that doesn't mean much." Only a small part of the island, including the boat landing and helicopter pad, was visible on the camera monitors.

George licked his fingers. "Don't tell my sister, but you cook better than Mom did."

Rachel laughed. "Thanks. That's high praise, I'm sure. I've been thinking about your sister. Does she have children?"

"Yup. Two girls. Little live wires."

"Do they ride horses?"

"Of course. Cassie is nine. She's heavily into barrel racing. Abbey's twelve and a tad more serious. She has Olympic aspirations, so Judy's sending her out to some high-falutin' English instructor for dressage lessons."

"Every little girl's dream."

"I wouldn't know." He sipped his coffee. "They're cute, and they can ride circles around me."

"So, you went riding when you were at their place?"

"Every day."

"That must have been fun."

"It was fantastic. They live in the hills in northern California. Beautiful country. What are you making now?"

"Pumpkin pie. It went over so well at Thanksgiving, I thought we needed a reprise."

"Remind me not to eat breakfast."

She chuckled. "When you get up tomorrow, it will be time for Christmas dinner."

"Guess we'd better have everybody call home."

"That's a great idea."

He stood up. "I'd better get moving." He carried his dishes to the sink, and then he pulled out his radio and signaled for Andy. "That's funny."

He strode through the doorway to the sitting room, and reappeared a few seconds later, frowning.

"His radio's not in his room."

Rachel stopped stirring her pie filling. "Either he's left it someplace, or…"

"He can't be out of range on this island."

"Maybe he's in the shower."

"I just came from there, but I'll check."

⁇

He left her again, going rapidly down the stairs. No one was in the shower area, or any other part of the first basement. He went on down to the control room.

"Hey, Miguel! You seen Andy?"

"No, sir."

"Did you talk to him this morning?"

"No, I was outside for a while, but I didn't run into him."

Rachel was in the doorway, and George turned to her, hoping she had news.

"I just came down to see if you knew anything," she said. "My pie can wait. I'll help you look for him."

George looked from her to Miguel and back. "If we've got another broken leg, we'll look pretty incompetent. All right, Miguel. You got your portable radio?"

Miguel turned part way toward them and looked at George for an instant. "Yes, sir."

"Rachel, where's yours?"

"It's upstairs. I'll get it and my jacket and meet you in the sitting room."

George turned back to Miguel. "If he shows up here, or if you hear from him or see him on one of the monitors, call me immediately."

"Yes, sir." Miguel met his eyes briefly and then turned back to the console.

George bounded up one flight of stairs, grabbed the first aid kit, and then hurried to his room. Rachel was just coming from hers.

"Get binoculars, kiddo."

She turned back to her bedroom.

George pulled on a sweatshirt, then his camouflage jacket and cap. Apprehension was making the back of his neck prickle. He added a sheathed hunting knife to his belt. On top of the dresser was the tiny package he had brought for Rachel. *Great way to spend Christmas Eve.* He seized his binoculars and went to meet her.

"Where do we start?" she asked.

"At the bottom of the cliffs, I guess. Worst-case scenario."

"The tide's pretty high, George."

He nodded. They both knew an injured person was at great risk along the shore. If Andy fell near the water that morning, they might never find him.

"Want to separate?" Rachel asked.

"No. Stay with me."

She nodded and reached out to grasp his fingers for an instant. "It's okay, George. We'll find him. Tonight we'll be laughing about this and singing 'The Wassail Song.'"

"I hope you're right. Come on."

He led her down the cliff path. The tide was too high to let them climb around the shore at the base. He tried to stop his imagination from picturing Andy's skinny body being dragged out by a breaker.

Rachel said soberly, "We'd better get around the perimeter as fast as we can."

George tried again to raise Andy on the radio with no success.

"Maybe he dropped his radio. I dropped mine the day—" She glanced up at him. George nodded, wishing he could erase the awful memories from her mind and the troubled look from her face. The best way to do that would be to find Andy.

"Let's move."

Their search of the rocky shore was limited because the water was so high. Even so, it still took them more than an hour to encircle the island and make a cursory search of a thousand places a person could fall.

"What's left?" Rachel panted when George sat down on a rock near the boat landing and motioned for her to sit too.

"The interior." He smiled at her expression. It was such a formal word for the tiny bit of ground between the shores of Frasier.

"George, do you think there could be another enemy hiding on the island?"

"No. I've been over every inch several times in the last few weeks just to be sure. The man Pierre shot was alone, and if any vessels had come near here since then, we'd know it." He lifted his radio to his cheek. "Miguel, any word from Andy?"

"No, sir."

"Anything unusual on your monitors?"

"No, sir. Some porpoise to the northwest of us."

"Keep me posted."

George stared out over the sea, and Rachel waited. He was worried now. Very worried. The wind was picking up, and the waves were growing larger. If they didn't find Andy soon, he'd have to call Pearl Harbor.

"Let's check the spring." He stood up.

She followed him to the windmills and the helicopter pad, and then down the steep path to the spring in the ravine. George walked slowly, looking at the ground, and Rachel followed suit, starting out in a spiral from the spring.

"Stay in sight," George called, as he worked toward the jungle, and she edged on along the faint path that headed toward the coffee bush.

"George!" She was calling him on his radio, and he turned, surprised at how far away she was. He could barely see her, nearly at the banana grove. He strode quickly to her, and she pointed to a trail of flattened plants leading off to the left. The dried stems were bent over and broken.

"What do you think?"

"You been out here lately?"

"No."

❧

They advanced slowly, and George went to his knees after a few yards. Rachel crouched beside him, trying to force down her fear. He reached out to touch a dark spot on the leaves and then raised his hand to look at it.

She swallowed hard. One finger was smeared with blood.

They looked at each other.

"Stay here." He got to his feet and followed the faint trail. It took him to a rocky ledge that overlooked the north shore. They had searched below it earlier, closer to the water.

Rachel watched him move along the ledge, silhouetted against the sky. She put her hand to her pistol, just for reassurance, and glanced over her shoulder, back toward the path. George stooped on the ledge and looked over the rim, and then he stood up and beckoned to her. She ran to him and looked down, seeing nothing unusual.

"He's down there," George said. "I'm going to bring him up."

"Do we need a rope?"

"I don't think so. I can climb down over there." He gestured to the right, where the drop was less steep.

"Do you want me to call Miguel?"

"Not until I see what's what."

She stood shivering in the wind. It wasn't Oregon mountain cold, but her lightweight wool jacket wasn't enough to warm her on this bleak day. George worked his way down to a thicket of evergreen bushes, and suddenly she recognized what he had seen: Andy's boots, protruding just a bit from the bushes.

George dragged him from the thicket and then knelt beside him, checking for a pulse. Rachel stood fifteen feet above, waiting with dread. When he glanced up, she lifted her radio. George shook his head. She raised her eyebrows in confusion.

George raised his radio to his mouth. "No sign of him, Rachel."

Her heart skipped a beat. She pushed the button on her unit and replied, "I copy."

George gave her a silent thumbs-up, and dragged Andy's body back into the thicket.

Rachel's heart pounded. She was scarcely able to believe what was happening. When George reached her, he grabbed her hand and hurried her along, back to the path and then to the edge of the jungle.

"Get under cover," he said in low, tight tones.

She faced him under the trees, looking for comfort in his eyes.

"Andy's dead," she said.

"Yes."

"You don't think Miguel—"

George put his hands on her shoulders. "Sweetheart, he was shot. If not Miguel, then who?"

She swallowed hard. "I guess either it was him or there's someone else on the island."

George nodded. "And I don't buy that scenario this time."

"We've searched just about everywhere," she said.

"No, not really. We've searched all the places an injured man might be, not the places a desperate man could hide."

"So you think there's a slight possibility it wasn't Miguel?"

"The very slightest. Like maybe one tenth of one percent chance."

"What do we do?"

"I'll need to call Pearl Harbor right away."

Rachel brightened. "Right. So we go back to the house and you…if you call from upstairs, Miguel can hear you, can't he?"

"Yes. I'll have to go down to the control room. I need to assume Miguel did it and take him into custody first. If I don't restrain him and he knows we're onto him, he might try something."

She nodded. "I'll follow your lead."

"All right. I go in first."

"If he did this, will he just sit there waiting for you?"

"I'm hoping he doesn't know yet that we found the body."

"But still—if you leave Miguel alone and Andy never shows up, he might incriminate himself. Maybe come out tonight when you're on watch and try to move the body. Dump it into the water."

George shook his head. "Too risky."

"He came in at noon wearing his jacket," Rachel said suddenly. "He was nearly late."

"But you didn't notice anything—blood, for instance, or the smell of gunpowder?"

"No, but I wasn't thinking about it. I was thinking about making pies."

"Let's go," George said grimly. "I don't dare leave him on the loose. I'll restrain him and then call Pearl."

They entered the house cautiously. The idea that Miguel might have left the control room appalled Rachel, but if he'd committed murder, deserting his post would be a small infraction. George set the first aid kit down.

"Stay behind me," he said as they entered the stairway.

The security door at the bottom of the first flight was closed.

Rachel looked at George apprehensively. He pulled out his keys and approached it.

"Get back!"

She backed up so fast on the landing that she sat down hard on the bottom step.

"I smell smoke," George whispered.

She sniffed. "I smell it too."

George went silently to the door and felt it. Then he inserted his key into the lock. He opened the door cautiously. The smoke smell increased, and the air beyond the door was hazy.

"Stay here."

He went down the steps cautiously, his gun drawn.

Rachel squinted, trying to see if the lower door was closed. Her eyes began to water. George paused briefly at the bottom of the stairs, and then he came bounding back up. He closed the door at the landing and pulled her up toward the main level.

"Come on!"

He held her hand tightly in his as he charged into the sitting room and made for the radio.

"I was afraid of that."

Rachel stared at the radio set. The cover was off, and several parts were detached and scattered over the floor.

"The bottom door was hot," George said. "I could hear the fire inside."

She stared at him. "Was Miguel in there?"

"I doubt it. He probably smashed all the equipment, started the fire, and got out."

"But if there are intruders—"

"It's possible. They could have overpowered him. I couldn't open the door to find out."

"All right, Lieutenant. What now?"

"We'll need our survival kits. You got camos?"

"A shirt."

"Andy had some sweats," George said. "Come on."

She followed him into the tiny corner room, and George pulled Andy's camouflage sweatpants from his sea bag. He made a quick sweep of the galley and headed down the hallway, checking the bathroom and Miguel's room.

He quickly searched Rachel's room and then stood at the door with it open six inches, looking down the hall.

"Get changed. Put your camo shirt on over your jacket if it will fit."

She pulled Andy's sweats over her jeans and took the camo shirt from its hook. It was too snug to go over her wool jacket. She unbuttoned the navy blue coat quickly and pulled two sweatshirts over her T-shirt and then the camo shirt. She delved into her sea bag for her compact survival kit.

"All set," she said, going to stand behind George.

He threw her a quick glance. "Hat? Gloves? We'll be out all night."

"This whole place will burn? The control room is down inside the rock."

"There are enough combustibles that I think it will all go. That door was radiating heat three feet."

As he spoke, she donned a knit cap and gloves. She'd told herself she was foolish last spring to pack a winter hat, but now she knew better.

"Anything else?" she asked.

"This place is burning. Is there anything in this room that you want to salvage? Your sketchbook, maybe?"

She smiled, surprised that he'd thought of that. "It's not critical."

"Well, why don't you slip it inside your clothes if you can? I'd hate to think you lost all that hard work. It may be the only thing you have left when we're done."

She slipped the sketchbook between her layers of shirts and tucked in the waist. Maybe someday she'd frame a couple of the drawings. It pleased her inordinately that George found her art worth saving.

"I'm ready," she said.

"Follow me."

They went across the hallway to George's room.

"Watch the door."

She didn't ask questions, but stood with her back to him, peering out into the hallway with her 9 mm Beretta at the ready.

❧

George rummaged in his dresser for his survival kit and extra clips for the guns. He hesitated, trying to think what else would be worth carrying. The short-range radios were perhaps not, especially when Miguel might be listening to anything they said. Still, he decided to keep them for now.

His eye fell on Rachel's Christmas present, the tiny box from the jewelry store, wrapped in silver paper. It struck him suddenly that they were going to lose everything they owned, and he shoved the box and the small souvenir chunk of firene into his jacket pocket, along with a snapshot of Judy's two girls. The compact Bible found a spot, too.

"George, I smell smoke again."

"Yeah, we've got to get out of here." He stepped up behind her and touched her shoulder. "Are you sure you have everything?"

She turned wide eyes to stare at him. He'd half expected to see terror in her eyes, but as he reached to touch her smooth cheek, a flicker of fear was replaced with steady trust.

"I'm all set, George. I've got you."

TWENTY-EIGHT

It was a six-foot drop from George's window. He went out first, after a hard look around. Rachel lowered herself from the sill, and he pulled her quickly around the corner of the house. They stealthily made their way away from it, toward the east tip of the island. It was slow going, avoiding the paths and trying to stay in cover.

Rachel asked none of the questions that whirled in her head but stuck to his heels, determined not to slow him down. As they ran, she fired abbreviated prayers heavenward.

On the eastern basalt cliffs they took cover and sat silently between some large rocks, their heads low. George kept a grim vigil, watching the way they had come and turning frequently to check every possible approach.

When they had sat for half an hour, Rachel began to wonder if they would stay there all night. She rose on her knees, her eyes just above the edge of the black rock, and looked southwest, toward the setting sun. The windmills thrust up beyond the jungle, whirling madly in the strong wind, and she thought a faint column of smoke drifted upward beyond them.

"We'll move when it's dark," George said quietly. "I can't chance anyone seeing where we go."

She nodded. He smiled just a little then, and reached for her hand. His right hand still grasped the pistol, and his eyes went immediately back toward the high end of the island.

"Long, long thoughts, kiddo?"

"Yes."

"We'll talk when we get to my stash."

She settled down between the rocks again and rested her head against his leg.

⸎

George leaned on the rock, waiting and thinking. As the light faded, he tried to stay even more alert. What was Miguel doing now, right this minute? And was he alone?

Finally it was time. He put his hand gently on Rachel's head, and she stirred. She inched up beside him, and he bent close to her. "Gun ready?"

"Yes."

He looked around one more time and climbed out of the hiding place. He led her by the easiest route, not the most direct. They circled low beyond the cliff to a rock-covered slope. It was getting cold, and the wind had picked up. Again he stopped and sat silent for several minutes in a declivity before he led her on to the entrance of the refuge.

From the sea it was invisible. They scrambled over several large rocks, and then George paused above the entrance.

"I'll go in first," he said, near her ear. He opened his survival pack and took out a small but powerful flashlight and then lowered himself between two rocks. The gap was barely large enough to admit him, but at the bottom the cave's mouth opened to the side.

Rachel eased herself into position after him. She saw that the cavern wasn't large, roughly six feet by ten, scooped back into the rocky slope. George couldn't quite stand up straight in the highest spot. Still, it was well above the high tide line and the floor was dry.

He shined the light around the chamber. Three wooden crates were stacked inside. He turned his light toward the aperture, and Rachel crawled in, the beam of her flashlight catching him in the eyes. She turned it off quickly and stood up, staring around her.

"Well, it's not the Ritz, but this is it," he said.

"It's really something."

"Hold this for me." He handed her his flashlight and holstered his pistol. Then he set the top two crates down to the stone floor. "Have a seat."

She sat on one and aimed the beam of the flashlight on the one he knelt to open.

"What have we got?" she asked.

"All kinds of goodies," he said in a teasing tone. She trained the light on the side of the crate that read *Meals Ready to Eat.*

"MREs! Yummy!"

He laughed. "Hungry, gorgeous?"

"I thought my name was *kiddo.*"

"Sorry. *Ensign* seems a little impersonal now."

He pried the top of the box off with his knife, revealing two dozen MRE's and four quarts of water. "It's been sitting a while," he warned. "The water's probably stale."

He started on the second crate. "Here we go!" He lifted out a small device that looked like a walkie-talkie.

"What's that?"

"A radio distress beacon. The battery may be dead."

He fished a battery from the crate and held the beacon in the light, fiddling with the cover to the battery compartment and the switch.

"How can you tell if it's working?"

"There's supposed to be a little red light when it's on."

"But there's not."

He sighed. "I was hoping."

"Do we have any other way to make outside contact? These portables aren't good for any distance."

George shook his head. "Can't think of anything, other than the signaling mirrors in the survival kits. Unless this thing will take the batteries from the portables."

Rachel pulled her radio from her belt and opened the battery compartment while George opened the one on the beacon.

"Looks like a match. Your radio's good for something besides leading Miguel to us."

She caught her breath. "What do you think happened? I called to you when I found the bent foliage. Do you think Miguel heard me and knew we were close to finding the body?"

"Maybe." George wished he hadn't mentioned it. Now she would feel responsible. "It's possible it wasn't he who killed Andy, but that's highly unlikely. We had all that surveillance equipment. I can't believe they got a sub or a helicopter past us."

He took a battery from her radio and fumbled with the beacon.

"If Miguel is in league with the cartel, they could have sent a submarine in on his shift." Rachel leaned closer, adjusting the flashlight beam for his task, and George was very conscious of her nearness.

"I don't know. They'd have had to be within our surveillance range during your watch," he said. "I suppose Andy could have missed something significant on his shift, but I don't think you would. They'd have to zoom in and out of here really fast."

"How about if they hid below the firene ledge, or below the cliffs on this end of the island?"

"Maybe. But if there were a large landing force, we'd have encountered them tonight."

"Miguel couldn't be working alone," she insisted. "If so, why would he destroy the house and all the supplies? That doesn't make sense."

"True."

"Maybe he was dead in there. Invaders went in while we were looking for Andy, killed Miguel, and started the fire." She shuddered.

"They had to use an accelerant," George mused. "That fire was hot and fast, and most of the stuff in that room wasn't especially flammable."

"There was fuel for the generators in the storage room."

"Yes. Either Miguel set the fire to aid his friends, or someone else surprised him." George slid the battery cover into place and flipped the switch. A red dot of light shone in the dimness.

"All right!" Rachel said fervently. "How far does the signal throw?"

"Five hundred miles."

"Even from inside a cave?"

"Let's hope so."

"Can the bad guys track it?"

He hesitated. "Let's hope not."

"And if Pearl Harbor can't pick it up?"

"A ship or a plane?" he suggested.

"So, this isn't a sure thing. Is that what you're telling me?"

"That's right."

"You think we're safe here?"

"I do. Nothing's been disturbed in here, and the entrance is well hidden. But I'll stand watch just in case. No way can they get in here if I'm awake." He took another pistol and several ammo clips from the crate, loaded the gun, and put it in his jacket pocket. "You got a knife?"

"Yes."

He put an extra one from the crate in his pack.

"When do we eat?" Rachel asked.

He chuckled. "You want chicken or corned beef?"

"Definitely chicken."

It was like a picnic, sitting on the boxes with Rachel and eating by the light of a candle he took from the crate to save the flashlights. She ate every bit of the unappetizing food. He tried not to think of the Christmas dinner they had lost.

"You get some sleep. I'm used to sitting up all night." He rose and bent over his crate, pulling out two wool blankets. "Lie on one of these and pull the space blanket from your survival kit over you."

"What am I sitting on?" she asked. "You didn't open this box yet."

"That, my dear, is our secret weapon."

She turned on her flashlight and examined the box closely. "It's pretty big."

"All in good time."

"You've got me curious."

"Curiosity killed the cat."

"Oh, now we're back to pet names." But she was smiling this time.

She spread the blankets and lay down. George blew out the candle and sat listening to the rhythmic waves and the howling wind. He reached in his pocket and touched the leather cover of his Bible.

You and me and Rachel on Christmas Eve, Lord. Thank You. Help me be as competent as she thinks I am.

❧

In the utter darkness, Rachel felt the old claustrophobic panic and pushed it down. She listened for George's breathing but couldn't hear it. All she could hear was the muffled wind and distant breakers. She knew he was only a few feet away, but her heart began to hammer, and her breath grew choppy.

"George?"

"Hmm?"

She rolled up onto her knees. "Where are you?" She reached out in the blackness, groping for him, touching nothing.

His flashlight beam shone out suddenly, and she crawled over to him, dragging the thin, shiny space blanket. He said nothing when she settled beside him, but moved over a little on the crate and tucked her blanket around her shoulders. The light went off. She leaned back against the rock wall.

"Couldn't sleep?" he asked softly.

"No. It was too dark."

"It's going to be dark for a long time."

"It's okay, now that I know where you are."

"Try to sleep."

Rachel sighed and leaned her head against the cold rock behind her, trying to breathe slowly and evenly. "Can't the Navy tell when our radio is down and our missile launchers are disabled?"

"No. But when Earl tries to call me, he'll know something's not right. Of course, there's a storm coming in. He might figure it's interfering with our signal."

"Tropical storm Kayla," she said. "They upgraded it to a typhoon this morning. Do you think he'll try to call you tonight?"

"Hard to say. He often does, late in my shift. He might call tonight to wish me a merry Christmas."

"You seem like good friends."

"We're more than that."

She puzzled that out in her mind. "You worked closely with him for a while, you told me that once."

"Yes, and…we're family."

"You're related to Commander Norton?"

"He's my father-in-law."

It stunned her, but it made sense. The ring, the deference Norton had shown him.

"I was assigned to his office six years ago," George said. "He and his wife, Camilla, had all the staff out to their place for a party. That's when I met Pam." He sat in silence for a long time.

"What was she like?" Rachel asked at last.

"She was gorgeous." He stirred. "Have you seen Mrs. Norton?"

"No. I've never even seen the commander."

"Pam looked a lot like her mother. Blond, green eyes. A button taller than you."

"A button?" Rachel lifted her head and stared, although she couldn't see him.

"She came up to the top button on my jacket. You only make it to the second one."

She smiled. "So, you fell in love with your CO's daughter."

"Yeah. Big time."

"What was she really like? I mean, inside?"

"Generous. Gracious by nature."

Not like me, Rachel thought.

"She couldn't cook worth beans."

"No?"

"No. We ate out a lot. I used to get up and make eggs in the morning."

"Did she work?"

"Yeah, she was a librarian. Can you believe that? A school librarian. And she played the flute."

"The flute? That's nice."

"Yeah. She played with the base orchestra."

"So, what happened?" Rachel asked, adding hastily, "If you don't mind telling me."

He leaned back with a deep sigh. "We wanted to have kids. We'd been married a couple of years, and nothing was happening, so she went to the base doctor, and he sent her to a civilian specialist. They did some blood work and found out her white cell count was way high."

"Leukemia?" Rachel guessed.

"Yeah." He shifted his position. "You warm enough?"

"Yes."

"It didn't hit us at first. The doctors were optimistic that her type could be cured, but…she was in the percentage that didn't make it."

"George, I'm so sorry."

"It was tough," he admitted. "She was skin and bones at the end. Lost all her hair. She was so sick. Letting her go was the hardest thing I ever did, but…I couldn't wish her to go on like that."

Rachel reached out in the darkness and found his hand. She gave his fingers a gentle squeeze, and he clung to her when she would have withdrawn her hand. They sat without talking for several minutes.

"Well, anyway," George said at last, "Earl was in charge of this missile site. He sent me out here with the engineers when they first decided to build it. I think he put me on the project more as a distraction than anything. I was in the angry stage of my grief then."

"And you loved this island."

"I don't know as I loved it then, but it seemed like the ideal assignment for me. Remote, isolated. Demanding, but without the pressure of being under Earl's eye every minute. I begged him to let me supervise the unit."

"And then they found the firene."

"Yes. I wanted to stay here more than ever. And he let me."

She closed her eyes against the blackness and thought about George's need to please Earl Norton. She knew from their recent talks that his own father had been dead a long time, and she supposed Norton filled that role for him now.

George held the commander in great esteem, she could tell, in spite of his excruciating memories. The anguish of Pam's illness and death bound the two men together tighter than their professional relationship or their friendship ever could. Earl had expedited George's career when he could, and had allowed him to grieve privately, in his own way. Now George felt obligated to make this mission succeed on every level. She hoped his father-in-law felt the urge to talk to him tonight, on Christmas Eve.

"George?"

"What?"

"Your Christmas present is burning up."

"Don't worry about it."

"Okay."

He squeezed her hand, and they were silent again. Rachel smiled in the thick darkness. Frasier might be going up in flames all around them, but she had never been so happy.

"What was it?" he asked.

"A sweater to match your eyes, only it wouldn't, quite."

He leaned toward her, and she felt his scratchy cheek against her forehead. "Merry Christmas, Rachel."

"Thanks. You too."

"You want to sing?"

"They might hear us."

"I doubt it."

"Let's not."

"All right. You want your present now?"

She laughed. "Is it in that crate over there?"

"No, it's in my pocket."

She turned on her flashlight. George blinked and held his hand over the end of the light.

"Sorry," she said. "I had to see if you were serious."

"I'm dead serious. Do you want it or not?"

"Of course I do."

He shifted and pulled a small box from his jacket pocket.

"Maybe a little squished." He handed it to her and took the flashlight in his left hand, still holding the gun in his right.

She bent her head over the gift and tore at the paper.

"Real wrapping paper. Where did you buy this?"

"At a mall near my sister's."

She had the box free and opened it carefully. He shined the light on a sterling silver pendant, and the stone gave off a lustrous gleam.

She caught her breath. "It's blue."

"Like your eyes on a sunny day."

"Is this what they call a star sapphire?"

"Yes."

"Oh, George."

He was smiling, and the fatigue lines at the corners of his eyes deepened. Her pulse raced as she soaked up the affection shining from his face.

"My sister suggested a suede jacket, but if I'd got you that, it would be ashes by now."

"I love this."

"I'm glad."

"Help me put it on?"

It was a struggle, but at last he managed, and she turned toward him, fingering the sapphire.

"Hold this." He put the flashlight in her hand and fixed one of the wool blankets so they could sit on several layers on the cold floor, then brought the other over and wrapped it around her shoulders, tucking the edges of the space blanket under it. He sat down beside her, shook out his own space blanket, laid it over his lap, and then he put his arm around her, blankets and all.

"Sleep now. That's an order," he said gruffly, taking out his pistol again.

"Yes, sir." She snapped off the flashlight, and he pulled her head onto his shoulder, bending down to brush her lips with the softest of kisses.

TWENTY-NINE

Rachel awoke hours later, stiff and cramped. She was curled up with her head resting on George's knee. With his left hand, he lightly stroked her hair. It was still pitch dark in the cave, but a faint grayness showed where the entrance was. The noise of the wind and waves was so loud that she wondered how she had slept. Over it all was the lashing of a savage rain against the rocks.

She sat up slowly. Her head ached, and she had a sore spot on her hip.

"Good morning," George said softly.

She pushed the light button on her watch. 0615.

"The typhoon," she said, rubbing her temples.

"Yes. I don't think we're going anywhere today."

"But Miguel—"

"This wind would blow us off the island."

"Where do you suppose *he* is?" she asked.

"I don't know. I'm betting he's not as comfortable as we are."

"Maybe his friends picked him up last night."

"No. We'd have seen a helicopter before dark, and the wind was too high after that. There's no way a small boat could navigate these waters in this storm. Unless they've got a teleporter, there's no other way off here."

"Maybe he's hiding in the jungle."

"I think we've got the only dry spot on Frasier," George said smugly. "He's probably wishing he hadn't burned the house."

Rachel stretched. "I'll bet he's curled up under the boat shelter, like that other guy."

"You may be right. If he is, he's miserable. No floor in that thing, and a whole lot smaller than this cave."

"How did you ever find this place?"

"Out exploring. I was sitting on those rocks by the entrance, and I dropped my pocket knife down between them."

"You wouldn't do anything so clumsy."

He sighed. "I wish I were half as wonderful as you think I am."

She gave his arm a squeeze. "Well, if we've got to wait the storm out, you should sleep. Let's eat breakfast, and I'll stand guard while you take a nap."

George didn't argue, so she went to the crate of MRE's and pulled two out.

"Hey, turkey and rice, with fruit cup. You didn't offer me that last night." She opened the first aid kit and took out the aspirin bottle. "Think that three-year-old water will kill me?"

"Nah."

After they had eaten, George crawled through the entrance for a look around and returned dripping wet.

"It's ugly out there," he said, stripping off his jacket. "As bad as I've ever seen it."

"Their timing wasn't so great," Rachel said, handing him a blanket.

"I didn't think this storm was moving in so fast. Guess they didn't, either. Someone told Miguel to put things in motion, and once they realized they couldn't land in the storm, it was too late."

Rachel raised her chin. "Well, if I were a spy, I'd keep my roof over my head until my friends arrived. He could have locked himself in and stood us off for days."

George laughed. "Miguel knew I'd find a way in. Now, if you and I had holed up in the control room, that might have been a different story. They could burn the house over us, and we'd survive. That place is built to withstand bombs and fire. But not when the fire starts inside."

"You're sure Miguel did this, aren't you?"

"Well, I spent most of the night thinking out the possibilities. If Miguel is innocent, there had to be a landing force that arrived before noon. That's extremely unlikely, with the surveillance equipment we had and the storm approaching faster than expected."

"If a sub sent out a Zodiac, we'd have found it when we swept the perimeter, looking for Andy."

"Hard to hide a rubber boat once it's inflated," George agreed.

"But a diver or two, maybe?" she hazarded.

"Come on, you had the morning watch. Could a sub get in here then? I *know* none came near here during my watch the night before."

She sighed, gathering up the food containers with the aid of her flashlight. "So Miguel was the advance man, preparing for the arrival of an occupation force. But they jumped the gun and told him to execute the plan with the typhoon coming."

"I think so. They probably were planning on keeping the surveillance equipment and missiles and using them against our forces, but Miguel made a very big mistake."

Rachel frowned. "He didn't kill you."

"Right. I think he planned to, but he didn't have a chance. I surprised him when I went downstairs to ask him about Andy, and I was wearing my sidearm. He couldn't stop us from going out to look for him. And then he guessed that I was on to him. With me loose, he had to destroy everything, or I'd have used it to get him and ruin their whole plan."

"You'll still get him."

"I'm counting on it."

Rachel tried not to think of Andy's body, drenched and abandoned. "You think Miguel's still alone out there."

"I do. They planned for him to clear the way so they could move in to get the firene. They don't really need to occupy the island, except to keep our forces at bay. But we've shown them they can't get at the firene with us here. I'm guessing they figured to get rid of us, come in quickly, grab as much as they could before the cavalry came galloping in, and then disappear with it. Even if they only got a hundred pounds or so, they'd have world-class weapons in a short time."

"He could have shot me when he came on duty," she said.

"He had to be sure he had me first. And with us both out of the house, he probably made radio contact with his friends. Most likely, destroying the equipment was their contingency plan. They would rather have kept it intact, I'm sure, but we found Andy's body. Miguel didn't misjudge me. If he'd left that equipment there, I'd have found a way to take it back and use it."

"Do you suppose he's got a long-range radio on him now? He destroyed both the ones in the house."

George considered. "Possible. He didn't seem to have any extra gear with him when he arrived, but who knows? I never went through his stuff. I wish now I had, but there really was no reason to do that. He's of Cuban descent, and I didn't want any possibility of a discrimination complaint, so even though I didn't really like him, I tried extra hard to be fair and treat him the same as I treated Andy. And Earl promised me a replacement for him by the middle of January."

"Did Miguel know that?"

"No, unless he eavesdropped on my conversation with Earl."

She frowned. "How did they ever get him in here? It was a last-minute thing."

"I'm guessing they had him in place in the Navy to get whatever information he could. When Chadwick was injured and Norton started looking for a quick replacement, someone with ties to this hostile group took advantage of our weak moment."

"You think someone with influence in the Navy is in on it?"

"Well, somebody somewhere pulled some strings and got Garcia assigned here. Why send us him and not some sailor in Pearl Harbor? You could pick any seaman off the *Bush,* and he'd have been as good for the job. When we get off here, I'll have some questions for Earl."

"It's not possible Commander Norton—"

"No, it's not," George said emphatically. "But he's done favors for me before. I don't deny it. He's a nice guy. So, maybe he did a favor for somebody else." He said slowly, "Of course, there's one other possibility. This guy might be a ringer for the real Miguel Garcia."

"You mean…they killed him and put their own man in his place?"

"Could be."

"Did they ever find out how word leaked out about the firene in the first place?" Rachel asked.

George was silent for a moment. "Yeah. They told me in Washington. One of our guys who knew about it was bought."

"Someone you knew?"

"Yes. I'm taking this personally, Rachel." His voice held a warning, along with grief.

"I'm sorry." She went toward him, stumbling over the corner of one of the crates.

"Careful."

"I know," she said ruefully. "No broken legs."

She sat down beside him and snapped off her light, reaching toward him in the darkness. Her fingertips found his scratchy cheek. He put his arms around her and pulled her close. "He was my friend. Matt Rubin. We were here for a year together. I just can't believe it."

"I wish I could fix it for you." She kissed him, just in front of his ear, and he sighed deeply.

"Who can you trust?" he asked softly.

She leaned her forehead against his cheek. "You can't quit trusting people. It's too lonely."

"Yeah. I know you're right." He squeezed her. "Imagine if they told us Pierre went bad. It's like that."

"I…can't imagine it."

He sighed. "I trust you."

"Good, because I'm going to keep watch while you sleep."

It was past noon when he stirred. She turned on her light. He was sitting up on the pad of blankets on the rocky floor.

"It's quieter," he observed.

Rachel got up from the crate and stretched. "The rain's not so bad, and I think the wind's let up."

"I'll take a look." He pulled on his damp coat and went to the entrance, returning shortly. "Let's eat something and then I'll reconnoiter. We may be in the eye."

Rachel said nothing while they ate the MREs and drank a small amount of the stale water.

"All right, I'm going out," George told her. "You stay put. I'll call your name when I come back."

"I'm going with you."

"No, you are not."

"Yes, I am."

He sighed. "Rachel, please. You're comparatively safe here."

"I don't want to be safe. I want to know where you are."

"That's silly. Come on, be reasonable. I can go quicker alone, and the chances are less that I'll be seen."

Rachel took a deep breath. She felt again the way she had when the stranger confronted her on the path and George was thousands of miles away. Waiting for him in the dark, dry cave, wondering if he were dead or alive, was unthinkable.

"I don't want to stay here alone. You said your friend Matt knows about this cave."

George turned away from her, and she waited, frightened by his silence.

"You're right." He slumped against the wall. "It's possible the enemy knows about it now."

"I'm sorry, George." She stepped up to him, reaching toward him. "Call me insubordinate or call me a weakling, I don't care. I really think we're better off together."

"You may be right." He turned off his flashlight and pulled her into his arms. She pressed her face against the damp front of his jacket and tried to stifle the sob that escaped her.

"Don't cry, sweet Rachel."

"I'm not crying."

They both knew that was a lie.

"Matt could be with them right now, telling them what to do and how to get the best of me."

"Don't think that," she said.

"I have to. I have to consider every angle now, or we'll never step off Frasier."

"God will help us."

"Yes, I'm counting on that. But Matt knows me better than anyone else, with the possible exception of Pierre. He knows how I think, and what my resources are."

"George, I'll do whatever you think will give us the best chance."

He took a deep breath. "All right, get your survival pack and your gun. And you do what I tell you, you hear?"

"Yes, sir!"

He went out first and then motioned for her to follow. She climbed up out of the hole between the rocks, and they bent low and ran up the slope through the drizzle.

At the top, they moved cautiously from rock to rock until they were near the vegetation. George crept through the wind-battered jungle. Rachel looked around constantly as she dogged him, but only the movement of branches in the light wind drew her eyes, and the only sounds were the wind and the soft patter of rain on the leaves.

George halted at the edge of the trees. She moved up beside him and looked down toward the spring. Fresh water, the one thing everyone on the island would need. There was no sign of life. Her eyes traveled up the steep path beyond to the ridge.

"One windmill's down," she whispered.

George nodded. "Come on."

They dodged in spurts toward the high bluff, first crossing the ravine, then climbing the hillside, but staying off the path.

They crouched at the base of windmill number two, taking in the sight of the other tower, laid neatly across the helicopter pad.

"Score one for us," George breathed in her ear. "They can't land a chopper."

Rachel swallowed hard. Smoke hung in the air beneath the low, brooding clouds. The place above them, where the house should have been, was strangely bare. Little puffs of smoke rose from the foundation and fluttered in the wind. The rain had slackened to a mist.

George led her cautiously toward the smoldering ruin of the house and along the side toward the cliff path. At the head of it he stopped, looking down toward the shore.

He turned suddenly and pushed her back. Fear seized her, and she stumbled until they could huddle together behind some bushes, where she had planned to have her greenhouse. Amazingly their clothesline still hung, worrying back and forth uneasily in the wind.

"You saw him?"

George nodded. His eyes were hard and calculating now. "He's got a rifle. One that was in the storage room, I guess. He was looking out to sea with binoculars."

"He's expecting a ship."

"That or a sub."

"They won't come yet."

"I don't think so. The storm's not over." He squinted up at the sky. "No. We're in the eye. Could be worse later."

"What do we do?"

"If I thought I could get within range, I'd take him out."

Rachel winced. She'd known George was capable of such a mindset. She'd trained for it herself. When she'd had to defend herself, she had done it, but she wasn't sure she could do this. *Miguel killed Andy. He'll kill us if he gets a chance.*

George shook his head regretfully. "No way I can get him from here."

Rachel said, "What happens if his people get here before ours do? Do we just lie low?"

"I'm not letting them get the firene," George said between his teeth, and she was sure that somehow he would stop them.

"Let's go." He stood up and went quickly by way of the path. Rachel knew Miguel could not possibly see them now from his perch on the low rocks. They ran back to the spring, and George watched the back trail while she quickly filled one of the plastic water bottles.

They bypassed the thick stand of jungle and made a straight line from the coffee bush to the eastern point, then down the slope to the cluster of rocks that looked like so many others in the jumble on the shore. Below them, the rocks sheared away to meet the water, forming the easternmost end of the hostile island.

"I don't know if I could have found this place without you," she admitted.

"I'm glad it wasn't necessary."

Inside the cave, he went immediately to the third crate and pried off the top. She bent low with her flashlight.

She laughed when he removed the packing material.

"A rocket launcher? We've got a rocket launcher! George! The odds just got better!"

"Only four rounds," he said apologetically.

"But, still!"

He shrugged. "I could take down a helicopter with one, but it won't do much good against a destroyer or a submarine."

"But if they come by ship and try to land troops by helo—"

"Yes. So long as they don't have too many choppers."

"They won't try to land a boat," she said.

"Who knows? I wish I knew if Miguel took the diving equipment."

"Think he'd try to swim out to them? It would be suicidal."

"Not if the weather calms. Say a sub surfaces right over the firene. It could be done easily on a nice day. Getting beyond the surf is the tricky part. Pierre and I dove out there several times to install equipment. And they could put out a Zodiac to pick him up."

George carefully stowed the ordnance in their packs. "When

we go out again, I'll carry this thing. You bring the survival packs. Let's make sure we've got knives and extra clips. Every weapon we own."

He made her take the extra pistol and checked their survival kits again. The wind's whining increased to a roar, and the muffled tumult of a violent downpour reached them.

"The back side of Typhoon Kayla!" Rachel had to shout to make him hear.

"We may as well rest," George replied. "Take off your wet stuff."

She peeled off the camouflage shirt and sweatpants and spread them out, pessimistic about their chances of drying. Her jeans were damp, and but the layers of sweatshirts had protected her. She shed one and wrapped a wool blanket around herself. George laid his jacket, cap, and sweatshirt aside.

"You'll freeze," she scolded, shining the flashlight his way.

"I'm all right." He took the other blanket and draped it over his shoulders. "Come here, Rachel. There's one more thing we need to do."

She went to him without hesitation. "What?"

"We pray."

❦

Far into the night the storm raged over the island. Waves dashed high against the cliffs, but the cave stayed dry. George dozed fitfully, waking to distant crashes of thunder. He crawled to the entrance once and found water pooling between the rocks just outside. Rachel slept leaning on one of the boxes, her head cradled on her arms. He pulled one of the space blankets over her to supplement the wool blanket. He sat down beside her with his back against the wall. His toes were cold. He wiggled them and thought about taking his boots off as he laid his head back and closed his eyes. *Dry socks. I should have put some socks in the crates.*

Rachel woke him by tousling his hair and calling softly, "George, honey, come on! The sun's out."

There was no time to savor the moment. He sat up quickly and stared at the entrance. The sun was definitely out. He checked his watch and found it was nearly 0700.

"Oh, boy, I slept that time!" He had planned to be outside before full daylight, but it was too late now. "Get ready. Put your things on. We ought to eat something too."

He wondered if the Navy would reach them before the MREs ran out. If not, he guessed they could get by for several days. It would be tough, but Rachel would hold up well. She wasn't a complainer. She was an improviser who turned adversity into adventure, and he had the impression she was willing to face anything with him.

"Do we have a plan?" she asked, buttoning her still clammy camo shirt over her layers.

"Try to find out if the enemy has arrived, and if they have, try to stop them."

"You just tell me what to do, George. If two people can do it, we will."

He reached for her hand. There was a lot he wanted to say to her, but this wasn't the time. He almost regretted not keeping her awake to talk far into the night, planning a future together, but she seemed rested and alert. *Get this job over with,* he commanded himself. *There will be time for other things later.*

After their prayer together the evening before, he had gone over and over the facts in his mind. Somehow during that last, refreshing period of deep sleep, peace had come to him.

"The Lord can save by many or by few," he said.

She frowned in bewilderment. "What does that mean?"

"Have you read about Jonathan in the Bible?"

"I guess not."

"He said that, just before he and his armor bearer whomped an enemy garrison and sent the entire army running."

"We can do that?"

"I believe we can. Stay close to me."

He carried the rocket launcher to the entrance and laid it on the floor. "I'll go out first and take a look. When I tell you, push it out in front of you, and I'll hoist it up out of the rocks."

"Got it." She stared at him, wide-eyed in the dimness. He stooped and kissed her gently, and then he crawled out of the cave.

He waited until his eyes adjusted to the brightness and then stood up, peering toward the jungle first and then around toward the sea. He scaled the rocks and looked again, using his binoculars. The sun on his face felt good. It seemed ages since they'd had a bright day.

He hopped back down and crouched at the cave entrance. "Okay, let's have it."

Rachel shoved the launcher toward him, and he grasped it and hefted it up onto the rocks. Then he climbed up and sat watching the slope while Rachel came out.

When they were both out of the rock pile, he loaded the rocket launcher. "Let's go. Keep close, and keep your gun ready."

They went slowly, stopping frequently to listen and look. The island was dripping and bedraggled. When they entered the jungle, they had to fight their way over downed trees and broken branches. George stopped near the edge of the trees, and Rachel leaned to peer around him.

"Half the banana trees are down!" she whispered in amazement.

"Worst storm we've had," George agreed. "Hey! Look! Windmill number two is still up!"

"Incredible."

He stood for a moment looking at it, a lone sentinel over the devastation brought by fire and storm.

"All right, we go fast across the ravine." He adjusted the launcher on his shoulder. "He's most likely on the west end of the island. We need to get to high ground so we can see if there's enemy craft in the area."

She nodded.

"Stick with me, sweetheart."

"You couldn't lose me if you wanted to."

He smiled at her and then took off in a zigzag path, dodging from the trees to an outcropping of rock and then on toward the ridge.

Fifteen minutes later, Rachel crouched beside him behind a rock on the edge of the bluff. The charred hole where the house had stood gave off a strong acrid smell. George frowned as he gazed out from the cliff, beyond the jagged rocks and pounding surf. He raised his binoculars for a better look, but there was no doubt.

An aging battleship lay a quarter mile offshore.

THIRTY

"They're putting Zodiacs in the water," George said grimly.

"You're sure it's the enemy?"

"I don't recognize their colors." He studied the flag fluttering in the breeze. "It's not the Stars and Stripes."

"We're not using battleships anymore, and anyway, one of our ships wouldn't travel alone," Rachel agreed.

"This one looks like they salvaged it off a scrap heap."

"Think they'll send a landing party?"

"I don't know. They can't land down there."

Rachel crept up beside him to look. "Wouldn't Miguel tell them which side the boat landing is on?"

"Those are diving crews," George said. "See?"

She focused her binoculars on the figures climbing down the ship's ladder to the small boats bobbing below.

"Going after the firene already?" she gasped.

"Not wasting any time."

"Do you think they've picked Miguel up yet?"

"Maybe."

They watched in silence for a few more seconds, and then George lowered his binoculars. "Guess it's now or never." He picked up the rocket launcher and eased it onto his shoulder.

"What are you going to do? You can't sink a battleship with that!"

"No, but I can blow their divers and equipment out of the water before they start. Once the divers are submerged, I can't get them."

Rachel gulped. "Okay. I guess we have to."

"If we don't, they'll make off with enough firene to destroy America as we know it."

"Once you fire that thing, the surprise is over."

"Right," George agreed. "I'm hoping the two boats will line up so I can get them both with one round. I don't need to kill all the men, just disable the Zodiacs and dump the diving gear in a hundred feet of water."

He sighted with excruciating patience. Rachel held her breath. Their four rockets seemed pitifully inadequate now.

George flipped on the guiding laser, and she knew he was aiming the dot at the nearest inflatable. It carried six men, two of them wearing wet suits and air tanks. She watched through her binoculars. If he waited too long, the divers would be over the side and out of his range. But the second boat was puttering gradually into a position that would allow him the two-for-one kill, if he could just wait a bit longer.

She jumped as the rocket whooshed from the launcher's tube. Two seconds later, havoc erupted in the Zodiacs. Bodies and equipment flew in all directions. The nearest boat was ripped to shreds, and the second hung half submerged on the surface. Men on the deck of the ship began to shout, and dozens of sailors rushed to peer over the side.

"What if they start shelling us?" Rachel asked, suddenly terrified.

"Then we move back. I've got to reload this thing."

"I haven't seen Miguel." While he worked, she craned her neck to look around at the path and toward the rocks where they had seen Miguel the day before.

"Maybe Typhoon Kayla got him," George said dispassionately.

She focused her binoculars on the ship again. "They're wondering where it came from and what to do about it. One guy is pointing right at me and yelling at an officer."

"Get down!" George pulled her below the rock. "They may have seen the glare on your lenses."

She swallowed. "Sorry."

"Get on your belly and crawl around the rock. They've got a couple of choppers on the deck. Tell me if they're moving."

More cautiously, she crawled through the sodden weeds and wriggled toward the brink of the cliff. When she could again see the ship, she carefully raised the binoculars.

"There are men swarming around one of the choppers. It looks like an antique."

She crawled back into position beside him.

"There must be a way to put them out of commission," George muttered, as he rearmed the rocket launcher. "Stay down. I'm going to take a look."

He moved forward, and then he came back with a pensive expression.

"Isn't it kind of like shooting an elephant?" Rachel asked.

"Yeah, with a pea shooter."

"I mean, isn't there one vulnerable spot, like the elephant's eye or something, where you can hit it and it will drop in its tracks?"

"Maybe, if we had an elephant gun."

She laid her hand gently on his arm. "They know we're here, George. If we can't stop them, at least let's make a good accounting of it."

He nodded. "Keep praying."

Suddenly the cliff shuddered, and a shell burst drowned the sound of the surf for an instant.

"Quick!" George hefted the rocket launcher. "Grab my pack. We're too close to the cellar hole. If they're going to shell the cliff, they might bury us."

They dashed eastward, away from the cliff face. George ducked into a cluster of rocks near the top of the path to the boat landing. Rachel dropped beside him panting. Another boom resounded behind them.

George rested his hand lightly on her back. "I'm going to try something. It may not work. Check the north side of the island. No ships off the boat landing, are there?"

Cautiously, she stood up and scanned the water.

"As far as I can tell, that battleship's alone."

He rummaged in his pockets and grinned up at her. "Let's go elephant hunting." He pulled the nugget of firene from his jacket pocket and set it carefully on the rock in front of him. She stared at it and then at him, her mind racing.

"Take the launcher," he said. "Get it into position on your shoulder. If they send a chopper over, you know what to do."

Rachel took a deep breath and hoisted the bulky weapon. She glanced at George. He was pulling another of the rockets from his pack.

"Do we know what we're doing?" she asked timidly.

"Not really. The rocket detonates on impact, and that will set it off—" He looked up at her. "I need all your matches."

"Matches?"

"From the survival kits. Quick, now. It's the chemical reaction with the sulfur that does it. I'm not sure it will work. This will be pretty crude, but…" He shrugged. "It's worth a try."

She rested the rocket launcher on the largest rock and fumbled to unfasten the survival packs.

George pulled his dog tags from beneath his clothing and grasped the gold ring, grimacing as he tugged at it.

"What are you doing?" Rachel asked.

"Zinc makes it more powerful. There's zinc in the gold alloy."

Rachel watched in amazement as he dug part of the solid explosive from the rocket's load with his knife and shoved the firene and the ring inside.

The philosopher's stone. Only it doesn't turn base metals into gold. Gold turns this rock into fire.

"Matches, sweetheart." He held out his hand.

"George, I love you whether this works or not."

He smiled up at her for an instant. "If we get out of this thing alive, will you marry me?"

"Yes." She opened the matchboxes and dumped all the matches

in his cupped hand. He winked at her and then turned back toward his work as she shouldered the launcher once more.

He was rapt in his concentration when a shot rang out. George jumped a little, and Rachel automatically swung the rocket launcher around, searching for a sniper.

"George!"

"Get down!" It was almost a gasp, and she looked sharply at him. He was leaning heavily on the rock, and the matches were scattered on the ground.

"You're hit, aren't you?"

"Afraid so. He winged me. Get down."

She knelt against the lower rock on the seaward side, knowing they were at least partially exposed to the shooter. Another bullet struck the rock between them, throwing off chips of basalt. One hit the back of her hand. She glanced down at the trickle of blood and then looked all around. Adrenaline pumped through her veins. *This is it. We're going to die.*

She looked over at George, half expecting to see him swooning, but his gray eyes were alert as he scanned the ridge.

"Well, well. He's on the windmill."

She saw Miguel then, forty feet above the earth, clinging to the steel ladder. One arm encircled the vertical support and steadied the gun barrel, and the other held the stock. Slowly she brought the muzzle of the rocket launcher up.

"Give it here," George urged.

"No time." Even as she flipped the aiming laser on, Miguel was taking aim again through the scope of the rifle. She made the dot of light touch his torso and held her breath. *If I miss...* She wouldn't think about that.

Whoosh!

"Yes!" George shouted. He leaped up and clapped her on the shoulder as the windmill tipped. The support on one side was sheared off where Miguel was perched. The rifle fell first, and then his mangled body left the steel framework and plummeted to the rocky path. The top half of the tower hung drunkenly for an instant, and then it tilted and swooped toward the earth. The mass of metal struck the ground with a jarring thud, and all was still except the wind.

George had his pistol out.

"Stay down."

She obeyed him this time, sinking to the ground and leaning the rocket launcher against the rock. She wrapped her arms around herself and tried to stop the shaking that overcame her.

She was still trembling when George returned. The sight of his blood-soaked sleeve pulled her from her panic. She flung herself at him, and he gathered her into his embrace, drawing her down in the shelter of the rocks.

"It's okay, Rachel. It's okay."

"You're bleeding."

"It's just a flesh wound."

"How can you tell? Take your coat off and let me look. Oh, George, we left the first aid kit in the cave."

Huge sobs shook her. He held her close, rubbing her back and murmuring in her ear, "I'll be all right. I promise."

She gulped air and squeezed handfuls of his jacket.

"Okay," she said at last, drawing one more choppy breath. "Okay. Let's go elephant hunting."

He pulled back and studied her face, and then he nodded. "Come on."

Together they gathered up the matches and broke off the heads. George reassembled the rocket and then armed the launcher with his modified load. They bent low as they dashed back along the side of the burnt-out house to the cliff top. The ship's guns had fallen silent.

"George, hurry!" she whispered, peering out at the gray hulk floating so solidly.

Faintly she heard the whine of a helicopter engine. George took up his position as the outmoded chopper lifted slowly, a foot, then two, off the deck.

"Say a prayer," he said, aiming the rocket launcher. For an instant it seemed everything froze, and she thought she might never breathe again.

Whoosh!

Rachel stared in disbelief. The destruction of the windmill was nothing compared to the cataclysm that unfolded before them. One moment the ship was there with the helicopter hovering just above it. The next, a monstrous cloud of smoke and flying debris obliterated it. At the edges of the cloud, she saw the stern and bow of the battleship lift impossibly high. What she thought must be a blade from the helicopter's rotor flew toward them and splashed into the water below the cliff. The shock of the blast hit her, and she fell back, her ears ringing. George flung the rocket launcher to the ground and dove toward her, covering her head with his body as pieces of debris rained down around them.

THIRTY-ONE

A cloud of acrid smoke roiled up the cliff face and lifted over the island. A cinder landed on Rachel's sleeve, and George slapped it away, coughing.

What did I do? He remembered bits of articles he had read about volcanoes, about how the fumes alone killed thousands of people.

"Sweetheart, I'm sorry," he said in her ear.

Rachel wriggled from beneath his weight and onto her side. She wrapped her arms around him.

"George, we're alive. The island's still here. It's okay."

The rumbling stopped. It was very quiet, except for the breaking waves.

George raised his head and stared into her bloodshot china blue eyes. He swallowed and then rose and walked numbly toward the edge of the cliff. Rachel followed.

The cloud lifted slowly. The waves above the firene ledge were large for such a calm day, but they were empty. He didn't see any swimmers. A few pieces of debris floated, but they were very small.

He sank back against a rock, afraid his knees would buckle under him.

"I was afraid for a second—" He lifted his cap and wiped his brow.

"It also crossed my mind that the whole mass of firene would explode."

He nodded, staring out at the place where the ship had rested. Unbelievable that it had gone down so fast. Flakes of ash floated down around them like discolored snow.

She smiled suddenly. "You sure know how to kill elephants, George!"

&

"Let me look at that wound now," Rachel said.

"Let's get down to the spring. My throat's killing me, and maybe the smoke won't be so bad down there."

They walked slowly. George insisted on bringing the rocket launcher and the one remaining rocket. Rachel carried the survival packs. They climbed over the skeleton of windmill number one. The bottom third of the second tower still stood, truncated and jagged against the sky. He guided her in a wide berth around the body of Miguel Garcia, crushed beneath the steel bars.

George was staggering by the time they arrived at the spring. He sank to the ground, dropping the rocket launcher, and lay back on the turf. Rachel pulled a telescoping cup from one of the packs and filled it with cool water.

"Drink this," she commanded.

He opened his eyes and looked at her blankly. She put her arm under his head and raised him a little. His left hand came up to take the cup, and he downed the water in one gulp and then lay back with a soft groan.

"I need to get the first aid kit," she said. George didn't answer. She was suddenly afraid. She didn't dare leave him for the half hour it would take her to get to the cave and back.

"George, wake up! Come on, you've got to take your jacket off! If you can't, I'll cut it off you. You're losing too much blood."

"All right, all right." He pushed himself up on his left elbow. "It's just a flesh wound."

"You said that, but I am *not* going to let my fiancé bleed to death after all we've been through!"

He smiled faintly and fumbled with the buttons. "Don't cut it, sweetheart. It's my favorite jacket."

"You mean your only jacket."

He wriggled his left arm out of the sleeve, and she eased the fabric off over the right. He winced, but his eyes were clear.

"Oh, George, there's gallons of blood!" She pulled off her camouflage shirt and her first sweatshirt, took her knife, and hacked a sleeve off the sweatshirt.

"What are you doing?"

"I'm sacrificing my Mount Hood sweatshirt to stop the bleeding."

"Don't try to tourniquet me," he warned. "I'm telling you, it looks worse than it is."

"You were about to pass out!"

"I was a little wobbly, is all. Come on, pressure on the wound, that's all I need."

She swabbed the oozing entrance and exit wounds in his upper arm with fresh water, and found two gauze pads in the survival gear. She wrapped them tightly against the wounds with strips of cloth from her sweatshirt.

"Are you sure nothing's broken?"

"I'm positive. I'd let you know."

"It didn't hit an artery?"

"I'd be dead by now if it did."

She sat leaning against the steep slope at the edge of the stream, cradling his head in her lap.

"Should we go to the cave?" she asked, smoothing back his dark hair. In spite of the chilly wind, sweat beaded on his forehead.

"Maybe after a while. Let's rest here. I think the air is clearing." He looked up at the sky, and Rachel followed his gaze.

"I can feel the sun again," she said. "I hope we don't have to spend another night here."

"We have to be prepared in case they send reinforcements," George said.

Fear washed over her at the thought. They were down to one rocket and the pistols. Maybe they could salvage Miguel's rifle.

George managed to bring his right hand up to rest on her forearm. "Let's not wait a long time, Rachel."

"I thought you wanted to rest," she whispered, her eyes full of fear.

"I mean to get married. Let's take the first chance we get."

She smiled then and stroked his cheek. "You going to shave first?"

He laughed. It would be easy to stay here, looking up at her forever. She had a grubby smudge beside her nose, but he didn't tell her. He turned his head slightly, into her hand, and kissed her palm.

"It will be complicated, you know," she said. "New assignments."

"Don't worry. I'll jump through any hoops they give me to stay close to you."

She stroked his hair. "All right. The first chance. Rest, then, sweetheart."

He closed his eyes and let go of all the anxiety, thinking only of God holding them safe in His palm.

He awoke some time later, how long he wasn't sure, but he was cold and stiff, and the shoulder wound stabbed when he moved and throbbed when he didn't. He groaned and sat up, clutching the makeshift bandage. The sun had dropped behind the ridge.

"Rachel?"

"Hear that chopper? I've got to load this thing!" She was kneeling by the rocket launcher, struggling to bring the last round out of his pack.

He heard it then, the unmistakable whir of a helicopter.

"They'll be looking for a place to land!" She slid the rocket into place just as the helicopter lifted over the edge of their little valley and soared above them with a deafening roar. The wind from the blades blew her hair out in a swirling cloud as she gritted her teeth and lifted the heavy weapon.

"Rachel, no!" George dove toward her and carried her and the launcher to the ground.

The rocket went off with a whine and struck the earth across the stream, a hundred feet away, throwing clods of dirt as it exploded. He pulled her head down as he had earlier, covering the upper half of her body with his own.

The helicopter moved on over the jungle, circled, and came back toward them.

"It's one of ours," he yelled, letting her sit up.

"I wasn't going to fire." She turned wide, stricken eyes on him. "We almost killed them!"

George wrapped his good arm around her and pressed a kiss to her forehead.

"Where can they land?" she screamed, as the chopper came over again, low.

He shrugged, gritting his teeth.

She grabbed her survival kit, pulled out the silver space blanket and shook it out, flapping it high above her head. The chopper flew over, circled, and came back lower. She stood with George, looking up helplessly.

A petty officer hung out the side with a bullhorn. "We'll send a boat in for you!"

George waved, and the helicopter lifted above the ridge and turned to the north.

It wasn't until they had climbed the hill again that Rachel saw the full battle group lying off to the north. She went down the treacherous path to the landing, and George came after her, alternately holding his shoulder and reaching out to stop himself from pitching forward. A small boat was already motoring toward the cove. The pilot cut the motor and let it ride the surf in.

Rachel waded out to meet them, and a seaman hauled her into the boat. George tumbled in beside her and lay gasping for breath.

"How long have you been here?" Rachel yelled to the seaman beside her, as they headed back out to the *Bush*.

"Just arrived, ma'am. Captain Gallant sent the chopper out as soon as we spotted Frasier. We could see that the windmills were down, and when we got closer we saw the house was gone too. Looking for survivors was the captain's first priority."

"Commander Norton sent you," she guessed.

"Yes, ma'am. We were on our West Pac, but the word came that you were in trouble out here. The commander's on the *Bush*."

"Norton's with you?" George growled from the bottom of the boat. The medic had insisted he lie down and have his wound looked at right away.

"He came aboard by jet, just before we spotted Frasier."

"Hey, hey!" George jerked his arm away from the medic's grasp, wincing in pain.

"Just going to start an IV, sir. You're a little dehydrated."

"It can wait. You're not carrying me off this boat."

The medic appealed silently to Rachel, but she shrugged. "He's still in charge, trust me."

It was two hours before she saw George again. At the commander's insistence, he was whisked off to sick bay the moment they were on deck. Rachel was interviewed intensively by Norton. She went over the chain of events that led up to their final battle. He asked her many probing questions about Andy's disappearance, Miguel's betrayal, the battleship, and George's simplistic reverse alchemy. Rachel decided she liked him. He was tough, he was thorough, but he was behind her and George one hundred percent. At last he released her into the care of a female ensign, detailed to escort her to private quarters.

"Welcome back, Ensign!"

Rachel gasped. "Heidi!"

Her friend drew her quickly around a corner and embraced her. "Are you all right?"

"Yes!"

"I've been praying for you. When we saw the smoke on the island, I was afraid you were dead."

"God brought us through."

As they crossed the deck, Rachel saw that the other vessels in the group had moved into position at the western end of the island. Several small boats patrolled the water, and helicopters beat the air over the island and the firene ledge.

"You can get cleaned up now," Heidi said. "I brought a couple of khaki uniforms for you to try. I wasn't sure of the size."

"Thank you." Rachel realized she must look a fright. She found not only clothing, but clean towels, toiletries, a robe, stationery, and a basket of fresh fruit waiting for her. The cabin was larger than any she had ever been in on a Navy ship.

"Is there anything else I can do for you?" Heidi asked, as Rachel looked around the cabin and private bathroom with wonder.

"Yes. You can tell me why I'm in here."

"This is the VIP suite. Captain Gallant's orders."

Rachel gulped. "Guess I'll have to write him a thank-you note."

"I brought you this." Heidi held out a small, leather-bound New Testament.

"Thank you! My other Bible is toast." Rachel hugged her again. "I'm so thankful to be here. There were moments when we weren't sure we'd make it."

"I'm so glad you did! You'll have to tell me all about it later. May I ask you something?"

"Of course."

"Did you enjoy the assignment on Frasier Island?" Heidi asked. "Except the last of it, I mean?"

Rachel smiled. "I wouldn't trade it for anything."

When she had showered and dried her hair, she put on the size eight uniform and surveyed herself critically in the mirror. Her eyes were still a little red and rimmed below with dark half circles. She looked longingly at the inviting bunk, but her desire to see George was stronger.

She was about to go in search of him when there was a brief knock at the cabin door. She opened it warily, and found George waiting outside, his right arm cradled in a sling.

"They let you go!"

"Rachel!" His eyes glittered with appreciation as he appraised her. "You look fantastic."

She laughed. "You look pretty good yourself." The crisp uniform fit him perfectly, and his clean-shaven face looked smooth and touchable. She sobered as he bent toward her. His kiss was fleeting but held a tantalizing promise.

"I brought you something." He eased her sketchbook from behind the sling. "It's a little damp."

"Incredible!" She reached for the battered tablet and flipped the pages. Pierre, the nesting plovers, the greenhouse, the sei whales. The latest of her many portraits of George. "How did you get this?"

"The recovery crew. I told them where to look. It took them a while, but they found the cave." He smiled with satisfaction. "Oh, and Norton wants to see us."

"He already debriefed me."

"Can't help it. He sent word for both of us to see him in the captain's quarters."

He held her hand firmly as they went to keep the appointment.

"Well," Norton said, smiling as they entered. "George, you look a sight better now."

"Thank you, sir."

"Sit down. I want to discuss the immediate future with you both.

George, I'll want some time with you after dinner, and, of course, you'll write a full report before you leave the ship."

George nodded. He and Rachel took seats at a small table, across from the commander. "What's the status of the recovery, sir?"

"Four survivors so far."

"You're joking!" George leaned toward the commander. "I can't believe it!"

"The cruiser picked them up south of here. They seem to be the lucky few with life jackets who were thrown clear of the blast. The recovery crew have found some remains, and the *Preston's* divers have located several large pieces of the ship lying on the ledge where she sank. The bow and the stern, but very little in between. I'll need you to give us some details on the load you used. We haven't tested it on a large scale yet. Our scientists will be very interested."

Rachel suppressed a shudder.

"We've recovered the bodies of Greene and Garcia." Norton frowned. "George, I owe you an apology. No, much more than that. Son, if I'd had any idea!" His head drooped in anguish.

"You couldn't know, sir."

"Perhaps not, but—" He raised his chin and met George's eyes. "My own aide, George. It was Shaw."

"Warrant Officer Shaw?" George's pain was evident. "He's the one who took care of our supplies, and he took me to the airfield last fall."

"That's right." Norton sighed. "I told him to line up a replacement for Chadwick, and he came up with this Garcia. I didn't question his judgment. It never occurred to me that he was manipulating the assignments."

"Why?" George asked.

"I hate to say it, but he was paid."

George frowned. "Why is protecting your country not good enough?"

"I don't think he realized it would affect national security." Norton's voice was low and contrite. "He was bribed into helping someone get the son of a friend into a plum assignment. Not that it really matters. It was unconscionable." He shook his head. "When you were in the office, I knew everything was in order. Nothing's been the same since you left."

George said nothing, and Rachel wondered if he struggled with appropriate responses whenever he talked to his father-in-law. She prayed silently that George would be engulfed in peace.

Norton sat up a trifle straighter. "Anyway, I had to come out when I heard you'd activated a distress beacon. I thought maybe the typhoon had damaged the house or something, but then we got the satellite photos of the fire. When I saw that the house was burning…George, Ensign Whitney, I'm glad you both survived."

"Thank you, sir," Rachel murmured. George reached over and squeezed her hand.

"So, George," Norton said more cheerfully, "there was a personal matter about which you spoke to me not so long ago."

"Yes, sir." George glanced toward Rachel. "There's been some progress on that front."

"Indeed?"

"Yes, sir. I'll leave it up to you which one of us should be transferred to another chain of command. You see, this morning I laid my heart at this lady's feet, and she graciously agreed to become my wife."

Rachel held her smile back from becoming a giant grin. Graciously, indeed. George had tossed off his question in the middle of a battle, but she hadn't cared about the circumstances.

Norton beamed at them.

"Well, that's fine. Stressful circumstances. I don't think there will be any problems on that score. And I found Ensign Whitney to be lucid and insightful during debriefing. Very impressive, after what you've been through today." He smiled kindly at Rachel.

"Thank you, sir." She felt a flush rise in her cheeks.

Norton turned back to George. "May I ask what your plans are?"

"Well, we haven't had a chance to discuss it much."

"We'll be staying here several days, I think," the commander said. "I may even ask you to go ashore again with the recovery crew, George."

"As you wish, sir."

"We can't leave any men ashore now, but we've still got to protect that firene until it can be mined. Subs in the area, I think, and perhaps an amphibious task force. After I assess the situation, I'll speak to Admiral Ellison."

"Yes, sir," George said.

"It will be a while before this group pulls out, and then we'll touch at Guam. I'll leave the ship there and fly back to Pearl. That will be your first chance to fly home, I think. Of course, you could get married right now, if you want to."

"I—" George looked at Rachel. She knew the red in her cheeks was deepening.

"Captain Gallant could perform the ceremony," Norton continued, "or the chaplain of your choice. Once we touch land, it gets complicated, though. Residence requirements and all that. Of course, Ensign Whitney, you might wish to wait until your family can be present."

"Well, sir," she said, feeling she might choke, "we...we haven't really talked about that."

George was eyeing her closely, and she wondered if he felt her discomfort. There were a few things they needed to settle in private, not under the watchful eye of their commanding officer. As if sensing her mood, Norton rose, and George and Rachel jumped up as he rounded the table.

"Allow me to give you some time alone. When you reach a decision, let me know. You'll both have post-combat leave coming. Four weeks minimum. And, George, we'll talk later about the options available for new postings for both of you." Norton cleared his throat and consulted his watch. "Well, then, I'll see you at dinner in...twenty-three minutes."

George said, "Thank you, sir."

The door closed firmly behind the commander.

Rachel turned toward George, and he smiled in apology. "I think he's just trying to help. So…what do you say?"

"To which part?"

He reached for her hand. "When I asked you to marry me, it may have been a little sparse on aesthetics, but I meant it. I love you, Rachel."

She took a deep breath. "I love you too, George. I've loved you since—"

"Not since your first day on Frasier."

"Hardly. You were a chauvinistic bully. But maybe since day forty or so. For some time, anyway."

"So, what do you say, gorgeous?" George asked with a smile. "Do you want a church wedding? Candles and flowers and brides-maids—all that?"

She looked down at her hand, clasped in his. "That would mean guest lists and invitations and photographers and rehearsals."

"Complications," George agreed.

"My mother would want to help pick out the colors, and she'd hire a caterer and a wedding planner."

He nodded. "I'm sure Judy would want to be in on the fun too. Rachel, I know you told me you were willing to get married right away, but if you do want some time…"

"Would it be terrible of us to disappoint our families?"

"I know Judy would get over it, she'd be so tickled you said yes!" He put his good arm around her. "I'd be very happy if you'd allow Captain Gallant to marry us this evening, here, on the deck of the *Bush*."

It was hard to keep her breath steady as he leaned toward her.

"But if that's not what you want, I can wait," he whispered, kissing her temple lightly where the scar was. "We'll do things however you want."

"I don't want to wait. I just…"

He raised his eyebrows. "You've never hesitated to tell me what's on your mind. Let me have it."

She smiled at the memories that evoked. "All right. Everything's happening so fast. You said you'd stick with the firene project. Do you still want to be out here with the task force? And where will I be when that's happening?"

"Well, things have changed since we discussed that," George said. "I doubt I'll stay out here now. We'll have to see what the commander comes up with when we talk about new assignments for us. I get the feeling he'd take me back into his office in Pearl, if we flew back with him from Guam. He'll need to replace his aide right away. But whether he could find a spot for you in Pearl that wasn't in his chain of command, I don't know. If that's the way it is, then I'll ask him to send us both to San Diego or Seattle or…someplace." George frowned.

"I don't care where," she said, "as long as we can spend some time together."

He nodded. "And someday, when we're both free, I'd like to get a little place in the mountains and raise horses, if you think you'd like that."

"I'd love that. And the four weeks' leave we have coming now?"

"Wherever you say. We can take a leisurely honeymoon, and then visit your folks if you want."

She nodded. "All right. I say yes, let's be married tonight, but that's the only decision I want to make. You settle the rest with Norton and the captain. Please?"

"With pleasure." George smiled and drew her toward him.

"Do you think the commander would give me away?" she whispered.

"To me? Of course!" He pulled her closer.

"Then we'd better go tell him." She pushed away from his chest.

"What's your hurry?" George murmured. He grasped her hand and pulled it up around his neck. "We've got eleven minutes left."

"You want to leave it 'til the last minute?"

"I make all the decisions now, remember? I think we'll need pink flowers for the wedding, and candy corn, and lots of sparklers for the reception."

Joy obliterated any objections she might have made. He kissed her deliberately and decisively, and Rachel relaxed in his arms, reveling in his touch and losing track of the time without caring. But in the back of her mind she knew they would make it to the captain's table on time. George would make sure of that.

ABOUT THE AUTHOR

Susan Page Davis is the author of several novels, spanning categories such as historical, mystery, children, and romantic suspense. A former news correspondent, she and her husband, Jim, are the parents of six and the grandparents of four. Susan and Jim make their home in Maine.

Visit Susan at her website: www.susanpagedavis.com

Harvest House Publishers
Fiction for Every Taste and Interest

Mindy Starns Clark

**SMART CHICK
MYSTERY SERIES**
The Trouble with Tulip
Blind Dates Can Be Murder
Elementary, My Dear Watkins

Melanie Jeschke

**THE OXFORD
CHRONICLE SERIES**
Inklings
Expectations
Evasions

Debra White Smith

THE AUSTEN SERIES
First Impressions
Reason and Romance
Central Park
Northpointe Chalet

**THE SISTERS
SUSPENSE SERIES**
Amanda
Possibilities
Picture Perfect

Susan Meissner

A Window to the World
Remedy for Regret
In All Deep Places
Seahorse in the Thames

**RACHAEL FLYNN
MYSTERY SERIES**
Widows and Orphans
Sticks and Stones
Days and Hours

Sally John

**THE OTHER WAY
HOME SERIES**
A Journey by Chance
After All These Years
Just to See You Smile
The Winding Road Home

IN A HEARTBEAT SERIES
In a Heartbeat
Flash Point
Moment of Truth

THE BEACH HOUSE SERIES
The Beach House
Castles in the Sand

Brandt Dodson

**COLTON PARKER
MYSTERY SERIES**
Original Sin
Seventy Times Seven
Root of All Evil
The Lost Sheep

Gilbert Morris

**JACQUES & CLEO, CAT
DETECTIVES**
Cat's Pajamas
What the Cat Dragged In
When the Cat's Away

George Polivka

TROPHY CHASE TRILOGY
Legend of the Firefish
The Hand That Bears
   the Sword

Susan Davis

Frasier Island

Craig Parshall

Trial by Ordeal

**THE THISTLE AND THE
CROSS SERIES**
Crown of Fire
Captives and Kings

CHAMBERS OF JUSTICE SERIES
The Resurrection File
Custody of the State
The Accused
Missing Witness
The Last Judgment

Roxanne Henke

The Secret of Us

**COMING HOME TO
BREWSTER SERIES**
After Anne
Finding Ruth
Becoming Olivia
Always Jan
With Love, Libby

B.J. Hoff

MOUNTAIN SONG LEGACY
A Distant Music
The Wind Harp
The Song Weaver

A NOVEL

FINDING MARIE

SUSAN PAGE DAVIS
Author of *Frasier Island*

Marie didn't ask to be a courier for secret documents.

The men chasing her couldn't care less.
They just want to find her, dead or alive.

Marie Belanger, a naval lieutenant's wife, unexpectedly finds a computer flash drive in her carry-on luggage at the San Francisco airport. Moments later the woman she had been sitting with on the plane from Tokyo is murdered. Suddenly her journey from California to her home in Maine becomes a nightmare as Marie is forced to run for her life. Her husband, Lt. Pierre Belanger, contacts his best friend, George Hudson, and together they set out on a search for Marie that spans the country. Yet as hard as they try, they seem to stay one step behind their enemies, who are just one step behind Marie.

❧

Finding Marie is an engrossing novel of faith, honor, and courage against a backdrop of espionage and international intrigue.